STANDING IN ANOTHER MAN'S GRAVE

STANDING IN ANOTHER MAN'S GRAVE

Ian Rankin

WINDSOR
PARAGON

First published 2012
by Orion Books
This Large Print edition published 2013
by AudioGO Ltd
by arrangement with
The Orion Publishing Group

Hardcover   ISBN: 978 1 4713 2809 1
Softcover   ISBN: 978 1 4713 2810 7

British Library Cataloguing in Publication Data available

Printed and bound in Great Britain by
MPG Books Group Limited

RIP Jackie Leven

Prologue

I

He'd made sure he wasn't standing too near the open grave.

Closed ranks of the other mourners between him and it. The pall-bearers had been called forward by number rather than name—six of them, starting with the deceased's son. Rain wasn't quite falling yet, but it had scheduled an appointment. The cemetery was fairly new, sited on the south-eastern outskirts of the city. He had skipped the church service, just as he would skip the drinks and sandwiches after. He was studying the backs of heads: hunched shoulders, twitches, sneezes and throat-clearings. There were people here he knew, but probably not many. A gap appeared between two of the mourners and he caught a glimpse of the graveside. The edges of the grave itself had been covered with sheets of green cloth, as if to mask the hard facts of the matter. Words were being uttered but he couldn't catch all of them. There was no mention of the cancer. Jimmy Wallace had been 'cruelly taken', leaving a widow and three children, plus five grandkids. Those kids would be down the front somewhere, mostly old enough to know what was going on. Their grandmother had given voice to a single piercing wail and was being comforted.

Christ, he needed a cigarette.

How well had he known Jimmy Wallace? Hadn't seen him in four or five years, but they'd worked in the same cop shop a decade or more back. Wallace was uniform rather than CID, but the sort of guy you'd talk to anyway. Jokes and gossip and the occasional snippet of useful information. He'd retired six years ago, which was around the same time the diagnosis appeared, along with the chemo and hair-loss.

Borne with his trademark humour . . .

Maybe so, but better to be miserable and alive. He could feel the pack of cigarettes in his pocket, knew he could back away a few yards, maybe hide himself behind a tree and spark up. The thought reminded him of schooldays, when there had been bike sheds blocking the view from the headmaster's window. Teachers occasionally arrived and asked for a light, or a cigarette, or the whole damned pack.

A well-known figure in the local community . . .

Well known to criminals he'd helped put away, too. Maybe a few of the old-timers had come to pay their respects. The coffin was being lowered into the grave, the widow giving cry again, or perhaps it was one of the daughters. A couple of minutes later it was all over. He knew there would be a mechanical digger hidden nearby. It had dug the hole and would be used to fill it in again. The mound of earth had been covered with more of the green baize cloth. All very tasteful. The majority of the mourners didn't linger. One man, face heavily lined, mouth permanently drooping, stuffed his hands into the pockets of his black woollen coat and approached with the smallest nod of recognition.

'John,' he said.

'Tommy,' Rebus replied, with another nod.

'Got to be us one of these days, eh?'

'Not yet, though.'

The two men started walking towards the

4

cemetery gates.

'Need a lift?'

Rebus shook his head. 'Car's outside.'

'Traffic's a nightmare—as per.'

Rebus offered a cigarette, but Tommy Beamish told him he'd stopped a couple of years back. 'Doctor advised me they stunt your growth.'

Rebus lit up and inhaled. 'How long have you been out of the game now?' he asked.

'Twelve years and counting. One of the lucky ones. Too many like Jimmy—get the gold watch, and soon after they're on a slab.'

'A cheery prospect.'

'Is that why you keep working? I heard you were in Cold Case.'

Rebus nodded slowly. They were almost at the gates now. The first of the cars was passing them, family members in the back, eyes fixed on the road ahead. He couldn't think what else to say to Beamish. Different ranks, different cop shops. He tried to conjure up the names of colleagues they might both have known.

'Ach, well . . .' Perhaps Beamish shared his difficulty. He was holding out his hand. Rebus shook it. 'Till the next time, eh?'

'So long as it's not one of us in the wooden suit.'

With a snort, Beamish was gone, turning his collar up against the falling rain. Rebus stubbed the cigarette out beneath his heel, waited a couple of moments, then headed for his car.

The traffic in Edinburgh was indeed a nightmare. Temporary lights, road closures, diversions. Long tailbacks everywhere. Most of it to accommodate the construction of a single tramline between airport and city centre. While stationary, he checked his phone for messages, unsurprised to find there were none. No urgent cases required his attention: he worked with the long dead, murder victims forgotten by the world at large. There were eleven investigations on the books of the Serious Crime Review Unit. They went as far back as 1966, the most recent dating from 2002. Where there were graves to visit, Rebus had visited them. Families and friends still left flowers at a few, and the names on any cards had been jotted into his notebook and added to the file—to what end he wasn't entirely sure. When he turned on the car's CD player, Jackie Leven's voice—deep and visceral—emerged from the speakers. He was singing about standing in another man's grave. Rebus's eyes narrowed. For a moment he was back in the cemetery, content to be staring at heads and shoulders. He reached over to the passenger seat and managed to wrest the lyric booklet from its case. The track was called 'Another Man's Rain'. That was what Jackie was singing about: standing in another man's rain.

'Time to get your ears checked,' Rebus muttered to himself. Jackie Leven was dead, too. A year or so younger than Rebus. They shared a Fife background. Rebus wondered if his school had ever played the singer's at football—almost the only time kids from different schools might meet. It wouldn't have mattered: Rebus had never been picked for the first team, consigned instead to offering encouragement from the frozen sidelines as tackles and goals went in and insults were traded.

'And standing in every bastard's rain,' he said aloud. The horn was sounding from the car behind. Its driver was in a hurry. He had meetings waiting for him, important people he was letting down. The world would crash and burn if this traffic didn't start moving. Rebus wondered how many hours of his own life he had wasted like this. Or sitting on a surveillance. Or filling in forms, requisitions and time sheets. When his phone pinged with a message, he saw it was from his boss.

Thought you said 3!

Rebus glanced at his watch. It was five minutes past the hour. Twenty more minutes would see him at the office, more or less. In days gone by, he might have had a siren and flashing light. He might have pulled out into the oncoming lane and trusted to the fates that he wouldn't end up in A&E. But these days he didn't even have a proper warrant card, because he wasn't a cop. He was a retired cop who happened to work for Lothian and Borders Police in a civilian capacity. His boss was the only member of the unit who was still a serving officer. A serving officer and not at all happy about his latest posting nursing the geriatrics. Not happy either about the three p.m. meeting and Rebus's tardiness.

What's the rush? Rebus texted back, just to be annoying. Then he turned up the music, repeating the same track as before. Jackie Leven still seemed to be standing in another man's grave.

As if rain wasn't bad enough . . .

II

He shook himself free of his overcoat and let it drip across the floor of the office to the hook on the far

7

wall.

'Thanks for taking the trouble,' Cowan said.

'Apologies, Danny.'

'Daniel,' Cowan corrected him.

'Sorry, Dan.'

Cowan was seated on one of the desks, his feet not quite reaching the floor, exposing a pair of red paisley-pattern socks above gleaming black leather shoes. He kept polish and brushes in the bottom drawer of his desk. Rebus knew this because he'd opened the drawer one day when Cowan was out of the room, having already checked the two drawers above it.

'What are you looking for?' Elaine Robison had asked.

'Clues,' Rebus had replied.

Robison was standing in front of him now, handing him a mug of coffee. 'How did it go?' she asked.

'It was a funeral,' Rebus answered, placing the mug to his lips.

'If we can get started,' Cowan snapped. The grey suit didn't look right on him. Its shoulders seemed over-padded and the lapels too wide. He pushed a hand defiantly through his hair.

Rebus and Robison took their seats alongside Peter Bliss, whose breathing sounded laboured even when at rest. But he'd had the same wheeze twenty years ago, and maybe the twenty before that, too. He was just a shade older than Rebus and had been in the unit longer than any of them. He sat with his hands clasped across his prodigious stomach, as if daring the universe to spring on him something he hadn't seen before. He'd certainly seen plenty like Detective Sergeant Daniel Cowan,

8

and had told Rebus as much on Rebus's first day with the unit: 'Thinks we're beneath his station. Reckons he's too good, and the bosses know it and have shunted him here to take him down a peg or three.'

Prior to retirement, Bliss had reached the rank of detective inspector—same as Rebus. Elaine Robison had been a detective constable, and blamed the lack of higher achievement on the fact that she'd always put family before career.

'Quite right too,' Rebus had told her, adding (after he'd known her a few more weeks) that his own marriage had lost its fight with the job early on.

Robison had only just turned fifty. Her son and daughter had left home, graduated from college and moved south for work. There were framed portraits of them on her desk, alongside other photos showing Robison herself posing at the top of the Sydney Harbour Bridge and seated at the controls of a light aeroplane. She had recently started to dye her hair, not that Rebus saw anything wrong in that. Streaked grey, she would still have looked ten years younger than her age and might even pass for thirty-five—same as Cowan.

Cowan, he reckoned, had arranged the chairs. They sat in a straight line in front of his desk, so that they all had to look up at him.

'Wearing those socks for a bet, Danny?' Rebus asked from behind the mug.

Cowan deflected the comment with a thin smile. 'Do I hear right, John? You've applied to rejoin?' He waited for Rebus to acknowledge the truth of this. The retirement age had been raised, meaning those of Rebus's vintage could reapply. 'Thing is,'

9

Cowan continued, leaning forward a little, 'they'll come to *me* for a reference. Way you're going, it won't be a fan letter.'

'You can have my autograph anyway,' Rebus assured him.

It was hard to tell if Peter Bliss's wheezing had just taken on a different timbre or whether he was stifling a laugh. Robison looked down into her lap and smiled. Cowan shook his head slowly.

'Can I remind you all,' he said quietly, 'that this unit is jeopardised? And if it closes down, only one of us will be welcomed back into the body of the kirk.' He pointed a finger at his own chest. 'A result would be nice. Progress of any kind would be nice.'

They all knew what he was talking about. The Crown Office was setting up a specialist Cold Case Unit for the whole of Scotland. If it scooped up their workload, their jobs would be history. The CCU would have at its heart a database of ninety-three cases dating back to the 1940s, including all the ones from the Lothian and Borders police authority. With the CCU up and running, questions were bound to be asked about the usefulness of the smaller Edinburgh team. Money was tight. There were already mutterings that dusting off old unsolveds did little but drain cash from current (and more urgent) inquiries in and around the city.

'A result would be nice,' Cowan repeated. He leapt from the desk, strode around it and plucked a newspaper cutting from the wall, brandishing it for effect. 'Cold Case Unit in England,' he intoned. 'Suspect charged for the murder of a teenager committed almost fifty years ago.' He paraded the clipping in front of their faces. 'DNA

10

. . . crime-scene analysis . . . witnesses whose consciences have been gnawing away at them. We know how this works, so how about *making* it work?'

He seemed to require an answer, but none was forthcoming. The silence lengthened until Robison broke it.

'We don't always have the resources,' she countered, 'never mind the evidence. Hard to apply DNA tests to anything when the victim's clothing got lost somewhere down the line.'

'There are plenty of cases where we *do* have clothing, though, aren't there?'

'And can we demand that every male in a town gives us a DNA sample so we can try for a match?' Bliss added. 'How about the ones who've died or moved away in the interim?'

'That positive outlook of yours is why I warm to you, Peter.' Cowan placed the cutting on the desk and folded his arms. 'For your own sakes,' he said. 'Not mine—I'll be fine and dandy—but for *your* sakes.' He paused for effect. 'For your sakes, we need to make this work.'

There was silence in the room again, broken only by Bliss's breathing and a sigh from Robison. Cowan's eyes were on Rebus, but Rebus was busy draining the last of the coffee from his mug.

III

Bert Jansch was dead, too. Rebus had seen him play a few solo gigs in Edinburgh down the years. Jansch had been born in the city but made his name in

11

London. After work that evening, alone in his flat, Rebus played a couple of Pentangle albums. He was no expert, but he could tell Jansch's playing from the other guitarist in the band, John Renbourn. As far as he knew, Renbourn was still around—maybe living in the Borders. Or was that Robin Williamson? He had taken his colleague Siobhan Clarke to a Renbourn/Williamson concert once, driving her all the way to Biggar Folk Club without telling her why. When the two musicians stepped on to the stage—looking as though they'd just roused themselves from armchairs by a roaring fire—he'd leaned in towards her.

'One of them played Woodstock, you know,' he'd whispered.

He still had the ticket to the Biggar gig somewhere. Tended to keep them, though he knew it was just one more thing that would need to be binned when he was no longer around. Next to his record deck lay a plastic guitar pick. He had bought it years back, after wandering through a music shop, telling the young guy behind the till that he might be back later for an actual guitar. The assistant had mentioned that the pick was manufactured by a Scotsman called Jim Dunlop, who also made effects pedals. In the years since, Rebus had rubbed all the writing from the pick, but had never used it on a guitar of any kind.

'Never learned to fly a plane, either,' he said to himself.

He studied the cigarette he was holding. He'd undergone a medical a few months back and received the usual warnings. His dentist, too, was always checking for the first signs of anything nasty. So far so good.

'Every lucky streak comes to an end, John,' his dentist had told him. 'Trust me.'

'Can I get an each-way bet on that?' Rebus had replied.

He stubbed the cigarette into an ashtray and counted how many were left in the packet. Eight, meaning he'd smoked twelve so far today. That wasn't bad, was it? Time was, he'd have finished one lot and broken open another. He wasn't drinking as much either: couple of beers of an evening, with maybe a tot or three of whisky before bed. He had a beer open now—his first of the day. Neither Bliss nor Robison had fancied a drink after work, and he hadn't been about to ask Cowan. Cowan tended to hang around the office late. They were housed within Police HQ on Fettes Avenue, which gave Cowan the chance to bump into senior officers, people potentially useful to him who would notice how he kept a good shine on his shoes and always addressed them properly.

'It's called stalking,' Rebus had once informed him, having caught him laughing too heartily at an old joke one of the assistant chief constables had been telling in the corridor. 'And I notice you don't pull *him* up when he calls you Dan . . .'

In a way, though, Rebus felt sorry for Cowan. There were almost certainly less proficient officers around who had more successfully scaled the heights. Cowan certainly felt that, and it gnawed away at him, so that he was almost hollowed out by it. The team had suffered as a result, which was a pity. Rebus liked many aspects of the job. He felt a small tremor of anticipation whenever he undid the binding from an old case file. There might be boxes and boxes, each one ready to

13

take him on a trip back through time. Yellowed newspapers would contain not only reports of the crime, but also general stories of national and world affairs, plus sport and advertisements. He would get Elaine Robison to guess how much a car or a house had cost in 1974, and would read out the football league tables to Peter Bliss, who had a knack for remembering the names of players and managers. But then, eventually, Rebus would be pulled back to the crime itself, to the details, interviews, evidence and family testimony: *somebody thinks they got away with it* . . . *knows they got away with it*. He hoped all these killers were out there somewhere, growing more ill at ease with each passing year as they read about advances in detection and technology. Maybe when their grandkids wanted to watch *CSI* or *Waking the Dead*, they had to leave the room and sit in the kitchen. Maybe they couldn't bear the sight of newsprint, or weren't able to listen in peace to the radio or TV news, for fear of hearing about the reopening of the case.

Rebus had posited the idea to Cowan: get the media to report breakthroughs on a regular basis, real or not, just to put the wind up the culprits.

'Something might shake loose.'

But Cowan hadn't been keen: weren't the media in enough trouble already for fabricating stories?

'It wouldn't be them doing it,' Rebus had persisted, 'it would be *us*.' But Cowan had just kept shaking his head.

The record finished and Rebus lifted the needle from the vinyl. It wasn't yet nine o'clock, far too early to be considering bed. He'd already eaten; already decided there was nothing on TV worth

14

watching. The bottle of beer was empty. He walked over to the window and stared out at the tenement opposite. A couple of children in pyjamas were staring back at him from a first-floor flat. He waved, which sent them scampering away. Now they were circling one another in the middle of their room, bouncing on their toes, not at all sleepy, and he had been dismissed from their universe.

He knew what they'd been telling him, though—there was a whole other world out there. And that could mean only one thing.

'Pub,' Rebus said out loud, reaching for his phone and his keys. Switching off the record deck and amp, he noticed the pick again and decided it was coming with him too.

Part One

*A man disappears down bar steps
With a piece of wounded sky . . .*

1

He was the only person in the office when the phone rang. Cowan and Bliss had gone to the canteen, and Robison had a doctor's appointment. Rebus picked up the receiver. It was the front desk.

'Lady here wants to talk to DI Magrath.'

'Then you've got the wrong office.'

'She says different.'

Rebus watched as Bliss came into the room, carrying a soft drink in one hand, a sandwich in the other, and with the edge of a crisp packet clamped between his teeth. 'Hang on,' he said into the receiver. Then, to Bliss: 'Any ideas about a DI called Magrath?'

Bliss placed the sandwich on his desk and removed the bag from his mouth. 'He started this place,' he told Rebus.

'How do you mean?'

'First boss of SCRU—we're all his babies, in a manner of speaking.'

'How long ago?'

'Fifteen years maybe.'

'Someone downstairs is looking for him.'

'Good luck to them.' Bliss saw Rebus's look. 'He's not dead or anything. Took up his pension six years back. Bought a place up north on the coast.'

'DI Magrath hasn't worked here for six years,' Rebus explained into the mouthpiece.

'Can somebody else have a word, then?' he was asked.

'We're a bit busy up here—what's it about?'

'A missing person.'

'Not really our department.'

'She met with DI Magrath apparently. He gave her his card.'

'Has she got a name?' Rebus asked.

'Nina Hazlitt.'

'Nina Hazlitt?' Rebus repeated, for Peter Bliss's benefit. Bliss thought for a moment, then shook his head.

'What is it she thinks we can do for her?' Rebus asked the front desk.

'Wouldn't it be a lot easier for you to ask her that yourself?'

Rebus considered for a moment. Bliss was seated behind his desk, breaking open the prawn Marie Rose sandwich—same thing he always brought back from the canteen. Cowan would soon appear, his fingers scented by bacon-flavour crisps. Maybe a trip downstairs wasn't such a bad idea.

'Five minutes,' he said into the receiver, ending the call. Then he asked Bliss if the office had ever dealt with missing persons.

'You don't think we've got enough on our plates?' Bliss poked a toe against one of half a dozen musty-smelling storage boxes piled next to him.

'Maybe Magrath worked MisPers before he came here.'

'Regular CID as far as I recall.'

'You knew him?'

'Still do. He calls me at home now and again to check SCRU's still here. He was the one who signed me up—almost the last thing he did before taking the gold watch. After him came Eddie Tranter, and then it was Cowan's turn.'

'Are my ears burning?' Cowan walked through

20

the doorway. He was stirring a cappuccino with a white plastic spoon. Rebus knew he would proceed to lick that spoon until not a trace of foam was left on it, before depositing it in the bin. Then he would slurp the coffee while checking his computer for e-mails. And the room would fill with the aromas of smoky bacon and vinegary prawn.

'Cigarette break,' Rebus said, shrugging his arms into his jacket.

'Mind you don't take too long,' Cowan cautioned.

'Missing me already?' Rebus asked, blowing a kiss and making for the door.

*   *   *

The main reception area wasn't huge, and she was easy to spot, being the only person seated on the single row of chairs. She sprang to her feet as Rebus approached. The bag on her lap fell to the floor, and she crouched down, scrabbling for its contents. Scraps of paper, several pens, lighter, sunglasses and a mobile phone. Rebus decided to let her do it unaided, then get back to her feet, rearrange her clothes and hair, and compose herself.

'My name's Nina Hazlitt,' she told him, shooting out a hand for him to shake.

'John Rebus,' he replied. Her grip was firm, several gold bangles dancing on her wrist. Her reddish-blonde hair was cut in what Rebus would have called a bob. Late forties at a guess, with laughter lines either side of her pale blue eyes.

'DI Magrath's retired?' Rebus nodded by way of answer, and she handed him the business card. It was smudged from age, its edges curled. 'I did try

21

phoning . . .'

'Long time since those numbers were active. What brings you here, Ms Hazlitt?' He returned the card and slid his hands into his pockets.

'I spoke with DI Magrath in 2004. He was very generous with his time.' The words were tumbling out of her. 'He wasn't able to help in the end, but he did what he could. Not everyone was like that—and it's no different now. So I thought maybe I'd come to him.' She paused. 'He's really retired?'

Rebus nodded again. 'Six years back.'

'Six years . . .' She was staring past him, eyes unfocused, as if wondering where the time had gone.

'I was told you're here concerning a missing person,' he prompted her.

She blinked her way back into the here and now. 'My daughter Sally.'

'When did she disappear?'

'New Year's Eve 1999,' Hazlitt recited.

'No sign of her since?'

The woman lowered her head and gave it a shake.

'I'm sorry to hear that,' Rebus told her.

'I've not given up, though.' Hazlitt took a deep breath and met his gaze. 'That's something I can't do till I know the truth.'

'I can appreciate that.'

Her eyes softened a little. 'I've been told the exact same thing so many times . . .'

'I'm sure you have.' He turned his head towards the window. 'Look, I was just headed outside for a cigarette—maybe you could do with one too?'

'How do you know I smoke?'

'I've seen what you keep in your handbag, Ms

22

Hazlitt,' he said, ushering her towards the door.

They wandered along the driveway towards the main road. She had turned down his offer of a Silk Cut, preferring her own menthols. When his cheap lighter refused to work, she'd fished in the bag for her Zippo.

'Don't see many women with these,' he'd commented.

'It was my husband's.'

'Was?'

'He only lasted a year after Sally vanished. Doctors decided it was an embolism. They don't like putting 'broken heart' on death certificates.'

'Sally's your only child?'

Hazlitt nodded. 'She'd just turned eighteen. Six more months and she'd have finished school. University was next: she was going to study English. Tom was an English teacher . . .'

'Tom being your husband?'

She nodded. 'House full of books; hardly surprising she caught the bug. When she was little, Tom used to read her a bedtime story. I walked in on them one night, expecting it to be a picture book of some kind, but it was *Great Expectations*.' The memory caused her to smile, creasing her face. Although more than half her cigarette remained, she flicked it on to the roadway. 'Sally and a bunch of her friends had rented some sort of chalet not far from Aviemore. Our Christmas present had been her share of the outlay.'

'The Millennium,' Rebus commented. 'I don't suppose it was cheap.'

'It wasn't. But it was supposed to be for four people and six of them squeezed in. That helped a bit.'

23

'Was she a skier?'

Hazlitt shook her head. 'I know that's what the town's famous for, and at least two of the girls could ski, but Sally just wanted to hang out. They'd been in to Aviemore itself—got invites to a couple of parties. They all thought she must be at the other one. There hadn't been a row or anything.'

'She'd been drinking?'

'I would assume so.' Hazlitt buttoned her thin jacket against the chill. 'I'd expected a phone call at midnight, even though I knew the reception on her phone wasn't great at the best of times. Next morning her friends guessed she'd hooked up with someone and was sleeping it off elsewhere.' She stopped abruptly and met his eyes. 'Not that she was like that.'

'Did she have a boyfriend?'

'They'd split up that autumn. He was questioned at the time.'

Rebus didn't remember the case at all, but then Aviemore was a long way north of Edinburgh.

'Tom and I had to travel up to Scotland—'

'Where from?' Rebus interrupted her. He'd taken it for granted that though her accent was English, she lived in the city.

'London,' she informed him. 'Crouch End—do you know it?' Rebus shook his head. 'We were lucky—Tom's parents helped us buy the place when we were first married. They'd come into some money.' She paused. 'I'm sorry, I know none of that's relevant.'

'You've been told as much?' he guessed.

'By very many police officers,' she admitted with another rueful smile.

'So how did you end up talking to DI Magrath?'

24

Rebus asked, genuinely curious.

'I talked to *everyone*—everyone who had time for me. DI Magrath had been mentioned in a newspaper. He specialised in unsolved crimes. And after the second one . . .' She saw that she had his attention and took a deep breath, as if preparing for a recitation. 'May 2002, A834 near Strathpeffer. Her name was Brigid Young. She was thirty-four and worked as a chartered accountant. Her car was parked by the road. It had a flat tyre. She was never seen again. So many people go missing every year . . .'

'But something made this one stand out?'

'Well, it's the same road, isn't it?'

'Is it?'

'Strathpeffer is just off the A9—look at a map if you don't believe me.'

'Right,' Rebus said.

She gave him a hard stare. 'I recognise that tone. It means you're beginning to wonder about me.'

'Is that a fact?'

She ignored him and ploughed on. 'The third was in 2008 on the A9 itself—a garden centre between Stirling and Auch . . .' She frowned. 'The place with Gleneagles Hotel.'

'Auchterarder?'

She nodded. 'A twenty-two-year-old called Zoe Beddows. Her car was in the car park all the next day and the day after. That's when suspicions were raised.'

Rebus had smoked his cigarette down to its filter. 'Ms Hazlitt . . .' he began. She held her hand up to stop him.

'I've heard it too many times not to know what you're about to say. There's no evidence, no

25

bodies have ever turned up, so as far as you lot are concerned, there's no crime. I'm just a mother whose reasoning has disappeared along with her only child. Does that cover it, Inspector?'

'I'm not an inspector,' he replied quietly. 'I used to be, but these days I'm retired. I work for the police in a civilian capacity. Outside of Cold Cases, I have no authority, which means I'm not much use to you.'

'But what are these if they're not cold cases?' Her voice had risen and taken on a slight tremor.

'It's possible I can think of someone else for you to talk to.'

'You mean CID?' She waited for him to nod. Wrapping her arms around herself, she turned away from him. 'I've just come from there. The inspector hardly gave me the time of day.'

'Maybe if I speak to him first . . .' Rebus reached into his jacket for his phone.

'Not a him, a *her*. Clarke, she said her name was.' She turned her face back towards him. 'It's happened again, you see. And it's going to keep happening.' She paused and screwed her eyes shut. A single tear began to trace its way down her left cheek. 'Sally was only the first . . .'

2

'Hey, you,' Rebus said, stepping out of his car.

'What's wrong?' Detective Inspector Siobhan Clarke turned her head slightly to peer at the building from which she'd just emerged. 'Bad memories stopping you coming in?'

26

Rebus took a moment to study the dreary two-storey façade of Gayfield Square police station. 'Just got here,' he explained, though in fact he'd been sitting in the Saab for a good four or five minutes, hands playing with the steering wheel. 'Looks like you're off out . . .'

'Well deduced.' She gave a smile and took a couple of steps forward, pecking him on the cheek. 'How've you been?'

'Still seem to have that old lust for life.'

'Meaning booze and nicotine?'

Rebus gave a shrug, returning her smile but keeping quiet.

'To answer your question,' she said, 'I'm taking a late lunch. There's a café I usually go to on Leith Walk.'

'If you're asking me to join you, there are certain preconditions.'

'And what might those be?'

'No smoky bacon crisps or prawns.'

She seemed to consider this for a moment. 'Could be a deal-breaker.' She gestured towards his Saab. 'It'll get a ticket if you leave it there. There's pay-parking across the street.'

'At one eighty an hour? I'm on a pension, remember.'

'Want to see if there's space in the car park?'

'I prefer the whiff of danger.'

'That bay's for patrol cars—I've seen civilians get towed.' She turned and started back up the steps, telling him to give her a minute. He realised his heart was beating a little faster than usual, and placed a hand over it. She'd been right about his reluctance to enter his old station—it was where he'd worked with her, right up until retirement.

27

Half a lifetime as a cop, and suddenly the force apparently had no need of him. He thought of the cemetery again, and Jimmy Wallace's grave, and gave a small, involuntary shudder. The door in front of him was swinging open, Clarke waving something in his direction. It was a rectangular sign with the words POLICE OFFICIAL BUSINESS printed on it.

'Kept behind the front desk for emergencies,' she explained. He unlocked the Saab and placed it inside the windscreen. 'And for that,' she added, 'you're treating me to a baked potato . . .'

*   *   *

Not just any baked potato either, but one filled with cottage cheese and pineapple. There were sticky Formica-topped tables and plastic cutlery, along with paper cups for the tea, the drawstring hanging over the side of each.

'Classy,' Rebus said, fishing out his tea bag and depositing it on the smallest, thinnest paper napkin he'd ever seen.

'You not eating?' Clarke asked, making a professional job of cutting through the skin of her potato.

'Way too busy for that, Siobhan.'

'Still enjoying the life of an archaeologist?'

'There are worse jobs at sea.'

'I don't doubt it.'

'What about you? Promotion suiting you?'

'Workload's no respecter of rank.'

'Well earned, all the same.'

She wasn't about to deny it. Instead she took a sip of tea and scooped up a forkful of cottage

28

cheese. Rebus tried to remember how many years they'd worked together—not that long really, in the scheme of things. Didn't see nearly so much of one another these days. She had a 'friend' who lived in Newcastle. Weekends she was often down there. And then there were the times when she'd called or texted him and he'd made some excuse not to make a meeting, never quite sure why, even as he sent the message back.

'You can't put it off for ever, you know,' she said now, waving the emptied fork at him.

'What?'

'The favour you're about to ask.'

'What favour is that, then? Can't an old pal just drop by for a catch-up?'

She stared him out, chewing her food slowly.

'Okay then,' he admitted. 'It's someone who came to see you first thing this morning.'

'Sally Hazlitt?'

'Sally's the daughter,' he corrected her. 'Nina's the one you talked to.'

'After which she came running straight to you? How did she know?'

'Know what?'

'That we used to be colleagues.'

He'd thought for a second that she was about to say 'close'. But she hadn't; she'd opted for 'colleagues' instead, just as earlier she had used the word 'civilians'.

'She didn't. A guy called Magrath used to run SCRU and she was looking for him.'

'A sympathetic shoulder?' Clarke guessed.

'The woman's daughter hasn't been seen in a dozen years.'

Clarke looked around the cramped café to make

29

sure no one was eavesdropping, then lowered her voice anyway. 'We both know she should have put it behind her a long time back. Maybe that's not possible any more, but it's therapy she needs rather than us.'

There was silence between them for a moment. Clarke seemed to have lost interest in what remained of her meal. Rebus nodded towards the plate.

'Two ninety-five that cost me,' he complained. Then: 'She seemed to think you brushed her off too readily.'

'Forgive me if I'm not always sweetness and light at eight thirty in the morning.'

'But you did listen to her?'

'Of course.'

'And?'

'And what?'

Rebus let the silence lie for a few seconds. People were hurrying past on the pavement outside. He didn't suppose there was one of them without a story to tell, but finding a sympathetic ear wasn't always easy.

'So how's the investigation?' he asked eventually.

'Which one?'

'The kid who's gone missing. I'm assuming that's how she ended up speaking to you . . .'

'She told the front desk she had information.' Clarke reached into her jacket and produced a notebook, flipped it open to the relevant page. 'Sally Hazlitt,' she intoned, 'Brigid Young, Zoe Beddows. Aviemore, Strathpeffer, Auchterarder. 1999, 2002, 2008.' She snapped the book shut again. 'You know as well as I do it's thin stuff.'

'Unlike the skin of that potato,' Rebus offered.

'And yes, I agree, it's thin stuff—as it stands. So tell me about the latest instalment.'

Clarke shook her head. 'Not if you're going to think of it in that way.'

'All right, it's not an 'instalment'. It's a MisPer.'

'Of three days' standing, which means there's still a decent chance she'll wander home and ask what all the fuss is.' Clarke got up and walked over to the counter, returning moments later with an early copy of the *Evening News*. The photo was on page five. It showed a scowling girl of fifteen with long black hair and a fringe almost covering her eyes.

'Annette McKie,' Clarke continued, 'known to her friends as 'Zelda'—from the computer game.' She saw the look on Rebus's face. 'People play games on computers these days; they don't have to go to the pub and put money in a machine.'

'There's always been a nasty streak in you,' he muttered, going back to his reading.

'She was taking the bus to Inverness for a party,' Clarke went on. 'Invited by someone she met online. We've checked and it pans out. But she told the driver she was feeling sick, so he stopped by a petrol station in Pitlochry and let her off. There was another bus in a couple of hours, but she told him she'd probably hitch.'

'Never arrived in Inverness,' Rebus said, looking at the photo again. Sulky: was that a suitable description? But to his eyes it seemed overly posed. She was copying a look and a style, without quite living it. 'Home life?' he asked.

'Not the best. She had a record of truancy, took a few drugs. Parents split up. Dad's in Australia, mum lives in Lochend with Annette's three brothers.'

31

Rebus knew Lochend: far from the bonniest neighbourhood in the city, but the Edinburgh address explained Clarke's involvement. He finished reading the report but left the paper open on the table. 'Nothing from her mobile phone?'

'Just a photo she sent to someone she knows.'

'What sort of photo?'

'Hills . . . fields. Probably the outskirts of Pitlochry.' Clarke was staring at him. 'There's really not a lot for you to do here, John,' she said, not unsympathetically.

'Who said I wanted to do anything?'

'You're forgetting: I *know* you.'

'Maybe I've changed.'

'Maybe you have. But in that case, someone needs to quash the rumour I've been hearing.'

'And what rumour is that?'

'That you've applied to return to the fold.'

He stared at her. 'Who'd want a crock like me?'

'A very good question.' She pushed her plate away from her. 'I need to be getting back.'

'Aren't you impressed?'

'By what?'

'That I didn't drag you into the first pub we passed.'

'As it happens, we didn't pass any pubs.'

'That must be the answer,' Rebus said, nodding to himself.

*   *   *

Back at Gayfield Square, he opened the Saab and made to hand her the sign.

'Keep it,' she told him. 'Might come in handy.' Then she surprised him with a hug and a final peck

32

on the cheek before disappearing into the station. Rebus got into the car and placed the sign on the passenger seat, staring at it.

POLICE OFFICIAL BUSINESS

Was that grammatically correct? What was wrong with OFFICIAL POLICE BUSINESS? Or just POLICE? He kept looking at that word. He had given so much of his life to it, but with each passing year he wondered just what it meant and how he fitted. *There's really not a lot for you to do here* . . . His phone was letting him know it had a message for him.

Is it just me or is this turning into a world record attempt for slowest cigarette ever smoked?

Cowan again. Rebus decided against answering. Instead he took a business card from his pocket. He had swapped it with Nina Hazlitt for one of his own. On one side were the details for DI Gregor Magrath; on the other was a scribbled telephone number, with Hazlitt's name beneath it. He placed it on the seat next to him, tucked under the plastic sign, and started the engine.

3

It took the best part of a week for the first batch of files to arrive. Rebus had spent a whole day trying to find the right people to talk to in the right departments of Central Scotland Constabulary and Northern Constabulary. Central covered the garden centre near Auchterarder, though at first Rebus had been told he'd need to talk to Tayside Police instead. Northern covered both Aviemore and

Strathpeffer, but these involved different divisions, meaning calls to Inverness and Dingwall.

It was all about to get simpler—allegedly. There were plans to merge the eight regions into a single force, but this had been no help to Rebus as he felt the telephone receiver generate heat under his grip.

Bliss and Robison had asked what he was up to and he'd treated them to a drink in the cafeteria while he explained.

'And we're not telling the boss?' Robison had asked.

'Not unless we have to,' Rebus had replied.

After all, one folder looked much like any other, didn't it? The first to arrive had been dispatched from Inverness. It smelled slightly of damp and there was a faint bloom on its outer covering. It was the file on Brigid Young. Rebus spent half an hour on it and rapidly concluded that there was a lot of padding. Having no leads, the local cops had interviewed everyone within reach, adding nothing except pages of meandering transcript. The photos from the scene shed almost as little light. Young had driven a white Porsche with cream upholstery. Her shoulder bag hadn't been found and neither had the key fob. Her briefcase had been left on the passenger seat. No diary, but there was one at her place of work in Inverness. She'd had one meeting in Culbokie and been on her way to another at a hotel on the shore of Loch Garve. She hadn't used her phone to call anyone about the puncture or let the client at the hotel know she'd been held up, for the simple reason that she'd left it behind at her previous meeting. The folder included some family photographs and newspaper clippings. Rebus would have called her handsome rather than pretty: a strong square jaw and a no-nonsense way of looking at the camera, as if the photo was just another task to be ticked off her list. There was a note to say that the briefcase, together with everything else in the car, had eventually been returned to the family, along with the Porsche itself. No husband: she'd lived alone in a house on the River Ness. Mother resided locally, in the same house as Brigid's sister. The file had been added to sporadically since 2002. There had been an appeal for information on the first anniversary of the disappearance, plus a reconstruction on a local TV news programme, neither producing any new leads. The most recent update consisted of a rumour that Brigid Young's business had been in trouble, leading to the theory that she could have done a runner.

When the working day was over, Rebus had decided to take the file home with him rather than leave it where Cowan might find it. In his flat, he had emptied its contents on to the dining table in his living room. Soon after, he'd realised that it made sense not to haul it back and forth to Fettes; he found some drawing pins in a cupboard, and began pinning the photos and newspaper cuttings to the wall above the table.

By the end of that week, Brigid Young's photograph had been joined by those of Zoe Beddows and Sally Hazlitt, and the paperwork took up not just the table, but sections of the floor and sofa. He could see Nina Hazlitt in her daughter's face: same bone structure, same eyes. Her file included pictures of the search that had taken place in the days after her disappearance: dozens of volunteers scouring the hillsides, along with a mountain rescue helicopter. He'd bought

35

a fold-out map of Scotland and added it to the wall, highlighting with a thick red marker the route of the A9, from Stirling to Auchterarder, Auchterarder to Perth, and from there through Pitlochry and Aviemore to Inverness and beyond, ending on the north coast at Scrabster, just outside Thurso—nothing there except the ferry that would take you to Orkney.

Rebus was sitting in his flat, smoking and thinking, when he heard someone thumping on his door. He rubbed at his eyebrows, trying to erase a headache that was gathering between them, walked into the hall and opened the door.

'When's that escalator getting fixed?' A thick-built, shaven-headed man his own age was standing there, breathing heavily. Rebus peered past him at the two flights of stairs he had just climbed.

'Hell are you doing here?' he asked.

'You forgetting what day it is? I was starting to get worried about you.'

Rebus checked his watch. It was almost eight in the evening. There was this arrangement they had—a drink once a fortnight. 'Lost track of time,' he said, hoping it didn't sound too much like an apology.

'I tried phoning you.'

'Must be on silent,' Rebus explained.

'You're not lying dead on the living room carpet, that's the main thing.'

Cafferty was smiling, though his smiles had more threat to them than most men's scowls.

'I'll get my coat,' Rebus told him. 'Just wait there.'

He retraced his steps to the living room and

36

stubbed out the cigarette. His phone was under a pile of papers—switched to silent as he had suspected. One missed call. His coat was on the sofa and he started to shrug his way into it. These regular drinks had begun soon after Cafferty's release from hospital. He'd been told that he'd flatlined at one point and that Rebus had brought him back. Not the whole truth, as Rebus had stressed. All the same, Cafferty had insisted on a drink as a way of saying thanks, then had arranged for the same thing to happen a fortnight later, and a fortnight after that.

Cafferty had once run Edinburgh—the worst of the city, at least. Drugs and prostitution and protection. These days he took either a back seat or no seat at all: Rebus wasn't sure. He knew only what Cafferty chose to tell him, and could never bring himself to trust the half of it.

'What's all this?' Cafferty asked from the living room doorway. He was gesturing towards the display on the wall, his eyes taking in the files on the table and floor.

'I told you to wait outside.'

'Bringing the job home with you—never a good sign.' Cafferty, hands in pockets, entered the room. Rebus just needed his keys and lighter . . . Where the hell were they?

'Out,' he commanded.

But Cafferty was studying the map. 'The A9—good road, that.'

'Oh aye?'

'Used it myself, back in the day.'

Rebus had located keys and lighter both. 'That's us,' he said. Cafferty was, however, in no hurry.

'Still playing the old records, eh? Might want

to . . .' He nodded towards where the needle had reached the run-out groove of a Rory Gallagher album. Rebus lifted the tone arm and switched off the hi-fi.

'Happy now?' he asked.

'Taxi's downstairs,' Cafferty replied. 'These some of your cold cases, then?'

'None of your business.'

'Not that you know of.' Cafferty gave Rebus that smile again. 'All women, though, judging by the pictures. Never my style . . .'

Rebus stared at him. 'What did you use the A9 for exactly?'

Cafferty shrugged. 'Fly-tipping, you might call it.'

'You mean getting rid of the bodies?'

'Ever driven the A9? Moorland and forest, logging tracks leading to the middle of nowhere.' Cafferty paused. 'Beautiful scenery, mind.'

'Some women have gone missing down the years—you wouldn't know anything about that?'

Cafferty shook his head slowly. 'I could ask around, though—if you want me to.'

There was silence in the room for a moment. 'I'll think about it,' Rebus said eventually. Then: 'If you did me a favour, would that be us square?'

Cafferty made to place a hand on Rebus's shoulder, but Rebus shied away.

'Let's get that drink,' he said, ushering his visitor back towards the landing.

It was ten thirty by the time he returned to his flat. He filled the kettle and made a mug of tea, then returned to the living room, switching on just the one lamp and the stereo. Van Morrison: *Astral Weeks*. His downstairs neighbour was old and deaf. Upstairs was a group of students who never made much noise except for the occasional party. Through the living room wall . . . well, he'd no idea who lived there. He'd never needed to know. The area of Edinburgh he called home—Marchmont— had a shifting population. A lot of the flats were rentals, most of them short lets. Cafferty had made this point in the pub. *Everybody used to look out for everybody else . . . Say you did end up on that floor of yours, how long would it be before anyone came calling?*

Rebus had argued that it had been no better in the old days. He'd been inside plenty of flats and houses, the inhabitant dead in bed or in their favourite chair. Flies and odour, plus bills piling up behind the door. Maybe someone had thought to knock, but they hadn't done much more than that.

Everybody used to look out for everybody else . . .

'I bet you used lookouts, too, didn't you, Cafferty?' Rebus muttered to himself. 'When you were burying the bodies . . .' He was staring at the map as he sipped his tea. He had driven the A9 infrequently. It was a frustrating road, only some of it dualled. Lots of tourists, many of them hauling caravans, with regular bends and blind summits making passing difficult. Lorries and delivery vans, struggling up the inclines. Inverness was just over a hundred miles north of Perth, but it could take two and a half, maybe three hours to drive. And when you got there, to cap it all, you were in Inverness. One radio DJ Rebus listened to called the place Dolphinsludge. There were certainly a few hardy dolphins in the Moray Firth, and Rebus didn't doubt that sludge figured too.

Aviemore . . . Strathpeffer . . . Auchterarder . . . and now Pitlochry. He'd ended up telling Cafferty some of the story, adding the caveat about coincidence being a strong possibility. Cafferty had given a thoughtful pout, swirling the whisky in his glass. The pub had been quiet—funny how people tended to finish their drinks and move on whenever Cafferty entered an establishment. The barman hadn't just removed the empties from their chosen table but given it a bit of a wipe, too.

And the first two rounds had been on the house.

'I doubt I can help much,' Cafferty had admitted.

'I didn't say I was asking for help.'

'All the same . . . If it was villains going AWOL, people who might well have fallen out with people they shouldn't have . . .'

'Far as I can tell, these were just ordinary women—civilians, you might call them.'

Cafferty had begun to outline the sorts of punishment he felt might be deserved, should a single culprit come to light, and had ended by asking Rebus how he felt whenever people got less than they deserved—less of a jail sentence; less of a punishment.

'Not part of my remit.'

'All the same . . . Think of the number of times you saw me walk free from court, or not even make

40

it that far.'

'It rankled,' Rebus had admitted.

'Rankled?'

'As in: pissed me off. Royally pissed me off. And made me that bit more determined it wasn't going to happen next time.'

'Yet here we are, sitting enjoying a drink.' Cafferty had clinked his glass against Rebus's.

Rebus hadn't said what he was thinking: *give me half a chance, I'd still put you away.* Instead, he had finished his whisky and risen to fetch another.

Side one of *Astral Weeks* had finished, and what was left of the tea had grown cold. He sat down and took out his phone and the card Nina Hazlitt had given him, punching in her number.

'Hello?' It was a man's voice. Rebus hesitated. 'Hello?' A little louder this time.

'Sorry,' Rebus said. 'Is this the right number? I was looking for Nina Hazlitt.'

'Hang on, she's here.' Rebus listened as the phone was handed over. He could hear a TV playing in the background.

'Hello?' Her voice this time.

'Sorry to be calling so late,' Rebus said. 'It's John Rebus. From Edinburgh.'

He heard an intake of breath. 'Have you . . .? Is there any news?'

'Nothing like that.' Rebus had taken the plectrum from his pocket and was playing with it in his free hand. 'I just wanted you to know I hadn't forgotten about you. I've pulled the files and I'm taking a look.'

'On your own?'

'For the moment.' He paused. 'Sorry to interrupt your evening . . .'

'It was my brother answered the phone. He's staying with me.'

'Right,' Rebus said, not knowing what else to add. The silence lengthened.

'Sally's case is reopened, then?' Nina Hazlitt's voice was a mix of hope and fear.

'Not officially,' Rebus stressed. 'Depends what I turn up.'

'Anything so far?'

'I'm only just getting started.'

'It's nice of you to go to the trouble.'

Rebus wondered if the conversation would have been so stilted without the presence of her brother. Wondered too why the hell he had phoned her out of the blue—late at night, when the only reason for calling could be that there was news of some kind, something that couldn't wait until morning. Filling her with momentary hope.

False hope . . .

'Well,' he said. 'I'll let you get on.'

'Thanks again. And call any time, please.'

'Maybe not quite so late, though, eh?'

'Any time,' she repeated. 'It's nice to know something's happening.'

He ended the call and stared at the paperwork in front of him.

'Nothing's happening,' he muttered to himself, placing the plectrum back in his pocket and rising to fix the final drink of the evening.

5

The officer's name was Ken Lochrin, and he had been retired for three years. Rebus had been given his telephone number after a bit of pleading. Lochrin's name was in the Zoe Beddows file. He seemed to have done a lot of work on it. His handwriting and signature cropped up over two dozen times. Having introduced himself, Rebus spent the first five minutes discussing retirement itself, swapping stories and explaining how SCRU worked.

'Me, I miss the job not one jot,' Lochrin had said. 'Complete pain in the posterior by the time I emptied my desk.'

'Bit frustrating not to get a result on Zoe Beddows?'

'It's a lot worse when you feel you're getting close—that never happened with her. Gets to the point where you have to move on—unless cold cases is your job, of course. So you're part of this new Crown Office initiative?'

'Not exactly. I'm in a smaller team based in Edinburgh.'

'Then how come Zoe's turned up on your radar?'

'This kid who went missing on her way to Inverness.'

'Zoe was four years ago, though.'

'All the same . . .' Rebus liked it that Lochrin used Beddows's first name. It meant she'd become a person to him rather than a case number.

'I did wonder about that myself, actually.'

'What?' Rebus prompted.

'Whether there could be a connection. But like I say—four years . . .'

'There was another in 2002, up near Strathpeffer,' Rebus said.

'Sounds like you've been talking to that woman—the Aviemore one.'

'Nina Hazlitt?'

'Daughter went missing on Hogmanay.'

'You know her?'

'I know she used to haunt Central HQ in Stirling, after Zoe disappeared.'

'This isn't just about her, though,' Rebus felt it necessary to state. 'There's Annette McKie now.'

'Known by the nickname Zelda—I read two papers a day. Gets me out of the house as far as the newsagent's. I'd drive the wife daft otherwise.'

'I didn't ask where you live, Mr Lochrin . . .?'

'Tillicoultry—world famous for our soft furnishings warehouse.'

Rebus smiled. 'I think I've been there, actually.'

'You and half of Scotland. So you're trying to find a link between this new girl and Zoe Beddows? Plus maybe Strathpeffer and Aviemore?'

'Something like that.'

'And you want to ask me about the photo?'

Rebus was silent for a moment. 'What photo?'

'The one Zoe sent her friend. Didn't I just mention it? Probably a coincidence, but I suppose you have to check . . .'

*　　　*　　　*

'It was in Zoe Beddows's file,' Rebus explained to Siobhan Clarke. He ran his hand through his hair distractedly. 'I should have spotted it, but it was

44

buried in an interview transcript. Just the single mention. Not even one of her closest friends. And no message with it. Just the picture, sent the day she went missing . . .'

He was standing with Clarke in the corridor outside the CID suite in Gayfield Square police station. Clarke's arms had been folded as she listened, but now she held up a hand to interrupt him.

'You've got the files? *All* the files?'

'Yes.'

'And you've cleared this with DS Cowan?' She rolled her eyes at the stupidity of her own question. 'What am I saying? Of course you haven't—you're keeping it to yourself.'

'You know me too well.'

Clarke thought for a moment. 'Can I see the photo?'

'I need to speak to the recipient.' Rebus paused. 'Well, it doesn't have to be *me*, of course . . .'

'You think I'm going to do it for you?'

'Annette McKie sent a photograph from her phone the day she vanished. Back in 2008 Zoe Beddows did the selfsame thing from the selfsame road. You're telling me we should ignore that?'

'What about the others—Strathpeffer and Aviemore?'

'Brigid Young didn't have her phone with her. Besides, could you send photos from a phone back then . . . ?'

A man appeared in the nearest doorway. Tall, slim, good suit.

'There you are,' he said.

Clarke managed a half-smile. 'Here I am,' she agreed. The man was staring at Rebus, awaiting an introduction.

'John Rebus,' Rebus obliged, holding out a hand. The two men shook. 'I'm with SCRU.'

'This is DCI Page,' Clarke told him.

'James Page,' Page clarified.

'You've changed a bit,' Rebus said. Page looked at him blankly. 'Led Zeppelin,' Rebus explained. 'Guitarist.'

'Oh, right. Same name as me.' Page at last attempted a smile, before turning his attention to Clarke. 'Meeting of the control team in five.'

'I'll be there.'

Page's eyes lingered on hers a second too long. 'Good to meet you,' he said to Rebus.

'No interest at all in why I'm here?'

'John . . .' Clarke's tone was warning Rebus off, but too late. He'd taken a step towards Page.

'I assume you're in charge, so you should know that there could be a link between Annette McKie and a series of other MisPers.'

'Oh?' Page looked from Rebus to Clarke and back again. But the phone he was holding had started to vibrate, and he focused his attention on its screen. 'Need to take this,' he apologised. Then, to Clarke: 'Write me a short briefing, will you?' He turned back into the office, raising the phone to his ear.

There was silence in the corridor for a few seconds.

'Need any help with that briefing?' Rebus asked.

'Thanks for adding another brick to the hod.' She folded her arms again; he wondered if it was a defensive gesture. He hadn't paid much attention to the 'Reading Body Language' classes at police college. Through the doorway, Rebus had a good view of Page's back. Neat haircut, no creases in the jacket. He wouldn't be much more than thirty, maybe thirty-five tops. The DCIs were getting younger . . .

'Thought you had someone in Newcastle you were seeing?' Rebus asked casually.

Clarke glared at him. 'You're not my dad.'

'If I was, I might have a few words of advice at the ready.'

'You're really going to stand there and lecture me about relationships?'

Rebus pretended to wince. 'Maybe not,' he conceded.

'Good.'

'So the only thing we need to discuss is this briefing for Mr Dazed and Confused.' He tried for a conciliatory tone and a kindly face. 'You'll want it to be thorough. Nobody better placed than me to help with that, I'd have thought.'

She stood her ground for a further moment or two, then made a sound that mixed frustration with resignation.

'You'd better come in then,' she said.

The cramped office was busy with detectives on their phones or staring hard at their computer screens. Rebus knew a few faces and offered a wink or a nod. He got the feeling desks and chairs had been requisitioned from elsewhere. It was a narrow, mazy walk to Clarke's corner spot, with waste bins and electrical cables to be negotiated. She sat down and sifted through the papers next to her keyboard.

'Here,' she said, handing him a copy of a blurry photograph. It showed a field and a line of trees beyond, with hills in the distance. 'Sent from her phone at just after ten p.m. the day she went missing. Wasn't when the picture was taken, of course. I'd say late afternoon. Nobody on the bus remembers her taking pictures out of the window, but then nobody paid her much attention till she said she was going to throw up.'

Rebus studied the landscape. 'Could be just about anywhere. Have you released it to the media?'

'It's been mentioned in dispatches, but we didn't think it meant anything.'

'Someone out there is bound to recognise it. Grazing land—farmer will know it if no one else does. Could the woods be Forestry Commission?' He looked up and saw she was smiling. 'What?' he asked.

'It's just that I had the exact same thought.'

'That's because you learned from the best.' Her smile started to slide. 'Just joking,' he assured her. 'Great minds and all that.' He peered at the photo again. 'Who did she send it to?'

'A friend from school.'

'Best friend?'

'Just a friend.'

'Did she usually send them photos?'

'No.'

Rebus looked at Clarke. 'Same thing with Zoe Beddows—sent to someone she knew, but no more than that. And no message—same as this time, right?'

'Right,' Clarke agreed. 'But meaning what, exactly?'

'Sent in a panic,' Rebus speculated. 'Maybe a cry for help, and any recipient would have to do.'

'Or?' Clarke knew there was more. Their eyes met again.

'You know as well as I do.'

She nodded slowly. 'Sent by the abductor—a sort of calling card.'

'Bit of work to be done before we can say that.'

'But that doesn't stop us thinking it.'

Rebus waited a while before speaking. 'So do you want my help on this or not?'

'Maybe for a time.'

'Then you'll get Physical Graffiti to tell my boss?'

'You're going to run out of Led Zeppelin titles sooner or later.'

'But it'll be fun while it lasts,' Rebus said with a smile.

'This is all working out for you, isn't it? Means you don't have to explain to Cowan about the files. Plus you can keep in touch with Nina Hazlitt.'

'What makes you think I'd do that?'

'Because she's your type.'

'Oh aye? What type do I go for, then?'

'Confused, needy, damaged . . .'

'I'm not sure that's exactly fair, Siobhan.'

'Then why have you gone all defensive?'

She was looking at his arms, so he looked too. They were folded squarely across his chest.

6

The file on Zoe Beddows had a home address and telephone number for her friend Alasdair Blunt. When Rebus called, he got an answering machine. Man's voice; Scottish, with a good education: *Alasdair and Lesley are otherwise engaged. Leave a message or try Alasdair's mobile.* Rebus made a note

49

of the number, ended the call and punched it in. It rang and rang. He looked around the walls of his living room. Clarke had asked him to scoop up all the files and take them to Gayfield Square.

'Sure you've got the space?' he'd countered.

'We'll find some.'

No one was answering. Rebus stared out of the window, down on to the street. A parking warden was checking residents' permits and pay-and-display tickets. Rebus had left his Saab on a single yellow line. He watched as the warden glowered through the windscreen at the POLICE OFFICIAL BUSINESS sign. The man looked up and down the street. His jacket was several sizes too big for him, as was the peaked cap. He lifted his machine and started to process the infringement. Rebus sighed and turned away from the window, ending the call. He was starting to phone Blunt's answering machine again, this time to leave a message, when his mobile trembled. Incoming: number blocked.

'Hello?' Rebus decided this was as much information as the caller needed.

'You just phoned me.'

'Alasdair Blunt?'

'That's right. Who am I speaking to?'

'My name's Rebus, sir. I'm calling from Lothian and Borders Police.'

'Oh yes . . .?'

'It's concerning Zoe Beddows.'

'Has she turned up?'

'I just need to confirm a few details about the picture she sent you from her phone.'

'You mean the case is still open?' He sounded incredulous.

'Isn't that what her family and friends would

want?'

Blunt seemed to consider this, and his tone softened. 'Yes, of course. Sorry, rough day.'

'What is it you do, Mr Blunt?'

'I'm in sales. Though not for much longer if things don't pick up.'

'Might help if you answered your phone—I could have been a new client.'

'Then you'd have called me on my other mobile, the one I use for business. That's why I was busy when you rang.'

'Understood.'

Blunt exhaled noisily. 'So how can I help?'

'I've been looking through the records and there doesn't appear to be a copy of the photograph Ms Beddows sent you.'

'That's because it got deleted.'

Rebus rested his weight on the arm of his sofa. 'That's a pity. There was no message? Just a picture?'

'That's right.'

'Showing what exactly?'

Blunt seemed to struggle to remember. 'Hills . . . sky . . . a sort of track off to one side.'

'Trees?'

'Maybe.'

'You didn't recognise the spot?'

Blunt hesitated. 'No,' he said eventually.

'You don't sound sure.'

'I'm positive.'

Rebus stayed silent for a moment, inviting Blunt to continue.

'Are we done?' the man asked.

'Not quite. What time of day did you receive the photo?'

51

'Sometime in the evening.'

'Can you be more precise?'

'Nine, ten o'clock, something like that.'

'And when do you think the picture was taken?'

'I've really no idea.'

'Was it bright sunlight, or maybe the sky was growing dark . . .?'

'The quality wasn't great.' Blunt paused. 'Twilight, I suppose.'

Same as with Annette McKie, Rebus noted. Then: 'Can I ask, how did you know Ms Beddows?'

'She cut my hair.'

'But you were friends?'

'She cut my hair,' Blunt repeated. Rebus thought for a moment. How many hairdressers kept their clients' contact details on their mobile? How many forwarded them photographs . . .?

'Which of your phones was the photo sent to, Mr Blunt?'

'What does it matter?'

'Was it your wife who saw it when it arrived? Asked you who Zoe was? Then maybe deleted it?'

'This has got nothing to do with anything.' Blunt was sounding irritated again.

'But is that what happened? You'd been spending a bit of time with Zoe? Maybe in your car—a wee drive to a farm track somewhere . . .?'

'I wasn't sure at first,' Blunt said quietly. 'I don't *think* the photo meant anything to us. It wasn't anywhere we'd been . . .'

'Did any of this come out at the time?'

'Some.'

Rebus was looking at the Zoe Beddows file. Incomplete. Like most cases. You were a cop, at the end of another long day you wrote up only the

52

stuff you thought was important.

'There's not an easy way to put this, Mr Blunt, but were you ever a suspect?'

'Only in my wife's eyes.'

'But you got through it, you and Lesley?'

'Lesley came later. After Judith had walked out on me.' Blunt paused. 'Zoe had quite a lot of "friends", you know. We'd stopped seeing one another several months before she went missing.'

'And there's nothing else you can tell me about the photo?'

'Only that it ended my marriage.'

'Sure that wasn't *your* doing, Mr Blunt?'

The line went dead. Rebus considered calling Blunt back, but decided against it. He would almost certainly refuse to answer. Instead, he walked over to the Zoe Beddows file, its contents splayed across the dining table. He knew he would have to read it again, every single line of it. He was fairly confident there was nothing about Zoe and her 'friends'. If any more of them had been interviewed, their relationship to the MisPer had not been flagged up. Laziness, or a sense of propriety on the part of the investigators? They would have known what the media would have done with it: created a story; distorted the facts; sold the public another version. In the process, Zoe Beddows would have become slightly less mourned. Rebus had seen it a dozen times or more. Prostitutes were 'asking for it', 'putting themselves in danger'; anyone with a chaotic lifestyle could be pitied less than the newspaper's mass of readers, the ones with families and steady jobs, the ones who feasted on those same vicarious details.

Rebus reckoned it had been a conscious decision

on somebody's part to leave speculation out of the case. Which was problematic for anyone opening the files from cold: the whole story wasn't there. He thought about phoning Ken Lochrin again, but decided it could be done later. He called Clarke instead. She answered with a question.

'What?'

'I was just thinking,' Rebus said. 'The stuff at my flat, it's been sorted into piles and pinned up on the wall—wouldn't it be easier for us to work from here?'

'This is a police inquiry, John, not a hobby. It needs to be brought to the station.'

'Understood.' A caller was waiting. Rebus glanced at the display. 'I'll see you in an hour,' he told Clarke. Then, to Daniel Cowan: 'Rebus speaking.'

'I don't like this, John, not one little bit.'

'I take it DCI Page has been on the blower?'

'If it's a cold case, it should be run from SCRU. You should be *here*.'

'Believe me, sir, if it were up to me . . . ?'

'Your patter's pish, John. Is this your way of sucking up to the big boys?'

'I'm a team player, sir—ask Bliss and Robison, they'll vouch for me.'

'It's not them you need to win over. Don't forget what I said: without my approval, you're staying retired.'

'But your approval's all I've ever really craved, Danny . . .'

Cowan's voice was rising to something just short of a yell when Rebus ended the call.

'You can't just wander in, you know.'

It was the next morning, and the uniform behind the desk at Gayfield Square police station didn't like the look of Rebus. Rebus had some sympathy: his eyes were probably bloodshot, he had failed to locate a clean shirt, and his razor definitely needed a new blade. He had shown her his ID and waited to be buzzed through the locked door leading to the stairs.

'Who's your appointment with?'

'I'm on secondment to CID.'

'That's not what your card says.'

Rebus leaned forward until his face was almost touching the Plexiglas partition. 'Are we going to have this every morning?'

'He's with me, Juliet,' Siobhan Clarke said, coming in from outside. 'Might as well get used to his ugly mug.'

'He needs to sign as a visitor. Then I can give him a badge.'

Clarke stared at the woman. 'Really? I mean, *really*, Juliet? He's attached to the McKie inquiry until further notice.'

'Then I should have been told.'

'So someone cocked up—there had to be a first time, eh?'

'I'm right here, by the way,' Rebus interrupted, feeling left out.

The officer's face broke into an eventual smile— aimed at Clarke rather than Rebus. 'Some proper identification by the end of the day . . .'

'Girl Guide's honour.'

'I thought you said you'd never been a Girl Guide.' The smile was broadening as she pressed the button to let them through.

Clarke led Rebus into the heart of the building. 'You'll require a passport photo,' she told him. 'Got one handy?'

'Never felt the need.'

She looked at him. 'No passport?'

'Didn't bother renewing it. I'm perfectly happy where I am.'

She looked at him again. 'When was the last time you actually left the city—for pleasure, I mean?'

He gave a casual shrug as she continued to study him, this time taking in his clothes.

'James likes the officers under him to be presentable.'

'You might be under him from time to time—but not me.'

'Is this what I have to look forward to?' She gave him a stern look and asked where the files were.

'At home.' He saw that she was ready to remonstrate, so held up a hand. 'I'm not being obstructive. It's just that I was awake till three going through them again. Slept late and didn't have time to pack them away.'

'Making you the resident expert until someone else gets a look-in?'

'You might almost call me indispensable.'

'Not even close, John.' They were outside the CID suite. The door, as usual, was wide open, a couple of detectives already seated at their desks. Walking in, Rebus caught the aroma of freshly brewed coffee. The pot rested on top of a filing cabinet. Clarke poured for both of them.

56

'Anybody get milk?' she asked. There were shakes of the head.

'That must make me the cavalry,' James Page said, striding into the office. He carried a litre carton in one hand, brown leather satchel in the other.

'Hello again,' he said to Rebus.

'Morning, sir.'

'First names around here, John.' Page handed the milk to Clarke but kept his eyes on Rebus. 'Any news from those files of yours?'

'Only that they're far from complete. Zoe Beddows had been seeing a married man—that's who she sent *her* photo to. But I only found that out by speaking to him. File just names him as one of her friends.'

'And the photo itself?'

'He didn't keep it. From the description: hills, sky and a track.'

'Similar enough to the one Annette McKie sent,' Clarke commented.

Rebus felt compelled to qualify the statement. '*If* she sent it.'

'Let's not jump to conclusions,' Page countered. 'What about Aviemore and Strathpeffer?'

'I did a bit of digging on the internet,' Clarke said. 'You couldn't readily send a picture from one phone to another until 2005 or 2006.'

'Really?' Page's brow furrowed. 'As recently as that?'

'Might be worth showing the photo we *do* have to Zoe Beddows's lover,' Rebus suggested. 'Even if they're unlikely to be the same spot.' He paused. 'And if I can add something else . . .' He was aware that Siobhan Clarke was holding her breath, waiting

57

for him to say the wrong thing.

'Yes?' Page prompted.

'We also need to get the new photo circulated. It has to ring bells with somebody.'

'There's a press conference at twelve,' Page said, studying his watch.

'There is?' Clarke sounded annoyed at just finding out.

'The mother's putting up a reward. Ten thousand pounds, I think.'

'A fair bit of cash,' Rebus stated. 'For someone who lives in Lochend.'

'Do you want me at the press conference, James?' Clarke was asking.

'We'll all be there—need to let people know we're motivated.' Page broke off, noticing Rebus's shirt and stubble. 'Maybe not quite all of us, eh, John?'

'If you say so, James.'

'Public perception and suchlike . . .' Page gave a thin smile and turned away, heading for his own inner office. He had to put his coffee down and take a key from his pocket to unlock the door.

'I'm sure that was a cupboard when I used to work here,' Rebus said to Clarke, keeping his voice down.

'It was,' she confirmed. 'But James seems to like it.'

The door closed again, with Page behind it. The room had to be near airless, and with no natural light that Rebus could recall. Yet James Page appeared to flourish there.

'Did I pass inspection?' he asked Clarke.

'Just about.'

'It's only day one, remember—plenty of time for

58

me to start letting the side down.'

'How about not doing that, eh? Just for once in your life.'

8

The school's rector had offered them his office, but Clarke had declined. As she waited with Rebus in the corridor outside, she explained her reasoning.

'Too intimidating. When you're in that room, it's because you're in trouble. We want him a bit more relaxed and talkative.'

Rebus nodded his agreement. He was looking out of a window towards the playground. The window was double-glazed, but condensation had found its way between the panes. The wooden frame was spongy.

'Could do with a bit of TLC,' Clarke commented.

'Either that or knocking down.'

'New schools for all, once we get independence.'

Rebus looked at her. 'What's with the "we"? Are you forgetting that's an English accent you've got?'

'Reckon I'm for deportation?'

'We might just keep you at a pinch.' Rebus pulled back his shoulders as a teenager in school uniform entered the corridor, hesitated, then walked towards them. His hair flopped into his eyes, and he wore his striped tie with an oversized knot.

'Are you Thomas?' Rebus asked.

'Thomas Redfern?' Clarke added.

'Aye.' Redfern didn't seem to have any gum in his mouth, but he sounded as though he did.

'You're in Annette's class?'

Redfern nodded.

'You all right talking here?'

The boy shrugged and stuffed his hands deep into his trouser pockets.

'I've already told the polis—'

'We know that,' Clarke interrupted. 'We just need to clear a few things up.'

'Have you still got that photo?' Rebus asked. 'The one Zelda sent?'

'Aye.'

'Mind if I see it?' Rebus held out his hand. Redfern produced a phone from the top pocket of his blazer and switched it on.

'Sorry we had to pull you out of class,' Clarke said.

The boy gave a snort. 'Double chemistry.'

'You can always walk the long way back.'

He had found the photograph. He turned the phone around so they could see its screen. Rebus lifted it from between his fingers. He didn't think it was blurred enough to have been taken from a moving vehicle, or even from behind glass. He got a sense that the photographer had been standing up, and was probably around his height.

'How tall is Zelda?' he asked.

'Bit shorter than me.' Redfern was indicating his own shoulder.

'Around five six?' Rebus nodded to himself.

'She could be standing on a rock or something,' Clarke suggested.

'No message with it?' Rebus asked the boy.

'No.'

'Did she often send you stuff?'

'A text now and then—if there was a party

60

maybe.'

'Did you know she was going to Inverness?'

'She told everyone.'

'Nobody else from the school was invited?'

'Timmy was, but her parents wouldn't let her go.'

'The girls knew about the party from the internet?'

'Some guy they talked to on Twitter,' Redfern confirmed. 'Year older but still at school. We all told her . . .'

'Told her what?' Clarke asked.

'To be careful. People online, you know . . .'

'Not always what they seem?' Clarke nodded her understanding. 'Well, we've checked, and he's a sixteen-year-old called Robert Gilzean.'

'Aye, the other polis told me.'

While Clarke kept Redfern talking, Rebus flicked through some of the other photos on the phone. Kids making faces, kids making hand gestures, kids blowing kisses. None showed Annette McKie.

'How well do you know Zelda, Tom?'

He gave another shrug.

'Were you at primary school together?'

'No.'

'So you've been in the same class for . . . what . . . three years?'

'I suppose so.'

'Ever been to her house?'

'Couple of parties. She seemed to spend most of the time in her bedroom.'

'Oh aye?'

Redfern almost blushed. 'Online games,' he clarified. 'Showing off how good she was.'

'You don't sound impressed.'

'Games are all right, but I prefer books.'

'That's refreshing,' Clarke said with a smile.

'What did you think when you got the photo?' Rebus handed back the phone.

'Didn't really think anything.'

'Bit surprised, maybe? Ten o'clock at night—not the sort of thing she'd done before.'

'I suppose so.'

'And you texted her back?'

Redfern looked at him and nodded. 'I thought she'd hit the wrong button, meant it for someone else in her contacts.'

'But she never answered?'

'No. She'd been sending texts to Timmy from the bus. Last one just said she was feeling queasy.' The boy paused. He looked from Rebus to Clarke and back again. 'She's dead, isn't she?'

'We don't know that,' Clarke answered softly.

'But she is, though.' Redfern's eyes were fixed on Rebus, and Rebus wasn't about to lie.

*　　*　　*

Rebus tried the door to James Page's room, but it was locked. He was on his own in the CID suite. There was no TV, but Clarke had shown him how to watch the press conference on her computer. He opened a few desk drawers, finding nothing of interest. The press conference was coming from a hotel round the corner from Gayfield Square. Rebus had picked up a couple of chicken slices from Gregg's on the trip back from the school. They were long gone, though a few crumbs of pastry lingered on his shirt and jacket. Lothian and Borders Police had their own camera at the hotel, its unedited feed—minus sound—appearing on Clarke's monitor. Rebus had failed to find any kind of volume control, which was why he was prowling the office rather than sitting at the desk. He'd unearthed some Nurofen in Clarke's drawer and popped a couple in his breast pocket—always handy to have. He'd drunk enough coffee and there didn't seem to be any tea bags, other than mint and redbush.

Back at the monitor, proceedings had started. Rebus gave the plastic casing a thump, but there was still no sound. No sign of a radio anywhere either. He knew he could go listen in his car, but that was supposing one of the local stations was covering it. Instead he sat himself down and watched. Whoever was manning the camera needed either an instruction manual or a trip to Specsavers. The focus was all over the place, and Rebus was shown more of the table than the people seated behind it. Others were standing. Page was flanked by Siobhan Clarke and a detective constable called Ronnie Ogilvie. Behind Annette McKie's mother and the oldest of her brothers stood a man Rebus half recognised. The man squeezed the mother's shoulder whenever he sensed she was flagging. At one point she covered his hand with her own, as if in thanks. Annette's brother did some of the talking, too, reading from a prepared statement. He seemed confident enough, gaze surveying the room, giving the photographers plenty of opportunities for a decent shot while his mother dabbed her reddened, sore-looking eyes. Rebus didn't know the lad's name, guessed him to be seventeen or eighteen: short hair spiked at the front with gel, face bearing some residual acne. Pale and gaunt and streetwise. But now the camera was a blur of movement. It was Page's turn. He seemed ready—eager even—to start fielding questions. After a couple of minutes, however, there was an interruption, Page turning to his left. The camera caught Annette McKie's mother as she staggered from the room, hand held to her mouth, either overcome with grief or about to be sick. The man went with her, leaving her son still seated. He was looking towards Page, as if seeking advice: should he stay or should he go? The camera swept the room, taking in other cameras, journalists, detectives. The double doors had swung shut behind the mother.

Then the camera was pointing at the patterned carpet.

And the screen went black.

Rebus stayed where he was until the team started to drift back into the office. Ogilvie shook his head at him, saving himself the effort of saying anything. Page looked annoyed at having been cut off in his prime—if the TV news concentrated on anything, it would be the walkout. He stabbed the key into the lock, opened his door and disappeared into his cupboard. Clarke made her way between the desks, catching her foot only once on a trailing cable. She handed Rebus a chocolate bar.

'Thanks, Mum,' he told her.

'Did you see it?'

He nodded. 'No sound, though—did Page get round to mentioning the photos from the phones?'

'Seemed to slip his mind when the mother did a runner.' She unwrapped her own chocolate bar and bit into it.

'Who was the guy standing behind her?' Rebus

asked.

'Family friend.'

'Is he the one putting up the reward?'

Clarke looked at him. 'Okay, spit it out.'

'I've not started eating it yet.' When this failed to raise a smile, he relented. 'His name's Frank Hammell. Owns a couple of pubs and at least one club.'

'You know him?'

'I know his pubs.'

'But not the club?'

'It's somewhere out in bandit country.'

'Meaning?'

'West Lothian.' Rebus nodded towards the monitor. 'Pretty touchy-feely, I thought . . .'

'Not that sort of guy?'

'Not unless you're *really* close.'

Clarke's chewing slowed. She thought for a moment. 'And what does any of this add?'

'A note of caution?' Rebus answered eventually. 'If he's the mum's "friend" and she's upset, you can bet *he's* upset too.'

'Hence the reward?'

'It's not the reward we know about that worries me—it's the one he might be putting out on the quiet.'

Clarke glanced towards Page's door. 'You think we should tell him?'

'Your call, Siobhan.' While she considered this, Rebus had another question. 'Remind me what happened to Annette's father?'

'Did a runner to Australia.'

'What's his name?'

'Derek something . . . Derek Christie.'

'Not McKie?'

'That's the mother—Gail McKie.'

Rebus nodded slowly. 'And the lad at the conference . . .?'

'Darryl.'

'Still at school, is he?'

Clarke called across to Ronnie Ogilvie. 'What does Darryl McKie do?'

'I think he said he was a bar manager,' Ogilvie replied. 'And he calls himself Christie rather than McKie.'

Clarke looked at Rebus. 'Eighteen is a bit young for a manager,' she commented.

Rebus gave a twitch of his mouth. 'Depends whose bar it is,' he said, rising to give her back her chair.

9

'Just like old times, eh?' Rebus said. 'And at last I'm seeing a bit of Scotland.'

They were in Clarke's car, a new-smelling Audi. The trip had been Rebus's idea—take a look at the spot where Annette McKie had last been seen; check for possible matches to the photo. They had left Edinburgh, heading north across the Forth Road Bridge into Fife, crawling through what seemed like miles of roadworks with a 40 mph limit, then skirting Kinross on the way to Perth, where they connected with the A9. It wasn't dualled, and they seemed to have hit the mid-afternoon rush. Rebus took a CD from his pocket and swapped it for the Kate Bush album Clarke had been playing.

'Who said you could do that?' she complained.

Rebus shushed her and turned up the volume on track three. 'Just listen,' he said. Then, after a few minutes: 'So what's he singing about, then?'

'How do you mean?'

'In the chorus.'

'Something about standing in another man's rain.'

'You sure?'

'Am I hearing it wrong?'

Rebus shook his head. 'It's just that I thought he was . . . Ach, never mind.' He made to eject the CD, but she told him to leave it. She signalled and pulled out to overtake. The Audi had a bit of heft. Even so, she just made it, an oncoming vehicle flashing its lights in protest.

'Trying to prove something?' Rebus asked.

'I just want us arriving in Pitlochry much the same time she did. Isn't that the whole point?' She turned towards him. 'And aren't you supposed to be looking for where that photo might've been taken?'

'Nowhere around here,' he muttered. But he began to scan the overcast countryside anyway. They passed a sign to Birnam and a Beatrix Potter exhibition. Clarke overtook another lorry, then had to brake hard when she spotted a speed camera, causing the lorry to brake too, accompanied by a blast of its horn and an angry flash of headlights. The Jackie Leven CD had ended and Rebus asked if she wanted Kate Bush back on, but she shook her head.

'Where the hell are they all going?' Rebus was peering at the traffic ahead of them. 'Not exactly tourist season.'

'Not exactly,' she agreed. Then, too casually:

67

'How's Cafferty, by the way?'

Rebus stared at her. 'What makes you think I'd know?'

She seemed to take a moment deciding how to answer. 'I was talking to someone from the Complaints . . .'

The Complaints: meaning Internal Affairs. 'Fox?' Rebus guessed. 'I see him sliming his way around HQ.'

'The word is out, John—you and Cafferty, your little drinking sessions.'

Rebus digested this. 'Is Fox coming after me? You don't want to hang around with those scumbags, Siobhan. Might be contagious.'

'They're not scumbags, as you well know. And to answer your question: you're not a serving officer, meaning at the moment I doubt Fox could touch you even if he wanted to.' She paused, keeping her eyes firmly on the road ahead. 'On the other hand, you go back a long way with Cafferty.'

'So?'

'So, is there anything for the Complaints to find if they *do* come looking?'

'You know how I feel about Cafferty,' Rebus stated coldly.

'Doesn't mean favours haven't been swapped somewhere down the line.'

Rebus drank from a plastic bottle of water, bought when they'd stopped for petrol at Kinross.

'Fox wants you to grass me up, is that it?'

'He was just asking if I saw much of you these days.'

'And then he happens to drop Cafferty's name into the mix?' Rebus shook his head slowly. 'So what did you tell him?'

'He was right, though, wasn't he—about you seeing Cafferty?'

'The guy thinks he owes me for what I did at the hospital.'

'You're on free drinks for life?'

'I pay my way.'

She overtook a Tesco delivery van. There were three articulated lorries at the very front of the queue, slowing inexorably as the road hit an incline. A sign they'd just passed suggested that sluggish vehicles should pull over to allow overtaking, but that wasn't happening.

'There's some dual carriageway coming up,' Clarke said.

'We're almost at Pitlochry anyway,' Rebus countered. Then, lowering his voice a little, 'And thanks for the warning.'

She nodded, staring straight ahead, hands tensed against the steering wheel. 'Just make sure there's no ammo Fox can use, eh?'

'From the look of him, I'd say he's got a history of firing blanks. Any chance of another cigarette break?'

'You said it yourself: we're nearly there.'

'Aye, but they don't let you smoke in petrol stations.' Which was why he'd headed for the car park at Kinross, while Clarke filled the fuel tank and bought drinks at the shop.

'Five more minutes,' she told him. 'Just five more minutes . . .'

Ten minutes later—not that Rebus was counting—they turned off the A9 and took the slip road into Pitlochry, passing the petrol station where Annette McKie's bus had stopped to drop her off. Clarke drove through the town. There was just the one main street, with signs leading off to the Festival Theatre, the hydroelectric dam, and Edradour and Bell's distilleries.

'I went to the dam once when I was a kid,' Clarke commented. 'Supposedly to see the salmon leap.'

'No salmon?' Rebus guessed.

'No salmon.'

'On the other hand, you have to love a town with two distilleries . . .'

It took only a couple of minutes for them to reach the far end of Pitlochry. She did a three-point turn and headed back the way they'd come. There was a small police station on the main road, but not continuously manned. For protocol's sake, Clarke had phoned Tayside's Divisional HQ in Perth before setting out, alerting a local inspector to their trip. She had stressed that a welcoming party would not be necessary.

'It's really just a recce.'

She was signalling now to enter the petrol station's forecourt. As soon as the car stopped, Rebus undid his seat belt and got out, making for the pavement, cigarette and lighter at the ready. He watched as Clarke went into the shop. There was a middle-aged woman behind the till, and Clarke showed her her warrant card, followed by two photos, one of Annette McKie and one a copy of the picture Annette had sent to Thomas Redfern. Directly across from the petrol station was the Bell's distillery, and behind it the vast turrets of what Rebus guessed was a hotel. Another car had pulled into the forecourt. The man who got out looked like a salesman: white shirt, pale yellow tie. His jacket had been hanging from a hook inside the car, and he slipped back into it, warding off the cold air. He unlocked the car's petrol cap, but then glanced towards the pavement and saw someone smoking there. Readjusting his priorities, he headed in Rebus's direction, offering a nod of kinship before lighting up.

'There'll be frost tonight,' he offered.

'Just so long as there's not snow,' Rebus responded.

'Last thing I need is them shutting the Drumochter Pass.'

'Snow gates?' Rebus guessed.

'That's the ones. Last winter was a nightmare.'

'You going to Inverness?'

The man nodded. 'How about you?'

'Heading back to Edinburgh.'

'Civilisation, eh?'

'This seems civilised enough.' Rebus looked in the direction of town.

'Wouldn't know—I only ever stop to fill up.'

'You travel a lot?'

'Part and parcel, isn't it? Five, six hundred miles a week, sometimes more.' He gestured towards his vehicle. Behind it, Rebus could see the woman at the till shaking her head in reply to another of Clarke's questions. 'Car's not even two years old and it's on its last legs,' the salesman was saying. 'How's the Audi?'

'Seems okay.' Rebus finished his cigarette. 'What is it you sell exactly?'

'How long have you got?'

'Let's say fifteen seconds.'

'Then I'll give you two words: 'logistics' and 'solutions'.'

'I feel duly enlightened.' Rebus watched as Clarke made her way back to the Audi. 'Thanks for that.'

'No problem.' The man took out his phone and was checking for messages as Rebus headed across the forecourt.

'Anything?' he asked, sliding into the passenger seat.

'She wasn't working that day,' Clarke obliged. 'The staff who were have all been questioned. One remembered Annette coming in and asking to use the loo. She bought a bottle of water and headed off again into town.'

'Nice of the bus not to wait for her.'

'Actually, the driver's mortified. But he was obeying company rules.'

Rebus peered out through the windscreen in search of CCTV.

'Cameras caught her,' Clarke confirmed. 'Busy on her phone.'

'Could she have had a rendezvous?'

'No family or friends in Pitlochry.' Clarke thought for a moment. 'There's another camera on the main drag but it failed to pick her out, and none of the shopkeepers remember seeing her.'

'So she'd maybe found a lift straight off . . .'

'Maybe.'

'Could she have started walking across country?'

'She was a city girl, John. Why would she do that?'

All Rebus could offer to this was a shrug. Clarke checked her watch. 'It's half an hour later now than it was when she set off. She could have passed through town without anyone noticing, maybe not started thumbing till she reached the other end.' She started the ignition and put the car into gear. As they left the forecourt, the salesman gave Rebus a wave.

'He sells solutions,' Rebus explained to Clarke.

'He should be in here with us, then.'

Once they had passed through Pitlochry again, there wasn't much to do but rejoin the A9. They had the option: south towards Perth or north towards Inverness. Clarke hesitated.

'Let's give it a few more miles,' Rebus said. 'Scenery's changing; might get more like the photo.'

'We're not going as far as Aviemore, mind.'

'My skiing days are behind me.'

'You don't think it would impress Nina Hazlitt?'

'What? Me going skiing?'

'You being able to tell her you visited Aviemore as part of your mission.'

'Everything in its time.'

'After twelve years, though? You seriously think there's anything to find there?'

'No,' Rebus was forced to admit, turning the Kate Bush CD back on. She seemed to be singing about her love for a snowman.

10

The moment they rejoined the A9, they hit roadworks, traffic down to a single lane and moving at a crawl. A barrier separated their northbound lane from the ones heading south, meaning no opportunity for a U-turn.

'We're stuck,' Clarke commented.

'Major resurfacing,' Rebus explained, reading one of the signs. 'Expect delays for four weeks.'

'We might still *be* here in four weeks.'

'Just as well we enjoy each other's company.'

She gave a snort at this. 'At least they *are* working.'

This was true. In the lane that had been blocked off, men in yellow reflective jackets were carrying tools or operating diggers. The sky was filled with a pulsing orange glow from the warning lights atop the various vehicles. The speed limit had been reduced to thirty.

'Thirty would be luxury,' Clarke complained. 'Speedo says twenty.'

'Slow and steady wins the day,' Rebus recited.

'That's always been your motto, has it?' She managed a thin smile. Rebus was studying the workmen.

'How about pulling over?' he suggested.

'What?'

'If she hitched along here, no way they wouldn't have noticed.'

A line of cones separated inside and outside lanes, but they were well spaced and it was easy to negotiate the Audi between two of them. Clarke pulled the handbrake on.

'Not the worst idea I've ever had, then?' Rebus pretended to guess.

As they got out of the car, a man strode towards them. Clarke had her warrant card ready. The man stiffened.

'What's happened?'

He was in his mid fifties, curls of grey hair escaping from the rim of his hard hat. Rebus got the feeling there were many layers of clothing beneath the high-visibility jacket and the fluorescent orange work trousers.

'Did you hear about the girl who's gone missing?'

74

Clarke asked.

The man looked from Clarke to Rebus and back again, then nodded.

'I didn't catch your name,' Rebus added.

'Bill Soames.'

'You're in charge of the crew, Mr Soames?' Rebus looked over Soames's shoulder towards the workmen. They had stopped what they were doing.

'They're probably worried you're Revenue or Immigration,' Soames explained.

'And why would either of those be a problem?' Clarke asked.

'They wouldn't,' Soames stated, meeting her eyes. He half turned and gestured to the men that they should continue with their work. 'Best if we talk in the office, though . . .'

He led them past the Audi, along a carriageway stripped of its tarmac, chunks of which were piled up next to the verge. Temporary overhead lights, powered by diesel generators, had been switched on, adding to the noise and fumes.

'You work nights?' Clarke asked.

'Twelve-hour shifts,' Soames confirmed. 'The night crew are in there.' He pointed to a Portakabin they were just passing. 'Six beds, one shower, plus a kitchen best avoided.' There was a row of three portable toilets, then another Portakabin, its windows covered with protective grilles. Soames opened its door and ushered them inside. He switched on a light and an electric heater. 'I could probably rustle up some tea . . .'

'Thanks, but this shouldn't take long.' There were plans of the roadworks on the room's only table. Soames rolled them up, making space.

'Sit yourselves down,' he said.

'So the crew are Polish?' Rebus asked. Soames gave a questioning look, and Rebus nodded towards the dictionary on the worktop. English–Polish/Polish–English.

'Not all of them,' Soames answered. 'But some, yes. And their English sometimes falls a bit short.'

'So what's the Polish for tarmacadam?'

Soames smiled. 'Stefan acts as their foreman. He's got better English than I have.'

'They sleep on site?'

'Long way to travel home every day.'

'And cook meals here? Basically live by the side of the road?'

Soames nodded. 'That's how it is.'

'What about yourself, Mr Soames?' Clarke asked.

'I'm over near Dundee. It's a slog but I make it home most nights.'

'There must be a night-shift supervisor?'

Soames nodded and checked his watch. 'He'll be here in an hour and a half. I'd rather he didn't catch me having a chinwag when I'm supposed to be out there.'

'Point taken,' Clarke said, without making it sound like an apology. 'So you've heard about Annette McKie?'

'Of course.'

'Has anyone talked to you?'

'You mean police?' Soames shook his head. 'You're the first.'

'She was probably hitching north out of Pitlochry. That means she would have had to pass right by here.'

'If she was on foot, someone would have noticed.'

'That's what we were thinking.'

'Well, she didn't. I asked the men.'

'All of them?'

'All of them,' Soames confirmed. 'Time she was in the area, it would have been the day crew.'

'The night crew's Portakabin has windows, though,' Rebus countered. 'Did you ask them too?'

'No,' Soames admitted. 'But I will, if you like. Give me a number and I'll get back to you.'

'Be easier if you did it just now.'

'Some might still be asleep.'

'Wake them up.' Rebus paused. 'Please.'

Soames thought for a moment before making his decision. He pressed his palms against the tabletop and started rising to his feet.

'And while we're waiting,' Rebus added, 'maybe we could have a word with Stefan . . .'

When Soames had closed the door, Clarke moved closer to the heater, warming her hands.

'Can you imagine it? Working all hours and in all weathers?'

Rebus was doing a circuit of the room, examining health and safety notices pinned to a corkboard, letters and forms piled high next to the dictionary. There was a phone charger but no phone. The calendar showed a photo of a blonde model atop a bright red motorbike.

'It's a job,' he commented. 'These days, that's something.'

'So what's your thinking?'

'There's no way she could walk past here without being spotted.'

Clarke nodded. 'Maybe she took a detour across the field at the back.'

'Why would she do that?'

'To avoid the wolf-whistles.' She looked at him. 'It still happens.'

'You'd know better than me.'

'Yes, I would.' She looked around the room. 'What do you think they do here between shifts?'

'I'm guessing booze, card games and porn.'

'You'd know better than me,' Clarke was echoing as the metal door shuddered open. A grizzled man in his early forties stood there, eyes hooded and with a week's worth of stubble on his chin and cheeks. His gaze met that of Rebus.

'Hiya, Stefan,' Rebus said to him. 'Keeping your nose clean, I hope?'

*　　　*　　　*

Stefan Skiladz had lived in Scotland for more than half his life, spending three of those years in prison for a serious assault after a day's heavy drinking at a friend's flat in Tollcross. Rebus had been CID at the time and had given evidence in court, Skiladz having pleaded not guilty despite the blood on his clothing and his fingerprints on the kitchen knife.

Clarke listened to Rebus explain all of this as the three of them sat around the table. When he had finished, Skiladz broke the silence with a question:

'What the hell is this all about?'

Clarke responded by pushing the photo of Annette McKie across the table towards him.

'She's gone missing. Last seen in Pitlochry getting ready to hitch-hike north.'

'So what?' Skiladz had picked the photo up, his face showing no emotion whatsoever.

'Your guys must go into Pitlochry,' Rebus answered. 'Someone has to do the tobacco-and-vodka run.'

'Sometimes.'

'So maybe they took pity on her.'

'And dropped her here? Better to wait for someone to take her further.' Skiladz looked up from the photograph. 'No?'

'I suppose so.'

'Could you keep the photo, show it around?' Clarke suggested.

'Sure.' He took another look. 'Pretty girl. I have a daughter, not so very different.'

'Has that helped keep you out of trouble?'

Skiladz stared at Rebus. 'I stopped with the drink. I got my head together.' He tapped a blackened finger to his brow. 'And I stopped getting into arguments.'

Rebus thought for a moment. 'Any of the other lads got form?'

'Trouble with the law, you mean? Why would I tell you?'

'Because then we wouldn't have to come back here with immigration officers and maybe the tax man too. And while we checked every person's ID and history, we'd make sure your name was mentioned in dispatches . . .'

Skiladz's eyes drilled into Rebus. 'You were a bastard back then, too. Just not so fat and old.'

'Hard to disagree.'

'So what's your answer?' Clarke added.

Skiladz turned his attention towards her. 'One or two,' he said eventually.

'One or two what?'

'Have had some trouble in the past.'

She got up and found a pad of lined paper, placing it in front of him, making sure not to

79

obscure the photograph lying there.

'Write them down,' she said.

'This is crazy.'

She held out a pen and made him take it from her. When she retrieved the pad a minute later, it contained three names.

'Day shift?' she asked.

'Only the first.'

'Thomas Robertson,' she read out. 'Doesn't sound very Polish.'

'He's Scottish.'

The door opened again. Bill Soames was standing there. He watched as Clarke tore the sheet from the pad, folded it in half and slipped it into her pocket.

'Nothing,' he said, turning to close the door. 'No one saw her.' Then, laying a hand on Skiladz's shoulder: 'Everything all right, Stefan?'

'Can I go now?' Skiladz asked Rebus.

'Ask her, not me.' Rebus indicated Clarke. She nodded at Skiladz and he got up to leave.

'What's been going on?' Soames asked.

Rebus waited until Skiladz was outside. 'Mr Skiladz has been helping us with our inquiries,' he told Soames. 'Necessitating another visit.' He rose and held out his hand for Soames to take.

Soames looked as though he had questions, but Rebus was already opening the door. Clarke shook Soames's hand and asked a final question of her own.

'How far do we have to drive before we can start heading south again?'

'A bit over half a mile, if you don't mind doing a U-turn on a dangerous bend.'

'I don't mind that in the slightest.' Clarke gave

him a smile as she made to follow Rebus.

Back in the car, she asked him for his thoughts.

'We can't just barge in and interview them,' he obliged. 'Tayside Constabulary need to be told.'

'Agreed.'

'So you talk to Tayside in the morning and come back later in the day. That way everything's above board.'

'You don't want to be involved?'

Rebus shook his head. 'I'm just the hired help.'

'Earning your keep so far.'

'Maybe let Communication Breakdown know that.'

Clarke smiled. 'What about Stefan Skiladz?'

'Worth doing a background check, but I doubt anything will come up.'

She nodded to herself and started the car. 'I might have to buy you a pint when we get back to Edinburgh.'

'What makes you think I don't have plans?'

'You're not the type,' she answered, signalling to pull out, always supposing a gap would eventually emerge in what looked like a solid convoy of lorries.

11

Rebus let her buy him two drinks in the end. Afterwards, he walked her back to her car and turned down the offer of a lift home.

'It's hardly on your route,' he explained.

'So you're either going to take a taxi or keep on drinking.'

'Flexing those sleuthing muscles of yours, eh?'

'Today went pretty well. But if you start coming into Gayfield Square with the sweat of the previous night's ale on you . . .'

'Understood.' He gave her a mock salute, then watched until the Audi disappeared from view. The town was quiet, with plenty of cabs plying for the largely non-existent trade. Rebus held up a hand and waited. Twenty minutes later he was paying the driver his money, adding a quid as a tip, and stepping on to the pavement outside a pub called the Gimlet. It was situated next to a busy roundabout off Calder Road, one of the main routes into the city from the west. The area was a mix of commercial and residential—car showrooms, low-rise industrial units; but also two-storey terraces with the usual array of satellite dishes pointing up at the sky.

The Gimlet dated back to the 1960s. It was a squat, free-standing box of a place, with a sandwich board outside advertising quiz and karaoke nights and a cheap all-day breakfast. Rebus hadn't been there in years. He wondered if it still operated as a glorified bazaar for shoplifters and housebreakers.

'Only one way to find out,' he told himself.

There was music blaring from loudspeakers, and a glamorous blonde on the TV reading out the sports news. Half a dozen sullen drinkers examined Rebus as he made for the taps. He studied the available beers, then checked the glass-fronted chiller.

'Bottle of IPA,' he decided. The barmaid was young, with tattooed arms and an array of facial piercings. Rebus reckoned she had chosen the soundtrack, whether the punters liked it or not. As she poured his beer, he asked if Frank was coming in.

'Frank who?'

'Hammell—this is still his place, isn't it?'

'No idea.' She threw the empty bottle into a bucket with more force than was strictly necessary. Rebus handed her a twenty-pound note, which she checked beneath an ultraviolet scanner, prior to opening the till.

'How about Darryl?' Rebus tried again.

'Are you from the papers?' She placed his change on the bar top rather than handing it to him. It comprised a few coins, plus three of the ropiest-looking fivers Rebus had seen in quite some time.

'Guess again,' he said.

'He's a cop,' one of the drinkers called out. Rebus turned to face the man. He was in his sixties and nursing a glass of dark rum. There were three empties in front of him.

'Do I know you?' Rebus asked.

The man shook his head. 'I'm right, though.'

Rebus took a mouthful of beer. It was too cold, and a bit flat. A door to the left of him was rattling open. A sign explained that it led to the beer garden as well as the toilets. The man who walked in was coughing as he pocketed his pack of cigarettes. He was well over six feet tall, shaven-headed, and wearing a black three-quarter-length coat over dark trousers and polo-neck.

Stood to reason the Gimlet would have someone manning the premises. Rebus's arrival had coincided with a break, that was all. The man stared hard at him, knowing him for a stranger and sensing the atmosphere in the room.

'Problem?' he asked.

'Cop,' the barmaid answered.

The doorman stopped a foot or so from Rebus and studied him from top to toe. 'Too old,' he offered.

'Thanks for the vote of confidence. I was hoping to talk to Frank or Darryl.'

'Is it to do with Annette?' one of the other drinkers asked. The doorman warned him off with a look before turning his attention back to Rebus.

'There are official channels,' he said, 'and you're not following them.'

'I didn't realise I was speaking to one of Frank's legal team.' Rebus took another sip of beer and put the glass down, reaching into his pocket for his cigarettes. Without saying any more, he headed for the door, letting it swing shut after him. As he had guessed, the beer garden was a rectangle of cracked concrete with weeds growing through. No tables or chairs, just empty aluminium kegs and beer crates. The walled enclosure was topped with plenty of razor wire, stray ribbons of polythene snagged in it. Rebus lit his cigarette and walked in a circle. There was a high-rise block in the distance, a couple staging a shouting match on one of its balconies. The traffic at the roundabout would be oblivious. Just another small scene in a world full of them. Rebus was wondering if the door behind him would open. Someone might want a quiet word or a boxing match. He looked at his watch and his phone, just passing the time. With the cigarette reduced to little more than butt, he flicked it on to the concrete, where it joined dozens of others. Then he opened the door and went back inside.

There was no sign of the golem. Presumably he was back at his post. The barmaid was eating a bag of crisps. Rebus saw that his beer was no longer where he had left it.

'Thought you'd finished,' she took pleasure in explaining.

'Can I buy you one?' he asked.

She didn't manage to conceal her surprise, but eventually shook her head.

'Pity,' Rebus said, nodding towards her piercings. 'I wanted to see if you leak when you drink.'

Out front, the doorman was busy speaking into his phone. 'He's right here,' he said when he spotted Rebus. He handed the phone to him.

'Hello?'

'Donny's not convinced you're a cop.'

'Officially, I'm not. But I'm on secondment to the team investigating Annette's disappearance.'

'Any way you can prove that?'

'Talk to DI Clarke. Either her or DCI Page. Who am I speaking to, by the way?'

'Darryl Christie.'

Rebus remembered him from the press conference: spiky-haired and whey-faced. 'Sorry about your sister, Darryl.'

'Thanks. So what's your name, then?'

'Rebus. I was CID but now I work cold cases.'

'So how come Page and his lot need you?'

'That's something you'd have to ask them.' Rebus paused. 'You don't sound enamoured . . .'

'I would be if Page spent as much time grafting as he does on his skincare regime.'

'I'd probably be wise to offer no comment.'

Darryl Christie made a snorting noise. He didn't sound like an eighteen-year-old. Or rather, he sounded like an eighteen-year-old who had grown up fast and self-confident.

'Does Frank Hammell share your concerns about the investigation?' Rebus enquired.

'What's it to you?'

'I just reckon he's a man who has his own ways of getting to the bottom of things.'

'And?'

'And I think he should share whatever he finds. Might hamper the eventual trial otherwise.' Rebus paused again. 'Of course, Mr Hammell's probably of the opinion a proper trial won't be necessary, not when he can act as judge and jury.'

Rebus waited for Darryl Christie to say something. He had turned his back on Doorman Donny and walked with the borrowed phone towards the roundabout, watching the traffic negotiate its way in and out of town. Eventually he spoke into the silence.

'Frank Hammell's a man with enemies, Darryl. You know that as well as I do. Is that what he's thinking—one of them's got their hands on Annette?' More silence. 'See, my feeling is, he's wrong to head that way, and I don't want you and your mum following him.'

'If you know anything, spit it out.'

'Maybe I should talk to him first . . .'

'That's not going to happen.'

'Will you let me give you my number, just in case?' There was another pause on the line, before Darryl Christie told Rebus to go ahead. He recited his mobile number and spelled out his name. 'Frank might have heard of me.'

Christie took a moment to form his next question. Rebus watched the passing parade of headlamps while he waited.

'Are your lot going to find my sister?'

'We'll do our damnedest, that's the only promise I can make.'

'Just don't hold it against her.'

'Hold what against her?'

'That Frank Hammell's dating our mother.'

'That's not the way it works, Darryl.'

'Prove it, then. Get busy.'

The line went dead. Rebus got another cigarette going, while he replayed the conversation. There was steel to the kid, but brains, too. And plenty of concern for his sister. Rebus pressed a few buttons until the screen presented him with the number of the last call. He took out his own phone and entered the details into his contact list under the name Darryl. When the cigarette was done, he headed back to the Gimlet and returned the phone to Doorman Donny.

'That took a while.'

Rebus shook his head. 'Finished talking to your boss ages ago. Phoned one of those premium chatlines after. Enjoy your next bill . . .'

Part Two

I see the dead men shuffling in their bones
Young girls laughing on their mobile phones . . .

12

What was it about Cafferty?

Even in a busy mid-morning café, customers kept their distance. Rebus had found them a corner table. The table next to it, once vacated, stayed empty. People might head towards it, then glance up at the hulking figure in the black leather jacket and change their minds.

'Turn-up for the books,' Cafferty had said. '*You* asking *me* for a drink.' He had then demolished a flat white and requested another with the complaint that the cups were like something out of a doll's house.

He was pouring sugar into this second coffee when Rebus asked him about Frank Hammell.

'Hammell? Shorter fuse than I like to see on a man. Never a great one for realising that actions have consequences.'

'I forget, did he ever work for you?'

'Back in the day.' Cafferty's phone, which had been sitting on the table, began to vibrate. He checked who the caller was but didn't answer. 'Is this about the missing girl?'

Rebus nodded.

'Saw Hammell on TV,' Cafferty continued. 'That's some reward he's put up.'

'Why do you think he did it?'

Cafferty considered this. He knew what Rebus meant: a man like Hammell could get information without needing to pay for it. 'He loves her,' he answered eventually. 'The mother, I mean. This is his way of showing it. You know he put the frighteners on her husband?'

Rebus shook his head.

'That's why the poor sod scarpered to New Zealand.'

'Australia, I heard.'

'Same difference—other side of the planet. That's how far he needed to be from Frank Hammell.'

'What about the missing girl's brother?'

Cafferty thought for a moment. 'Enlighten me.'

'His name's Darryl Christie—kept his dad's surname. He spoke at the press conference. Manages at least one of Hammell's bars.'

'I didn't know that.' Rebus could see Cafferty storing the information away.

'Seems like a bright kid.'

'Then he should get out while he can.'

'How many places does Hammell own these days?'

Cafferty's mouth twitched. 'Hard to say, even for me. Half a dozen pubs and clubs. Fingers in a lot more pies than that, of course. He's had meetings in Glasgow and Aberdeen.'

Meaning meetings with men like himself.

Rebus watched as Cafferty stirred his coffee. 'You sound like you still take an interest,' he commented.

'Call it a hobby.'

'Some hobbies end up all-consuming.'

'Man's got to have something to fill his retirement. That's where you went wrong. Nothing to do with yourself all day, so you ended up back in the game.' Cafferty scooped up some of the mousse from the surface of his drink and spooned it into his mouth.

'Any idea who might bear a grudge against Hammell?'

'Present company excepted?' Cafferty smiled. 'Probably too many to count, but I doubt they'd bring a kid into it.'

'If they did, though . . .'

'Then any day now they'll get a message to Hammell, and that's when he'll go supernova. You'll want to know about it if that happens.'

'We should keep a watch on him?'

'You should be doing that anyway. I seem to remember a fair few surveillance operations mounted against *me* in the dim and distant past.'

'Caught you red-handed, too.'

Cafferty gave another twitch of the mouth. 'Best not to dwell on it.'

'Actually, I think we need to, just for a moment.'

Cafferty looked at him. 'And why's that?'

'Because the Complaints are keeping tabs on me.'

'Tut-tut.'

'They know, for example, that we've been out a few times together.'

'Someone must have told them.'

'Wasn't you, was it?'

Cafferty's face remained a mask.

'See, it makes sense to me,' Rebus continued. His hands were wrapped around his own mug of coffee, but he hadn't taken so much as a sip since sitting down. 'In fact, I can't think of a neater way of setting me up. You keep taking me out for these little drinks and chats, making everyone think we're bosom buddies . . .'

'I'm insulted.'

'Well, someone's been talking to them.'

'Not me.' Cafferty shook his head slowly as he placed his spoon on the table. His phone was vibrating again.

'Sure you don't want to answer that?' Rebus asked.

'I can't help it if I'm popular.'

'You might want to look that word up in a dictionary.'

'The shit I let you get away with . . .' Cafferty's eyes were sudden dark tunnels, leading to darker places still.

'There you are,' Rebus said, giving a thin smile. 'Knew you were still in there somewhere, waiting to come out and play.'

'We're finished,' Cafferty stated, rising to his feet and snatching his phone. 'You should try being nice to me, Rebus. Sometimes I think I'm the only friend you've got left.'

'We've never been friends, and never will be.'

'You sure about that?' Rather than wait for an answer, Cafferty started threading his way between the tables, nimble for such a big man. Rebus sat back and looked around him, studying the café's morning clients. He wished the Complaints had been watching and listening, just this one time; it might have put their minds at rest.

13

'Did you miss me?' Rebus enquired as he walked into the SCRU office.

'Have you been somewhere? Can't say I'd noticed.' Peter Bliss was hauling files and folders

94

from a large plastic container. Some sheets fell free, sliding across the floor. Elaine Robison helped pick them up.

'How are things at Gayfield Square?' she asked.

'Coffee's not a patch on here.'

'I meant the case.'

Rebus shrugged. 'I'm not sure anyone's convinced about the links to the other MisPers.'

'It was always going to be a hard sell, John.'

'I seem to be in luck here, though—no Cowan to speak of.'

'He's at some meeting,' Bliss explained, seating himself at his desk. 'Huckling for a move.'

'To the CCU,' Robison added, resting her hands on her hips. 'Seems there's a vacancy at the top table.'

'I was under the impression our dear leader hates cold cases.'

'But the one thing he does like is advancement. They'd have to promote him DI.'

'Fast track to DCI and above,' Bliss said with a shake of his head.

'Well, his wardrobe's good and ready, even if he's not.' Rebus turned to leave.

'Not staying for some of that famous coffee?' Robison asked.

'Places to go, people to see,' Rebus said by way of apology.

'Don't be a stranger,' she called to him as he headed out of the door.

ETHICS AND STANDARDS was what it said on the wall next to the office, but everyone called them the Complaints. Rebus tried the handle. It didn't budge. Combination lock. He knocked, pressed his ear to the door, knocked again. Further along the corridor was the Deputy Chief Constable's office, and the Chief Constable's beyond that. Rebus hadn't been hauled up here for a carpeting in quite some time. His years on the force, he'd seen the pen-pushers come and go. They were always full of new ideas, tweaks they were keen to make, as if you could change the job by means of strategy meetings and focus groups. The Complaints was part of that—every year or two, their name seemed to change—Complaints and Conduct; Professional Standards; Ethics and Standards. One cop Rebus had known, the Complaints had gone after him because a neighbour had complained about the height of his leylandii. The whole process had taken the best part of a year, after which the cop had decided he didn't like the job any more.

Another result for the Complaints.

Rebus gave up and took the lift down to the cafeteria. Bottle of Irn Bru and a caramel wafer. He walked over to a table by the window. The window looked on to the sports field, where you could sometimes see off-duty officers playing rugby. Not today, though. The chair made plenty of noise as Rebus pulled it out from the table. He sat down and returned the stare of the man sitting there.

'Malcolm Fox,' he stated.

Fox didn't deny it. He was twenty years younger than Rebus, and a stone and a half lighter. A bit less grey in his hair. Most cops looked like cops, but Fox could have been middle management in a plastics company or Inland Revenue.

'Hello, Rebus,' Fox said. There was a plate in front of him, nothing on it but banana peel. The glass next to it contained tap water from the jug by

96

the cash till.

'Thought maybe we should meet properly.' Rebus took a mouthful of Irn Bru and stifled a belch.

'I'm not sure that's such a good idea.'

'We work in the same building: any reason we can't be sitting together?'

'Every reason.' There was nothing confrontational in Fox's style, no emotion when he spoke. He had the casual confidence of someone who knew they were on another plane from those around them.

'Because you're putting together a file on me?'

'Today's police force is very different from the one you got used to. Methods have changed, and so have attitudes.' Fox paused. 'Do you really think you'd fit in?'

'You're telling me not to bother reapplying?'

'That's a decision only you can make.'

'Who was it told you about me and Cafferty?'

Fox's face changed slightly, and Rebus realised he'd made a mistake. The man knew where Rebus had got that gen: Siobhan Clarke. A black mark against her.

'Ask yourself this,' Rebus ploughed on. 'Could it have been Cafferty himself? Using an intermediary? Just to screw up my chances.'

'Better if you'd simply kept clear of him in the first place.'

'Hard to disagree.'

'So why didn't you?'

'Maybe I was hoping he might let something slip—I work cold cases, remember.'

'And has he?'

Rebus shook his head. 'Not so far. But the

97

amount of skeletons around Cafferty, there's always a chance.'

Fox looked thoughtful as he sipped his water. Rebus unwrapped the wafer and bit into it.

'The file on you,' Fox said eventually, 'goes back to the 1970s. In fact, to call it a 'file' is doing it an injustice; it takes up one whole shelf.'

'I've been called into the headmaster's office a few times,' Rebus conceded. 'Never been given my jotters, though.'

'I wonder: is that down to luck or guile?'

'There was always a good reason why I did what I did—and it got results. The High Hiedyins recognised that.'

' "Room should always be made for one maverick",' Fox quoted. 'That's what a former Chief Constable wrote about you. He underlined the "one".'

'I got results,' Rebus repeated.

'And what about now? Think you can break cases without bending a few rules along the way? We've no room for even one maverick these days.'

Rebus shrugged. Fox spent a moment studying him.

'You're on secondment to Gayfield Square,' he said. 'That brings you back into contact with DI Clarke.'

'So?'

'Since you retired, she's managed to unlearn some of the stuff you taught her. She's going to keep rising through the ranks.' Fox paused. 'Unless . . .'

'You're saying I'm a bad influence? Siobhan's her own woman. That's not about to change just because I'm around for a week or two.'

98

'I hope not. But back in the day, she covered up for you a few times, didn't she?'

'I've no idea what you're talking about.' Rebus tipped the bottle to his mouth again.

Fox managed to force out a smile, studying Rebus the way a sceptical employer might an underqualified job candidate. 'We've met before, you know.'

'We have?'

'Sort of—we were on the same case one time, back in my CID days.'

'I don't remember.'

Fox shrugged. 'Not so surprising really—I don't think you made it to a single briefing.'

'Probably too busy doing real work.'

'With a mint on your tongue to mask the smell of booze.'

Rebus gave him a hard stare. 'Is that what this is about—me not giving you the time of day? Did I nick your sweets in the playground and now you need to get your own back?'

'I'm not that petty.'

'You sure about that?'

'Quite sure.' Fox was rising to his feet. 'One more thing,' he said. 'You know there'll be a physical? If you go ahead with your application, I mean.'

'Constitution of an ox,' Rebus declared, thumping his chest with a fist. He watched the other man leave, then finished his caramel wafer before heading outside to the smoking zone.

14

Rebus had brought the MisPer files with him to Gayfield Square. He made sure Page saw him lugging them to Siobhan Clarke's desk. It took three trips, the Saab parked out front with its POLICE OFFICIAL BUSINESS sign prominent.

'Thanks for the help,' Rebus said to the room at large. He was sweating, so removed his jacket and draped it over Clarke's chair. A female officer came across to ask him about the boxes.

'Missing persons,' he explained. 'Three of them, between 1999 and 2008. All last seen on or around the A9, just like Annette McKie.'

She lifted the lid of the topmost box and peered inside. She stood a little over five feet tall, short dark hair in what Rebus might have called a pageboy cut. She reminded him of an actress—maybe it was Audrey Hepburn.

'I'm John,' he said.

'Everybody knows who *you* are.'

'Then I'm at a disadvantage.'

'Detective Constable Esson. But I suppose you can call me Christine.'

'You always seem to be glued to your computer,' he told her.

'That's my job.'

'Oh?'

She placed the lid back on the box and gave him her full attention. 'I'm our link with the online community.'

'You mean you send e-mails?'

'I contact networks, John. Missing persons

networks. I've been posting on Twitter and Facebook, plus updating the L and B website.'

'Asking for sightings?'

Esson nodded. 'Making sure her photo is disseminated as widely as possible. An ask can circulate the globe in seconds.'

'These networks,' Rebus asked, 'would they have details of historic cases?'

Esson looked at the boxes again. 'Might well have—want me to check?'

'Could you do that?'

'Give me their names and dates of birth, photos if you have them . . .' She paused. 'I thought your theory was they're all dead?'

'As of now that's all it is—a theory. Worth challenging, wouldn't you say?'

'Sure.'

'Names, DoBs, photos?'

She nodded. 'And anything else relevant: distinguishing marks; where they were last seen . . .'

'Got it,' Rebus said. 'And thanks.'

She accepted this with the beginnings of a blush and retreated to her desk. Rebus found a pad of paper and began to write down a few salient details about Sally Hazlitt and the others. Twenty minutes later he took the information, along with a selection of photos, over to Esson. She seemed bemused.

'Ever heard of e-mail?'

'Is there something wrong with my handwriting?'

She smiled and shook her head, then read out a line from his notes on Zoe Beddows. '"Liked the men"?'

'I'm sure you can find a way of rephrasing it.'

'I certainly hope so.' She studied the

101

photographs. 'I'll scan these in as best I can. Nothing a bit more high-res?'

'Afraid not.'

'Oh well.'

'I see you've met Christine,' Siobhan Clarke said, approaching the desk. She had a bag slung over one shoulder and a laptop tucked under her other arm. 'Don't let her challenge you to one of her shoot-em-up games. She's lethal.'

Esson was blushing again as Rebus followed Clarke to her own little parcel of land.

'How was Pitlochry?' he asked.

'Fine.'

'The police station?'

'Serviceable.' Clarke looked over towards Esson. 'Thing about playing games online,' she went on, 'you get to know people.'

'Annette McKie played online games,' Rebus commented.

'And Christine's been in touch with dozens of people she played with. If any of them hear a peep from their friend Zelda, Christine will know about it . . .' She broke off and stared at the boxes. 'Well done you, by the way. Though now they're here . . .' She made show of scanning the office for a spare desk.

'Is there another room we could use?' Rebus suggested.

'I'll look into it.' She shrugged herself free of her coat and sat down heavily, before noticing his jacket draped over the chair.

'Let me get that,' Rebus said.

'No, leave it.' She was opening the laptop. 'Got the interviews on here,' she explained. 'Audio only.'

'Was there someone there from Tayside Police?'

'An inspector, all the way from Perth. We didn't exactly hit it off.'

'But you spoke to everyone you needed to?'

She nodded and rubbed her eyes, the fatigue obvious.

'Want me to get you a coffee?' Rebus suggested.

She looked at him. 'So it's true what they say—there *is* a first time for everything.'

'And a last, if you're going to have a go at me.'

'Sorry.' She allowed herself a yawn. 'The two Poles work the night shift. Stefan Skiladz did the translating. Both were involved in petty crime in their younger days, back in the homeland. Gang stuff. Fights and pilfering. They swear they've kept their noses clean since coming here. I'll run their names through the system, just to be sure. I already ran a check on Skiladz, and he was telling us the truth—never a hint of back-pedalling since he got out of jail.'

'Why do I get the feeling you're leaving the interesting stuff till last?'

She looked up at him. 'Maybe I will take that coffee,' she said.

Rebus obliged. On his return, he saw that she was busy on her desk computer. She accepted the mug with a nod of thanks.

'Thomas Robertson,' she said, 'works the day shift. Doesn't like nights; prefers to spend them in the watering holes of Pitlochry. There's a particular barmaid he's keen on, though he didn't say if the feeling is mutual. He told me he was in trouble just the once, resisting arrest after a fight with a girlfriend outside a club in Aberdeen.'

'And?'

'He wasn't telling the whole truth.' She tapped

103

a fingernail against the computer screen and angled it a little so Rebus could have a better view. Robertson had been charged with attempted rape, the victim someone he'd met that night, the assault happening in an alleyway behind the club. He'd served two years in HMP Peterhead, and had been out of prison less than twelve months. Rebus did a quick calculation in his head. Zoe Beddows had vanished in June 2008, only a couple of months prior to Robertson's arrest.

'What do you think?' Clarke was asking.

'What does he say about Annette McKie?'

'Denies seeing her. Says they were working flat out that afternoon. He doubts he'd have noticed a supermodel strolling past.'

Rebus was looking at Robertson's mug shot: short black hair, plenty of stubble, and a scowl. Dark-brown eyes, chiselled features.

'I think we need to talk to him again, a bit more formally,' Clarke was saying. 'And maybe have a team search the area around the roadworks. It's a mix of woodland and fields, plus a stretch of river.'

'Needle-in-a-haystack stuff,' Rebus commented. He realised Christine Esson was standing just behind him, holding out some sheets of paper. He took them from her.

'Two essays,' she explained. 'Both looking at where killers choose to leave their victims. Bit of light reading for you.'

'Any chance of you giving me the gist?'

'I've not looked at them, just printed them off. Plenty more like them out there if you're interested.'

Rebus was about to tell her that he really wasn't, but he noticed the look Clarke was giving him.

104

'Very helpful,' he said instead.

'Thanks, Christine,' Clarke added, as Esson returned to her desk. Then, to Rebus: 'She's like that.'

'There's about thirty pages here, half of it equations.'

Clarke took the two documents from him. 'I know one of the authors—by reputation, I mean. I wonder if James has considered bringing in a profiler . . .'

'And maybe a ouija board at the same time.'

'Times have changed, John.'

'For the better, I'm sure.'

She made to hand the essays back to him, and he wrinkled his nose.

'You take first look,' he said. 'You know how much I value your opinion.'

'Christine gave them to *you*.'

Rebus looked over to Esson's desk. She was watching. He managed a smile and a nod as he placed the printouts on top of one of the storage boxes.

'Want to come with me while I tell James the news?' Clarke asked.

'Not really.'

'I suppose I should have asked you what *you've* been up to.'

'Me? Not much.' Rebus paused. 'Apart from dropping you in it with the Complaints. So I should probably say sorry for that . . .'

Clarke stared at him. 'Tell me,' she said.

15

That evening, Rebus barely had time to open the day's post and stick an album on the deck before his phone rang. He checked the number: not recognised.

'Hello?' he said. He was in the kitchen, staring at the meagre contents of the fridge.

'Rebus?'

'Who's asking?'

'Frank Hammell.'

'Darryl gave you my number?'

'Get your arse down to the Gimlet. Let's do some talking.'

'Before I can agree to that, I've got a question.'

'Go ahead.'

'Does the Gimlet do food this time of night?'

*　　*　　*

Takeaway pizza was the answer. It was waiting in a box for him, still warm, at a corner table. There was no one else in the place, just Donny on the door. No TV or sound system, no one serving behind the bar.

'Right little *Mary Celeste*,' Rebus commented, lifting a slice of pizza from the box and heading towards the bar. Hammell stood behind it, arms stretched along the polished surface. He was around five ten, with a look that mixed entrepreneur with scrapper. He wore a dark blue shirt, open at the neck, and his sleeves were rolled up. His thick salt-and-pepper hair was well groomed. Close up, Rebus could make out scarring leading from his top lip to his nose. One eyebrow had a permanent nick in it. Here was a man who tended not to back down when things got heated.

'I'll have a malt, if you're asking.'

Hammell turned and reached for a bottle of Glenlivet, the stopper squeaking as it was removed. He didn't bother measuring, just poured freely. 'I'm guessing no water,' he said, placing the drink in front of Rebus. Then, palm extended: 'That'll be five on the nose.'

Rebus stared at him, then smiled and handed over the money. Hammell didn't ring it up; just stuffed it into his pocket. There had been no sign of surveillance outside, and Rebus had to wonder what it would do to Malcolm Fox's head if he ever learned of this meeting.

'So you're John Rebus,' Hammell said. His voice was a deep gargle; sounded as if his throat needed clearing. Rebus had known a con once who'd sounded like that because someone had tried to strangle him with a towel in his cell.

'I suppose I am,' he said. 'Just like you're Frank Hammell.'

'I used to hear about you. You know I worked with Cafferty?'

'Way he tells it, you worked *for* him rather than with him.'

'Back in the day, he hated you with a vengeance. Should have heard the things he was prepared to do to you and yours . . .' Hammell gave this time to sink in. He walked to the corner table and retrieved the pizza, placing it on the bar top and helping himself to a slice.

'It's not bad,' Rebus informed him.

'Better not be. I told them what I'd do to them if the cheese was too stringy.' He took a bite. 'I can't abide stringy cheese.'

'You should write restaurant reviews.'

There was silence for a moment as the two men ate. 'Know what I think?' Hammell said eventually. 'I think they left the cheese out altogether.'

'One solution to the problem,' Rebus stated.

'So you and Cafferty,' Hammell went on, dabbing at his mouth with the back of his hand, 'best of pals these days, eh?'

'News gets around.'

'Ever wondered what his game is?'

'All the time.'

'Bastard says he's retired—as if carpet bowls and a pair of slippers were ever his style.'

Rebus took out his handkerchief to deal with the grease on his fingers. One slice of the pizza was enough.

'You don't like it?' Hammell asked.

'Not as hungry as I thought.' Rebus lifted the whisky to his lips.

'Darryl tells me you're working cold cases. So how come you're suddenly interested in Annette?'

Rebus considered how to answer. 'There may be a pattern.'

'What do you mean?'

'Other young women have vanished down the years. Three that we know of, the first in 1999. All of them were on the A9 or near it at the time.'

'First I've heard.'

'I wanted you to know.'

Hammell stared at Rebus, narrowing his eyes a little. 'Why?'

'Because you're probably drawing up a list of

enemies, thinking one of them might have her.'

'What makes you think I've got enemies?'

'Business you're in, I'd say it's an occupational hazard.'

'You think I'll go after your old pal Cafferty? Is that what this is about—you covering his arse?'

'If you want Cafferty, be my guest, but I think you'd be making a mistake.' Rebus put down the half-empty glass. 'How's Annette's mum doing?'

'How do you think? It's ripping her to shreds. You really reckon there's some sick bastard out there who's done this before? How come he's kept himself under the radar?'

'As of now, it's only a theory . . .'

'But you believe it?'

'It's a theory,' Rebus repeated. 'But one you need to be aware of, if things aren't to get ugly.'

'Fair enough.'

'How long has Darryl been working for you?'

'Since before he left school.'

'I notice he kept his dad's surname.'

Hammell glowered at Rebus. 'Kid can do what he likes—free country last time I looked.'

'I assume the dad knows about Annette?'

'Of course.'

'You've known the family a while.'

'What business is that of yours?'

Rebus offered a shrug and watched Hammell do some thinking.

'Anything I can do to help?' the man asked eventually. Rebus shook his head. 'A bit of cash, maybe? Case of hooch?'

Rebus pretended to consider this. 'Maybe just don't charge me for the pizza.'

'What makes you think I paid for it in the first

place?' Frank Hammell answered with a snort.

16

Siobhan Clarke lived in a high-ceilinged first-floor flat that was part of a Georgian terrace just off Broughton Street. A five-minute walk took her to work each morning, and she liked the area's mix of bars and restaurants. There was a cinema complex at the top of the hill, a concert venue nearby, and every kind of shop you could ever wish for on Leith Walk. The flat shared a drying green at the back of the building and she'd got to meet most of her neighbours down the years. Edinburgh had a reputation for being cold and distant, but she'd never found that. Some residents were shy or quiet, just wanting to get on with their lives without fuss or incident. Her neighbours knew her as a police officer, but had yet to ask for help or a favour. When one of the ground-floor flats had been broken into, everyone had gone out of their way to let Clarke know they didn't blame her for the eventual lack of a result.

She had been thinking about an evening visit to her gym, and had even changed in readiness before slumping on the sofa and checking the TV schedules instead. When her phone let her know she had a message, she decided to ignore it. Then her door buzzer sounded. She went into the hall and pushed the button next to the intercom.

'Yes?' she asked.

'DI Clarke? It's Malcolm Fox.'

Clarke sucked air in between her teeth. 'How do

you know where I live, or is that a stupid question?'

'Can I come in?'

'No, you can't.'

'Any particular reason?'

'I'm expecting someone.'

'DCI Page, perhaps?'

Christ, the Complaints really did know everything . . .

'Something to hide, DI Clarke?' Fox was asking.

'I just like my privacy.'

'Yes, me too. And that time we happened to bump into one another—I was trusting that you'd have understood our little chat was meant to be kept private.'

'Then you should have said.'

'Still, I can appreciate that John Rebus is an old and dear friend. You probably feel no qualms about sharing information with him.' Though two doors, seventeen stone steps and a passageway separated them, it felt as if his mouth was only an inch or so from her face. She could hear each of his individual breaths.

'John Rebus is proving invaluable to the McKie inquiry,' she stated.

'You mean he's not gone out on one of his famous limbs yet—not as far as you're aware.'

'Why can't you just leave him alone?'

'Why can't *you* see that he's the same liability he's always been? Don't tell me life wasn't simpler before he managed to inveigle his way on to the McKie case . . .'

'What do you mean?'

'Why do you think he's there? What titbits might he be passing back to his good friend Cafferty? Working cold cases is one thing, but now he has

111

access to an entire floor of CID offices in Gayfield Square.'

'You don't know what you're talking about.'

'I know a cop gone bad when I see one. Rebus has spent so many years crossing the line, he's managed to rub it out altogether. As far as he's concerned, his way's the right way, no matter how wrong the rest of us might know it to be.'

'You don't know him,' Clarke persisted.

'Then help me *get* to know him—talk me through some of the cases the pair of you worked.'

'So you can twist it all around? I'm not that stupid.'

'I know you're not—far from it—and this is your chance to prove it to the people at the top, the people I talk to each and every day.'

'I grass up my friend and you put in a word come promotion time?'

'John Rebus should be extinct, Clarke. Somehow the Ice Age came and went and left him still swimming around while the rest of us evolved.'

'I'd rather bludgeon Darwin with a claw hammer than evolve into *you*.'

She heard him give a sigh. 'We're not so different,' he said quietly, sounding weary. 'We're both conscientious and hard-working. I can even see you joining the Complaints—maybe not this year or next, but sometime.'

'I don't think so.'

'My instinct's usually right.'

'And yet you couldn't be more wrong about John Rebus.'

'That remains to be seen. Meantime, take care around him—I mean that. And feel free to call me any time you think he's floundering—floundering

112

or diving to the bottom . . .'

She released the intercom button and walked back into her living room, crossing to the window and peering down on to the street, craning her neck left and right.

'Where the hell did he go?' she said to herself, failing to see Malcolm Fox anywhere. Then she looked at the message on her phone: *I'm 5 minutes away and hope we can discuss your friend some more—Fox*.

They had her home address *and* her mobile number.

And they knew about Page.

She sat back down in front of the TV, but her head was swimming.

'Gym,' she said, rising again and looking around for her holdall.

17

Rebus was most of the way home when he got a text message. It was from Nina Hazlitt:

Missoni Hotel. Too late for a drink?

He stayed on Melville Drive and took a left at the junction with Buccleuch Street. Then he thought of something and pulled over. Checked his phone again and opened the list of recent callers, adding Hammell's mobile to his contacts page. Five minutes later he was parking on George IV Bridge. A member of the hotel staff asked him if he was checking in. The man was young and toned and wearing a kilt with a zigzag pattern. Rebus shook his head.

'Just visiting,' he said.

There was a bar off the main reception. Rebus couldn't see Nina Hazlitt, so he texted to let her know he had arrived. The people in the bar seemed to have a thirst for cocktails. Rebus decided one more whisky wouldn't do any harm, except to his chances of passing a breathalyser test. Two minutes later, Hazlitt joined him, pecking him on the cheek as if it was the most natural thing in the world.

'Have you eaten?' she asked. 'The restaurant's supposed to be good—or there's a fish place next door.'

'I'm fine,' Rebus assured her. 'How about you?'

'I ate on the train.'

One of the bar staff asked her what she was drinking. She studied Rebus. 'Not really your kind of place?' she guessed.

'Not really,' he agreed.

'Maybe we should go somewhere else.'

'There's the Bow Bar, right around the corner.'

She waited for him to finish the whisky, and placed her arm in his as they exited the hotel.

'How's your brother?' Rebus asked.

She looked flustered, as if trying to remember how Rebus knew about him.

'He answered the phone that night,' Rebus explained.

'Ah,' she said. Then: 'He's all right.'

'Does he have a name?'

'Alfie.'

'Is he just visiting, or . . . ?'

'Are you always this inquisitive?' she asked with a laugh. Then, stretching out an arm to point at the Bow Bar: 'Is this the place?'

Rebus opened the door for her. She took one

look at the interior and declared it 'charming'. There was a table by the window, recently vacated. Rebus took the empties to the bar and ordered IPA for himself and a vodka tonic for her. The place was just noisy enough—no chance of anyone eavesdropping on their conversation. Back at the table, they chinked glasses.

'So, how are things?' she asked.

'Things are interesting. I've got a foot in the door with the Annette McKie inquiry.'

'They accept there's a connection?'

'They accept the possibility.'

'Well, that's progress.' She seemed immediately more energised, pulling her shoulders back, eyes gleaming.

'There's no proof yet. And to be honest, the McKie case is throwing up other possibilities. The photos are the real link.'

'Photos?'

He realised she didn't yet know. 'Annette McKie's phone was used to send a photograph of a landscape at dusk. Same thing happened with Zoe Beddows.'

She took a moment to digest the information. 'That can't be coincidence. What about Brigid Young?'

'The technology wasn't around back then.'

'Sally had her phone with her in Aviemore.'

'Yes, I remember you saying.'

'I don't think it could take pictures though . . .' She thought for a moment. 'Some of the people she knew at school keep a page for her on Friends Reunited.'

'That's kind of them.'

'It has photos of her—school trips, parties,

115

concerts . . .'

'Any way to know who visits it?'

'I don't think so.'

'Might be worth finding out.'

She stared at him, eyes narrowing. 'Why?' But before he could answer, she had worked it out. 'You think someone took her? One person stalking all these girls and then sending out photos? And he might have gone online posing as a friend . . .?' Her voice was rising, and Rebus gestured for her to bring it down a little. She took a couple of sips of her drink, trying to compose herself.

'I'll ask,' she said, voice trembling. 'I'll ask Sally's friends.'

Rebus thanked her and decided to try for a change of tack, asking what brought her back to Edinburgh.

'You, of course,' she eventually answered.

'Me?'

'You're the first person in such a long while who's taken me seriously. And when you phoned the other night . . .'

'You decided to drop everything?'

'I'm self-employed. Wherever I lay my laptop, that's my office.'

'What do you do?'

'Publishing, sort of. I edit people's books, do proofreading, sometimes research.'

'Sounds interesting.'

She managed a laugh. 'You're not a very convincing liar—but it *can* be interesting. Last book I did was an encyclopaedia of myth and legend. It covered the whole of the British Isles—quite a lot from Scotland.'

'Oh aye?'

'Did you know there's a dragon buried beneath the Royal Mile?' She did a quick calculation. 'We might be perched on one of its wings.'

'No shortage of stories in this city—I've heard alibis that were harder to swallow.'

She smiled. 'I was a teacher for a while, same as Tom, except primary school. Used to love telling my class a folk tale. Once you had their attention, you kept it.' Her voice trailed off. He knew she was thinking of her daughter again; doubted Sally was ever out of her thoughts for more than a few minutes at a time on any given day. She kept threatening to place her glass on the table, but it hadn't quite happened yet. It was almost reduced to ice in any case.

'Get you another?' Rebus asked.

'My turn.'

'I'm fine,' he said, having hardly touched the pint. 'Got the car outside, and this isn't my first tonight.'

She decided to have another drink anyway, reaching into her bag for money. Rebus played with a beer mat while he waited for her to return.

'So, anyway,' she said, squeezing around the table and sitting down again, 'you've managed to unearth the files on those other poor women?'

'The records aren't as complete as I'd like.' He saw her look. 'It happens—things get mislaid; notes that should have been written up aren't . . .'

'Oh.'

'Not that there were gaps in Sally's case,' he sought to reassure her.

'Is there any possibility that I . . .? No, I suppose not.' She lowered her eyes.

'I doubt they'd come as any consolation. You

might find them a bit . . .'

'Upsetting?'

'I was going to say "cold". Nobody working the case *knew* Sally, you see.'

She nodded her understanding. 'You're trying to protect me.'

'I'm not sure I'd put it like that.'

They focused on their drinks for a minute. Rebus didn't know what else to say to her. He didn't like to think of her as being trapped in limbo, but that's where she was. The past had its grip on her and wasn't letting go. He worked with the past, too, but he could always put it back in a box and have it delivered to a storeroom or warehouse.

'Is there a draught?' he asked.

'I don't think so.'

'Thought you were shivering.'

'It happens sometimes. You know that saying about someone walking over your grave?'

'Never really understood it, though.'

'Now you come to mention it, I'm not sure I understand it either. Sure you don't want another?'

'Trying to get me arrested for drunk-driving?'

'Couldn't you talk your way out of it?'

'Not these days.'

She grew thoughtful again. 'Working cold cases, you must meet a lot of families who've lost loved ones . . .' She watched him nod. 'I talk to a lot of them, too. Over the internet mostly. You know that in England and Wales they can't issue a death certificate, no matter how long the person's been missing? It's hell for the families—means they can't sort out the estate. Up here, you wait seven years and the court gives you a Presumption of Death certificate.'

'And that's what happened to you?'

She shook her head. *'Presumption*'s not what I want. I need to know what happened to her.'

'Even after all this time?'

'Even after all this time,' she echoed. Then she sighed, finished her drink in two gulps and asked if he would walk her back to the hotel.

'My pleasure,' he said.

As they walked back up Victoria Street, he told her he'd not been in the Missoni before.

'I doubt I'd be able to afford it normally,' she explained, 'but I got a late deal.'

The kilted doorman didn't seem to be around. They stopped at the steps, both lighting cigarettes, standing in companionable silence as the traffic and pedestrians rolled past.

'The rooms are nice,' she said eventually. 'In fact . . .' She looked in her bag. 'There was something I wanted to give you, but it's upstairs.' She looked up at him. 'Do you want to . . .?' But he was already shaking his head.

'Then will you wait here while I fetch it?'

'Sure.'

So she stubbed out her cigarette and headed indoors. Three minutes later she was back, holding a book.

'Here,' she said, handing it over.

Rebus read the title aloud: *'The British Isles: Myth and Magic.* Is this the one you did research for?'

She nodded, watching as he flicked through a few pages.

'Thanks,' he said. 'I mean it. I'll start it tonight.'

'Look, about earlier . . . I hope you don't think I was trying to proposition you?'

119

He shook his head again. 'Not a problem, Nina. It would have been flattering if you had. Are you heading back in the morning?'

She gestured towards the building across the street. 'Bit of research I need to do.'

'The National Library?'

'Yes.'

'Is this for work?'

She nodded. 'I was thinking of staying another night . . .'

There was an invitation there—or at least an opening—but Rebus ignored it.

'You know you'll be the first person I call—supposing I make any progress,' he said instead.

'You seem to be my best hope, John. I can't thank you enough.' She moved forward to kiss him, but he leaned back a little at the waist, and instead took her hand in his, shaking it. Her grip was almost fierce. Her whole body seemed to be vibrating.

'Maybe next time we can compare myths and legends,' he said.

She nodded, averting her eyes, then turned and hurried back into the hotel. Rebus got into his car, turned the key in the ignition and signalled to make a U-turn.

All the way home he was anticipating her call, but it never came.

18

Lochend at midnight.

Darryl Christie slipped out of the house. He'd

120

been home less than an hour. His mum was dead to the world, having been prescribed sleeping pills. Darryl's two younger brothers, Joseph and Cal, shared the bedroom next to Annette's. Darryl's own room was downstairs, in what had been built as a conservatory. He'd added blackout blinds when he'd taken it over. Several times Frank Hammell had offered to find them a bigger and nicer place, but Darryl's mum had grown up in Lochend, as had her parents before her. All her friends lived within walking distance of the house—and besides, Darryl and Annette would be moving out before long. Growing up, with their own lives to live.

Darryl had examined every inch of his sister's bedroom, finding nothing to help explain her disappearance. He'd even contacted a few of her very closest pals, but nobody seemed to have any ideas. It had been Darryl, too, who had broken the news to his father, having reminded Gail that someone needed to do it.

'You're the man of the house, Darryl,' she'd said, reaching for the vodka bottle.

The house had seen more than its fair share of visitors. Faces Darryl hardly knew wanted to offer sympathy, sit with Gail for a while and feed on her grief. Her closest friends had become like bodyguards, fending off curious neighbours and rubberneckers. The landline rang dozens of times a day, and Gail's mobile was always needing to be recharged.

Darryl had tried his best to stay out of it, retreating to his room. He could hear the voices in the living room and kitchen, and often they tried offering him tea and beer and a sandwich, tapping on his door and calling out to him. And when

121

everyone had departed for the day, the house felt cold and empty, Joseph and Cal walking on tiptoe so as not to disturb their mother, doing homework without needing reminding, making their own dinner if necessary. When Darryl was required elsewhere, he would tell them: 'You're in charge. Anything urgent, phone me.'

Frank Hammell had asked him if he needed time off, but he had shaken his head.

'Cops are useless, Darryl,' Hammell had said. 'But I've got feelers out. We'll get to the bottom of this, one way or the other . . .'

Outside the house, Darryl paused to examine the sky overhead. You never saw many stars—too much light pollution. There was the beginning of an overnight frost on the pavement and the car windscreens. Plenty of people still awake—TVs glowing from living room windows; some music from a distant party; a dog barking, desperate to be allowed back indoors. Darryl walked to the corner and shook the hand of the man standing there.

'I thought we might walk,' Cafferty said. 'Not far—just to stop us freezing our backsides off.'

'Sure,' Darryl said, slipping his hands into his pockets.

'We've not met before, have we?' Cafferty asked him.

'No.'

'It's just that sometimes I forget a face, and that looks like a lack of respect next time I see the person.' He glanced towards the young man. 'Don't want that happening between us, Darryl.'

'Okay, Mr Cafferty.'

'How long have you been working for Frank?'

'A while.'

'*He* used to work for me, you know.'

'Your name's been mentioned.'

'Probably not with any great enthusiasm.' A taxi rumbled past, driver's-side window down, seeking an address. Cafferty watched it, as did Darryl.

'Can't be too careful, eh?' the older man said with a thin smile. Then: 'I should have said at the start, I'm sorry about your sister. Anything I can do to help, you only have to ask.'

'Thanks.'

'Frank doesn't need to know—it can be between us. If that's okay with you, Darryl.' Cafferty seemed to study the young man. 'I met your dad a few times, back in the day.'

'Really?'

'Just in the pub, you know. He was friends with Frank.'

'Aye, he was.'

'But then they say love's no respecter of friendship.' Cafferty turned a corner and Darryl realised they were doing a little circuit that would bring them back to his house. 'I like that you kept your dad's surname,' Cafferty was saying. 'Are you still in touch with him?'

Darryl nodded.

'Well, tell him I said hello.'

'I'll do that. Look, I hope you don't mind me asking, but why are we out for a walk together at the dead of night?'

Cafferty chuckled, then sniffed and reached into his pocket for a handkerchief.

'You know a cop called Rebus?' he asked as he wiped at his nose.

'I've spoken to him.'

'He mentioned your name to me. I've got a lot

123

of friends in this town, people who make sure I'm as well informed as I need to be. You might think Frank has a lot of friends too, but they're not the sort that can always be trusted. What do you think he would do if it turned out one of them had snatched your sister? What if they were using her as a bargaining tool of some kind?'

'That's not what the cops think happened.'

'And they're always right, are they? Come on, Darryl, we know better than that. But I'm hearing that you're a bright one, and that's why we're out here together tonight. Frank Hammell's enemies are going to see *you* as their enemy, too. Which means a friend like me makes sense. That's all I'm asking.' Cafferty stretched out his arms to consolidate the point. 'Anything you feel able to share, I'll listen. Later on, it might be that you're ready to step out from Frank's shadow . . .'

'And you'll be there to help?'

'I'm here for you and your family, Darryl. Any time you feel you need me.'

'Frank says you're retired.'

'Maybe I am.'

'So why the interest?'

'Let's just say there's a bit of history between us.'

'A score to be settled?'

'Maybe . . .'

Outside the house, they shook hands again.

'Still living at home, eh?' Cafferty commented.

'For the moment.'

'I've got a few flats I could let you take a look at.'

But Darryl shook his head.

'You know your own mind—I like that about you too.' Cafferty patted the young man's arm and turned, starting to walk away. Darryl watched him disappear slowly into the darkness then angled his head towards the night sky again. There were stars up there, plenty of them. You just had to believe . . .

19

'I've always liked Perth,' Siobhan Clarke said. 'Just maybe not this particular bit of it.'

She was standing outside the divisional police HQ with Rebus, keeping him company while he smoked a cigarette. The building itself was a tall concrete lump hacked up from the 1960s or 70s. Tenements across the street and a petrol station next door.

'When are you ever in Perth?' Rebus asked.

'Away games. St Johnstone's ground is just off the M90.'

'You go to away games?' Rebus sounded disbelieving.

Clarke supported Hibernian FC. Time was, she'd taken Rebus to a few home matches, back in the days when you could smoke in the stadium. He couldn't remember ever seeing a goal, just a succession of nil–nil draws made bearable by nicotine and the half-time pie.

'There's a game in Edinburgh this weekend if you fancy it,' she was saying. 'Thought not,' she added, seeing the look on his face. 'So what did you get up to last night?'

'I had a quiet one—just a bit of reading.'

'Those papers Christine got off the internet?'

'Christ, no.'

'What then?'

'Hell are you smiling for? I *can* read, you know.'

Someone behind them cleared his throat. He stood in the doorway, doing everything but tap his watch.

'When you're ready,' he told them.

He was a uniformed inspector by the name of Peter Lightheart, same cop who had been with Clarke the previous day at Pitlochry. Clarke had introduced Rebus to him on their arrival this morning, Rebus taking the proffered hand briefly before advising that he would need a quick cigarette before they got started.

Lightheart's demeanour belied his name. Clarke had already warned Rebus that the man lacked patience, wit and cunning: 'So we need to crowd him out of the interview if we can.'

'Two ticks,' Rebus told Lightheart, indicating that he'd almost finished with the cigarette. To deflect the man's attention, Clarke asked if the search team had been given its orders.

'Of course,' Lightheart replied. 'Probably been at it for the past hour.'

'How many officers?'

'A dozen.'

'Search warrant for the sleeping quarters?'

Lightheart nodded, looking annoyed that she would think it necessary to check.

'Why here?' Rebus asked, getting rid of his cigarette butt.

'Sorry?' Lightheart enquired.

'Doesn't Pitlochry have a perfectly usable cop shop? We could have talked to him there.'

'No proper interview room,' Clarke explained. 'And no technology.'

Meaning: video camera and audio equipment. A uniformed officer was checking both as Lightheart, Clarke and Rebus filed into the ground-floor room. There was nothing on the cream-coloured walls except a No Smoking sign and some attempts at scratchwork graffiti. The camera was high up in a corner, pointing towards the table and three chairs. Thomas Robertson was seated, hands gripping the edge of the table, one knee bouncing nervously. He would be thinking to himself: this is all looking serious. Which was the whole point, of course.

'All set?' Lightheart asked the officer.

'Yes, sir. Already recording.'

Lightheart settled himself opposite Robertson, Clarke taking the only free chair left. That was fine with Rebus. He rested his back against a wall, facing Robertson and quite visible to him. Lightheart waited for the officer to leave, then got busy with the formalities: making introductions for the benefit of the camera, and announcing location, date and time. As soon as he was finished, Robertson spoke.

'They're going to kick me off the job,' he complained.

'Why's that?'

'Twice in two days you've dragged me away from my shift.'

'There's a reason for that, Mr Robertson,' Clarke told him. She had printed out the details of his arrest and conviction. 'If you'd told us the truth yesterday, we might not be here.'

'I did tell you the truth.'

'Let's be charitable and say you played down the seriousness of the assault.' Clarke began to read from the charge sheet. Robertson's eyes met

Rebus's, but saw no sympathy in them. When Clarke had finished, the room was silent for a moment.

'Resisting arrest after a fight with your girlfriend?' Clarke commented. 'No, Mr Robertson—attempted rape of a woman you'd only just met.'

'It wasn't like that—we were both smashed. She was keen enough at the start . . .'

Clarke held up a photograph, taken at the victim's hospital bedside.

'Cuts, bruises, abrasions and a black eye. You're not telling me she was keen on *that*?'

'Things got a bit . . .' He shifted in his chair. He was the same man as in the mug shot Clarke had shown Rebus, but something in him had changed. Life had roughed him up a bit. Maybe prison, where he would have been segregated with the other sex offenders. Maybe just the passage of time. He had been handsome, but was rapidly losing those looks.

'Where did you grow up?' Clarke asked, pretending to sift her notes for the details. Quick change of tack: classic interview technique. Robertson was going to be kept on his toes. Rebus had never seen Clarke lead an interview before. Lightheart had, having spent the previous day with her, and Rebus hoped the man knew there was nothing to be gained from interrupting.

'Nairn,' Robertson told her.

'Not too far from Inverness?' she checked.

'Far enough,' he said.

'What road is that?'

He looked quizzical. 'The A96.'

'You were born in 1978?'

128

'That's right.'

'In Nairn?'

'Correct.'

Clarke made show of studying her notes again. Robertson ran his tongue over his lips, dry-mouthed.

'Do you remember the Millennium, Mr Robertson?'

Lightheart failed to hide his surprise at the question, half turning his head in Clarke's direction.

'Eh?' Robertson asked.

'Hogmanay 1999—everybody remembers where they were.'

Robertson had to think. 'Aberdeen probably. With mates.'

'"Probably"?'

'I'm sure it was Aberdeen.'

Clarke wrote this down. She was still writing as she threw out her next question. 'Any partners since you got out of jail?'

'Women, you mean?'

She looked up at him. 'Or men.'

He gave a snort. 'No thanks.'

'Women, then,' she conceded.

'There've been a few.' He ran his hands down either side of his face, making a rasping sound of palm against stubble. There were home-made asterisk tattoos on his knuckles.

'And now there's this barmaid in Pitlochry?'

'Gina, yes.'

'She knows you've done jail time?'

'I told her.'

'Same story you told us?' Clarke was staring at him across the table. 'Maybe I should just check that . . .'

129

'Look, I've already said—I never saw that girl!'

'Let's try and keep calm,' Lightheart advised.

'So, 2008, you were living in the north-east?' Clarke asked into the silence.

'What?'

'The attempted rape—it took place at the back of a nightclub in Aberdeen.'

'So?'

'So you were living there?'

'Sort of.'

Clarke read from her notes: '"Sleeping on friends' floors"—you were unemployed at the time?'

'That's right.'

'But looking for work?'

'Yes.'

'Travelling about a bit?'

'What is all this?' Robertson looked at all three of them in turn. 'What are you trying to do here?'

'How well do you know the A9, Mr Robertson?'

When he didn't answer, Clarke asked again.

'I fucking work on it, don't I?' he spat.

'Easy,' Lightheart said in warning.

'Look, yesterday it was all whether I'd seen that girl or not, but now it's 1999 and 2008 and God knows what. Okay, I spent some time in the nick. Okay, I didn't tell you the whole truth—it's not something I go around shouting from the rooftops.' He leaned forward. 'It's not something I'm proud of,' he stressed. Having made his point, he sat back again, the chair making a single creak of protest.

Clarke let the silence lie, studying the paperwork again.

'You didn't spend the Millennium in Aviemore?' she eventually asked.

130

'No,' Robertson answered, sounding suddenly tired.

'You're sure about that?'

'Why the hell would I go to Aviemore?'

'Maybe someone invited you.'

'They didn't.'

'It's not *that* far from Aberdeen.'

Robertson just gave a slow shake of the head.

'Strathpeffer?'

He looked at her. 'Couldn't even place it on a map.'

'Auchterarder?'

'Nope.'

'And you didn't see Annette McKie the day she disappeared?' Clarke held up the photo of the missing girl so it was facing Robertson.

'For the hundredth time—no.'

'We've got some officers going through the Portakabin where you sleep. Want to tell us what they'll find there?'

'Dirty washing.'

'Anything else? A bit of hash, or speed?'

'I wouldn't know anything about that.'

'Porn maybe?'

'One of the lads has a laptop.'

'Then it'll be taken away and examined.'

'Making me Mr Popular.'

'Do your workmates know why you went to jail?'

'Something tells me they'll be finding out.' The look he gave Clarke had hardened. 'You can't pin the girl on me, so something else will have to do. And if all else fails, at least you'll see me kicked out of a job.'

'You're not being charged.' Clarke gathered up her papers.

'Is that it, then?' Robertson looked around the room. Clarke nodded towards Lightheart and he formally concluded the interview.

'Did you bring him here in a patrol car?' she asked.

'Yes,' Lightheart replied. 'Send him back the same way?'

Clarke stared at Robertson. He was wiping perspiration from his palms on to his trousers.

'He can catch a bus,' Clarke said, striding from the room.

20

'Not a good sign,' Clarke said, entering the office at Gayfield Square. DC Christine Esson was standing next to Clarke's desk, looking fretful.

'What is it?' Clarke asked her.

'Best if you come see.'

So they followed Esson to her computer and stood either side of her as she sat down and got busy.

'Twitter?' Rebus said.

Clarke looked at him. 'You know what it is, right?'

'Of course,' Rebus said.

'There's a missing persons network,' Esson explained. They use Twitter to get information out. Annette McKie's got her own hashtag . . .'

Clarke gave Rebus another glance. 'It's how you get something trending,' she explained.

'Uh-huh.'

The screen was filled with messages, all of them

132

ending #annettemckie.

'Mostly,' Esson said, 'they're linking to Annette's profile, just trying to get her description out there. But look at this one.' She zeroed in on a particular message.

Police i/ving road crew A9 north of Pitlochry! #annettemckie

'Then there's this,' she added, highlighting another.

Police team scouring woods near A9 north of Pitlochry—loads of them #annettemckie

'Posted by different people,' Clarke commented.

'Locals, by the look of it,' Esson added. 'Here's another.'

Cop car near totalled me doing a U-turn, heading S from roadworks. Siren and lights—they've got s/o!! #annettemckie

'Looks like Tayside Constabulary went about things with their usual subtlety,' Rebus muttered, straightening up.

'I don't think you realise, John.' Clarke turned to Esson. 'Show him.'

With a few deft clicks and taps, Esson did just that. 'Half a dozen blogs are on to it,' she said, 'plus local media. Ronnie has had to fob off a couple of reporters already.'

As if on cue, the phone rang again on Ronnie Ogilvie's desk. He picked it up, said a few words, then put the receiver down. Rising to his feet, he walked towards them.

'BBC,' he said. 'Wanting to know if it's true we're connecting Annette McKie to three other disappearances.'

'They didn't get *that* from Twitter,' Esson said.

'Nina Hazlitt?' Clarke guessed, eyes fixed on

133

Rebus. He offered a shrug.

'Spoken to her recently?' Clarke persisted.

'Last night,' Rebus conceded.

Esson was studying the BBC Scotland news feed on her monitor. 'Here it is,' she declared.

It was only a paragraph of text—no video or photo to accompany it.

The mother of a teenager who disappeared from Aviemore at Hogmanay 1999 says detectives in Edinburgh are probing links between that mystery and missing schoolgirl Annette McKie, who vanished a fortnight ago while travelling from Edinburgh to Inverness. It is believed that other women have gone missing from the same stretch of road, one in 2002 and another in 2008. Nina Hazlitt, whose 18-year-old daughter Sally disappeared from a New Year's holiday in Aviemore, hopes that fresh clues—including photos sent from the victims' phones—can help provide answers to what she calls 'the A9 Abductions'.

There was a link to the McKie press conference, accompanied by a still of Gail McKie fleeing the room. Ogilvie's telephone was ringing again. So was Clarke's mobile. She was looking in the direction of James Page's door.

'In for a penny,' she said. But there was no need. The door was flung open and DCI Page stood there, his own phone pressed to his ear as he listened. His pointed finger seemed to include Rebus, then jerked in the direction of the corridor. Clarke led the way, Rebus following close behind.

Once they were outside the office, Page ended the call and closed the door. Then he folded his arms.

'Explain,' he said.

'Explain what, sir?' Clarke countered.

134

'Maybe you were huddled round Christine's screen to look at cats being funny on the internet.'

'No, James. We were looking at Twitter and the BBC.'

'Then you know what I'm talking about.'

'Of course—but I still don't see what needs explaining. Everyone's a reporter these days. A patrol car turns up at the same spot on the A9 two days running, people nearby are going to gossip about it. Used to be the garden fence would do, but now it's Twitter and the like. No way we can stop it.'

'In fact, we should do the opposite,' Rebus offered. 'Get tongues wagging, people's memories whirring . . .'

Page glowered at him. 'What about this Hazlitt woman? Where's *she* getting her information from?'

'Speculation rather than information,' Clarke jumped in. 'It's the same story she's always told. Only thing that's changed is there's a new MisPer for the media to hang it on.'

Page considered this, eyes still on Rebus. Clarke was looking at him too, willing him to keep his mouth shut.

'We need to get the photo from Annette McKie's phone out there,' Rebus stated, ignoring her. 'If the public want a story, we should give them one, get them working for us. Looks like our only hope anyway of finding out where it was taken.'

'And you should give a statement to the press,' Clarke added, turning her attention to Page. 'Just you this time. Set the record straight.'

Page tried not to seem overly keen on the idea. 'You think so?'

135

'Definitely,' Rebus added. 'Dampen down some of the wilder speculation, make sure everything's kept in proportion.'

'Nothing too formal,' Clarke went on. 'Maybe outside the station . . .'

'It's not very photogenic,' Page argued. 'HQ, maybe? Can you get on to our media people, Siobhan?'

'Sure.'

'Show the press the photo at the same time,' Rebus nudged. 'They'll lap it up.'

Page seemed to be visualising the scene. He nodded slowly.

'Has to be today, though,' Clarke prompted. 'While the story's still hot.'

'I'll need a full briefing from the pair of you. Full *and* quick.' He thought of something else and looked down at the clothes he was wearing.

'Your suit looks fine,' Clarke reassured him.

21

After the briefing in Page's airless office, Rebus headed outdoors for a cigarette. He punched Nina Hazlitt's number into his phone, but she wasn't answering. He was in the car park, just about invisible to prying journalists. For some reason he had an image in his mind of the tattoos on Thomas Robertson's knuckles. There had been no mention of them on the original charge sheet, and he wondered if they had been part of the prison experience. Robertson had barely been out of his teens when Sally Hazlitt had vanished; not that this meant he couldn't be responsible. Zoe Beddows had disappeared not long before he'd attacked the victim outside the nightclub. The thing was, the nightclub attack had been brutal and stupid— he'd been apprehended straight away by people nearby who had heard the screams. Could the same person have plucked four women from the world without leaving evidence behind? Rebus doubted it. But that didn't mean he hadn't done something to Annette McKie. Spotted her, gone after her, left her somewhere. Sometimes you had to allow for coincidence—the same road; photos sent from mobile phones. A song jumped into his head—'Connection'; not the version by the Stones, but a cover by a band called Montrose. He had bought their album thinking they came from the town, but they were American. Connection versus no connection. Just random events, given shape by sheer force of a mother's will. On cue, his phone rang and he placed it to his ear.

'Hello,' he said.

'Sorry,' Nina Hazlitt explained, 'I had to come outside. They're not keen on phones in the library.'

'You've been doing your research, then?'

'Yes.'

'But leaving enough time to talk to the BBC?'

'A news agency, actually. They must have passed it along.'

'Everything you told them, it could only have come from me.'

'Oh.' She paused. 'Are you going to get in trouble?'

'Would that bother you?'

'Well, yes, of course.'

'I'm not so sure, Nina.'

He waited for a response, but heard only the passing traffic on George IV Bridge.

'You know that book you gave me?' he continued. 'I started it last night. A lot of things people used to believe turned out to be just stories.'

'Feel free to mock me, John—don't imagine for a second that you're the first.'

'I'm not mocking you.'

'You think I'm seeing things that aren't there.' She paused. 'I don't have time for this. The agency are taping an interview with me in an hour. Everyone needs to be aware, John. Someone out there *knows* what happened.'

'I'm on your side, Nina.'

'I don't *need* anyone on my fucking side! I've managed this far with a minimum of effort from the likes of you . . .' Her voice had grown shrill. It cracked on the last few words.

'Nina?'

'I didn't mean that.' She took a deep breath, composing herself. 'You know I didn't.'

'It's okay.'

'If you don't want me to talk to them, just tell me.'

'DCI Page is about to give a statement. See what he has to say, then make up your own mind, okay?'

'Okay.'

'You're still staying in town tonight?'

'Changed my mind—I'm on the six o'clock train.' She hesitated. 'I should have thought before I spoke to that journalist. I hope you'll still feel able to trust me.'

'Let's see.'

'You promised I'd be first to know, John. I'm assuming you always keep your word.'

138

'Say hello to your brother for me.'

'I hope I'll see you again sometime, John. Remember to keep in touch.'

He ended the call.

*　　　*　　　*

Back in the CID suite, there was no sign of Page or Clarke. Rebus went over to Christine Esson's desk and asked if she wanted a coffee.

'Don't drink the stuff.'

'Tea?'

She shook her head. 'Hot water, that's what I like. You should see the looks I get in cafés.'

So he made himself a coffee and brought her her chosen drink.

'You're a cheap date,' he commented. She seemed to have Twitter up on her screen again.

'How does it work?' he asked, drawing over a chair.

So she showed him, and he told her to get the photo from Sally Hazlitt's phone up there.

'Twitter, Facebook, YouTube—and anywhere else you can think of.'

'No problem,' she said. 'And the message to go with it . . .?'

'We need to know where it was taken, that's all.'

'Anything else?'

Rebus thought for a moment, then nodded. 'Any way I can watch Custard Pie while he does his thing for the great unwashed?' She looked uncomprehending. 'Page's meet-the-press,' Rebus elucidated.

'Shouldn't be a problem,' Esson said.

'With sound, if at all possible.'

139

'Of course.' She paused, her eyes narrowing. 'Custard Pie?'

'Page and Plant,' Rebus said. Then, seeing the look on her face: 'Never mind. Just get me that feed, eh?'

22

Rebus spent the early evening reading more of the book Nina Hazlitt had given him, concentrating on the Scottish chapters, filling his head with stories of cannibals, shape-shifters, witches and monsters. When the buzzer sounded, telling him someone was outside the main door of the tenement, he went to the window. He couldn't quite make out the figure, but it wasn't Cafferty. His phone pinged with a text. It was from Clarke.

Going to let me in?

Rebus went into the hall and pressed the button next to the intercom. As he opened his own door, he could hear her pushing at the main door. He went out on to the landing and leaned over the rail.

'What happened to you after the press conference?' he called out.

'Summoned to the Chief Constable's office. He wanted a briefing of his own.' She took the two flights of stairs at a canter. He knew she used a gym sometimes, or had done in the past.

'Still go jogging?' he asked.

'Some weekends—nothing too strenuous.' She looked over his shoulder towards the flat's interior. 'Do I wait for an invite, or . . .?'

Rebus hesitated for a second, then led her inside.

140

As they reached the living room, he asked her if she wanted a drink.

'I'm okay,' she said.

'Just a social visit, is it?'

She shrugged, seeming distracted. 'The photo from Annette McKie's phone is out there now.'

'Yes,' Rebus said. 'Now we wait for someone to pinpoint where it is.' He paused. 'There's something you want to tell me.'

'While we were at Fettes,' she eventually explained, 'Malcolm Fox happened by.'

'Oh?'

'As you guessed, he wasn't exactly thrilled I'd been talking to you.'

'I'd say he's the type who's seldom "thrilled" by anything.'

'He had a word with James, too, asked why you'd been brought in to the McKie case.'

'Is he trying to get me thrown off it?'

'I'm not sure.'

'But at the very least, Page now sees me as a bigger liability than ever?'

'I did have to fight your corner.' She had settled on the arm of the sofa, as if planning only a short stay. Rebus's book was on the floor by his chair and she angled her head to read the cover.

'*Myth and Magic*?'

'And old wives' tales,' Rebus added. 'So did you manage to convince your boss?'

'I think so.'

'And did that involve using your feminine charms?'

She gave him a cold look.

'Sorry,' Rebus apologised. 'It's just that he's a showroom dummy—I know it and you know it.'

141

'But he's not. You're seeing what you want to see. Has there ever been anyone of a higher rank that you've not dismissed out of hand?'

'Plenty.' Rebus paused. 'In the old days.'

'These aren't the old days, John. And James is good at what he does. You've seen the team he's put together—do they seem unmotivated?'

'No,' Rebus was forced to admit.

'Is there anything they're not doing that they should be?'

'No,' he repeated.

'Well then.'

'Page is one of the good guys, that's what you're saying . . .'

But her attention had been diverted to the wall above the dining table and the large map of Scotland pinned there, the route of the A9 marked in red highlighter.

'Meant to take that down,' Rebus said. Clarke was walking towards the map, looking not at it but at the three large shopping bags sitting on the table.

'Stuff needs putting away,' Rebus said casually, but he wasn't fooling her. She pulled a few sheets of paper from the first bag.

'You made copies,' she stated. 'All those files you brought to the office . . .'

'Not all of them,' Rebus countered. 'Just the official reports and statements. I skipped the newspaper cuttings.'

'Jesus, John.'

'You've seen what the office is like, Siobhan. I lugged all those boxes in there, and they've not been opened yet.'

'You might not have noticed, but we've been a bit busy.'

142

'You were going to find another room we could use.'

'And I *will*, given a bit of time.' She paused. 'But that's not what this is about. You made the copies before you handed the boxes over. You never intended to let them go, not completely.'

'I get bored, Siobhan. A bit of reading whiles away the hours . . .'

She gave him another look. 'This sort of thing, it's meat and drink to the Complaints.'

'Only if they find out about it.'

'What makes you think they won't?'

Rebus shrugged. 'This is the way I've always worked, Siobhan—you know that.'

'It's also why people you work with tend not to last long. Remember Brian Holmes and Jack Morton?' She watched as his face darkened. 'Okay, sorry, that's a low blow.'

'Did Fox just happen to drop those names into your wee chat?'

'He's out to get you, John. He even came to my flat.'

'When?'

'Last night. Warning me off, telling me I should be on his side rather than yours.' She began to slide the sheets of paper back into the shopping bag, then asked him if he'd seen Nina Hazlitt's interview.

'Was it on TV?'

Clarke shook her head. 'Webcast for some news agency. She thanked us for everything we were doing.'

'Nice of her.'

'She handles herself well in front of a camera. No sign of craziness.'

'She's not crazy.' But Rebus was remembering her last phone call, voice verging on the hysterical.

'She still needs reining in, if at all possible.'

'And I'm the man for the job? Is this your thinking or Page's?' Rebus waited for an answer, but none was forthcoming. 'He told you to come here?' He walked to the window and peered down on to the street. 'Is he waiting in his car? What does he drive?'

It was a BMW, double-parked twenty yards up. There was someone in the driver's seat.

'Why didn't you bring him in? Afraid it might have diluted those feminine charms of yours?'

She glowered at him. 'This was my idea, John. And if I *had* brought him up, you'd be off the case right now.' She pointed towards the shopping bags.

'He wouldn't have got over the threshold.'

She closed her eyes for a second. A text arrived on her phone.

'That'll be him,' Rebus muttered. 'Wondering what's taking so long.'

Clarke read the text and turned towards the door. 'I'll see you in the morning,' she said quietly.

'Is he dropping you at yours, or is it back to his?'

She didn't rise to it, just walked out of the room. Rebus stayed by the window, watching her exit the tenement and head towards the car. Its lights came on as she approached, picking her out as though she were an actor making her entrance. The passenger-side door opened and closed, the BMW remaining motionless as a dialogue took place. Then it began to crawl down Arden Street's gentle slope towards the junction, passing Rebus's building in the process, driver and passenger staring straight ahead. He willed Clarke to look up, but she

144

didn't.

'Played that with your usual charm and grace,' he muttered to himself. Siobhan Clarke was stuck somewhere between Page and Fox and he could see how much it was hurting her.

How much *he* was hurting her.

Good at her job, ready for the next step up, life on an even keel—and then in walks John Rebus, not even bothering to wipe his shoes, leaving bits of muck everywhere without even noticing.

Aye, nicely played, John.

He lit a cigarette and poured himself a whisky, stopping when the liquid was halfway to the top of the glass. He sat himself at the dining table, eyes focused on the road map. After a while, the glass needed refilling and the ashtray emptying. Without music, he realised how empty the room felt, but he couldn't find an album to match his mood. He thought of calling Siobhan Clarke, apologising for everything. Or maybe a text—keep it short and sweet. Instead of which he ended up in his armchair with the book Nina Hazlitt had given him. There were no serpents buried beneath Edinburgh, and no monster swimming in Loch Ness. It was all just superstition and the basic human hunger for explanations, answers, reasons.

When his eyelids began to droop, he decided that was fine. Just one more night when he wouldn't quite make it as far as the bedroom.

23

The guardian of the front desk at Gayfield Square still showed reluctance to allow Rebus entry. Each morning she printed him a fresh visitor's pass, and at the end of each day she needed him to return it.

'Be easier doing me one for a week,' Rebus suggested, trying to remember her name.

'You might not be here a week,' she countered.

'Think of the environmental damage you're doing.'

'I recycle them.' She handed him that day's pass. 'Needs to be worn at all times, remember.'

'Absolutely.'

As he climbed to the first floor, he unclipped the badge and stuffed it into his jacket. The office had just started work for the day. He nodded towards Ronnie Ogilvie and, passing Christine Esson's desk, asked her if she had any new wonders to show him.

'Just these,' she said.

He took the sheets of paper from her.

'They're e-fits,' she explained. 'There's a guy I know on a force down south, he's a dab hand with the software.'

Rebus stared at the three faces in turn. Sally Hazlitt, Brigid Young and Zoe Beddows had been aged so that each photo showed them as they might look in the present day. Hazlitt was the most changed—not surprising, since she had been missing the longest. A woman of thirty, eyes and cheekbones still much like her mother's. Beddows and Young were more recognisably the same women who had disappeared. A few lines had been

146

added to Young's face, her eyes hollower, mouth sagging slightly. Beddows was shown in her late twenties, still sharp-featured but losing some of her spark.

'What do you think?' Esson was asking.

'Pretty good,' Rebus admitted.

'He did some others—different hairstyles . . .'

Rebus nodded, and she knew what he was thinking.

'Pretty pointless if they're dead,' she commented.

'I think you should circulate them. But get Page's permission first.'

'Mr Trampled Underfoot?' She gave Rebus a smile. 'I did my research last night.'

Page's door opened and he fixed his eyes on Rebus, then gave a little flick of the head by way of summons. Rebus helped himself to a mug of coffee first, then knocked and went in. There was no space for a chair for visitors. Yesterday, with three of them in there, it had been a sweat box. Yet somehow it suited Page, a man who liked his parameters tight, no room for manoeuvre.

'John,' he said, sitting down behind his laptop.

'Yes, James?'

'Good to see you here so early.'

Rebus just nodded, ready for whatever was coming.

'Shows motivation, but we need focus also.'

'Absolutely.'

Page's words were just filling time while he considered how to broach the real subject. Rebus decided to spare him any more effort.

'Is it to do with the Complaints?' he guessed.

'In a way.' Meaning: yes, specifically and definitely.

'Sorry if I seem to be bringing a bit of baggage with me,' Rebus said. 'Rest assured it won't interfere with my work.'

'Good man. And how's that work going?'

'Slower than I'd like.'

'You appreciate that Annette McKie has to be our priority?'

'Of course.'

'And we can't let your historical cases get in the way.'

'Nina Hazlitt isn't going to take a telling from me. She's been waiting years for this opportunity.'

'Is she still in Edinburgh?'

'As far as I know, she went back to London last night.'

'Well, that's something, I suppose.' He pressed his palms together as if in prayer, resting his mouth against the tips of his fingers.

'Don't suppose you've seen Siobhan this morning?' Rebus asked, trying to keep his tone casual.

Page shook his head and checked his watch. 'Not like her to be tardy.'

'Unless she was late to bed.'

Page stared at him. 'I dropped her home at quarter past nine, if that's what you're getting at.'

Rebus pretended to show surprise. 'No, nothing like that. I just thought—'

He was interrupted by his mobile phone. Siobhan Clarke's name was on the screen.

'Talk of the devil,' he said, pressing the phone to his ear.

'Where are you?' Clarke asked.

'In the office. Why?'

'I'm parked outside. Better get down here.'

148

'What's happened?'

'Robertson's bunk's not been slept in. He didn't get back to the camp last night . . .'

24

The M90 again, but only once they'd escaped the sluggish morning traffic in Edinburgh. Heading towards Perth and the A9. A quick pit stop to pick up beakers of tea and dry croissants. Kate Bush still singing about snowmen. As they crossed the Forth Road Bridge, Rebus asked Clarke if she noticed anything different. She studied him and shook her head.

'No scaffolding on the rail bridge.'

She looked to her right and saw this was true.

'Can't remember the last time I saw it without,' he added.

'Yes,' she agreed. Then: 'Look, I'm sorry about last night.'

'Me too. Hope you didn't have words with James afterwards.'

She glanced towards him. 'What makes you think that?'

'Nothing.' He paused for effect. 'It's just that I was in his bolt-hole when you phoned . . .'

'And?'

'He was giving me a slap on the wrist about the Complaints.'

'And?' she repeated, growing a little more irritated.

'And nothing,' Rebus stressed. 'I just got a feeling the two of you had . . . you know . . . maybe had words . . . before he dropped you at your flat. And if that's the case, I'm sorry I was the cause.'

'You can be a real bastard sometimes, John.' She shook her head slowly.

'It has been said,' he admitted. 'And believe me, I'm not proud of the fact.'

'Thing is, though, you *are* proud of the fact.' She looked at him again. 'You really are.'

They drove in silence after that, Rebus staring at the scenery—the elongated stretches of hillside near Kinross; the merest glimpse of Loch Leven; the way the view opened up as they rounded a curve in the road and entered Perthshire, snow visible along the topmost ridge of the distant Ochils. (He guessed they were the Ochils; didn't feel like checking with Clarke.) When her phone rang, she pressed a button on the steering wheel and answered with a voice raised above the engine noise.

'DI Clarke,' she informed the caller.

'It's Lightheart.' The inspector's dull drone seemed to emanate from the same speaker as Kate Bush. Clarke pressed another button to mute the CD.

'Give me an update,' she said.

'He seems to have got on the bus all right. It dropped him near the works. Some of the men gave him short shrift, though—didn't like that their Portakabin had been searched. So he didn't hang about, told them he was going into Pitlochry. That was the last they saw of him.'

'He's done a runner,' Clarke confirmed.

'Looks like.'

'Anyone talked to his girlfriend?'

'The barmaid, you mean? Not yet.'

'Could he be shacked up with her?'

'It would solve all our problems.'

'And if someone had checked first thing, it would be saving me this bloody drive.'

'Want me to do it then?'

'No, I'll talk to her when I get there.'

Rebus took note of that—*I*, not *we* . . .

'Are you in Pitlochry?' she was now asking Lightheart.

'Yes, but I need to head back to Perth—eleven o'clock meeting I can't be late for.'

'You do that then. We'll talk again after.'

She ended the call and signalled to overtake the lorry in front.

'Want the CD back on?' Rebus eventually asked.

Clarke shook her head. A little later, she decided to put a question to him.

'You don't think it's him, do you?'

'No.'

'Because he's got a short fuse and that's not the sort of person who goes years between victims?'

'Right,' Rebus agreed.

She nodded slowly. 'So why did he run?'

'It's what people like him do—act on instinct; no forethought.' Rebus decided it might be okay to throw in a question of his own. 'Did the search turn up anything?'

'They want to know if it's worth putting a couple of frogmen in Loch Tummel.'

'And is it?'

'James's call.'

'What about Robertson's stuff?'

'Pretty much as you said. Half an ounce of cannabis, a few knock-off DVDs.'

'Porn?'

'Some.'

'Hard core?'

'No S and M, if that's what you mean.' She looked at him again. 'This from the man who doesn't rate profilers.'

'Common sense comes cheaper.'

She managed a smile. The ice between them was melting. 'That book in your flat—did Nina Hazlitt give it to you?'

'How did you know?'

'It's on her Facebook bio that she edits books, including myths and legends.'

'Did you know that "Ring-a-Roses" is about the plague?'

'I thought everybody knew that.'

Rebus decided to try again: 'Sawney Bean?'

Clarke thought for a moment. 'Cannibal?'

'Except he probably never existed. It was anti-Jacobite propaganda, according to one theory. Doesn't take much to get a rumour started.'

'Is the Burry Man in your book?' Clarke asked.

'He is—you ever seen him in the flesh?'

'Last August. Took the car to Queensferry and watched him marching around, taking a drink from anyone that offered. Covered top to toe in burrs: no idea how he managed to pee . . .' She paused. 'Could Nina Hazlitt be putting together a new bogeyman?'

'I as good as asked her the same thing.'

'And?'

'She wasn't happy about it.'

'She's an editor by trade.'

'So?'

'She creates order, John. If there's one person responsible for all these disappearances, that gives

152

some sense to what's otherwise senseless.'

'And we're back to psychology again.'

'Not got much else, have we?'

'We've got a lot of people who don't seem to be around any more.'

'There is that.'

When she asked him if he wanted to choose a CD, he knew he'd been forgiven his latest transgressions.

25

The Tummel Arms wouldn't open for business for another hour, but its door was unlocked. It was a bright, bustling morning on Pitlochry's Atholl Road. Neighbours stood on the pavements, grocery bags or dog leads in hand, and shared the local gossip. They were used to visitors, and hadn't paid Clarke and Rebus a moment's notice.

'Hello?' Clarke called out, pushing open the pub door. The place smelled of bleach. Stools and chairs had been placed on tables so the floor could be sluiced. A woman appeared from the direction of the ladies' loo, toting a mop.

'We're looking for Gina Andrews,' Clarke explained.

The woman pushed a stray hair behind one ear. 'She's at the baker's. Won't be long, though.'

'We'll wait, if that's okay?'

The cleaner shrugged, then disappeared again.

'Trusting souls up here,' Rebus remarked, eyeing the unguarded row of optics on the gantry.

'Not really,' Clarke replied, nodding towards

the CCTV camera above the door. The door itself swung open and another woman negotiated her way inside, carrying a large plastic tray piled high with individually bagged rolls and sandwiches. She heaved it on to the bar and exhaled noisily.

'Police?' she said, turning towards her visitors.

'That's right,' Clarke said.

'About Tommy?'

'Thomas Robertson, yes.'

'His car's still parked out the back.'

'How long has it been there?'

'Only since last night.'

'He was in here, then?'

Gina Andrews shook her head. She was in her thirties. Short and stocky, with shoulder-length blonde hair. She had that attitude necessary to good bar staff the world over: fair, but firm when the need arose; someone it wouldn't be wise to get on the wrong side of.

'He must have driven here, but he didn't come in. One of the regulars told me his car was there, so I sent him a text.'

'Nothing back?'

She shook her head again and started transferring the rolls to a metal salver. There was a printed label on each packet, identifying the filling.

'How much do you know about him, Ms Andrews?'

'He's all right. Likes a drink and a laugh.'

'Is he your . . .?'

Andrews looked up from her work. 'My bidie-in? Nothing that serious.'

'Just a friend, then?'

'Most nights.'

'Would you say he had a temper on him?'

154

'If the wind's blowing in the right direction.'

'Do you know where he was yesterday morning?'

'No.'

'He was answering some questions at a police station in Perth.'

'About the girl who went missing?'

'What makes you say that?'

Andrews gave a snort. 'You're not exactly in downtown Chicago. She counts as big news. Word's out that the police were up at the construction site.'

'Did you know that Mr Robertson has a criminal record?'

'He told me he'd been in jail.'

'Did he say why?'

'Rammy outside a nightclub. Tommy steps in and ends up being the one you lot lift.' She had filled one tray and was starting on another.

'It was attempted rape,' Rebus told her. She froze for a moment.

'Victim was pretty traumatised,' Clarke added.

'And that makes him a suspect?' She had gone back to the task, but with slightly less enthusiasm.

'He's always been okay with you?' Clarke enquired.

'Nice as ninepence.' She thought for a second. 'Did you tell him you were going to put me in the picture?'

'Does it matter?'

'Might explain why he lost his bottle. Got as far as the car park but couldn't bring himself to face me.'

'So why abandon the car?' Clarke asked.

'No idea.'

'Mind if I take a look at it?' Rebus added.

'Help yourself.'

155

Clarke nodded at Rebus to let him know he could go. She would be staying; questions still to be asked.

Outside, Rebus got a cigarette lit and made for the rear of the building. The gravel car park had space for only four vehicles, a sign explaining that it was reserved for staff. That wouldn't have bothered Robertson: as far as he was concerned, he was practically family. The only car there now was a beat-up Ford Escort, mostly blue in colour, though one door panel and a front wing were of different shades. The rear bumper was missing, one tail light smashed. It was a private enough spot, no buildings overlooking it. Rebus examined the gravel surface around the car for any obvious signs of a struggle, then peered in through the windows. The car itself was locked, the interior messy: empty crisp bags and soft-drink cans; newspapers and petrol receipts. He jotted down the details of the licence plate and did another circuit of the vehicle. The tax disc's time was almost up, and it would take a friendly mechanic and possibly a backhander to see the Escort through any MOT. At least two of the tyres were balder than Bobby Charlton on a windy day. When he planted the toe of his shoe against the modified exhaust, it wobbled badly.

Back inside the pub, the cleaner was taking her leave. Rebus held the door open for her. Andrews had finished one chore and started another, loading clean glasses into their shelves. Rebus gave Clarke a shrug to let her know he had nothing for her. She responded with the exact same gesture.

'He wouldn't happen to be hiding out at your place?' Rebus asked Andrews.

'Your pal here just made the selfsame

156

accusation.' She turned towards them and folded her arms: nothing defensive about the body language; quite the opposite, if her face was anything to go by.

'I'll take that as a "no", then.' Rebus pointed towards the display of rolls. 'Mind if I buy one?'

'You can get them at the bakery.'

'The roast beef with horseradish,' he told her.

Their staring contest lasted a good ten seconds, during which time he placed some money on the bar. She relented and handed him the first roll that came to hand. It was ham and mustard, but Rebus thanked her anyway.

'Ms Andrews,' Clarke informed him, 'was telling me she reckons he'll have headed back to the north-east. He has friends there he keeps in touch with.'

'Any names?' Rebus asked.

'Not that she can recall.'

Rebus's look said it all: *that's a big help*.

Then he bit into the roll.

*   *   *

Their next stop was the road crew, Bill Soames and Stefan Skiladz providing another less-than-enthusiastic welcome.

'You planning to scare off every man I've got working here?' Soames asked, hands stuffed into jacket pockets. The traffic was its usual diesel growl, choking the air and ensuring they had to shout. The weather was closing in, the temperature dropping and fog creeping towards them across the valley.

'Way it looks to me,' Clarke responded, 'it was

157

his workmates who sent him packing.'

'Tommy never needed much excuse to go into the town,' Skiladz said.

'There's been no word from him?' Rebus asked.

'Nothing.'

'His car's at the back of the Tummel Arms.'

'No surprise there.'

'He didn't go in, though,' Clarke added.

'Well he didn't come back here either.'

'Sure about that?'

Soames gave Rebus a hard stare. 'You saying we're lying?'

Rebus tried to make his shrug seem casual. 'Or being lied to, maybe. Is any of his stuff missing?'

Soames left it to Skiladz to answer.

'Nothing,' the Pole said.

'See, if I was thinking of doing a runner,' Rebus went on, 'I'd want to pack a few things first.'

'Maybe he wasn't thinking straight,' Soames said. 'You lot had just given him a grilling, dredging up his past . . .'

'And it was all tea and sympathy when he got back here?' Rebus's smile was thin and humourless.

'We're not covering for him. Look around you.' Soames made a sweeping motion with one arm. 'Piss-poor place for a game of hide and seek.'

'Did your search team find anything?' Skiladz interrupted.

'No,' Clarke admitted.

'Because there's nothing to find. You're wasting time and effort and I don't think the girl ever made it this far—not on foot.'

'And that means you've fucked over an innocent man,' Soames added. Then, with a glance towards Clarke: 'Pardon my French.'

'We're wasting our time here,' Clarke told Rebus.

'Isn't that what Stefan just said?' Soames commented.

But Clarke was already heading back to the car.

26

James Page had been busy.

Esson's e-fits of the missing women had been released to a few favoured media outlets. TV liked them, and that evening's Scottish news would carry them. The public had also started suggesting locations for the photo sent from Annette McKie's phone. Some had even submitted their own photos to back up their hunches. Page had made space on a wall of the CID room, and Esson had pinned them up. More were arriving all the time. Page led Clarke and Rebus into his office.

'Is he a serious suspect?' was Page's first question.

'I'm not sure,' Clarke admitted.

'The fact that he ran . . .'

'He's the type who acts without thinking.'

'A wanderer,' Rebus added. 'Never seems to stay anywhere for long.'

'Do we have any idea where he would go?'

'Aberdeen or thereabouts,' Clarke speculated.

'Worth letting Grampian Police know they should keep an eye out?'

'Wouldn't do any harm.'

Page glanced at his watch. 'I'm briefing the Chief in an hour. Is there anything more substantial I can give him?'

'Everybody's working flat out.'

'Thus far without a result. And the longer that situation persists . . .'

'If Annette got a lift,' Rebus said, 'it would be in a vehicle heading north. Any of the suggestions or photos from that stretch of the A9?'

'Between Pitlochry and Inverness, you mean?' Page checked his computer screen. 'Not that I can see,' he concluded.

'A nice big wall map is what we need,' Rebus told him. 'That, and plenty of drawing pins . . .'

*   *   *

Throughout the rest of the day, people phoned and e-mailed their thoughts and suppositions. Some had no firm ideas, but just wanted to say the team were doing a grand job. At which point they'd be thanked and gently nudged off the line with the explanation that other callers were waiting.

Rebus had driven home and returned with his own map, sticking it to the wall with Blu-Tack.

'I see you've already highlighted the A9,' Esson commented. 'That was fast work.'

Yes, and there were pinholes, too, near Auchterarder, Strathpeffer and Aviemore.

'Okay,' Esson said, taking a sip of hot water before beginning to recite the list: 'Appin, Taynuilt, Salen, Kendal, Inveruglas, Lochgair, Inchnadamph . . .'

'Slow down,' Rebus complained. 'I don't know where half these places are. And you made that last one up.'

'I've been to Inchnadamph,' Ronnie Ogilvie

160

piped up, his hand smothering the mouthpiece of his phone.

'John's got a point, though,' Clarke said. 'Let's pinpoint them on Google Maps, and when we know where they are, we flag them up on the wall.' She looked around the room. 'Everyone happy with that?'

There were nods of assent.

'Divvy the list up, Christine,' Clarke told Esson. She saw that Rebus was studying the photos submitted by the public, comparing them with the one from McKie's phone. 'Any of them take your fancy?'

'A couple.' He tapped them with his finger. Clarke had to agree.

'Where are they from?' she asked.

'One's the A838 south of Durness.'

'That's way up in the north-west, isn't it?'

Rebus showed her on the map. 'Miles from anywhere.'

'What about the other?'

'The A836. Little place called Edderton.'

'Where's that?'

Rebus shrugged, so Clarke went to her computer and let it do the work. Two minutes later she had her answer.

'The Dornoch Firth,' she said. 'Not more than a couple of miles off the A9, just north of Tain.'

'Where they make Glenmorangie?' Rebus asked.

'You'd know better than me.'

Rebus traced the A9 north from Inverness. It cut across the Black Isle and skirted the Cromarty Firth, heading inland again until it reached the Dornoch Firth, hugging the coast from there until Wick. Tain was marked, and so was the A836. Not many major roads up that way, and thousands upon thousands of inland acres of wilderness.

'We've got plenty more contenders,' Clarke cautioned, as Ogilvie's telephone rang again. 'So let's just keep at it.'

27

By the end of the day, they felt numb. Ogilvie said he was willing to stay another hour by himself, manning the phone. Clarke shook her head.

'We all need a break. I've asked one of the uniforms to take over until nine. After that, the switchboard will make a note of numbers and say we'll call them back in the morning. Good work, though, everybody—I mean it.'

These would normally have been Page's words, but he was at Fettes HQ, attending yet another briefing. Clarke rubbed tension from her forehead as she walked over to the wall map. Rebus was standing in front of it, looking thoughtful.

'There'll be more to do tomorrow,' he advised, 'with a bit of luck.'

'The e-fits of the three women? You really think we'll get sightings?'

'It would be nice to think so.' He turned towards her. 'So what do you make of it?'

She studied the map. 'How many votes does that make for Edderton?'

'Four and counting.'

'Must be just about the whole population.'

Rebus managed a smile. 'Three for Lochgair, but it's way over on the west here.' He tapped the map.

'Next to Loch Fyne.'

'And a couple for Durness,' Clarke added. The map was studded with drawing pins, and a further cluster had been added to the wall beneath the map's bottom edge.

'Offerings from England?' Clarke surmised.

'And Wales and Northern Ireland.'

She puffed out her cheeks and expelled a blast of air. 'Isn't this the sort of thing profilers are supposed to be good at?'

'Don't start.'

'I'm just saying.' She gave a weary smile. Then, studying the map again: 'You're still thinking the A9?'

'Or just off it.'

'So that's—what?—six suggested locations.'

'Six and counting.'

She nodded slowly, glancing behind her to ensure no one else in the team was close enough to hear. All the same, she lowered her voice. 'What if it doesn't mean anything? We narrow it down, maybe even convince ourselves we've got the right spot . . . what if it tells us nothing?'

'Then we try something else.'

'What, though?'

'Have a bit of faith, Siobhan. If you can say at the end that you put in the hours and tried your damnedest . . .'

'I'm sure the family will send us a nice Thank You card.'

'They might and they might not.' Rebus placed a hand on her shoulder. 'Whatever you do tonight, make sure it's a long way from this.'

She nodded her agreement. 'Same goes for you,' she told him.

163

'Absolutely,' he said. 'I might even have a nice wee drive out into the country . . .'

* * *

A couple of city pubs first, though. There was a different face on the door at the Gimlet. He was on his phone and didn't seem to sense any threat in Rebus. The pub itself was busy, same barmaid as on his previous visit. He gave her a wink of recognition but didn't stay for a drink. His second watering hole of choice was even less gentrified. The Tytler sat in the middle of a housing scheme in the north of the city, half of which was due to be torn down. The Tytler's clients looked similarly ready to have a demolition notice slapped on them. Again Rebus chose not to linger; a quick word with the monosyllabic barman and he was off again. A longer drive this time, heading west out of the city into the badlands of West Lothian. Broxburn, Bathgate, Blackburn and Whitburn. Tribal towns; ex-mining communities. Jo-Jo Binkie's was the name above the door of a converted art deco cinema on a main street predominated by closed businesses and For Sale signs. Three hulking doormen gave him their best stare. They all bore armbands on their coats identifying them as SECURITY, and earpieces with a thin cord which disappeared into the space between neck and collar.

'All right, pal?' one of them asked Rebus. Plenty of scar tissue on the man's face, and a nose that had been broken at least once.

'Fine,' Rebus said, making to pass him. But a hand stopped him.

'Meeting someone?' the doorman enquired.

164

'Maybe.'

'See, it's Couples' Night, so unless it's a threesome you're after . . .?'

'Old folks' home is down the road,' one of the other bouncers added. 'They might do a bit of dancing there.'

Rebus broke into a smile. 'Mind if I steal that one for my book?'

'What book would that be?'

'I'm calling it *Fuds Say the Funniest Things*.'

The young man moved closer. 'Fud, am I? Maybe we should go round the back and find out . . .'

The third bouncer, who looked the most experienced, had kept his counsel thus far, but now he patted his young colleague on the back.

'Easy there, Marcus. Our friend's a police officer.'

Rebus stared Marcus down. 'He's right, you know. And the reason I've got to the age I have is that I never start a fight I can't win. Little tip for you there . . . wee man.'

Rebus turned his attention to the leader of the group.

'Who is it you want to see?' the man asked. Shaven head; neat moustache/beard combo peppered with grey. He too was a survivor.

'Mr Hammell,' Rebus told him.

'He knows you're coming?'

'Not exactly.'

'Might not want to see you, then.'

'Maybe if you tell him it's about Annette.'

The doorman chewed this over, at the same time working the gum in his mouth.

'Does Mr Hammell know you?'

Rebus nodded.

'Okay then. Follow me.'

Inside the foyer lay an acre of red carpet. There were tiny twinkling lights set into the ceiling, and the old box office was where you still paid your entrance money. Behind two sets of swing doors, Rebus could hear pounding dance music and a few drunken female whoops. The doorman had stopped long enough at a narrow stairwell in one corner to unhook a red rope. The sign next to it said STAFF ONLY. They climbed to the balcony area, the walls throbbing from the sound system.

'That Marcus needs a bouncer of his own,' Rebus commented.

'It's turning into a young man's game, same as everything else.'

Emerging at the top of the stairs, Rebus saw that some of the old cinema seating remained, rows of plush velour awaiting an audience that would never come. A mirror ball was working hard at entertaining the dancers below. Red and blue lights pulsed. The doorman led Rebus past the back row of seats to an office, where he knocked and entered without waiting to be asked, stranding Rebus on the door's other side. Half a minute later, he was back, leaving the door open this time and signalling for Rebus to go in.

'Thanks,' Rebus said. 'I mean it.' The doorman nodded, aware that he was now owed a favour, something he could tuck away in his back pocket for the future.

The office surprised Rebus by being large, bright and modern. Pale wooden furniture, ochre-coloured leather sofa. There were framed publicity shots for old films on the walls, including

166

many Rebus had seen in his youth.

'Found them when we bought the place,' Frank Hammell explained. 'Hundreds of them left to rot in the roof space. I think they were supposed to be insulation.' He had come from behind his desk to shake Rebus's hand. He held on to it and asked if there was news.

'Not much,' Rebus conceded. 'Mind if we sit?'

Hammell took one end of the sofa and Rebus the other. Tonight Hammell was wearing stonewashed denims with brown brogues. A silver-tipped belt strained in combat with the gut it encircled. White short-sleeved shirt open at the neck. He ran a meaty hand through his hair.

'Rob's a gent,' he told Rebus, nodding towards the door.

'Certainly seems to have a bit more grey matter than Doorman Donny at the Gimlet.'

'Brains and brawn don't always mix. It's getting harder to find good guys.' Hammell gave a dismissive wave of the hand. 'Anyway, I leave the hiring and firing to Darryl. So what brings you here, Rebus?'

'I was hoping you could tell me where Thomas Robertson is.'

'Mind if I ask *you* a question first?'

'Go ahead.'

'Who the hell is Thomas Robertson?'

Rebus tried staring him out, but Hammell seemed to have played the game before. 'He's someone we were questioning,' he eventually decided to explain.

'Okay.'

'And now he's gone missing.'

'You think he's the one who took Annette?'

167

'No, but I'm pretty sure *you* think he did.'

Hammell stretched out both arms, palms upwards. 'Never heard of him till you walked in,' he protested.

'He was part of a road crew working north of Pitlochry. Drove into town and that's the last anyone saw of him.'

'So he's a fugitive?'

'He's not been charged with anything.'

'How come he ended up on your radar, then?'

'He has a bit of previous.'

'Abduction?'

Rebus shook his head. 'Assault.'

'And now you've questioned him and let him go?'

'We searched his sleeping quarters. Didn't find anything linking him to Annette.'

Hammell was thoughtful. 'How exactly am I supposed to have known about him?'

'There was some gossip on the internet.'

'Only net that interests me is the away team's at Tynecastle.' He paused. 'I saw on the news . . . photos of those other women. And the picture Annette sent . . . Is there anything I can tell Gail, just something to chase the gloom?'

'We've had plenty of suggestions. Tomorrow or the day after, we'll be checking the shortlist personally.'

'No sightings of Annette, though? Her picture's been everywhere . . .'

Rebus didn't say anything to this. Hammell got up and walked behind his desk, opening a drawer and bringing out a bottle of vodka.

'Want one?'

When Rebus shook his head, Hammell lifted

a single glass from the drawer and poured an inch into it.

'How's Annette's mother doing?' Rebus asked.

'How do you think?'

There was no knock at the door. It just opened, and a young man Rebus recognised as Darryl Christie was standing there. He saw that Hammell had a visitor and began to mutter an apology.

'The two of you should meet,' Hammell said, gesturing for the young man to come in. Rebus reckoned Christie merited standing up for.

'We spoke on the phone,' he explained, extending his hand. 'I'm John Rebus.'

'Is it to do with Annette?'

'Just a progress report,' Hammell reassured him. 'Nothing to worry about.'

Christie's phone buzzed and he checked the message on the screen. He was a handsome enough lad, and his tailored suit looked brand new. A suit was an interesting choice. It belonged to the world of grown-ups, of serious business. Hammell dressed sloppily because he could afford to: no one was going to misjudge him, whatever he chose to wear. Darryl had to work that bit harder. In denims, there was always the chance he would be mistaken for a nobody.

'What's this I hear about photographs?' Christie asked.

'Your sister sent one,' Rebus explained. 'Or at least, one was sent from her phone. Same thing with a missing person from a few years back. Right now, that's about as much as we have.'

'Plus a suspect who's gone AWOL,' Hammell interrupted. 'We've not got him locked in the cellar, have we, Darryl?'

'Not last time I looked.' Christie's phone buzzed again, alerting him to a new message.

'Always the fucking texts,' Hammell complained. 'Take him to a show or the best restaurants, he hardly looks up from that bloody phone.'

'It's how business gets done,' Christie muttered, his fingertips busy on the touchscreen.

Hammell wrinkled his nose and caught Rebus's eye. 'People like you and me, we prefer things face to face. That was all you had in the old days. Tonight you could have phoned me, but you came in person.' He nodded his approval. 'Sure you won't take that drink?'

'I'm fine,' Rebus said.

'You could offer me one,' Darryl Christie commented.

'But then I'd have to pour you into a cab at the end of the night.'

Christie ignored this. He waved his phone in his employer's direction. 'I have to deal with this,' he said, turning and exiting the room.

'Not even a word of goodbye, eh?' Hammell shook his head in mock despair. 'He's a good kid, though.'

'How long have you known his mother?'

'Didn't you ask me that already?'

'I don't recall you answering.'

'Maybe because it's still none of your business.'

'Line of work I'm in, every little detail counts. You knew Darryl's dad?'

'Derek was a mate.' Hammell offered a shrug.

'Any truth in the rumour you ran him out of town?'

'Is this coming from your mouth or your pal Cafferty's?'

'I've told you, he's not my pal.'

Hammell poured himself another generous shot of vodka. Rebus could smell it. Wasn't the worst aroma in the world . . .

'Cafferty's finished anyway. Game over.' Hammell tipped the glass and drained it.

'Can you tell me what Annette's like?' Rebus asked. 'Or is that none of my business either?'

'Annette's a proper little madam—always needs to get her own way.'

'I was thinking that,' Rebus said, nodding his agreement. 'Her bussing it to Inverness . . .'

'One of my guys would have *driven* her!' Hammell growled.

'You suggested as much?'

'But she had to do it *her* way—and see where that got her!' Hammell made an exasperated sound and started refilling the glass again.

'You blame her?'

'If she'd just listened to reason, none of this would be happening.' He paused, stared down into his glass, swirling its contents. 'Look, you know me, right? You know who I am . . . It *annoys* me that I can't do anything to help.'

'You put up the reward.'

'And all that's done is flushed out every nut job and greedy bastard in a four-hundred-mile radius.'

'I doubt you could be doing anything we're not. It only gets problematic if you decide to go your own way.'

'I'll say it one more time: I don't know anything about this guy Robertson. But if you need a hand getting him back . . .' Hammell fixed Rebus with a look.

'I don't think that's necessary—or wise.'

171

Hammell gave a shrug. 'The offer's there. And how about that bonus? Bankers can't be the only ones, eh?' He had reached into one of the pockets in his jeans and produced a fat wad of what looked like fifty-pound notes.

'No,' Rebus said.

'Aye,' Hammell stated, reckoning he knew the truth of it. 'Cafferty already pays you a big enough retainer.'

Rebus decided it was time to go, but Hammell had other ideas.

'I'd been told you're like him, and it's true. You could almost be brothers.'

'Now I'm feeling insulted.'

Hammell smiled. 'Don't be. It's just that *one* like Cafferty has always seemed too many.' He stared into his drink before lifting it to his lips. 'Shame you didn't leave well alone in that hospital when you had the chance.'

28

It was two a.m. when Darryl Christie got back to the house in Lochend. His mother had dozed off in front of one of the TV shopping channels. He roused her and sent her to bed, though she'd demanded a hug first. The hug had been forthcoming, in exchange for a promise to take things easy with the booze and the pills.

Joseph and Cal had tidied the kitchen and washed up after dinner. Darryl checked the fridge—plenty of ready meals and milk. He'd placed a twenty-pound note on the table for groceries, and it was still there. Upstairs his brothers were in their bunk beds, but the small TV was warm to the touch and there were video games strewn across the floor. Some of them looked like they belonged to Annette. Joseph had asked permission to borrow one or two, and Darryl had agreed.

'I hope you two are asleep,' he warned them, though they weren't about to open their eyes and give up the pretence. Closing the door, he slipped into his sister's room and switched on the light. The walls had been painted black, but then decorated with posters and stickers. There were little stars and planets on the ceiling that glowed in the dark—those had been a Christmas present from Darryl. He sat for a moment on her single bed. He could smell her perfume, reckoned it was coming from the pillow. He lifted it and sniffed. There was no real sense of absence—at any moment she could come bounding in, demanding to know what he was doing there. They'd been competitive when younger, landed a few slaps, kicks and bites. But not recently, having come to inhabit different worlds.

'Just come home, you silly bitch,' Darryl said quietly, rising to his feet and heading back downstairs. He lay down fully dressed on his narrow bed, leaving the lights off in the conservatory so he didn't need to close the blinds. Then he tapped a name into his phone and waited until his father picked up.

'It's me,' he said.

'Any news?'

'Nothing.'

'It's been two weeks.'

'I know.'

173

'How's your mum?'

'Not great.'

'I can't come back, Darryl.'

'Why not? Hammell wouldn't dare touch you.'

'This is my life now.'

Darryl Christie stared at his faint reflection in the glass panels overhead. Light pollution again: no stars visible.

'We miss you,' he told his father.

'*You* miss me,' Derek corrected him. 'Is Frank still treating you right?'

'Yes.'

'And Cal and Joe?'

'They're okay.'

There was silence for a moment. 'Is Frank there tonight?'

'Not since Annette went missing.'

'His choice or your mum's?'

'I'm not sure.'

They spoke for a few more minutes, until Derek Christie reminded his son how much the call was costing.

'I keep telling you,' Darryl said, 'it's Frank's tab.'

'Even so . . .'

And that was that—goodbyes and talk of the trip to Australia Darryl would someday make. Afterwards he swung his feet on to the floor and sat on the edge of the bed. He had been lying to his father: he did have a phone paid for by Frank Hammell, but this wasn't it. This belonged to Darryl, which was why he used it to send a text message to Cafferty. He reckoned the old boy would be sound asleep. Maybe it would wake him and maybe it wouldn't. He punched it in anyway and hit 'send'.

Your pal Rebus has taken a shine to Hammell. He was at Jo-Jo's tonight.

Proper spelling and punctuation—only the best for Mr Cafferty. Darryl switched to his other phone to send one final text. Afterwards he might manage a few hours' sleep. A few hours seemed to be all he ever needed. By six or six thirty he'd be on his laptop, at the start of a new working day. He checked the wording of the message and made sure it was going to the right number, then pressed 'send' and lay back on his bed again, eyes open. He reached for the remote and used it to close the blinds around and above him. The system had cost a fortune—more than three times what he'd told his mother—even after Frank Hammell had negotiated a hefty discount. Darryl started to unbutton his shirt. Judging by the illuminated screen, a message had arrived already on one of his phones . . .

Part Three

And looking from a low ridge
To loch waters in the west
Where darkened hills are dreaming . . .

29

It was, as Rebus had explained to James Page, a no-brainer.

'You've got the engine here, running beautifully. Me, I'm by way of a spare light bulb in the glove box. I'm the part you can afford to be without.'

And Page had agreed, despite Clarke's protestations, which was why Rebus had filled his Saab with petrol and hit the road north again. Perth with its roundabouts, then Pitlochry and the roadworks, and on to House of Bruar, where he stopped for lunch. His parking bay was right outside the menswear shop, and he glanced at the window display, deciding that he was still not ready for strawberry-coloured cords. A sign at the Drumochter Summit informed him he was 1,516 feet above sea level. The mountains either side of him looked forbidding, yet hill-walkers had set out for the day—their cars parked in lay-bys—or else were returning to their vehicles, cheeks ruddy, breath visible in the air. At Aviemore, he signalled right, deciding on a detour through the town. There wasn't much to it, but it was bustling. Loch Garten was signposted. He recalled taking his daughter there thirty years before. The RSPB had built a hide, complete with telescopes and binoculars, but there had been no sign of the famous ospreys—just an empty nest. How old would Sammy have been? Five or six. A family driving holiday. These days he had to call her Samantha, on those rare occasions when he called her at all. She preferred sending her father texts, rather than actually engaging in a conversation. Rebus couldn't blame her, not when the conversations—his fault—almost always ended up in another petty disagreement. He had told Nina Hazlitt that he couldn't know what she'd been going through, but more than once he had almost lost Sammy.

He had to wait at the T-junction before he could rejoin the A9, losing count of the number of lorries and vans he was now going to be tailing, some of which he was sure he had overtaken on a stretch of dual carriageway many miles back. He had to remind himself that he was in no rush. He had plenty of CDs with him, and a box of chewing gum purchased at the petrol station. A spare packet of cigarettes and a half-litre bottle of Irn Bru. When he passed a turn-off to the Tomatin distillery, he gave it a little salute, having done the same for Dalwhinnie fifty miles or so back. Despite Inverness being only ten miles away now, and the road mostly dualled, it seemed to take an age to reach its outskirts. Culloden battlefield was nearby—another site they'd visited on that holiday. It had been a bleak place with a small visitors' centre in a building no bigger than a bothy. Sammy had kept saying how bored and cold she was.

The four p.m. news was on the car radio as Rebus entered Inverness. Traffic here was more congested still, and he made no friends by getting himself into the wrong lane then trying to get out of it again so he wasn't forced into the city centre. He crossed the Kessock Bridge on to the Black Isle, then another bridge across the Cromarty Firth, where he had to salute another distillery—Glen Ord. He knew this route from the fold-out map, but had bought another map before leaving Edinburgh.

180

There seemed to be four huge construction platforms in the water to the right. Rain was falling, and the windscreen wipers provided a hypnotic rhythm. It took a moment for him to realise what the sound reminded him of: waking up to the stylus still plying its course around an album's run-out groove. Alness was fourteen miles south of Tain and boasted Dalmore distillery, while Tain itself had Glenmorangie. At the next roundabout he left the A9 for the A836, signposted towards Bonar Bridge, Ardgay and Edderton. He had a phone number for a local farmer and punched it into his mobile.

'Five or ten minutes,' he told the man, ending the call.

And five or ten minutes was all it took. The farmer's name was Jim Mellon, and he was waiting with his venerable Land Rover. He signalled for Rebus to park by the side of the road.

'We'll take mine,' he called out, having decided that the Saab might not be up to the task.

Rebus got out and locked the car, the farmer smiling at what he probably saw as a 'townie precaution'. He was younger than Rebus had expected—clean-shaven, fair-haired and handsome.

'I appreciate you doing this,' Rebus said. 'And thanks for taking the trouble to get in touch in the first place.'

'You said on the phone I wasn't alone?'

Rebus nodded his agreement. 'A few others are of the same mind as you.'

'Well, let's see what you think.' Mellon gestured towards the Land Rover. 'Not allergic to dogs, are you?'

In the back of the vehicle sat a collie—Rebus

guessed a sheep dog. Intelligent eyes, and not about to demean itself by looking for a pat from a stranger. The engine started with a roar and they headed up the narrow muddy road, past a sign warning them that if its lights were flashing, the snow gates ahead were closed.

'How often do vehicles use this route?' Rebus asked.

'A few times a day,' Mellon speculated. 'Not much up here.'

'It's signposted to Aultnamain.'

'Not much there either—but we're not headed that far.' He was turning on to a single-track road, punctuated by passing places. It was tarmacked, but with grass sprouting through cracks in the surface. Only a minute or two later, he brought them to a juddering stop and pulled on the handbrake. 'I'd say this is it.'

Rebus opened his door and got out. He produced a copy of the photo from his pocket. The sky was darker now, but not too dark. Mellon was pointing out the direction to him. Rebus gazed, then held up the photo, his eyes moving between the image and the real thing.

'Could have been taken at any time, mind,' Mellon cautioned.

Rebus knew what the man meant: there was probably little in this landscape that had changed in a hundred years or more.

'The thing is,' Rebus said, 'this time of day, she couldn't have been much further north than Pitlochry. By the time she got here, it would have been pitch black.'

'Then the photo can't have been taken here, can it?'

But Rebus wasn't so sure. He got out his own phone and snapped the view. It wasn't professional quality, but he started sending it to Clarke anyway. His phone, however, had other plans.

'No signal,' Rebus commented.

'It's usually pretty good. You just have to find the right spot.'

'So even if the photo was taken here . . .'

'She might have had trouble sending it.' The farmer nodded his understanding. 'Do you have other locations that could fit the bill?'

'One or two.'

'Any of them near where she was last seen?'

'They're not as good a match as this.' Rebus was looking around. Some would call it a peaceful spot, others a lonely one. The wind was whistling around them. Rebus didn't quite know what he was looking for, other than a sense of the why and the who: why here, and who had chosen it?

'I don't suppose you've seen anything suspicious?' he asked Mellon. 'Any strangers stopping for longer than usual?'

The farmer plunged his hands into the pockets of his Barbour. 'Nothing like that. And I've asked around, everybody says the same.'

'Tyre tracks where there shouldn't be any?'

The farmer shook his head.

'And at the top of the road?'

'Left at the junction brings you back to Alness eventually.'

'And if you turn right?'

'You join the road to Bonar Bridge.'

'What are the chances of a stranger finding this road, Mr Mellon?'

The man shrugged. 'It's on the maps. I dare say

satnav has it too.'

Rebus was taking a couple more photos, but it was getting too dark for them to be of any use. He just felt he should be doing *something*.

'You've come a long way,' the farmer said. 'There's tea at the house if you want it.'

'Thanks, but I've got a few miles ahead of me.'

'And have you seen enough?'

Rebus surveyed the horizon—as much of it as he could make out. 'I think so.'

'You reckon the poor lassie's out here somewhere?'

'I don't know,' Rebus admitted.

Back at the Land Rover, the dog gave him what could have been taken for a sympathetic look.

30

For some reason—mostly because he had failed to make any other decision—he was back on the A9, but heading further north. Soon though he turned off into Dornoch, passing what he assumed must be its cathedral (though no bigger than a village kirk) and stopping in the near-deserted square. A hotel and a shop seemed to be open, but the streets were empty. He found he could get a signal, and got out of the car to walk up and down a bit while he made the call.

'Well?' Siobhan Clarke asked.

'I'm pretty sure.'

'But not absolutely certain?'

'No.'

'So what now?'

'I've taken a few photos on my phone so you can see what I mean.'

'Are you heading back?'

'Not quite yet. I've stopped in Dornoch.'

'At this rate you'll not be home till midnight.'

Rebus thought of the overnight bag on the Saab's back seat. 'Thing is, Siobhan, there's no way she could have sent that picture on her phone. Not from Edderton, not at the time she did.'

'Okay.'

'So how else could it have been sent? All I can come up with is it's not an actual photo as such.'

'What is it then?'

'A *photo* of a photo. Might explain why it looks slightly blurry.'

'And sent why?'

'To throw us off the scent. Because we'd then spend days scouring the countryside around Pitlochry looking for it, reckoning it for the crime scene.'

Clarke was silent for a moment. 'We could check that,' she said. 'Just need someone who knows about photography.'

'Agreed.'

'So it doesn't really get us anywhere?'

'It tells us we're dealing with someone who puts a bit of thought in. And whoever they are, looks like they have this calling card. That's two things we didn't know before.'

'I'd probably trade them for a name and address, though.'

'You and me both.' He had crossed the road and was standing beneath a signpost. *To The Beach* was one option.

'Isn't Dornoch where Madonna got married to

that film director?' Clarke was asking.

'I'll ask next time I see her. Meantime, any news your end?'

'Still no sign of Thomas Robertson. But other locations for the photo are coming in.'

'Any good ones?'

'Nothing we haven't heard before. Durness got another vote, though.'

'Does that put it level with Edderton?'

'Just tucked in behind. Oh, one other thing—you remember Alasdair Blunt?'

'The charmer who reckons Zoe Beddows ruined his marriage?'

'We showed him the photo from Annette's phone.'

'And?'

'He said he couldn't be sure.'

'I'll tell you who might have a better memory of it . . .'

'His ex-wife? Her name's Judith Inglis.'

'You're earning your sweeties today, Siobhan. What was her opinion?'

'A pretty good match, she reckons. I mean, it's far from definitive . . .?' Rebus grunted a response and she changed the subject, asking him if he'd seen any dolphins: 'There are supposed to be some up that way.'

'Bit dark now,' he replied. 'Have you clocked off for the day?'

'More or less.'

'Lucky you.'

'I seem to remember the road trip was your choice.'

'It was.'

'And you wanted to do it alone.'

'What are you getting at?'

'Just wondering if you maybe had another navigator in mind.'

'Nina Hazlitt, you mean?'

'Did I say that?'

'Nice to be held in such low esteem.'

'You really are on your own there?'

Rebus looked up and down the empty street. 'I really am,' he said.

'She mentioned you by name in one of the interviews she gave. Surprised your ears weren't burning.'

'What did she say?'

'Apparently you're one of the very few "persons in authority" to take her seriously.'

'I'm a person in authority?'

'Don't believe everything you hear. Besides, it'll probably count against you with James.'

'Because he's not the one getting the plaudits?'

'We're all working hard, John. Nobody likes it when one figure gets picked out.'

'Understood.' He ended the call with a promise to send her his photos from Edderton. He did so while he still had a signal, noting that his phone's battery was getting low. Back at the car he started the ignition and headed down a narrow lane, which widened as it passed a caravan site and a coastguard station. The wind off the firth buffeted the Saab, the track ahead covered in a shifting, swirling layer of sand. He found himself in an empty car park, a steep grassy slope behind him. There were steps down to the beach, and the moon revealed the tide line. From what little he could see, the beach stretched for hundreds of yards. Rocky outcrops jutted from the sand. The waves had that insistent pulse to them, never quite the same twice. He felt utterly alone in the world. No traffic sounds; no other humans; nothing but clouds visible in the sky overhead. Only his car to remind him what century this was—that and his phone, which rang obligingly. It was Nina Hazlitt.

'Hello?' he said, answering.

'Reception's terrible.'

'It's the wind, I think. I'm heading back to the car.'

'Are you on top of a mountain or something?'

'At the coast, actually.' He climbed the steps, opened the driver's-side door and got in. 'Is that better?' he asked.

'Weather sounds foul up there.'

'We're used to it. What can I do for you, Nina?'

'Nothing, really. I just wanted a chat.'

'I'll warn you—I've not much battery left.'

She paused, as if seeking the right gambit. 'How are you getting on with the book?' she offered.

'Really interesting.'

'You're just saying that . . .'

'The Burry Man versus the Green Man, selkies versus mermaids . . . I remember the selkie in that film *Local Hero*.'

'Wasn't she a mermaid?'

'Maybe she was.'

'Sounds like you *are* reading it, though.'

'Told you.' He peered out towards the swell of the sea. Dolphins? Not tonight. And selkies, shape-changers? Not in a million years.

'Is there any . . . progress?'

'A bit,' he conceded.

'Do you have to keep it secret from me?'

'It's more to do with Annette McKie.' Rebus

188

thought for a moment. 'Did you get a chance to ask Sally's friends?'

'None of them remembers anyone out of the ordinary visiting the Friends Reunited page.'

'It was always a long shot.'

'Long shots seem to be my speciality.'

'Mine, too. I'm a long way from giving up on this.'

'I hope that's true, John.'

'But it might help if you didn't mention my name to the media.'

'Oh?'

'Doesn't go down well with the other troops.'

'I didn't realise.' She paused again. 'I seem to keep letting you down, don't I?'

'You weren't to know.'

The call lasted a few more minutes. It seemed to him that despite the presence of her brother in her life, the woman was lonely. Friends had probably fallen away as her range of interests had narrowed. He was relieved when his phone beeped, telling him the battery was about to give out.

'Any second now, my phone's going to die,' he explained to her.

'In other words, you're fobbing me off.' Her tone had stiffened.

'Nothing like that, Nina.' But she'd already hung up on him. He exhaled noisily and began to reverse out of his parking spot, but then stopped again and reached for the road map. Durness was on the A838, which ran along Scotland's jagged northern coastline. To get there, all he had to do was follow the A836, the same road that ran through Edderton. How long that journey might take was another matter. His phone summoned up just enough life for an incoming text from Siobhan Clarke: *Dear David Bailey, hard to tell—looks promising though x*

He headed back into the centre of Dornoch and saw that the hotel opposite the cathedral was brightly lit and inviting. There would be beer there, and a good range of malt whiskies. Hot food, too, if he was lucky. He had filled his wallet before setting out, knowing a night away was probable, so he parked the Saab directly outside the hotel's front door and got his bag from the back seat.

31

He was awake early and first into the breakfast room. A fry-up, two glasses of orange juice and a couple of cups of coffee dealt with a head thickened by one whisky too many. There had been a slight frost overnight, and a milky sun was doing its best to penetrate thin layers of cloud. The citizens of Dornoch were readying for the day's business or returning home with their newspapers of choice. Rebus dumped his overnight bag in the Saab, scraped the frost from the windscreen with his credit card and started the engine.

The A836 started off as a two-lane road, busy with local traffic but few tourists. Heavily laden logging lorries squeezed past Rebus's car as they headed south. He refilled the fuel tank at the first petrol station he saw, unsure when there might be another. The attendant didn't seem to know either.

'Depends which roads you're taking.'

'True enough,' Rebus responded, unable to fault

the young man's logic. Then, realising how much each litre was costing, he requested a receipt. Back in the car, he looked at the map book again. The peaks all had Gaelic names, none of which he'd heard of: Cnoc a Ghiubhais; Meall an Fhuarain; Cnoc an Daimh Mor. There was a whisky called anCnoc, so 'Cnoc' had to mean something. Maybe next time he would take the trouble to read the label on the bottle. After the village of Lairg, the road narrowed to a single lane with passing places and the terrain became more desolate. Cloud covered the tops of peaks whose steep slopes were dusted with snow. He passed conifer plantations and the remains of such plantations, stumps like tombstones in a vast cemetery. The sky was leaden, and weathered signs warned of lambs on the road. At Altnaharra, the hotel was open all year round. He saw that a few cars had parked up, walkers and climbers prepping for the rigours ahead. He pulled over and sat for a few minutes with his windows down, overhearing snatches of conversation and watching as they set out for the day. Some had Ordnance Survey maps strung around their necks, protected from the elements by clear plastic pouches. Their backpacks bulged with provisions and waterproofs, and most carried a long pole— and sometimes two—to help take the strain. He waited until the last one had clambered over the stile and had their back to him before he lit a cigarette, blowing smoke into the crisp, unpolluted air.

Half an hour later, he was driving into the village of Tongue, where he would join the road west along the coast to Durness. But he had one detour to make. There was a photograph in his jacket pocket. It had been sent to him a few years back, and he used it to find where he was looking for. The village itself was off to the left of the road, but Rebus headed for the causeway across the Kyle of Tongue. The bungalow was next door to a youth hostel. There were no names next to the doorbell. He pressed and waited, then pressed again. The view was breathtaking, but the house had been battered by the elements and would be again. He peered in through the living room window, then walked around to the back. No fence separated the property from the field behind it. The kitchen showed signs that someone had been home earlier: cereal packet next to the table, milk waiting to be returned to the fridge. Rebus went back to the Saab and sat there wondering what to do now. He could hear seabirds and gusts of wind, but nothing else. He tore a page from his notebook and jotted a message, returning to the front door to push it through the letter box.

He drove off again in silence, not in the mood for a CD or whatever radio reception could be mustered. Soon he was entering something calling itself 'North-West Highland Geopark'. The landscape grew more alien, almost lunar, rocks barely covered by any form of vegetation. But now and then there would be a spectacular cove with pristine white sand and blue sea. Rebus began to wonder if he'd ever been further from a pub in his life. He checked petrol gauge and cigarette packet both. Durness was still some miles off, and he had no idea what he would find there. He skirted Loch Eriboll and headed north again. Durness wasn't quite at the tip of Scotland—if you reckoned your vehicle up to the task, you could follow a track all the way to Cape Wrath. Rebus had a phone number for one of the locals, but no signal as yet. Durness itself, when he reached it, consisted of a few cottages and larger modern houses, plus a smattering of shops. There were even a couple of venerable petrol pumps. He stopped next to them and crossed the road to the Spar, where he asked the shopkeeper if she knew where Anthony Greenwood lived.

'He went to Smoo this morning,' she told him. 'I'm not sure if he's back.'

Rebus then showed her the photo.

'You're the police?' she surmised. 'From Edinburgh? Anthony told us all about it. The spot you're looking for is just by Keoldale.'

Two minutes later, armed with a fresh pack of cigarettes, he was back in the Saab and driving a further couple of miles, following her precise—almost too precise—instructions. But as he neared the site, he knew it was wrong. Not *all* wrong; just wrong enough. Gusts snapped at him as he gazed down towards the Kyle of Durness, then up the slope towards the bare hillside beyond a row of embattled trees, some of which looked permanently stooped.

'No,' he said. The hillside was too steep.

But then he'd known that all along, and even more so since Edderton. He drove slowly up and down the road, just in case he was missing something, but the shopkeeper in Durness had sent him to the right place.

It just wasn't the *right* place.

He consulted his map again. He could go back the way he'd come or keep going. The road made a circuit of sorts before joining the A836 again.

Rebus had never been one to retrace his steps, so headed south-west towards Laxford Bridge. The route was still narrow, dotted with passing places, but there was no traffic. Rebus reckoned he'd come a hundred miles or more since leaving Dornoch and not once had he been stuck behind a vehicle of any kind. There was sporadic tourist traffic, along with a few delivery vans. But everyone was very polite, flashing their headlights to let him know they had pulled over and he didn't need to, or acknowledging him with a wave whenever the roles were reversed. Having crossed to the west coast, he found himself heading inland again, south and east past miles and miles of nothing but scenery and sheep. Twice he had to stop for ewes on the road, and once he caught sight of a large bird of prey gliding over one of the distant summits. There were patches of snow up there, and a huge greasy sky. He passed lochs with wildfowl resting on the glassy surface, and his tyres pressed ancient roadkill further into the tarmac. He had just reached a narrow, dog-leg-shaped loch when his phone sounded. He had one missed call. He pulled over and returned it. The signal was fine.

'Dad?' It was Samantha's voice. 'Where are you? I got back and saw your note . . .'

Rebus had got out of the car. The air was clear and sharp as he inhaled. 'Would you believe I was just passing?'

'No.' She was stifling a laugh.

'Happens to be the truth. There was something I had to check in Durness.'

'How did you find the right house?'

'That picture you sent.' He held it up. Samantha was standing in front of her bungalow, arm around the waist of the tall young man next to her.

'So where are you now?' she asked.

'Nowhere. Quite literally.' He looked around him, saw the hillside reflected in the still surface of the loch. 'If I remembered any of my geography classes, I might be able to describe it.'

'Too far south to turn around?'

'I'd say so. I think I'm about sixty miles from Tongue.'

'That's a shame.'

'Next time, eh?' he said, rubbing at his forehead with the meat of his thumb. 'Or maybe if you're ever in Edinburgh. How are things anyway? It's a beautiful location . . .'

'You looked in the windows, didn't you? Place is a right tip.'

'No worse than mine. How's Keith doing?'

'He's okay. Got some work on the decommissioning project at Dounreay.'

'Do you check him for radioactivity?'

'I don't need a bedside light any more,' she joked. Then: 'You should have told me you were coming.'

'It was more of an impulse thing,' he lied. 'Sorry I've not phoned for a while.'

'You're kept busy. I saw that woman mention you on the news.' Meaning Nina Hazlitt. 'Is that why you were in Durness?'

'Sort of.'

'So that means you might be back?'

'I don't think so. But everything's all right with you and Keith?'

'We . . . we're trying IVF.'

'Oh, aye?'

'At the Raigmore Hospital. First one didn't

195

'take.'

'Sorry to hear that.'

'We're not giving up—not yet.'

'Good for you.' He closed his eyes and opened them again. The scenery took its time coming back into focus.

'I wish I'd been here. I was only out seeing a friend. Her baby's nine months . . .'

'At least I know where you are now. When we're on the phone like this in future, I can picture the view from your window.'

'It's a nice view.'

'It really is.' Rebus cleared his throat. 'I'd better get going. This is supposed to be me working.'

'Take care, Dad.'

'You too, Samantha.'

'I'm touched you came to visit. Really I am.'

He ended the call and stood there staring ahead of him without taking any of it in. Why hadn't he told her he'd be dropping by? Did he want to see the look on her face so he could judge whether she was pleased or not? Probably. But then there was the other possibility: that he'd *not* wanted her to be home. That way they couldn't end up falling out. He had made the effort, without any of the possible repercussions. Ever since Durness had been mentioned, he'd thought about Samantha, seeing an excuse to visit her without it looking as though he had gone out of his way.

Just passing.

'You're a basket case, John,' he told himself as he headed back to the idling car. 'And who wants a basket case as a grandad?'

IVF: she'd not mentioned it before, never really talked about kids. He wondered what the problem

196

was. She'd been hit by a car a decade or so back—could that have caused complications? Or maybe it was Keith and his job. They'd already had a shot at IVF without telling him. Wanting to surprise him maybe? Or did he just not figure in their lives to that extent?

At Bonar Bridge, instead of taking a right and passing through Edderton again, he headed along the northern side of the Dornoch Firth, picking up the A9 at Clashmore.

'Hello again,' he told the road. He was driving south now, through Tain and Inverness and Aviemore and Pitlochry. No room in his stomach for a late lunch, but he refilled the Saab's tank at a petrol station and bought a paper and a bottle of water. There was a veritable convoy on the opposite carriageway, led by a transporter with earth-moving equipment on its trailer. The traffic on Rebus's side of the road was moving more freely, for which he was grateful. Just south of Aviemore, he pulled into a lay-by behind an articulated lorry and a delivery van, getting out for a stretch and a rolling of the shoulders. Busy as the route was, he got the feeling he could walk a few dozen yards into the hills and be stepping where no feet had ever passed. The wilderness remained wilderness precisely because nobody bothered to stop. He turned at the sound of the van's door opening, the driver jumping down.

'Any chance of sparking me up?' the man said, waving a cigarette.

Rebus obliged.

'The dashboard lighter's buggered,' the man explained, nodding his gratitude before inhaling greedily.

'What about the HGV?' Rebus asked.

'Driver's dead to the world. Curtains shut and everything. We could be in the back, emptying the container, and he'd still be snoring.'

Rebus managed a smile. 'Sounds like you've given it some thought.'

'Not really. Dutch number plate, meaning you're more likely to get a few buckets of flowers than a flat-screen television.'

'You really *have* thought about it.'

The man laughed and took another drag on his cigarette.

'How do you know he's all right?' Rebus asked, meaning the lorry driver.

'If he drives those things every day, he's *far* from all right.' The man tapped a finger to his temple, then asked Rebus if he was in sales.

'Just had to go up north,' Rebus answered, keeping it vague.

'Inverness?'

'Further.'

'Wick?'

'North-west, towards Cape Wrath.'

'I didn't think there was anything up that way.'

'You're well informed.' Rebus paused as an artic rattled by, followed by a stream of cars. There was a change in air pressure, as if some force were trying to suck him on to the carriageway.

'It's worse on motorways,' the van driver said. 'Try taking a piss on the M8 hard shoulder.'

'Duly noted. You use this road a lot?'

'Like clockwork: Inverness–Perth–Dundee– Aberdeen. I could drive it blind.'

'Maybe not when I'm in the vicinity, eh?'

'Worried I'd dunt your Saab?'

Rebus shook his head. 'Worried I'd have to

32

Edinburgh again.

Long tailbacks into the city, a forty-mile-per-hour limit enforced by average speed cameras. Bloody roadworks. And then, as he entered the city itself, signs warning him about the tram project with its diversions and road closures. His back was on fire. Too much time at the wheel, and hardly the most relaxing of drives. At Gayfield Square he stuck the POLICE sign on the dashboard before getting out, patting the Saab's roof in thanks for not breaking down on him. Then he headed inside, expecting his nemesis to be waiting. Instead, there was a new face behind the Plexiglas, and she accepted Rebus's ID at face value, buzzing him through. He climbed the stairs and entered the CID office. Everyone was clustered around Christine Esson's computer.

'What have I missed?'

Page looked up briefly. 'Welcome back,' he said, gesturing for Rebus to come and look.

'It's the CCTV from the bus station,' Siobhan Clarke explained. It had been looked at before, but only to make sure Annette really did board the Inverness coach. 'Christine had the idea of winding it back a bit . . .'

Esson was using her mouse pad to move the action forwards and backwards, a few frames at a time. Annette skipped towards the bus queue, then seemed to retreat until she left the frame altogether. There was a cut to another camera, showing her from further away. Different angle, but obviously shot at the same time. Back, back, back towards the glass doors of the bus station. The door opening as she got closer to it, closing as she went through it, her hand pressed to the metal handle. She was on the pavement now, their view of her opaque, glass in the way.

'Can we zoom in?' Rebus asked.

'Not necessary,' Page said. 'Watch what happens.'

A figure was approaching her, speaking to her. Rebus sucked air through his teeth. It was recognisably Frank Hammell. His hand was grasping her arm. And then the pair of them moved out of shot again. Esson paused the recording, then played it forward in real time. Hammell and Annette walked into shot, his hand grabbing her as if reluctant to let her go. She shrugged him off and pushed open the door, striding purposefully across the concourse. Cut to the other camera. Was that relief on her face? She was up on her toes, a bag slung over one shoulder, joining the short queue to board the single-decker coach, glancing back just once to see if Hammell was there.

'The one and only,' James Page said, straightening up. He rested his palm on Esson's shoulder. 'Good work, Christine.' Then he clapped his hands just once, keeping them pressed together. 'So now we bring Mr Hammell, that good friend to the McKie family, in for a little chat.'

'He never mentioned being at the bus station?' Rebus guessed.

Clarke answered with a shake of the head. 'And we've just managed to get an itemised list from

200

Annette's mobile network. She sent a dozen texts from the bus—ten to her pal Timmy, the other two to a phone belonging to Frank Hammell. Only time her phone was used after that was for the photo to Thomas Redfern.'

'Incoming calls?'

'We don't have those.'

'Be interesting to know if Hammell texted her back.'

'We'll ask him,' Page responded crisply. 'This is a man with a criminal record, isn't that right, John?'

'He's a criminal all right, but as yet we've never nailed anything on him.'

'Well, he's lied to this inquiry, and that's quite enough to be going on with.'

'Obstruction at the very least,' Ronnie Ogilvie agreed.

Page nodded slowly. 'Back to your desks then, everyone. Siobhan, get on the phone to Mr Hammell and request his company.' Page caught Rebus's eye, gesturing towards his office. Rebus followed him, not bothering to close the door. He'd had enough of close confines for one day.

'How did it go?' Page was asking.

'I'm convinced the photo was taken at a place called Edderton.'

'Siobhan seems to agree. But she also said something about it being some sort of hoax . . .'

'Not exactly. But I think the abductor's playing a game with us.'

Page took a moment to digest this. 'And Hammell?' he asked.

'Needs to be interviewed.'

'He could have followed her to Pitlochry . . .'

'He could,' Rebus admitted.

Page remained thoughtful. 'How was the rest of your trip?'

'Largely uneventful.' Rebus handed over the petrol receipt. 'Expenses,' he explained.

Page studied it. 'Dated today.'

'That's right.'

'I thought you went yesterday?'

'The trip took longer than expected.'

'You were away overnight?'

'A hotel,' Rebus said.

'Receipt?' Page held out a hand, but Rebus shook his head.

'On the house, as it were.' He turned to go, but Page hadn't quite finished with him.

'Nina Hazlitt picked you out for praise.'

'I'm sorry about that.'

'As long as it doesn't go to your head.'

'Quite the opposite, James, I assure you . . .'

Back in the body of the kirk, it struck Rebus once again that he had nowhere to sit, not when the team was accounted for. There was a metal-framed chair that had come from the interview room, but no desk to go with it. Rebus placed it next to Clarke and checked that the legs were not going to collapse beneath him.

'Somewhere to put the boxes?' he hinted, prodding one of them with his finger.

'All in good time.'

'Otherwise I've busted a gut lugging them here for nothing.'

She stared at him. 'Poor you.' Then, turning back to her computer: 'How was the rest of the trip?'

'I took a look at Durness.'

'Thought as much. Explains why you're only just getting back.'

'It's not a contender.'

On her screen, she had found a contact number for Frank Hammell. She pressed her phone to her ear and waited.

'Mr Hammell?' she said. 'DI Clarke here. Do you think we could have a word at the station . . .?' She tapped the nib of her pen against a notebook next to her keyboard. 'Today, if at all possible.' She listened to his response, then asked when he would be back. 'Well, if that's the best you can do, sir. Noon tomorrow. We'll see you then . . .'

She ended the call and looked at Rebus again. 'He says he's in Aberdeen on business.'

Rebus pursed his lips. 'Thomas Robertson business?'

Clarke shrugged. Rebus was studying the map on the wall. More pins had been added, new locations suggested. The biggest cluster was still around Edderton. Christine Esson was approaching. 'Have you told him?' she asked Clarke.

'Told him what?'

'The sightings.'

'Oh.' Clarke opened her mouth to speak, but Page called out from his doorway, gesturing for her to join him in his office. 'You better do it,' she said to Esson, rising from her chair and squeezing past Rebus.

'I'm all ears,' Rebus offered.

'You know we put out the e-fits of the missing women?' Esson obliged.

'Yes.'

'We've had some sightings.'

'Okay . . .'

'And interestingly, most are of Sally Hazlitt.'

'Why is that interesting?'

203

'Because she's been missing the longest. Means the e-fit is less likely to be accurate. Easier to age a photo a couple of years than a dozen.'

Rebus nodded his acceptance of this. 'So where did all these sightings take place?'

She went back to her desk, returning with a pad of paper covered in her writing.

'Brigid Young was spotted last year working in a bar in Dublin. She now has an Australian accent, by the way.'

'Are you okay if we discount that one?'

Esson smiled. 'I think we can scratch most of them.'

'But not all?'

She looked at her notes again. 'Zoe Beddows has been seen in Brighton, Bristol, Dumfries and Lerwick—all within the past three months.'

'She gets about a bit.'

'And as for Sally Hazlitt . . .' She did some addition, her mouth forming the numbers. 'Eleven sightings in total, everywhere from Dover to Dundee.'

'There's something you're not telling me.'

'Two people claim to have seen her in Inverness, working in a hotel.'

'Same hotel both times?'

Esson nodded. 'The two callers don't know one another, and they stayed there on different weeks. One was in September, the other October. It's got to be coincidence, right? I mean, Inverness being on the A9 . . .'

'What's the hotel called?'

'Whicher's. It's part of a chain. I don't know much more than that.'

'Was she a chambermaid?'

'Receptionist.' Esson paused. 'I'm sure it's nothing.'

Rebus nodded slowly. 'And this is the only example where two people have come forward with the exact same information?'

'So far, yes.'

'Well, I suppose it's worth checking.'

'Not a priority, though?'

'What do you think?'

'I think they're long dead.'

'And Annette McKie?'

'There's still a chance—albeit a slim one.'

'Which is why the focus needs to be on her,' Rebus said. 'That was good work, by the way—the bus station CCTV. Shows what happens when you're thorough.'

Her head dropped just a fraction. 'To be honest, I feel a bit bad about it.'

'Why?'

'Because it wasn't picked up straight away.' She glanced in the direction of Page's closed door.

'It was Siobhan who looked at the footage originally?' Rebus guessed. Esson gave the slightest of nods. 'You reckon she's in there getting a spanking?' Rebus watched as the colour rose to the young woman's cheeks. 'I still think you deserve a prize—what do you say to a nice big mug of hot water?'

33

The Oxford Bar was mid-evening quiet. Rebus was seated in the back room with an IPA and the

Evening News when Siobhan Clarke arrived. She asked him if he wanted a refill.

'Have I ever been known to refuse?'

She retreated and returned a couple of minutes later with a fresh pint and a glass full of something green-tinged and fizzy.

'Lemonade and lime?' he guessed.

'Gin, lime and soda,' she corrected him, raising the glass and taking a gulp, exhaling noisily afterwards.

'Sign of a tough day,' he commented.

'We can't all go swanning off around the Highlands.'

'Did Page have a go at you?'

'About what?'

'Not spotting Hammell at the bus station.'

She looked at him. 'Christine told you,' she surmised. Rebus gave a shrug and waited for her to answer. 'I think he was more annoyed that he can't get his teeth into Frank Hammell until tomorrow.'

'Am I invited to that interview?'

'No.'

'Just you and Physical Graffiti? That'll be cosy.'

'Don't start.'

He held up his hands in a show of surrender. They sat in silence for a minute or two. Eventually she asked if there was anything in the paper.

'Not much.'

'Christine told you about the e-fits?'

He nodded.

'They got me thinking,' she went on. 'Maybe the accountant had money worries. And the hairdresser might've decided she'd had enough of married men . . .'

'And Sally Hazlitt?'

206

Clarke shrugged. 'Lots of people go missing, John, for all sorts of reasons. Look at Annette McKie. Bit of a wild child. She has a falling-out with her mum's boyfriend and decides to hide out for a while—maybe to punish him or put her mum through the wringer.'

'And the photo?'

'Might have nothing to do with anything.'

'Meaning I'm seeing things?'

'Your job is tying up loose ends. Maybe these are just random threads.'

He concentrated on finishing his first pint so he could get started on the second.

'It's something we have to consider, John.'

'I know that.' He wiped a line of foam from his top lip. 'So is this you politely telling me my services are no longer required?'

'It's not up to me.'

'Page, then? Are you running his errands to get back in his good books?'

She glared at him. 'James doesn't think you've got anything. Meantime *he's* got Thomas Robertson and Frank Hammell to be getting on with.'

'Why would Hammell abduct his lover's daughter?'

'We'll have to ask him.'

Rebus shook his head slowly, then asked her if she wanted another. She checked the time on her mobile phone.

'I need to be heading off,' she said. 'Are you planning on hanging around?'

'Where else am I going to go?'

'Home, maybe.'

'I was thinking of inviting you to dinner.'

'Not tonight.' She paused. 'Another time,

207

though, for definite.'

'Christine Esson's worried about you,' he stated as Clarke began to get to her feet.

'Worried?'

'That you'll blame her for getting called to the headmaster's office.'

'It wasn't her doing.'

'Maybe you could tell her that when you see her tomorrow?'

'Sure.' She slung her bag over her shoulder.

'How long do you reckon I've got, before Page sends me packing?'

'I don't know.'

'A day? Maybe two?'

'I really don't know, John. I'll see you in the morning.'

'Let's hope so.' Rebus raised his glass, toasting her as she turned her back on him and made for the exit. He was on his own again, the other tables wiped clean and awaiting customers. He finished the paper, while sounds of laughter came from the bar area. The usual crew were in: half a dozen familiar faces. Some of them, he didn't even know what they did for a living. It didn't matter in here. And although some regulars were given nicknames hinting at their jobs, no one had mooted this for Rebus—not to his face, at any rate. He was always just John. When he looked at the table in front of him, the pint Siobhan had bought him was down to its dregs. He lifted the empties, preparing to join the throng in the front room. Then he paused, remembering the drive to Tongue and back: the isolation and stillness, the sense of a world unchanged and unchanging.

Where are you?

Nowhere. Quite literally.

'But I prefer it here,' he told himself, making for the bar.

34

'Just a few questions, Mr Hammell,' Page said. The suit he was wearing seemed more tailored than ever.

'This place smells like a wrestler's kecks,' Hammell replied, his mouth twisting in distaste.

'It's not great,' Page agreed, casting an eye around the interview room's scarred walls. 'But it's what's available.'

'So not just psychology, then?'

Page looked at him, all innocent. 'Sorry?'

'Thinking it might unnerve me, get me to say something I shouldn't?'

Siobhan Clarke looked down at the floor and pretended her tongue was dislodging something from between two teeth. It was the only way to stop from smiling. Hammell had read Page's thinking to the letter.

'Anyway, many thanks for sparing the time,' Page said. 'Just want to clear up a slight discrepancy.'

'Oh?' Hammell sat low on the chair, legs splayed in front of him, like a boxer at rest between rounds.

'What we're wondering,' Clarke interjected, 'is why you didn't tell us you were at the bus station with Annette.'

'I don't remember anyone asking.'

'You didn't need to be *asked*, Mr Hammell.'

'Who says I was there anyway?'

'CCTV,' Page interrupted, trying to wrest the interview back from Clarke. 'Looks like you were having a few words with her.'

'The camera doesn't lie. I'd told her one of my guys would drive her to Inverness, but she didn't want that.'

'Might I ask why not?'

'Because she's a stubborn little madam, and she thought she might have to say thanks.' Hammell's tone betrayed his irritation. 'Didn't turn down cash for the train, though. Next thing I know, she's at the bus station—cheaper than the train and she can pocket what's left.'

'Were you following her?' Clarke asked.

'Sort of.'

'Why?'

'To make sure she was telling the truth. Way she is, it was just as likely she was going to see one of her junkie pals in Sighthill and crash there for a few days.'

'So you followed her to the bus station?'

'To Waverley first. She checked the train prices on one of the machines, then didn't bother buying a ticket. Trailed her to St Andrew Square and . . . well, you've got that on camera, right?'

'An argument,' James Page said.

'Just me telling her to catch the bloody train. But she dug her heels in.'

'And you didn't tell us any of this because . . .?'

'For one thing, it's not relevant.'

'And for another?' Clarke asked.

There was a moment's flickering self-doubt in Hammell's face. 'I didn't want Gail to know.'

'Why not?'

Hammell shifted in his chair. 'I wasn't sure how

210

she'd take it—me snooping like that. But it's how I am. I need to have a bit of control over a situation.'

Page considered this, leaning back and folding his arms. He was about to ask something, but Clarke got there first.

'What can you tell us about Thomas Robertson?'

'Look, I'm giving it to you straight—not holding back.'

'And we appreciate that, Mr Hammell,' Page assured him.

'Okay then.' Hammell paused. 'He's the one you think snatched Annette.'

'Is that why you were in Aberdeen?'

'Robertson has previous.'

'Not in the abduction line he doesn't.'

'No, but he probably knows a few villains up where he comes from.'

'You were finding out if one of them might have taken her? Why would they do that?'

'To get at me.'

'And did you make any progress?'

'Nobody's talking. But Robertson's name's out there now—they know I want a word with him . . .'

The room fell silent again until Siobhan Clarke asked a question.

'Who told you Thomas Robertson was of interest to us?'

'What?' Hammell's eyes narrowed.

'It's not common knowledge.'

'Isn't it?'

'No,' Clarke stated.

'Well, his name's out there.'

'Yes, but who told *you*?'

His eyes met hers. 'I don't remember,' he said, his voice level and emotionless.

211

And for some reason, Siobhan Clarke knew.

Who else was it going to be, after all?

* * *

'What are you doing here?'

Rebus looked up from his toasted sandwich. 'It's a café,' he replied. 'I'm having something to eat.'

'The usual?' the guy behind the counter called to Clarke.

'Just a flat white,' she told him, sitting down opposite Rebus.

'Didn't realise you had a monopoly on this place,' Rebus commented, glancing through the window towards Leith Walk.

'I don't.'

'But you're annoyed I'm here.'

'I'm annoyed at you full stop.'

Rebus put down the sandwich and wiped his fingers on the tissue-thin napkin. 'What've I done now?'

'You went and talked to Frank Hammell, didn't you?'

'Is that what he says?'

'He didn't *have* to say it.'

'Does Page know?'

He watched her shake her head. The coffee arrived. It was instant, some granules floating on the surface.

'Are you going to tell him?'

She glanced up at him. 'This is the sort of thing that would have Fox and his team dancing in the street.'

'When Thomas Robertson went AWOL, my first thought was that Hammell had nabbed him.'

'Something you decided to keep to yourself.'

'I went to see Hammell. He denied it.'

'So you gave him Robertson's name?'

'Half the internet knew we'd lifted someone for questioning. It would have taken him ten minutes to find out what I told him.'

She placed her elbows against the edge of the table and leaned in towards him. 'You're not CID, John. This isn't your job any more.'

'So people keep reminding me.' He had prised open the remains of the toastie in order to study its contents: a processed cheese slice and thin, pallid ham. 'Did your own chat with Hammell shed any light?'

'He says they argued because he'd given her money for the train.'

'Did you ask him what he was doing in Aberdeen?'

'He was looking for Robertson.'

Rebus stared at her. 'He admitted it?'

She nodded. 'Meaning he doesn't *have* Robertson.'

'Always supposing you take him at face value.'

'Which you don't, I suppose?'

'Odd that he'd just come out and tell you. If anything *does* happen to Robertson . . .'

'Hammell's just put himself forward as chief suspect.' Clarke was thoughtful. Rebus lifted his beaker of tea, but a cooling scum had gathered on its surface.

'I need a drink,' he said.

'You really don't.'

'I think I do, otherwise I'm going to be tasting that ham all afternoon. You coming?'

'I'll stick to coffee.' As he started to get up, she

gripped his forearm. 'If Page smells it on your breath . . .'

'That's why pubs sell mints, Siobhan.' And with a wink and a smile, he was gone.

She picked up the coffee and blew on it. Fox was right, of course: John Rebus was the loosest of cannons, and no constabulary had room for those any more. He'd also warned her that Rebus's mere proximity might damage her chances of further promotion. And hadn't everything been fine at Gayfield Square until Rebus had barged his way in? A good team, a great boss, and no errors of judgement. Not that Rebus had had anything to do with her missing Hammell on the CCTV: she alone was to blame, and she'd apologised again that morning to James Page. Malcolm Fox's words were sloshing around in her head: *Call me any time you think he's floundering—floundering or diving to the bottom . . .*

But that was how Rebus worked: kicking up all the sand and sediment, then studying what effect it had and what was uncovered in the process.

'It's too hot?' the guy behind the counter called over to her. She realised she was still blowing on the coffee, blowing so hard some had sloshed over the side.

'No, it's fine,' she assured him. And to prove it, she took a sip.

In truth, the liquid in the beaker was lukewarm at best, but she drank it anyway.

35

It didn't help that Rebus was doing a good impression of a man coughing up his lungs when Page encountered him in the corridor outside the CID suite.

'You all right, John?'

'Never better,' Rebus replied, wiping a hand across his eyes. 'Something stuck in my throat.'

'The butt of a cigarette, maybe?' Page made show of sniffing the air. 'And Polo mints for lunch? Interesting diet you have there.'

'Works for me.' Rebus pulled back his shoulders.

'Well, I wanted a word with you anyway . . .'

'Is this me getting my jotters?'

'You've done good work here, John, but the inquiry seems to be moving in different directions.'

'While I'm stuck on the hard shoulder trying to thumb a lift?'

'I wouldn't have put it *quite* like that. But it's true that I'm starting to think your time here may be drawing to a close.'

'In which case, I've a favour to ask.'

Page's eyes narrowed slightly. 'Yes?'

'Don't tell SCRU just yet. I need a bit of time to shift those boxes.' Rebus gestured in the vague direction of Clarke's desk.

'Shouldn't take more than an hour or two,' Page countered. 'I can get one of the team to help you.'

Rebus was shaking his head. 'Not your best use of resources, James. I'm happy to move them myself. I'll be out of your hair by this time tomorrow.' He held out a hand, which Page studied for a moment before extending his own to meet it.

Ten minutes later, Rebus was on Leith Walk again with a takeaway coffee and a box of paracetamol from the local pharmacy. He swallowed two, and browsed the windows of local shops. One of them sold second-hand vinyl, but he knew he didn't have time for a browse. Having convinced himself that he was fit to drive, he headed to his car, tucking the POLICE OFFICIAL BUSINESS sign under the passenger seat and turning the ignition. It was approaching three p.m. and he was going to meet the rush hour somewhere on his route, but all the same . . .

'Back in the saddle,' he told his car, patting its dashboard for luck.

I could drive it blind . . . He remembered the van driver's words as he headed for the M90. Escaping the city centre provided the usual problems: temporary traffic lights; teams digging up the roads. Many a potential rat-run had been blocked off, meaning little was to be gained by diverging from the main route north out of the city. Traffic slowed again on the approach to the Forth Road Bridge, and remained heavy until he had passed the turn-offs to Dunfermline and Kirkcaldy. He stopped at the Kinross services for fuel. The woman behind the till gave a little nod of recognition. Maybe she had a good memory, but it was more likely he had taken on the tics and rhythms of the regular traveller, and she was merely acknowledging him as a member of the tribe.

Perth, with its busy roundabouts, and then the end of the dual carriageway and the sense that time was working against each and every traveller on the road. Turbo-charged BMWs and Audis weaved in and out of the procession, driven by men in shirts and ties, any one of whom could have been the man he'd talked to at the petrol station in Pitlochry, the one with 'solutions' to offer.

Pitlochry itself eventually arrived, bringing a welcome stretch of dual carriageway, though this was also when slow lorries decided to overtake other slow lorries, Rebus yelling curses at them as he was forced to brake. He studied the roadworks as he passed them. Men in high-vis jackets and hard hats were still busy with their tools and machines. He couldn't make out Bill Soames or Stefan Skiladz. When the Michael Chapman CD finished, he swapped it for Spooky Tooth, and reached over to the passenger seat for a slug of water from the bottle he'd bought. Darkening skies and no sign of any hill-walkers today. No stopping at Bruar: on to Glen Truim and past Newtonmore. Aviemore to his right, where he prayed for more lorries to turn off than actually did, then Tomatin and another salute in the direction of its distillery. Evening now, the sky over Inverness illuminated by sodium, feeder roads still busy with the remnants of the homeward rush. It was only as he approached the city that he thought: I could have taken the train. But he liked his car too much, and patted the dashboard again to convey this feeling to it. Ten minutes later, he was in the car park at Whicher's Hotel, rolling his shoulders and clicking his spine back into place while listening to the Saab's engine start to cool.

He paused long enough for a cigarette, taking in his surroundings. There was a new-looking shopping mall within walking distance, plus business units, some of them not yet leased. This was an area of the city for sales reps rather than

217

tourists. When he eventually headed indoors to reception, he noted that the carpet was tartan and there was a stag's head on the wall. Plenty of wood panelling and piped music. A man in a pinstripe suit was checking in.

'Your usual room, Mr Frazer,' the receptionist was assuring him.

The receptionist was young—early twenties, maybe even late teens. Curly blonde hair and lashings of aquamarine eyeshadow. Behind her, a man much the same age was busy with paperwork. When Rebus's time came, she had the same smile as for Mr Frazer. It faltered only when he showed her his ID and the e-fit of Sally Hazlitt.

'Recognise her?' Rebus asked.

'Looks a bit like Susie,' the receptionist said. 'What do you think, Roddy?'

The young man turned from his work long enough to give a crisp nod. Rebus noted that he was wearing a waistcoat of the same tartan as the carpet.

'Susie works here?' Rebus asked. The receptionist's badge identified her only as Amanda.

'Yes.'

'Do you know if anyone showed her this photo? It's been on the news.'

'She's a different shift from me.' She was growing wary now.

'When was she last seen?'

She had picked up the phone next to her. 'You need to speak to the duty manager . . .'

The duty manager's name was Dora Causley and she sat with Rebus in the lounge as a pot of tea was fetched. She held the e-fit and studied it carefully.

'It's very like her,' she admitted.

218

'Susie?'

'Susie Mercer. She's been with us nearly nine months.'

'Not at work today, though?'

'She phoned in sick a few days back. By rights, she should have produced a doctor's line by now . . .'

'I'd like to speak to her.'

Causley nodded slowly. 'I can get you her details.'

'Thank you. And do you happen to know if anyone might have shown her this photo or mentioned the likeness to her?'

'No idea, sorry.'

She left him to his tea and shortbread, returning a few minutes later with a slip of paper: home address and phone number.

'Do you know where this is?' Rebus asked.

Causley shook her head. 'I've only been in Inverness a couple of years. Amanda can find it for you on the computer.'

Rebus nodded his acceptance of this. 'What about Susie Mercer? Is she a local?'

'English accent,' Causley said. 'No shortage of them in these parts.'

'Is she married?'

'Don't remember seeing a ring.'

'She must have a personnel file—any chance I could take a quick look?'

'I'd need authorisation for that.'

'My word's not good enough?'

The firmness of her smile was answer enough.

Armed with a route map printed from the internet by Amanda, Rebus set out to the car park. The Saab's bonnet was still warm to the touch.

'Sorry, old-timer,' he apologised. 'We're not quite done yet.'

The address was a flat above a charity shop in the city centre. Rebus pressed the bell and waited. He had been forced to leave his car on a double yellow line. Parking didn't seem to be possible otherwise. He pressed the bell again, checking the name beneath it: Mercer. There was one other buzzer, the name next to it scored out. Rebus tried it anyway, and a minute later the door opened. A man in his mid twenties stood at the foot of the stairs, chewing a mouthful of dinner.

'Sorry,' Rebus said. 'I was looking for Susie Mercer.'

'Haven't seen her today.'

'She's been off sick. Workmates are a bit worried.'

The man seemed to accept this. 'I'm in the flat next to hers. I can usually hear her television.' He was leading Rebus up the narrow flight of uncarpeted stairs. There were two doors at the top, one standing open, revealing what looked to Rebus like a bedsit: sofa, bed, cooker all visible. The man tapped on Susie Mercer's door. After a moment, Rebus tried the handle, without success. There was no letter box for him to peer through.

'When was the last time you saw her?'

'Few days back. You think she's in there?'

'Could be.'

'I hope she's all right.'

'Is there a landlord? He'd have a key, wouldn't he?'

The tenant nodded his agreement. 'Want me to fetch him?'

'He lives nearby?'

'Few streets away.'

'I'd appreciate that. Sorry again to interrupt your dinner.'

'It's fine,' the man said, heading indoors to fetch his jacket. He hesitated, about to lock his door, then told Rebus he could wait inside if he liked.

'That's good of you,' Rebus said, accepting the offer.

The room was small, the only available window open a few inches, presumably to release the smell of cooking. Looked like chilli from a tin, with a bag of nachos to accompany it. There was no TV, just a computer on a desk, and the bowl of leftover food next to it. A movie had been paused. Rebus recognised the actor but couldn't put a name to him. He plucked a nacho from the bag and popped it into his mouth. From envelopes on a ledge behind the door, it seemed the tenant's name was G. Fortune. Rebus could only presume the G stood for something other than Good.

Next to the narrow single bed were a reading lamp and some well-used paperbacks. Thrillers, picked up for between ten and fifty pence, possibly from the charity shop downstairs. No music system other than an MP3 player attached to a large pair of headphones. No wardrobe either, just a rail for jackets, shirts and trousers, and a chipped chest of drawers for everything else. Rebus heard the downstairs door open and close, and two sets of feet begin to climb the stairs.

The landlord took Rebus's hand when it was offered, but he had a question ready.

'You're from the hotel?'

'I never said that,' Rebus commented.

'Geoff here says you did.'

Rebus shook his head. 'He may have got that impression.' He took out his ID. 'I work for the police, Mr . . .?'

'Ralph Ellis. So what's going on here?'

'Just a few questions for Ms Mercer. She's not been seen at work for a few days. Called in sick but hasn't provided a doctor's line.'

'You think maybe she's . . .?' Ellis nodded towards the locked door.

'Only one way to find out, sir.'

Ellis debated with himself for a few seconds, then produced a bunch of keys from his pocket and found the right one, opening the door, calling out to Susie Mercer as he did so.

The room was dark. Rebus switched the light on. The curtain was closed, the bed unmade. The place was very similar to Fortune's, down to the clothes rack and chest of drawers. But the hangers had been stripped and the drawers emptied.

'Looks like she's done a flit,' Fortune said.

Rebus made a circuit of the room and the shower room off. Toiletries gone. Some women's magazines left on the floor next to the bed. Pinholes on the wall above the headboard of the bed. Rebus pointed to them.

'Any idea what the pictures were?'

'A couple of postcards,' Fortune said. 'One or two photos of her and her friends.'

'What friends?'

Fortune shrugged. 'I never saw them in the flesh.'

'What about a boyfriend?'

'I've heard guys' voices from time to time—'

'Well,' the landlord interrupted, 'she's not here and she's not dead, so I think we can lock up again.'

He looked at Rebus. 'Unless you've brought a search warrant with you . . .'

Rebus didn't want to leave. On the other hand, he couldn't see anything worth lingering for. 'Is the TV hers?' he asked.

'I think so,' Fortune said.

'It's not mine,' Ellis added.

'It might be now,' Rebus said quietly. Susie Mercer had left in a hurry, taking only what she could carry. He handed business cards to both men.

'In case she gets in touch,' he explained.

'You don't think she's coming back, though?' the landlord asked.

Rebus shook his head slowly in reply. Not now her e-fit was out there . . .

36

He sat in his car and considered the situation. Then he remembered the cop he'd spoken to in Northern Constabulary, when he'd been tracking down the case files on Sally Hazlitt and Brigid Young. He had a name and contact number in his notebook, so he made the call. The police switchboard answered and he told them who he was and that he needed to speak to Sergeant Gavin Arnold.

'He's not on shift,' he was eventually told.

'It's a bit urgent. Would he mind you giving me his home or mobile number?'

'We can't do that.'

'Maybe if I give you my number then, and you can get a message to him?'

'I'll see what I can do.'

After ending the call, Rebus knew that all he could do was wait. In Inverness. Aka Dolphinsludge. On a dreich weekday evening with the temperature falling rapidly. He drove around without taking much of it in. A couple of supermarkets were open and looked busy. Men stood outside pubs, sucking hard at cigarettes, keen to get back inside. When his phone rang, he pulled over to the kerb.

'What is it I can do for you?' Gavin Arnold asked.

'Do you remember me, Sergeant?'

'You're the reason I spent almost half a day covered in the dust of ages while I hunted those damned files. Haven't stopped sneezing yet.'

'I'm grateful to you.'

'So has there been some progress?'

'It'd be easier if I explained in person.'

'You're planning to drive up?'

'I'm already here.'

'Man, you should have said—I'm at the Lochinver, just along from the railway station.'

'If it's a pub, I think I passed it a couple of minutes ago.'

'I'm towards the back of the main room, next to the dartboard. Do you play?'

'Not really.'

'Pity. It's a league night and we're a man down . . .'

More double yellow lines outside the bar—every legal parking spot filled. Rebus left the sign on the dashboard, locked the Saab and pushed open the door of the Lochinver. Arnold waved to him from the bar. The two men shook hands.

'What's your poison?' Arnold asked.

224

'Just a lemonade.'

'Got the car, eh?' Arnold looked sympathetic. He was in his mid forties, slim and tall. Dressed in dun-coloured chinos and an open-necked white shirt. His cheeks glowed, but that could have been the result of one whisky too many.

'Your turn, Gavin!' came the call. Arnold gave Rebus an apologetic smile. 'This takes precedence, I'm afraid.'

'Fine by me,' Rebus said. He rested his weight on a bar stool and watched the game. Arnold was good, but his opponent had the edge. The players' team-mates offered noisy encouragement from their tables. Arnold lost to a single eighteen/double-top out-shot and the two men shook on it.

This, it turned out, had been the fixture's decider. After a bit of banter between the teams, Arnold slid on to the stool next to Rebus.

'Unlucky,' Rebus offered.

'I've never beaten the swine yet,' Arnold replied, his voice betraying his irritation. But he shrugged it off, ordered another whisky for himself and turned his attention to Rebus.

'What brings you all the way from Edinburgh?'

'What brought you all the way from Lancashire?'

Arnold grinned. 'Yorkshire, actually. Some days you'd swear the English outnumber the Scots up here. Not that you can always tell by appearances.' He gestured towards the barmaid and she approached with a smile.

'Sue,' he said, 'this is a friend of mine. His name's John.'

'Nice to meet you, John.' She reached between the pumps to shake his hand. 'Any friend of Gavin's, as the saying goes.'

225

'Sue owns this place,' Arnold informed Rebus. Then, to Sue: 'John here reckons he can place an accent.' He looked at Rebus. 'Go on then— where was Sue born? I'll even give you a clue—her surname's Holloway.'

Rebus studied Sue Holloway. Her smile told him this was a game he was fated to lose, though it was incumbent on him to try.

'Manchester?' he offered eventually.

'Tell him, Sue,' Arnold said.

'You're almost right, John,' Holloway obliged. 'But I was born in Kirkcaldy.'

'Makes you a Fifer, then,' he said. 'Same as me.'

'You've probably been back more regularly than I have.'

'Of late, only as far as the M90. But you grew up in Manchester, right?'

'Right,' she conceded. 'And for that, you get a drink on the house. Are you sure you want to stick to lemonade?'

With fresh drinks in front of them, Rebus warned Gavin Arnold that the tale he was about to tell might take a while.

'As long as you like,' Arnold reassured him.

So Rebus laid out the whole story, finishing the lemonade and accepting yet another. Arnold's darts team had drifted away, the bar only half full by the time Rebus finished. He ended by saying he would let Arnold mull it over while he stepped out for a cigarette. But Arnold followed him into the cold and stood there with him.

'So you think Mercer might be the Hazlitt lassie?'

'She might,' Rebus conceded, blowing smoke into the night air.

226

'And when those photos were published, she decided it was time to leave?'

'It's a possibility.'

Arnold thought for a moment. 'Could be a few clues in her personnel file.'

Rebus nodded. 'You're local, I'm not. Easier if you were the one to do the asking.'

Arnold looked at his watch. 'Bit late now . . .'

'There must be a night manager at the hotel,' Rebus suggested.

'Even so . . .'

'I'd really appreciate it.'

'My one bloody night off,' Arnold muttered, but he was smiling as he said it.

'There's a whisky on me afterwards,' Rebus said by way of encouragement.

'That seals the deal,' he was told.

They took the Saab, and stopped at Arnold's police station on Burnett Road long enough for him to change into his uniform.

'Looks better that way, more official,' he explained.

Then, with Arnold navigating, they headed to Whicher's. The night porter had started his shift, but said there was nothing he could do. The office was locked until Dora Causley arrived in the morning.

'How do you contact her in an emergency?' Rebus asked.

The porter plucked a card from one of the pockets in his tartan waistcoat.

'Call the number,' Rebus commanded. Arnold was standing at his shoulder, saying nothing but looking stern and definitely not to be messed with. The porter did as he was told, his eyes on both men.

'It's gone to voicemail,' he said eventually.

Rebus gestured for the receiver, took it, and told Causley she should call him 'as a matter of urgency'. He recited his mobile number, then handed the receiver back and told the porter they'd wait.

'Bar still serving?'

'Guests only,' the man explained.

Arnold took a step forward and glowered at him until it was decided he might be able to bend the rules just this once.

A single malt for Arnold, and tea for Rebus. They sat in the lounge. Leather chesterfield chairs, piped music. Only three guests were in there with them, huddled around the remains of their drinks, discussing as best they could the next day's business meetings, voices slurred, eyes drooping.

Arnold had removed both jacket and tie, but was still recognisably an officer of the law. He asked Rebus how long he had left until the gold watch.

'I'm already retired,' Rebus admitted. 'Cold case unit's staffed by crocks like me.'

'You never told me that.' Arnold seemed to be weighing up whether to take offence or not. Eventually he chuckled into his glass. 'I never even asked for ID, did I? You could have been anybody.'

'Sorry,' Rebus said.

Arnold chuckled again, but more wearily this time. He looked at his wristwatch. 'Can't wait here all night, can we?'

'I suppose not.'

'She could be out on the town.' Arnold yawned, stretching both arms wide, straining the buttons of his shirt. 'You planning on heading back south?'

'That was the general idea.'

'I could get the stuff in the morning and send it to you.'

But Rebus was thinking of something else. He hadn't brought his overnight bag with him this time, but all the same . . .

'One for the road?' he asked Arnold, signalling for the barman. When he ordered whisky for both of them, Arnold knew he could no longer rely on his designated driver to get him home.

37

Another dining room breakfast.

There was no sign of the businessmen from the lounge bar. Most of the guests seemed, like Rebus, to be travelling solo. It was half past seven, and Amanda on reception had informed him that Dora Causley didn't get in until eight. He'd texted this information to Arnold, along with the offer of bacon and eggs. When Arnold arrived, however, in full uniform and showing no hint of the previous night's intake, he wanted nothing but coffee and orange juice.

'Don't do breakfast,' he informed Rebus as he pulled out the chair across the table.

'Me neither, unless it's already paid for.' Rebus polished off the last triangle of toast. 'Sleep all right?'

'Like a baby—wet the bed three times.'

Rebus smiled, as he felt was expected.

'How about you?' Arnold asked.

'I never seem to be able to sleep late in hotel rooms.'

229

'That's hardly fair, is it?'

'Hardly,' Rebus agreed.

Their waitress was pouring refills when Causley, forewarned by the front desk, marched towards them, eyes only slightly bloodshot.

'Good morning,' she said.

Rebus was about to say something about her inability to check her phone for messages, but Arnold had sprung to his feet and was shaking her hand. 'Sergeant Arnold,' he reminded her. 'We met when you had that break-in.'

'Yes, of course.'

'Good job it was kept out of the papers, eh?' Arnold turned towards Rebus. 'Turned out to be one of the housekeeping staff.'

Causley busied herself trying not to squirm. Arnold was still holding her hand, and she knew what was expected.

'You'll be wanting to see that file,' she said.

'If it's not too much trouble,' Arnold replied, only now loosening his grip.

*　　　*　　　*

Having played his part, Arnold had headed off to work, and half an hour later, Rebus was checking out of the hotel, taking with him photocopies of Susie Mercer's CV, application letter, references and twelve-week performance review. He sat in the Saab and went through everything for a second time. The references were from other hotels, one in Northern Ireland and one on Mull. Mull was the more recent, and Rebus called the number. Yes, he was told, Susie Mercer had worked there the previous summer. The hotel in Northern Ireland, on the other hand, had no record of her.

'Though we did have a Susan Merton here around that time.'

Rebus waited for the woman to pull Merton's photograph from her personnel file, then described Mercer to her.

'Sounds about right,' she conceded. Rebus asked if a copy of the photo could be sent to him. She snapped it with her phone and a couple of minutes later it arrived on his screen. It was blurry, and the cut and colour of the hair were different, but he'd bet his pension Susan Merton and Susie Mercer were the same person. He had tried Mercer's number half a dozen times, leaving messages when prompted. Now he punched in a text and sent it, asking her to get in touch without revealing who he was.

Looking down the CV, he saw more hotel and restaurant work, plus stints in department stores and as an office temp. High school in Aylesbury; further education college in the same town. Rebus had only the vaguest notion that Aylesbury was somewhere near London. Her date of birth was June 1, 1981, while Sally Hazlitt's was the reverse— January 6. 6/1 and 1/6—easy to remember. When his phone rang, he answered automatically. It was Peter Bliss.

'Someone's looking for you,' Bliss said, keeping his voice down.

'Cowan?'

'Gayfield Square told him you'd be back here first thing.'

Nicely played, Page: just a smidgen of revenge . . .

'I'm in Inverness,' Rebus confided. 'I'll be another three hours at least.'

231

'Inverness?'

'It's a long story.'

'You should call in on Gregor Magrath.'

It took Rebus a moment to place the name. 'The guy who started SCRU?' He remembered the card Nina Hazlitt had given him, the one with Magrath's number on it.

'He lives up that way.'

'You reckon Cowan would be happier if I told him that was what I was doing?'

'Probably not.'

'Well, thanks for the warning anyway.'

'So we'll see you this afternoon?'

'Will there be bunting?'

Bliss was stifling a laugh as he ended the call.

38

Cowan was on the phone when Rebus walked into the SCRU office. Bliss gave Rebus a wink and Elaine Robison added a little wave, their attitude suggesting that the workload had been managed more than adequately in his absence.

'He's here now,' Cowan was saying into the receiver, eyes on Rebus. 'Better late than never, I suppose.' He paused as he listened. 'Yes, I'll tell him. Straight away, yes.'

He ended the call and told Rebus not to bother taking his coat off. 'DCI Page wants to see you. Any idea why that might be?'

Rebus was stumped. All he could come up with was that the case files were taking up space and needed to be moved.

'Where the hell have you been anyway?'

'Didn't realise you would be pining for me, Dan . . .'

Out in the car park, Rebus apologised to the Saab one more time before starting the engine. There was a single dry cough of complaint before the motor caught. He got on the phone to Siobhan Clarke. Before she could speak, he told her that he'd just been to Inverness.

'And the thing is, I think Sally Hazlitt's definitely still alive. Soon as that e-fit went public, she did a runner. I don't suppose it counts as conclusive, but all the same . . .'

'Throwing into doubt your whole serial-killer theory?'

'Yes.'

'Thing is, John, there's a problem with that—it's why James wants to see you.'

'Oh?'

'Couple more victims by the look of it. We'll tell you all about it when you get here.'

*　　*　　*

Two of the Gayfield Square detectives would be 'hot-desking', so that Rebus could have the one going spare. The boxes had been piled next to it and on it.

'The desk drawers are out of bounds, I've been told to advise you,' Page said. 'DC Ormiston's keeping his stuff in there for the duration.' They were in his office, Page seated behind his desk, Siobhan and Rebus standing. 'Siobhan tells me you've changed your thinking about the first victim.'

'She tells *me*,' Rebus countered, 'that there may

be others.'

Page nodded and picked up a sheet of paper, reading from it.

'It's the photo sent from Annette McKie's phone. It chimed with a couple of families. Both have lost teenage daughters in the past five years. Suspected drownings, neither body recovered.'

'They sent photos from their phones the day they vanished?' Rebus guessed.

Page nodded slowly. 'In one case, the photo no longer exists. But the parents swear it was the same as the one they saw on the news.'

'And the other family?'

'Kept all their daughter's things. Here's the picture they were sent.' Page was tapping the screen of his computer. Rebus walked around the side of the desk so he could see it.

'Christ,' was all he could think to say.

It was Edderton, no doubt in his mind at all.

*   *   *

That night, Rebus stayed late at the office. Clarke had volunteered her services and the two of them were giving some order to the boxes, sorting out what might be important. Page wanted a precis, something he could take to the Chief Constable. Northern Constabulary would need to be persuaded to cooperate in the inquiry—the area around Edderton searched; local people questioned at length and in detail—and that meant putting together the facts, while trying to predict queries and problems, then prepping possible responses. Clarke was working on the timeline.

'Do we add Sally Hazlitt or not?' was one of her

questions.

Rebus didn't really know.

'1999, 2002, 2008 and 2012. To which we can add 2007 and 2009.' She stared at the figures. 'I know what a profiler would say.'

'Enlighten me, if you must.'

'They'd say serial offenders start out slow, then become more prolific the longer they get away with it.'

'Oh aye?'

'Three possibilities: one, it's because they want to be caught; two, it's precisely because they're *not* being caught; three, it's because they're becoming addicted to it—each new victim satisfying them for a shorter time.'

'Is that the sort of stuff you need to know these days to be a DI?'

'I think it's worth looking at those essays Christine printed out. Our guy has given us one big problem: no disposal sites to work with. But we *do* have Edderton. It has to mean something to him.'

'Unless he chose it at random to throw any police investigation off the scent. Could be somewhere he stopped just the once. Maybe someone else snapped the original picture and he got hold of it somehow.'

Clarke considered this, trying not to look too disheartened. They worked in silence for a few more minutes until she asked him about Inverness and he filled her in on the details of his trip.

'And the Saab didn't break down?'

'Not ready for the knacker's yard just yet.'

'Apparently not.'

Rebus stretched his spine and rolled his shoulders. 'We about done here?'

'I should type all this up.'

'Ready to present to Page first thing?'

'It would make sense.'

'A cold drink would make sense, too.'

'Give me another half-hour.'

'And what will I be doing all that time?'

'Getting your Inverness adventure down on paper,' Clarke suggested.

Afterwards, they walked to a bar on Broughton Street, Clarke sucking in lungfuls of the night air as if tasting freedom after long captivity.

The pub was well lit and filled with conversation rather than music. A pint of beer and a gin, lime and soda. Rebus, feeling reckless, even threw in salted peanuts and a bag of crisps.

'How are you feeling?' Clarke asked as they clinked glasses.

'I'm all right.'

'I meant with all the driving you've been doing.'

'You offering to apply the Deep Heat?'

'No.' She smiled and took a sip.

'It's weird up there,' Rebus said. 'Beautiful and bleak and eerie, all at the same time.' He swallowed a mouthful of beer. 'One particular stretch south of Durness—I doubt it's changed since the time of Sir Walter Scott.'

'You should have taken a navigator.'

'I really did think you were needed here.'

'And I know that's not the whole truth.' She paused, inviting him to comment, but he opened the crisp bag instead.

'What about Edderton?' she asked eventually.

'Farming and tourism, I'd say. A distillery an easy commute away. Plus some rigs in the Cromarty Firth.'

'Dornoch?'

'Nice wee place. Good-looking beach. No sign of Madonna.' He wiped foam from around his mouth. 'Everything seemed so . . . normal.' He shrugged. 'Just normal.' His phone went and he checked the screen. 'Nina Hazlitt,' he informed Clarke.

'You going to answer?' She watched him shake his head. 'Why not?'

'Because I'd probably lie to her, tell her there's no news.'

'Why not the truth?'

'Because I want to be a hundred per cent sure— maybe a hundred and ten.'

They waited until the phone had stopped. It sounded once more to tell Rebus he had voicemail.

'If Sally is alive,' Clarke said, 'what do you think her story is?'

'I've no idea.'

'What was her place like in Inverness?'

'Pretty anonymous. I think she moves around a lot, never stays anywhere long.'

'Maybe it's like the song says—she hasn't found what she's looking for.'

'Who has?' Rebus said, lifting the pint to his mouth again.

'You're not doing too badly,' Clarke commented, causing him to raise an eyebrow.

'This case,' she explained. 'It's put a spring in your step.'

'I'm a regular Fred Astaire all right.'

'You know it's true, though . . .'

He managed to lock his eyes on to hers. 'I don't think it is. The job's changed, Siobhan. Everything's . . .' He struggled to find the words. 'It's like with Christine Esson. Ninety per cent of the stuff she

237

does is beyond me. The way she *thinks* is beyond me.'

'You're vinyl, we're digital?' Clarke offered.

'Contacts used to be the way you got things done. The only network that mattered was the one out there on the street.' He nodded towards the pub window, thinking that Frank Hammell had said much the same to him that night in Jo-Jo Binkie's, after Darryl Christie had gone.

'Your way works too, John—Edderton; Susie Mercer. Those were shoe-leather results. So don't go thinking you're obsolete.' She pointed to his near-empty glass. 'Are we having another?'

'Might as well, eh?'

He watched her as she queued at the bar. Then his phone rang again, and he decided he might as well answer.

'John?'

'Hello, Nina.'

'I called you a few minutes back.'

'Signal's patchy here.'

'You sound like you're in a pub.'

'Guilty as charged.'

'You sound tired, too. Is everything all right?'

'As well as can be expected.'

'And the inquiry?'

'See my previous answer.'

There was silence on the line for a moment. 'Do you mind me calling?'

He closed his eyes. 'No,' he told her.

'And when you get news, you'll tell me?'

'Didn't I promise?' *I think your daughter's alive* . . .

'Promises aren't always kept, John. Should I come north again? I'd like to see you.'

238

'I don't think that's a good idea.' *Your daughter's alive, but why did she leave?*

'You sound . . .'

'Tired?'

'No, not just tired—strange. Are you sure you're all right?'

'I have to go, Nina.' *Why would she not get in touch when she knows you're out there, desperate and searching?*

'John, I—'

He ended the call just as Clarke returned to the table.

'Let me guess,' she said, watching him switch off the phone and place it on the table. Then, sitting down: 'You really don't want to tell her about Susie Mercer?'

'No.'

'I can see how it might make things worse. On the other hand . . .'

Rebus ignored her and picked up the fresh pint.

'Cheers,' he said. 'Here's tae us.'

As he drank, he couldn't help but think of the rest of the toast.

Wha's like us?

Gey few—

And they're a' deid . . .

39

Malcolm Fox's drink of choice was Appletiser. He never touched alcohol, not these days. He always recycled the empty bottles, along with paper, cans, plastic and cardboard. Now the council was asking him to recycle kitchen waste too, and he was running out of room in his bungalow for all the boxes and bags. He already had a compost bin in his back garden, though it was only ever added to in the summer—lawn trimmings and the few weeds he could be bothered to dig up. Fox wasn't convinced any of it made a difference, yet he found himself unable not to comply. Though the bungalow had no party walls, he always kept the volume low on the TV, and seldom listened to music. He liked reading—almost as much as he liked work.

It would have been against regulations to bring home the files on John Rebus, even if he could have carried them. But he prided himself on his memory and had jotted down pages of salient details, along with several decades' worth of supposition, rumour and claim. He felt he knew the man almost as well as anyone he'd ever met. Right now, Rebus would be in some boozer somewhere, probably running up a tab that would never require paying. Rebus wouldn't see that as either bribe or inducement, but rather as standard operating procedure. Time was, plenty of his fellow detectives would have felt the same, but those days were past, the combatants long retired from the field. Fox wished Rebus would just take his carcass overseas to some beachside taverna where he could pickle himself at his leisure while spending some of that accrued pension. Instead of which, he had reapplied for a CID posting.

The sheer bloody nerve of the man.

What was more, he still had at least one champion on the force—the Chief Constable had sided with him, and had told Fox that if the Complaints were going to raise an objection, they'd best build a bloody good case.

Look at the man's record, Malcolm. Who else managed to put Big Ger Cafferty away?

Yes, that counted as a big tick for Rebus, but Fox himself was suspicious. Cafferty hadn't served much of a stretch. How convenient to have someone on the force who seemed to be his nemesis. *Seemed* being the operative word. Who was to say the two hadn't been in cahoots? Cafferty had returned to the city apparently stronger than ever, his empire undiminished. How was that possible, and why had no one managed to put him back inside since? Come to that, wasn't it convenient that Rebus had been on hand at Cafferty's hospital bed, ready to give CPR when he flatlined? Would you bring your worst enemy back from the dead? The staff had had to drag Rebus away, such had been the intensity of his focus.

Enemies? Fox didn't think so.

The Chief Constable had challenged him to build a case, and Fox in turn had asked for permission to look at Rebus's phone accounts—landline and mobile. The Chief had been reluctant, but Fox had worn him down. The relevant paperwork was on its way. He was hopeful there might be a little bomb tucked away there.

Though he didn't like to admit it, there was something else about Rebus that gnawed at him. It was the lifestyle. The smell of smoke on the man's suits—always supposing he *owned* more than one suit. The pale, pasty face and the three or four extra stone he seemed to carry. And the drink.

The drink above all.

Fox had ceased to take alcohol because he was an alcoholic, while Rebus continued to sup for

241

the exact same reason. Somehow, though, Rebus still functioned, while Fox seldom had. Alcohol fogged his mind and made him short-tempered. It gave him the sweats and the shakes and nights of the worst possible dreams. Rebus was probably the kind who slept better after a dozen or so malts, damn the man.

Then there was the fact that Fox had seen Rebus in action. Their time together in CID had been short, but it had been enough, the preening ego obvious from the start—always late, or off somewhere, the paperwork piling up on his desk while he coughed his way to another cigarette break. If in doubt, Fox had been told, try the pub across the street, you can usually find him there, deep in thought with a whisky in front of him.

Did I nick your sweets in the playground and now you need to get your own back . . . ?

It wasn't that at all. The force had spent generations tolerating and turning a blind eye to cops like Rebus. Those men were gone now, memories of them fading, their foibles no longer humoured by officers of Fox's generation. Rebus was the last. He had to be convinced that his time was past. Then there was Siobhan Clarke, a good detective who had flourished once freed from Rebus's influence. Now that he was back, her loyalty to him could well prove her undoing. So Fox sat on his sofa with the TV news channel muted, sifting through his pages of notes on the man. Ex-army, divorced, one daughter. A brother who'd served time for drug-dealing. No current relationships, other than with the bottle and anyone who happened to sell tobacco. A flat in Marchmont, bought back when he was first married, that no cop would be able to afford these days. A string of one-time colleagues who had fallen by the wayside, including a couple killed in the line of duty. Whichever way you looked at it, Rebus was bad news. Siobhan Clarke had to know that. She wasn't stupid. The Chief Constable should know it too. Did Rebus have something on the boss—was that the explanation? Something buried in all the paperwork? And maybe there was some hold he had over DI Clarke, too—missed by Fox despite his diligence.

He knew what he had to do. Start reading again. Start from the very beginning . . .

*   *   *

Information was always worth paying for, that was the way Cafferty looked at it. The cop's name was Ormiston and he didn't come cheap, but he had delivered tonight. Cafferty tapped Darryl Christie's number into his phone and waited. The young man answered.

'You on your own?' Cafferty asked.

'Just driving home.'

'That's not what I asked.'

'I'm on my own.' It sounded like Darryl was using the car's speakerphone. 'I thought I'd have heard back from you before now.'

'It was certainly an intriguing text.'

'Reckon your man Rebus is in Frank's pay?'

'I wouldn't put anything past Rebus. But it's Hammell I'm phoning about.'

'Yes?'

'Police have got CCTV of him and your sister.'

'What do you mean?'

243

'At the bus station, arguing. Cops pulled Hammell in for questioning. Seems he'd tailed her from home to the train station and then on to St Andrew Square.'

'Why would he do that?'

'His story is she took money from him for a train, and he was annoyed she then went for the cheaper option.'

'You're well informed, Mr Cafferty.'

'Always, Darryl.'

'Is this coming from your man Rebus?'

'That would be telling. I just felt you ought to know. I'm not sure your mum does—and I'm guessing Frank's said nothing to you about it.'

'He hasn't,' Darryl Christie confirmed. 'Anything else?'

'A quid pro quo, maybe? What's your boss up to at the moment?'

'He's just been hosting a drinks party at his house.'

'Any faces I'd know?'

'A couple from up north—Calum MacBride and Stuart Macleod.'

'Alliances being forged?'

'I didn't hear much business being discussed.'

'Interesting, all the same. And how are things with the family?'

'Much the same.'

'Still keeping an eye on your mum?'

'We'll be fine.'

'Of course you will. But remember, anything I can do to help . . .'

'Thanks, Mr Cafferty.'

'Your dad would be proud of you.'

'My dad *is* proud of me.'

'Safe home then, Darryl,' Cafferty said, ending the call.

* * *

Darryl took a mug of tea into his bedroom. It was after midnight again. He'd phoned both pubs and the club—quiet nights in all three. He lay on his bed, phone active, checking the net while he played back the events of the evening. Frank Hammell lived in a mews house near Raeburn Place. He'd put Darryl in charge of the catering and welcoming the guests. Plus making sure glasses were kept topped up. That was fine by Darryl—he could listen in on as many conversations as he liked. The bottles of whisky, wine and champagne were stored in the room Hammell used as an office, meaning it was easy for Darryl to boot up his boss's laptop, get it working, and plug in the memory stick he'd brought with him. Left it to do its job while he poured more drinks. Frank Hammell enjoyed playing the host, treating Darryl like a lackey—more whisky, more samosas, more of those mini hamburgers. And Darryl was happy to look obliging. Hammell had even ruffled his hair at one point in front of Calum MacBride, calling him 'a good lad'.

A good lad, yes. A good lad who knew almost every aspect of the business and was learning more every day. A good lad who was paying off long-term employees and replacing them with leaner, hungrier models who knew where their loyalty lay.

Stretched out on his bed with his head supported by a pillow and his laptop balanced on his flat stomach, Darryl slotted home the memory stick. Financial records, not all of them password-protected. Those that were would be the kind the taxman never saw. Hammell had trusted Darryl with some passwords. The rest wouldn't be a problem. Darryl had a friend who spent his whole life hacking—one good reason Darryl himself would never succumb to online banking. Hammell had, however.

'Makes life simpler,' he'd said.

Simpler, yes, if you were stupid enough.

The blinds hadn't been closed yet and he glanced up at the sky. Overcast again; the house silent apart from the hum of his laptop's fan. He thought about his sister, taking cash from her mother's lover. She wouldn't have said please or thanks—Frank Hammell would have offered. But following her to make sure she got on the train? Arguing with her at the bus station? Darryl wondered what that was all about. No way he could ask without his employer asking in turn how he knew.

Then he remembered the package . . .

40

Page was just starting the briefing when Rebus arrived at Gayfield Square next morning. Christine Esson handed him nine sheets of paper held together with a staple. Rebus scanned them while Page spoke. The final five pages comprised the material gleaned the previous night from the files, but they were preceded by details of the two new MisPers.

August 2007, Jemima Salton, age fifteen, had failed to return home from a party, some of her clothing turning up in a picnic area on the banks of Loch Ness. The party had been held in Invermoriston and Jemima lived six or so miles away in Fort Augustus. Her plan had been to walk or hitch home in the early hours. Divers had been sent in, but the loch stretched for miles. Accidental drowning had been the verdict. No body ever turned up, and her phone and bag remained missing. Her family had maintained her bedroom almost as a shrine. The photo had been sent to them at three in the morning, though they hadn't seen it until later. No message. They'd checked the bedroom. No Jemima either . . .

November 2009, sixteen-year-old Amy Mearns had had an argument with her parents and gone to visit various friends in the village of Golspie. There had been a trip to a nearby beach, and at some point Amy had drifted away. Her jacket was found the following day, attached to a fence above the seashore, blown there perhaps. Amy herself had not been seen again.

'Accidental drowning,' Page intoned once more. Rebus could feel the man's eyes on him. 'You'll note from the map that Golspie is on the A9, north of Tain and Dornoch, while Invermoriston is on the A82, south of Inverness and within easy reach of the A9. Two patterns seem to be emerging—the photos, plus that road—and that means I'm taking them seriously.' He paused. 'Any thoughts so far, John?'

Rebus only now looked up from his reading. 'It's a busy enough route. Tourist traffic as well as vans and lorries. It also covers a lot of ground. Not easy to get an investigation going . . .'

'Nevertheless,' Page barked. But he didn't seem

247

to know what to say next. Clarke saved his blushes by suggesting that the various constabularies needed to be contacted and a summit of sorts held.

'All sorts of jurisdiction and protocol issues,' she said.

Page nodded.

'We also need to do what John did with the previous cases,' Esson piped up. 'Talk to families and friends, try to get a better sense of the MisPers' lives in general and their movements on the day they vanished.'

Page nodded at this, too.

'The photo is just about all we're left with,' Ogilvie added. 'If we're confident it's Edderton, we should organise a sweep of the area and interview anyone who lives locally or visits regularly.'

Page puffed out his cheeks, visibly daunted by what lay ahead.

'Something to bear in mind,' Rebus interrupted. 'The earliest victim we have is Sally Hazlitt, and I'm beginning to think she may still be alive. Same might go for one or more of the others.'

'How much do we let the media know?' Clarke asked Page.

'At this stage, as little as possible.'

'If we turn up mob-handed in Edderton, they may start to get an inkling.'

'We need to talk to Grampian Constabulary first—or is it Northern?'

'The latter,' Rebus answered.

'We also need to talk to the families of Jemima Salton and Amy Mearns as soon as possible,' Clarke said. 'For several years now they've been under the impression their daughters drowned. We've just put the idea in their heads that they may have been abducted and murdered instead.'

'Good point.' Page was rubbing a hand up and down his jaw. 'An order of priority is needed—can I leave that with you, Siobhan?'

She nodded her agreement. 'You'll be wanting to brief the Chief Constable,' she told him, trying her best to make it sound like a reminder rather than the strong suggestion it actually was.

'I'll call his office,' Page said, glancing at his watch. A moment later he had retreated to his cupboard. There was silence in the room, all eyes on Clarke. She, on the other hand, was staring in Rebus's direction.

'John,' she said, 'can you divvy up the cold cases? We need fresh interviews with all concerned. Did our abductor lie in wait, or had he met the women beforehand? Could he be in some job that took him to those specific places, or to those particular victims?'

'It's a tall order,' Rebus warned her.

'Worth a try, though, wouldn't you say?' Her look dared him to defy her.

'Absolutely,' he responded, the team gathering around him to receive their orders.

       *   *   *

Rebus had lost count of the number of cases he'd worked, cases often as complex as this one, requiring interview after interview, statement after statement. He thought of the material in the boxes, now being pored over by those around him—paperwork generated in order to show effort rather than with any great hope of achieving a result. Yes, he'd been on cases like that, and others where he'd despaired of all the doors knocked on, the blank faces of the questioned. But sometimes a clue or a lead emerged, or two people came forward to furnish the same name. Suspects were whittled down. Alibis and stories unravelling after the third or fourth retelling. Pressure was sustained, enough evidence garnered to present to the Procurator Fiscal.

And then there were the lucky breaks—the things that just happened. Nothing to do with dogged perseverance or shrewd deduction: just sheer bloody happenstance. Was the end result any less of a victory? Yes, always. It was possible that there was something he had missed in the files, some connection or thread. Watching the team at work, he couldn't decide if he would want them to find it or not. It would make him look stupid, lazy, out of touch. On the other hand, they needed a break, even at the expense of his vanity. So he watched them, their heads bowed as they sifted through the documents, chewing on their pens, underlining, making notes, or typing their thoughts into their computers. Putting together more detailed chronologies, deciding who should be questioned, ready to suggest some avenue that had been missed—either by the original inquiry or by Rebus.

More chewing of pens. More notes. Trips to the kettle and coffee pot. The occasional offer to fetch snacks from downstairs. Rebus was the only one who took cigarette breaks. During one, he made sure the cars in the car park were empty before tapping a number into his phone.

'I want to talk to Hammell,' he told the person who answered. 'Tell him it's Rebus.'

After a few seconds, the man's voice was back in Rebus's ear. 'He can't speak at the minute.'

'Tell him it's important.'

'He'll phone you back.'

And that was the end of the conversation. Rebus stared at the display, cursing under his breath. He lit a second cigarette and paced the car park. It was hemmed in by the two-storey police station and the back of a Georgian tenement. Lots of windows; no signs of life. Pigeons on the rooftops, just getting on with things. A large red-brick chimney belonging to some art studio on Union Street. A plane making a sharp turn, heading for the airport. Car horns sounding from the direction of Leith Walk, and a siren in the distance, failing to come any closer.

'Life's rich tapestry,' Rebus muttered, as if to the friendly cigarette held between his fingers. A couple of minutes later, he was readying to discard it when his phone rang. Not a number he recognised. He answered by giving his name.

'Something you've got to tell me?' Hammell enquired. All business; no time for chat.

'It isn't Thomas Robertson,' Rebus stated.

'So?'

'It just isn't. You need to let him go or stop hunting him down.'

'Which would you prefer?'

'Depends if you have him or not.'

'What makes you so sure he's not the guy?'

'He was in jail when one of the women disappeared.'

'Doesn't mean he didn't snatch Annette.'

'Yes, it does. We're pretty confident they're all linked.'

'Convince me.'

251

'Have you got him or haven't you?'

'This is bullshit, Rebus.'

Rebus pondered his options for a moment, then took a deep breath. 'It looks like there are at least two other victims we didn't know about. One was snatched in November 2009. Robertson was in Peterhead at that time. Both these new victims, photos were sent from their phones, same as with Annette.' Rebus paused. 'I could get in trouble for telling you this, but I need you to understand.'

'All right, I understand. But I never did find that little gobshite.'

Frank Hammell ended the call.

The rest of the day felt a lot like limbo. Things were happening, but not in the vicinity of Gayfield Square. Page had taken Clarke with him for his meeting at HQ with the Chief Constable. Rebus had asked her to text him updates, but she'd probably thought it bad manners to whip her phone out in the middle of the Chief's office.

Northern Constabulary had requested copies of everything Page's team had. Esson and Ogilvie were given the job of collating and sending it. Gavin Arnold called Rebus from Inverness to tell him the station was buzzing. Rebus decided the corridor was the best place to continue their conversation.

'We're having to draft officers in from all over,' Arnold went on. 'Dingwall's the nearest cop shop of any size, but it's too far from Edderton. It'll be Portakabins on site and a loan of some land.'

'I know a friendly farmer,' Rebus said, giving Arnold Jim Mellon's name and contact number. 'He's the one who recognised the locus in the first place.'

'Thanks, John—I might get a brownie point or

252

two for that.'

'One favour less I owe you.' Rebus peered through the doorway. The team was restless, impatient for the return of James Page with their instructions. 'How long till the media gets wind of it?'

'One of my colleagues is probably blabbing to the local paper as I speak.'

'Bound to happen, I suppose.'

'Will you be back up this way?'

'I'm not sure.'

'I remember that drowning—the one in Loch Ness. Nobody thought anything of it at the time.'

'No reason to. What about Golspie—any memory of that?'

'None. Slap-bang on the A9, though. Do you reckon that's what they'll call him: the A9 Killer?'

'I'm just hoping this is the end of it.'

'That depends on us catching him.'

'I suppose it does,' Rebus said.

'Positive news on that front is a chief super called Dempsey will probably head the case at our end.'

'Good, is he?'

'One of the best we've seen up here. Not a bloke, though—first name's Gillian.'

'My mistake.' Rebus watched as Page and Clarke reached the top of the stairs. 'I've got to go, Gavin.'

'Give me a bell if you hit town. And if I'm in your neck of the woods for a Caley away game . . .'

'The pies are on me,' Rebus confirmed, following two stern faces into the CID office. It took only seconds for everyone to gather around Page.

'Bottom line,' he began, 'Chief's not entirely convinced by Edderton. As he says, it's a photo of a photo—that's been confirmed, by the way. Could have been taken at any time and used merely to throw us off the scent. On the other hand, the A9 connection is too strong to dismiss, and since Pitlochry seems to be getting us nowhere, he's spoken with Inverness and requested a search of the area where the photo was taken, plus interviews with the locals. Northern Constabulary are already actioning this, but they may be short a few bodies, so we're going to pitch in. Christine and Ronnie, I want you to go talk to the parents in Golspie and Fort Augustus.'

'Northern are okay with that?' Esson checked.

Page gave a nod of confirmation. 'I'll be headed to Northern Constabulary HQ with Siobhan.' Page sought out DC Ormiston. 'Dave, you'll be running the show here.'

'Understood.'

Rebus caught Clarke's eye. She hesitated a moment before speaking.

'John has been to Edderton, spoken with people there. Might be useful to have him on the ground with us, at least at the start . . .'

Page fixed his gaze on Rebus while he made up his mind.

'Fine,' he said.

*   *   *

It was mid afternoon before Nina Hazlitt called. Rebus didn't answer, but listened afterwards to her message.

'Is it true they've found two more? The internet's full of gossip about it. I should have known. I can't believe I didn't spot them in the papers. But it means I'm right, doesn't it? Right about the A9, right about them all being connected.' She was sobbing between sentences. 'Please call me back— you promised you would. You said I'd be the first to know. I need you to tell me what's happening. Sally was the start of this, John—don't forget that. I have a stake . . . Do you hear me? Don't shut me out!'

Clarke emerged from Page's office and approached his desk, just as Nina Hazlitt broke down into sobs again and ended her call.

'Hazlitt knows about the two new additions,' he said.

'So soon?'

'All over the internet, apparently.'

Clarke gnawed at her bottom lip. 'As some might say, this shit just got serious.'

'It was always serious, Siobhan.'

'True,' she agreed. 'But now everyone's *taking* it seriously.'

'Did you get a rough ride at HQ?'

'Not particularly, though it was made clear that if we're reading more into this than is actually there . . .?'

'You can always lay the blame on me,' Rebus suggested.

'I'll bear that in mind.' She managed the beginnings of a smile. 'So . . . . Inverness in the morning.'

'It could almost be a country song.' Rebus paused. 'Thanks for inviting me along, by the way.'

'Least I could do.'

'And you almost didn't do it at all. It's as though my reputation precedes me.'

'Well, there is that.'

'Seems to me the focus has shifted from Annette McKie,' Rebus commented.

'Only because we've no new leads.'

'I can't see her family being thrilled about it.'

Clarke could do nothing but shrug. Then: 'Think I should talk to her mother?'

'Might be nice if someone did, before she hears about Golspie and Loch Ness.'

'Yes, you're right.'

'Maybe get Christine and Ronnie to do it, though—good training before they head north. And best be quick—news travels at broadband speeds these days.'

41

That evening, Cafferty turned up at the door of Rebus's flat.

'Can't be that time already,' Rebus complained.

'Just fancied a drink,' Cafferty responded. He was dressed as usual in a black leather jacket with a black polo-neck beneath.

'You seem happy,' Rebus said.

'I'm fine.'

Rebus had already finished packing and had been considering setting out on the road. A drink was a decent enough alternative. It would stop him driving, meaning he'd get to Inverness in daylight rather than the middle of the night.

'Somewhere walking distance,' he stipulated.

Cafferty bowed his head. 'I dare say you know the local hostelries.'

'I'll get my keys, then. And this time you stay that side of the threshold . . .'

The Tannery was fairly busy. There was football

on the TV, and most of the drinkers seemed to be there to watch it. Rebus and Cafferty found a spot at the far end of the bar. Not having a clear view of the screen, it was quieter than the rest of the pub. Cafferty insisted on buying the first round.

'I'm the one dragging you out, after all.'

A man had risen from one of the tables. He waited until he had their attention, then nodded towards the barman. 'He's too young to know who you are, but I'm not. We don't want any trouble here.'

Cafferty looked at Rebus. 'Is he talking to you or to me?' Then, to the man: 'Don't sweat it.' He stuck out a hand, which the man—presumably the landlord—took, before returning to his table, a relieved look on his face.

'Didn't even offer us one on the house,' Cafferty complained, demolishing his whisky and ordering another. 'So, is it true about all these poor wee girls?'

'Is what true?'

'The count's up to six now.'

'Is it?'

'I can use a computer, same as the next man. Silver surfers, they call us. So Annette McKie's just the last in a long line?'

'Looks that way.'

'Maybe that's the way it's *meant* to look.'

Rebus put his glass down. 'What are you saying?'

'She'd had an argument with Frank Hammell, hadn't she?'

'Who told you that?'

Cafferty just smiled. 'Could he maybe have followed her, with a view to settling it?'

'You'd like us to put Hammell in the frame?'

257

Cafferty laughed away the suggestion. 'I'm just speculating here.'

'So how did that photo end up getting sent from Annette's phone? How could Hammell have known about the others?'

'Frank has fingers in many pies.'

But Rebus was shaking his head. He lifted the pint again. 'He just didn't want her taking the bus. Turns out he was right, too—she probably wouldn't have got travel-sick on the train.'

'I still think it's too convenient,' Cafferty offered. 'Hammell's a player, and she's the next best thing he has to a daughter of his own. It can't be down to chance that she was snatched. Have you spoken to Calum MacBride or Stuart Macleod?'

'Never even heard of them.'

'They run Aberdeen. There's been a bit of tension between them and Hammell . . .'

'Same questions, then: why the photograph, and how did they know?'

'I'm not the detective here.'

'No, you're not. What you are, though, is the same conniving bastard you've always been. Six missing women and you're trying to conjure something out of it for your own entertainment.'

Cafferty's eyes darkened. 'Careful what you say, Rebus.'

'I speak as I find.' Rebus pushed his drink away and headed for the door. The landlord was outside, puffing on a cigarette and with his phone pressed to his face. He recognised Rebus and wished him all the best. As it dawned, however, that Cafferty was staying inside, he began to look a little more anxious. Rebus lit a cigarette of his own and kept walking.

Fox watched him leave. He was slouched in the passenger seat of a Ford Mondeo, parked across the street from the pub, outside a late-opening grocer's shop. His colleague, Tony Kaye, was inside the shop itself, making it look as though they'd pulled up to buy provisions. Kaye emerged toting a four-pack of beer and munching on a Mars bar. He dumped the cans on the back seat and walked around to the driver's side.

'Cafferty's still in there,' Fox told him. But only a minute or two later the man emerged. He must have phoned for a taxi, because one drew to a halt and he climbed in. A further figure left the pub straight afterwards and jogged towards the Mondeo.

'For me?' he said, climbing into the back and opening one of the beers.

'Better be worth it,' Kaye muttered.

Joe Naysmith was the youngest member of Fox's small team. He swallowed and stifled a burp before making his report.

'Football on the telly. Helluva din.'

'Could you make out *any* of what they were saying?' Fox demanded.

'Seemed to be about Frank Hammell. Him and the girl who went missing.'

'What about them?'

Naysmith offered a shrug. 'Like I say, it was noisy. If I'd got too close they'd have clocked me.'

'Useless,' Tony Kaye growled. He turned towards Fox. 'All this effort, Malcolm—for what exactly?'

'For a result.'

259

'Some result.' Kaye paused. 'Who tipped you off that they'd be meeting?'

'Text message. Number blocked.'

'Same as before, then. Makes you wonder, doesn't it?'

'What?'

Kaye gestured in the direction Rebus had taken. 'If he's being set up.'

Fox stared at his colleague. 'Am I missing something? Didn't a retired detective—a current police employee, by the way, with his nose deep in an ongoing case—just have a known gangster turn up at his door? And didn't the two of them then go out together for a drink and a catch-up?'

'It doesn't mean anything.'

'It means *everything*, especially when they start discussing the very case Rebus is working on. Throw Frank Hammell's name into the mix and it gets more interesting still.'

'I don't see it,' Kaye said, shaking his head.

'I do,' Fox retorted. 'And at the end of the day, *that's* what really matters.'

'Want one?' Joe Naysmith asked, holding out a can towards Kaye.

'Why the hell not?' Kaye snatched at it.

'In which case, I'm driving,' Fox said, pushing open the passenger-side door.

'Afraid we'll be pulled over? Why not take a risk for once?'

'We're swapping,' Fox persisted.

Kaye looked at him and knew the man wouldn't give up. He sighed and reached for the door handle.

PART FOUR

I took a jar of pain to the soaking field . . .

42

If he'd been putting together a mix tape for the journey, it would have featured plenty of songs about roads. Canned Heat and the Rolling Stones, Manfred Mann and the Doors. He refuelled at Kinross, checked out the roadworks north of Pitlochry, and stopped for tea and a cheese scone at Bruar, where he looked at his phone and found a missed call from Nina Hazlitt—making four in total—and a message from Siobhan Clarke telling him that rooms had been booked for a couple of nights at Whicher's. He doubted this was coincidence. Maybe it was the only hotel Clarke knew in Inverness. Inverness, however, was not his immediate destination. He stayed on the A9, crossing the Kessock Bridge. Alness, followed by Tain, and finally the turn-off to Edderton. Jim Mellon had been contacted, and he'd made sure the police located the spot. A Portakabin was being unloaded from a flatbed lorry, which would have the devil's own job reversing back to the main road. The crane arm dropped the Portakabin on to the narrow lane ahead of it. Maybe the fields were too marshy to take its weight. The end result was that diversions would be needed. No traffic was going to be able to pass this way until the police operation had finished. A uniform gestured for Rebus to lower his window. Rebus obliged, holding out his ID. Mellon was in consultation with a woman in a smart two-piece suit, the pair of them pointing towards the hills. The woman held a copy of the photo sent from Annette McKie's phone. She had come prepared: shoes swapped for green wellies. Rebus wished he'd thought of that.

He manoeuvred the Saab up on to what verge there was.

'Give me a shout when the lorry needs to get out,' he told the uniform. The man nodded, adding Rebus's licence plate to the clipboard he was holding. Mellon had recognised him and was giving him a wave. Rebus walked forward and shook hands. The woman was waiting for an introduction.

'I'm John Rebus,' he obliged. 'Attached to the Edinburgh inquiry.'

She nodded slowly. 'Mr Mellon was telling me about you. I'm DCS Dempsey.'

'Yes, ma'am.' They shook hands and sized one another up. She was around forty, buxom and bespectacled and with shoulder-length ash-blonde hair.

'Where's DCI Page?' she asked.

'On his way. What do you make of the comparison?' Rebus gestured towards the photo she was holding.

'I think it was taken pretty much where we're standing.' She paused. 'Though I'm still not sure what its significance might be.'

'Whoever sent it, if he's being really clever, then he's brought us here to waste our time and effort.'

She stared at him. 'We're praying he's not that clever?'

Rebus nodded.

'Then let's hope that's the case.' She gestured towards the line of police vans parked on the carriageway past the Portakabin. They would have to head towards Aultnamain and circle back towards home—no way they could squeeze past the obstruction. Officers were being arranged into groups and shown maps, presumably marked with the grid they would be covering. 'What is it they should be looking for?'

'Anything out of place,' Rebus advised. 'Scraps of clothing, cigarette ends, a discarded bottle or can.' He paused. 'How about the interviews?'

'A team of six,' she replied. 'There really aren't that many habitations for them to visit.'

'Would it be cheeky of me to ask them to check cafés and petrol stations too?'

'Within what sort of radius?' She had narrowed her eyes a little, as if reappraising him.

'Dornoch, Bonar Bridge, Tain—for starters, anyway.'

This merited the thinnest of smiles. 'You know this part of the world?'

'A bit.'

'What's your thinking?'

'A traveller—might not be someone who lives locally. But they must know the area.'

'We'll see what we can do.' She had been about to add his rank until realising she didn't know it.

'I rose to the giddy heights of detective inspector,' Rebus informed her.

'Past tense?'

He nodded again. There was an incoming text on his phone.

'Lucky you,' Dempsey said. 'I'm getting no signal.'

'Half a bar,' Rebus said. 'And as Mr Mellon will tell you, a gust of wind the wrong way and I'll lose it.'

The message was from Clarke, letting him know they'd reached HQ in Inverness and were about to

265

go into a meeting with 'the brass'. But Rebus knew that the only 'brass' worth dealing with was right there with him. When he looked up, Dempsey was on her way over to one of the search teams. They carried thin sticks and evidence bags and seemed enthusiastic about the task ahead of them. When Dempsey started giving them what Rebus guessed must be a pep talk, they paid close attention.

'A fine woman,' Mellon said in an undertone. 'You'd be proud coming home to that of an evening.'

The uniform with the clipboard was standing by Rebus's shoulder.

'Time to move your car, sir,' he said, as the air brakes on the flatbed gave a loud hiss. 'If you want it kept in one piece . . .'

43

Mid afternoon. Neither Page nor Clarke had put in an appearance. From her texts, it seemed to Rebus that this was not Clarke's favoured strategy, but Page had lined up a series of meetings, presumably so he could listen to his own voice, and Clarke had felt obliged to stick with him.

Sandwiches and bottles of water had appeared from somewhere. They filled the back of a patrol car, its doors wide open so people could help themselves. No hot drinks, though Mellon had offered to see what he could do. The Portakabin contained little more than a table and a couple of chairs. There was an Ordnance Survey map of the area on the table, the whole scene reminding

Rebus of that first trip to the roadworks outside Pitlochry. A generator was on its way, so that the structure could have both lighting and heat. Another half-hour or so and the search would be called off for the day. Light was fading—at least thirty minutes earlier than in Edinburgh. Rebus was sipping water when the van arrived. It parked at the rear of the line of vehicles. There was no sign of the officer on clipboard duty. A uniform emerged from the driver's seat and nodded a greeting towards Rebus. Rebus got a bit closer so he could read the writing on the van's side.

Grampian Police Canine Unit.

The back had been opened and a cage unlocked. A dappled springer spaniel emerged and began a keen examination of the road surface.

'Long way from home,' Rebus commented.

'Northern doesn't have anyone like Ruby,' the officer explained.

'You've driven here from Aberdeen?'

The man nodded, his attention focused on the dog.

'Left it a bit late.' Rebus studied the sky.

'Ruby's not using her eyes, though. Means she can work that bit longer. You in charge?'

Rebus shook his head. 'DCS Dempsey's the one you need, but she's had to head back to Inverness.'

'Maybe I'll just get started, then.' The dog handler looked like he came from farming stock: plenty of girth and a ruddy face, black hair swept back from his forehead. The gate to the field stood open, and Ruby was itching to explore, but she wasn't going anywhere until given permission.

'Don't you need . . .?'

'What?'

267

'A bit of cloth or something belonging to the MisPer?'

'That's not Ruby's speciality,' the officer said.

'So what is?'

'She's a cadaver dog.' He gave a signal to the spaniel and she bounded across the field in front of him. One of the search teams was arriving back from the hunt, meagre gatherings in their evidence bags. They headed for the Portakabin, so they could record what they'd found and leave the bags on the table. When they went over to the food car, Rebus took a look at their haul. A rusty bottle top, crisp bags and chocolate wrappers, an old paint can, half a brick . . .

Bits of twine . . .

A few shredded remains of a carrier bag . . .

A mouse skeleton . . .

Some feathers . . .

It was desperate stuff. If the team had looked full of energy at the start, they were now a lot more sombre, pessimism setting in. Rebus had lost sight of the dog handler, but he found him again: already halfway across the field, heading for the line of trees beyond. He was passing another of the search teams as it headed back. One of the officers bent down as if to stroke Ruby, but then straightened up—warned off, Rebus reckoned. Ruby had been trained for work, not play.

There were mutterings at the food car. Phones were being checked for messages, held high in the air as a signal was sought.

'Better luck tomorrow,' someone commented.

'As long as the weather holds.'

Rebus asked about the forecast.

'Grim,' he was told.

'Maybe sleet,' another voice added. Then: 'Are you from Edinburgh?'

Rebus nodded.

'I hate that place,' the cop said. 'Cannot bloody stand it.'

'I'm guessing you're from Inverness.'

The man scowled at Rebus. 'Hate *that* place, too. Dingwall's good enough for me.'

'Isn't it time for your meds, Bobby?' someone else enquired, causing a few tired smiles.

Half an hour later, the message came through from HQ: call it a day. Dempsey would not be coming back. Someone was given the task of locking the Portakabin.

'We're leaving the evidence here overnight?' Rebus asked.

'If you can call it evidence. The Chief will take a look at it in the morning and decide what to do.'

'How much more ground still to cover?'

'Plenty.'

Rebus watched the teams prepare their escape. There were mutterings from those whose vehicles were stuck the wrong side of the Portakabin— long detours lay ahead of them. Cars had to be manoeuvred past other cars. One got stuck, muddy tyres spinning, and had to be pushed off the verge. As the last patrol car reversed down the lane, the four officers inside gave Rebus a little wave. They were talking about him, breaking into grins. Rebus didn't bother waving back. The dog-handling van was still there, about twenty yards separating it from Rebus's Saab. These were the only two vehicles left. Dusk had descended, and Rebus could see about two thirds of the field. There was no sign of Ruby and her colleague. He leaned against

269

his car and smoked a cigarette, stubbing it out afterwards into the Saab's ashtray—didn't want to leave anything behind that could be misread as a clue. Not that this seemed to have occurred to the search teams. Crusts of bread and bits of sweetcorn were scattered on the roadway next to where the food car had been. There was even a discarded plastic water bottle in the ditch. Rebus picked it up and threw it on to his passenger seat.

A waste of time, maybe, but all the same . . .

Another fifteen minutes or so and it would be pitch black—no street light of any kind out here. He could already pick out a few stars in the sky, and the temperature was dropping. He sounded his horn three times, in the hope that the dog handler would get the message. When he heard a whistle, he reckoned it was in response, but it came again, and again after that—more urgently. It wasn't the sort of sound you made when you were communicating with your dog, and it was followed by a shout from somewhere the other side of the field. Rebus couldn't see anything. He knew from the search team's footwear that the field was far from dry. No torch in his Saab, meaning he'd only have the light from his phone's screen if he happened to get lost.

Another cry.

'Bollocks,' Rebus said to himself, setting out through the gate.

The field contained dips and shallow hollows, and this was where it was most treacherous. Rebus felt himself sink up to his ankles. He cursed again but kept moving, breathing heavily. A fence separated the field from the trees beyond. It was the best part of four feet in height, topped with a strand of barbed wire. Rebus peered beyond it.

'You there?' he called out.

'Here,' the dog handler said.

'Where?'

A thin beam of light appeared. The woods were deeper than Rebus had expected. Ruby and her master were somewhere within. Rebus looked at the fence, then to left and right, seeking a stile or another gate. Seeing neither, he shrugged out of his coat and draped it over the barbed wire, easing one leg over the fence, then the other. His trousers snagged on something and he heard them tear. One jagged tine had pierced coat and trouser leg both.

'Bastard,' he said under his breath. He sank up to his ankles again, almost losing a shoe as he pulled himself up a low bank and into the woods.

'Where the hell are you?'

'Here,' the dog handler said, shining the small torch again. 'Can you go fetch a team?'

'They've all gone.' Rebus could see both dog and man. Ruby was seated on the damp ground, tail wagging, tongue lolling. 'What is it?' Rebus asked, trying to catch his breath. In answer, the handler directed the torch to a spot just beyond Ruby. The dog turned her head in the same direction, licking her chops. The earth had been disturbed, and Rebus knew what it was he was being shown.

An all-too-human hand, jutting up from the makeshift grave.

'Christ,' he hissed.

'Thing is,' the officer said, playing the torch over the clearing, 'I don't think Ruby's done yet—not by a long chalk.'

44

The diesel thrumming of the generators. Half a dozen arc lamps illuminating proceedings. Officers reeling out lengths of crime-scene tape. A mud track led from the lane into the trees. This track was now out of bounds, bordered by the blue-and-white-striped tape. A vehicle must have been used; doubtful the bodies had been dragged or carried all the way.

'Has to be all-wheel drive,' Rebus had posited to Clarke. 'Mind you, that probably accounts for three quarters of the cars in these parts.'

She had nodded, staring at him.

'What?' he had asked.

'I just can't believe you were *here*.'

To which he had offered only a shrug.

Page was in consultation with Dempsey. He had done well to borrow boots from somewhere. Rebus's own shoes needed drying out—either that or chucking away. Clean socks wouldn't be a bad idea either, and as for his trousers...

'You bleeding?' Clarke asked as he checked the damage.

'Just a scratch.'

'Might need a tetanus shot.'

'Tot of whisky'll do me fine.'

They were discussing anything but what lay in front of them. Ruby had located three bodies so far, and was now on a break, her handler having fetched a bowl and a bottle of water from the van. The scene-of-crime team had arrived and were busy. A doctor had been found, and a couple of evidence officers were busy with video cameras.

'So how was your day?' Rebus made show of asking Clarke.

'Oh, you know, just the usual.' She folded her arms across her chest in an attempt to stay warm.

'Checked into the hotel yet?'

'Seems all right.' She shuffled her feet. They were standing well away from the three graves, there being not enough overshoes and the like to go round. Trace evidence again; the 'integrity of the locus' had to be maintained—Page had used those exact words when explaining to Clarke why she'd have to stay this side of the tape for now. Rebus hadn't merited any such apology, or even an acknowledgement of his existence.

Even though he'd been the one to call it in.

Or maybe *because* he'd been the one to call it in.

Dempsey had thanked him, though, Rebus reminding her that it was Ruby's result more than his.

'Sore point,' Clarke had said to him afterwards. 'As I was hearing at HQ, not much love lost between Northern Constabulary and their neighbours in Grampian . . .'

She was looking at her phone now, reciting the time. 'Ten fifteen.'

'Feels later,' Rebus offered.

'How long have you been out here?'

Rebus didn't like to think. Instead he moved aside to let more SOCOs through. They ducked beneath the tape, dressed in their hooded white overalls and elasticated shoe covers, making a rustling sound as they walked. They carried cases and folded plastic sheets. The mortuary van had yet to arrive. It would bring the body bags. But nothing

273

was being moved just yet.

Rudimentary tents had been erected over only two of the graves, someone having been dispatched to Inverness for more.

'This is interminable,' Clarke said, shuffling her feet again.

'We could sit in the car,' Rebus offered. She dismissed this with a firm shake of the head. 'If Page needs you, he'll know where to find you.'

'He'll find me right here,' she stated.

'Well, I'm going for a cigarette.' She nodded and he left her to it, emerging on to the road and lighting up. Looking back, he saw the long shadows of the players as they moved around the clearing. One of the generators was really making a hellish racket, but it was better than silence, better than overhearing snatches of the discussions the SOCOs would be having.

It was a lonely spot. He couldn't help wondering if they'd been brought here alive, bound and gagged perhaps, or in a stupor. Or maybe already dead. Trace evidence again—there had to be some of it in the vehicle. Fibres of clothing; strands of hair; maybe even saliva or blood.

Did they arrive here in daylight or at night? He guessed the latter. But a car left on the lane at night would look suspicious to anyone happening to drive past—another reason to take it into the woods.

Where it might have left tyre tracks, scrapings of paint against a trunk or branch.

The forensic team would get busy in the morning; they needed daylight for their work.

A cordon had been put in place at both ends of the road, diversion signs posted. When a man approached on foot, Rebus tensed. His shoes and trouser bottoms were soaked, meaning he'd got past the guards by crossing the fields.

Journalist.

He had his phone out, held in front of him to film what he saw. Rebus covered his face with his hand.

'Put that bloody thing away unless you want a night in the cells,' he barked. 'Then turn yourself around and bugger off the way you came.'

'Can I quote you on that, officer?' He was young, with fair curly hair spilling from the hood of a green Barbour jacket.

'I mean it.' Rebus checked and saw that the phone had been lowered.

'Big operation,' the reporter said, rising up on to his tiptoes to peer over Rebus's shoulder. 'SOCOs and everything. I'm guessing that means you've found something.'

'You'll know when everybody else does,' Rebus growled.

'What the hell's going on?'

Rebus turned in the direction of the voice. DCS Dempsey was striding towards him.

'Pond life,' Rebus explained, but her eyes were on the young man.

'Might have guessed you'd be first out of the traps, Raymond.'

'Anything you'd care to share, DCS Dempsey?' He was busy with his mobile's touch screen, turning it from camera to tape recorder.

'There'll be a press conference in the morning.'

'Too late for our early edition. Throw me a bone here, will you? The internet's killing us.'

Dempsey gave a theatrical sigh. 'There seem to be human remains, but we don't know much more than that. Now off you go.'

When the reporter tried asking a further question, she shooed him away. He gave a lopsided grin. 'See you at Mum's on Sunday, then?'

She nodded, avoiding eye contact with Rebus. The reporter was already on the phone to his newsroom, having turned back the way he'd come.

'Is Raymond his first name or his last?' Rebus enquired.

'First,' Dempsey confided. 'And before you say anything, he's my nephew. Doesn't mean he gets special treatment.'

'I thought he just did.' She made no response. 'Well,' Rebus went on, 'I hope he's got sharp elbows—when word gets out, there's going to be a media scrum.' They stood in silence for a moment. 'How many are we up to?' he asked eventually.

'Five, I think. Four in an advanced state of decay.'

'And the other?'

'I wouldn't bet against it being Annette McKie.'

Rebus watched as Page and Clarke emerged from the woods, Page removing his shoe protectors. Clarke was stony-faced as she checked her phone for a signal. Page looked pale and queasy. He turned away and dry-heaved, hand clamped to his mouth to muffle the sound. Rebus offered him what water was left in his bottle. Page accepted it with a nod of thanks. Clarke had got through and was talking to either Esson or Ogilvie, letting them know the game plan had just changed.

'I need to get back to Inverness,' Dempsey announced. 'Gee up some pathologists and see what can be done before morning.' She studied the three Edinburgh detectives. 'You lot should

get your heads down—big day in front of all of us
. . .?' She started walking towards her car, shoulders
slumped. Page was offering Rebus's water back to
him.

'It's yours now,' Rebus said. Clarke had ended
her call.

'Will the restaurant still be open at the hotel?'
she asked.

Rebus shook his head. 'A sandwich in the bar if
you're lucky. Crisps on the side.'

'Can you pair stop talking about food?' Page
requested, angling his head away from them as
another wave of nausea struck.

45

Almost two a.m.

Page had retired an hour back, and Esson and
Ogilvie soon after. The original plan had been for
the pair of them to head to Edinburgh at day's end,
but Clarke hadn't wanted either of them nodding
off at the wheel. Neither had seemed to mind. They
had interviewed the parents of the Golspie and
Fort Augustus victims, gleaning not very much in
the process.

'It was weird seeing Jemima's bedroom,' Esson
had said. 'It really is exactly as she left it. Some
people just can't let go, can they?'

Reception had doled out little toothbrush sets
for both Esson and Ogilvie, and found them a
couple of rooms at 'the last-minute rate'. Rebus
guessed the place might be busier next day,
depending on how many news channels decided to

cover the story. He was nursing his fourth whisky of the night.

'You thawed out yet?' he asked Clarke.

'Almost.'

'I've half a mind to head back out there,' Rebus told her.

'What good would it do?' She was staring at her phone's screen, using the hotel wi-fi to scour the internet for mentions of Edderton.

'None,' Rebus admitted. 'I'd just be in everyone's way. On the other hand, I don't think I'm going to be able to sleep.'

'Four's not enough any more?' She gestured towards his whisky glass.

'Never has been. This is just taking the edge off.'

She picked up a shred of lettuce from the plate in front of her. The sandwiches, crisps and cherry tomatoes had been dispatched, though Rebus had abstained, with the complaint that he'd already eaten his own weight in white bread that day.

'This is just beginning, isn't it?' Clarke speculated. 'Totally different case now.'

'Nothing's really changed,' Rebus countered. 'We've got confirmation, that's all.'

'You always knew it would turn out like this?'

'It was a possibility—we all knew that, whether we said so or not.'

'You've worked more of these cases than I have: where do we go from here?'

'Local interviews; crime-scene analysis; appeals for information . . .'

'What sort of person are we looking for?'

'Isn't that a question for one of your profiler chums?'

'I don't have any profiler chums. And it's out of

278

my hands anyway.'

Rebus looked at her. 'I'm not convinced our pal Page is up to the task. You might need to be at his shoulder.'

'James will be fine. He's just not been to many murder scenes.'

'He's an office manager, Siobhan—could be CID or a company selling fitted kitchens. This needs someone a bit different.'

'DCS Dempsey's at the head of the table.'

'That's a definite bonus. But even she won't have covered something like this before.'

'And you have? You're asking me to get you an invite into the boardroom?'

'More or less.'

'That might make it a bit crowded—unless you want *me* left outside?'

He shook his head. 'I just need to be there.'

'Won't always be possible, John.' She finished her orange juice and checked the time. 'What's the breakfast like?'

'Substantial.'

'I forgot to ask when they start serving . . .'

'Seven.'

She gave a tired smile. 'It's like sitting with the Michelin guide.' Then she rose to her feet, bidding him good night.

He sat for the length of one final drink, adding it to his tab. His phone was on the table in front of him. He picked it up and turned it over in his hand. He could call Nina Hazlitt. Or Frank Hammell. Or Darryl Christie. By morning the news would be out there, broken by Dempsey's nephew. No, he decided eventually—give them one last night of unknowing, one last sleep sprinkled with hope.

When he tried getting to his feet, the backs of his legs ached: too much standing around in the cold. There were some books on a shelf in the bar area, and he asked if it was all right to borrow one.

'That's what they're there for, sir.'

The one he picked—for its title more than anything—was *Cracking the Code*. He took it upstairs to bed with him, the barman's last words echoing in his head:

Pleasant dreams...

46

The first news crew arrived at breakfast time.

Rebus was out front, smoking a cigarette. Rain had arrived in heavy gusts, and he was sheltering next to the hotel's entrance. The crew chatted among themselves as they sprinted past him. They didn't have reservations, but were hopeful; an early check-in would be a bonus; quick shower and something to eat, then they could get on the road to Edderton. English accents; unshaven; bleary-eyed: Rebus got the idea they'd driven through the night to get there. He flicked away his cigarette and headed for the breakfast room. Page was busy on his phone, while Clarke started on the second pot of coffee.

'Slight problem,' Rebus told her, nodding towards the open doorway. Clarke had a clear view of the reception desk. One of the arrivals held a full-sized news camera at his side. Page saw it too, and told the person he was speaking to that he would call back.

'If they're staying, we're not,' he commented.

'Agreed,' Clarke said. Then: 'Any news from Dempsey?'

Page nodded slowly. 'First autopsy will start in an hour. Pathologist reckons it'll take a couple of days to get through them. Meantime, forensics are busy at the locus.'

'Weather won't be helping,' Rebus interrupted.

'They've covered what they can with plastic sheeting,' Page informed him.

'I need to buy some wellies,' Clarke said.

'Me too.' Rebus lifted one foot so she could see his rudimentary attempt at shoe-cleaning. 'And trousers, while I'm at it.' The reception desk had provided a needle and thread, but his repair wasn't going to hold.

'How about the tetanus?'

Rebus shrugged. 'What are the symptoms?'

'Headache, dry mouth . . .' She examined his sewing. 'Lack of hand/eye coordination.'

Page was busy checking messages. 'Are Christine and Ronnie on the road home?' he asked.

'Yes,' Clarke confirmed.

'Dempsey's going to want the families brought to Inverness,' Page said. 'It's a murder investigation now.'

'That reminds me, we should buy Ruby a nice juicy bone,' Rebus said.

All three of them watched as the news crew entered the dining room, grabbing a table before heading for the buffet. There was a swagger to them, as though they suddenly owned the place.

'I think that's our cue to make an exit,' Page said, getting to his feet.

They decided not to check out—not until they

281

knew there was somewhere else for them to go. There wasn't much leg room in the back of Clarke's Audi, but that was where Rebus ended up. On the way to Northern Constabulary HQ, Page decided to entertain them with a pep talk about protocol and how they were 'representatives' of Lothian and Borders Police so should 'showcase' their talents and not make 'waves'—or any foul-ups. Rebus got the feeling the speech was aimed squarely at him. He met Clarke's eyes in the rear-view mirror, but she wasn't giving anything away.

The building they were looking for was next to a roundabout and across the road from a twenty-four-hour Tesco. The police HQ was a modern three-storey construction of pink stone and smoked glass. There were journalists waiting on the roadway and pavement in front of it, setting up cameras or busy on their phones. A uniformed constable checked Page's warrant card before nodding the Audi in the direction of a parking space. Rebus spotted a sign next to the entrance with the motto *Protect and Serve* on it, written in Gaelic as well as English. Bit late for the 'protect' part; all that was left was the 'serve' . . .

Once indoors, they learned that Detective Chief Superintendent Dempsey had already left for the first autopsy. It was being held at nearby Raigmore Hospital. Rebus couldn't help thinking: same place as Sammy's IVF. Page was asking for directions when a text arrived on his phone.

'Dempsey,' he explained to Clarke and Rebus. 'Resident pathologist's apparently annoyed by the number of bodies—live rather than dead—and wouldn't welcome us adding to the total.' He gnawed at his bottom lip. Rebus knew what he'd be thinking. They were here as guests of Northern Constabulary. It wasn't *really* their case—not until Annette McKie was formally identified. Even then, common sense dictated that the McKie inquiry would be bundled with the others. With Edderton as the locus, it was Northern's case, no contest. If Page complained or made a fuss, they could be sent packing at a moment's notice. On the other hand, what use were they to anyone just hanging around, waiting to be told what had already happened in their absence?

'We could head out to Edderton,' Clarke suggested.

After a moment's consideration, Page nodded his agreement.

So it was back on to the A9, the rain growing heavier as they crossed the Kessock Bridge, side winds buffeting the car. Clarke had set the wipers to their maximum speed, but they still struggled to cope.

'Never did buy those wellies,' Rebus commented from the back seat.

'There's an umbrella somewhere at your feet,' he was told. He reached down and picked it up. It was pink and retractable, and looked to have a circumference no bigger than a drum cymbal.

'It's yours if you want it,' Clarke said.

'Thanks,' Rebus replied without enthusiasm.

The uniform at the cordon was dressed for the elements. He even had a plastic shield for his clipboard. Their names were jotted down, along with the Audi's registration number. A camera crew were sheltering in the back of their van, doors open so they could keep an eye on things. Raymond—Dempsey's nephew—was seated in his own car, a

283

white Volkswagen Polo. His window was down, and he offered a nod of greeting towards Rebus as the Audi crawled past the cordon and started to ascend the hill, rivulets of rainwater either side of it. The Portakabin had been unlocked and was providing shelter for those taking a break from the crime scene. SOCOs cupped their hands around beakers of instant soup, trying to get warm. Page decided to keep moving up the slope towards the locus. Clarke glanced back and saw that Rebus was happy where he was, but gesturing for her to stick with her boss.

There was just about room enough for Rebus inside the Portakabin. A couple of SOCOs were waiting for the kettle to boil, mugs at the ready. Bottles of water; empty Cup-a-Soup sachets. No sign of the evidence bags from the previous evening—the lab had probably taken them.

'Not the best of days for it,' Rebus said to no one in particular. 'And no sign of the heater we were promised.' Then: 'Have all the bodies gone now?'

There were nods of confirmation.

'Still just the five?'

'Just?'

'I'm thinking we should be thankful there aren't more.'

'They've brought the dog back for a final recce,' one SOCO said.

'Any effects in the graves?' Rebus asked, trying to keep his tone conversational.

'Sorry—who are you again?'

'I'm with the Annette McKie team. I was here when Ruby found the first of them.'

This seemed to satisfy the room—just about. 'No effects,' he was told. 'No clothing, no jewellery, nothing.'

'And one body a good bit more recent than the others?'

There were more nods.

'She should be easy enough to identify,' someone conceded.

'The others won't be?'

'Dental records maybe. Or a DNA match. Do you want some soup?'

The offer told Rebus that he had been accepted. 'Thanks,' he said, even though he was still full from breakfast.

'Grabs them from the A9,' another of the team was saying, 'buries them here and sends a picture—got to be local.'

'Might just be someone who knows the road,' Rebus cautioned. 'Any tyre tracks up there?'

'Nothing useful as yet.'

'Only three or so weeks since he was last here, though.'

'Ground might have been frozen—dipped below zero the night the McKie girl went missing.'

Rebus nodded his understanding. 'You'll keep looking?'

'Until we're told to pack up.'

'Clothing and personal effects might have been buried separately.'

'We've a metal detector coming later today, plus the offer of geo-phys if we want it.' The man's eyes were on Rebus, daring him to doubt the effort being made. Rebus blew across the surface of the soup instead. Reconstituted peas and carrots had never held such fascination for him.

47

Late in the afternoon they reconvened at Northern
Constabulary HQ in Inverness. Dempsey was due
to host a press conference at the top of the hour,
but wanted her team to hear the news first. The
mood was solemn. Photographs were handed
round. According to the pathologist's report, all
five corpses were women, but only one was readily
identifiable. Rebus stared at the face of Annette
McKie. Her eyes were closed and bits of earth still
clung to her eyelashes, hair and ear lobes.

'Manual strangulation,' Dempsey was intoning.
'We may even get lucky and come up with a
thumbprint. You'll see signs of bruising to the
neck, especially around the voice box. Large hands,
the pathologist says. Judging by decomposition
and insect activity, victim has been deceased for
between twenty and twenty-five days.' She looked
up at the room. 'Three weeks today since she was
abducted, so I think it's fair to say she wasn't kept
alive for long.' Dempsey returned to her notes.
'From the visual evidence, I'm prepared to name
the victim as Annette McKie, but the family are
on their way from Edinburgh to make the formal
identification.'

'Did the other victims die the same way?'
someone asked, interrupting Dempsey's flow. She
glowered at the miscreant.

'No way of telling. Deterioration is too advanced.
All the pathologist would say is that she can't see
initial signs of stab wounds or gunshots on any of
them. Regarding Annette McKie, there's probable

sexual activity, but as yet no indications of forced penetration. Pathologist's got a mountain ahead of her, however, and we can't expect a full report for a few more days. We have the particulars of the missing women provided by our friends at Lothian and Borders, and those will be useful in the preliminary stages. I have to stress that we don't know for sure who the other victims are. I don't want any of you jumping to conclusions.'

There were nods and grunts of acknowledgement. Clarke had raised her hand. Dempsey considered for a moment before deciding to grant permission for a question.

'Who's ID'ing Annette McKie?'

'One of her brothers, I think. Apparently her mother's in bits. Probably been watching the live feed on TV.' The mention of TV caused her to glance at her watch. 'I need to get ready to face the jackals,' she said. 'We can have another confab after. Meantime, thinking caps firmly on heads. I want constructive ideas—as many as you can throw at me. Now, back to your posts, everybody.'

As the meeting broke up, Page lunged forward, ready to press his case for inclusion in the media conference. Rebus turned to face Siobhan Clarke.

'We don't have "'posts", do we?'

She looked around the room. 'No,' she admitted, 'we don't.'

'Nor do we have a place to sleep tonight—unless we risk the hotel.'

'Another good point.'

'And the pair of us still need boots of some kind.'

She couldn't deny it: her shoes were caked with mud from earlier. 'Are you suggesting a shopping trip?'

287

'And maybe a quick visit to the tourist office—check out the bed-and-breakfast situation.'

Clarke was staring towards Page. Page was smiling at Dempsey, bowing his head in gratitude. He was in. 'We'll only be an hour,' Rebus pressed her.

'Fine,' Siobhan Clarke said through gritted teeth.

* * *

They were walking back into Northern Constabulary HQ with the address of a willing guest house when the press pack's interest was aroused. A car was arriving, a white Range Rover Sport with tinted rear windows. Frank Hammell was driving, Darryl Christie in the passenger seat, his attention focused on the screen of his phone. A few photos were taken, TV cameras hoisted to shoulders, but otherwise they were allowed some room and a bit of respect as they parked in the bay allotted to them and got out. No one thrust a microphone into their faces while demanding to know their reaction to the news. Rebus ended up holding the door open for Hammell and Christie, neither man seeming to recognise him, perhaps because they were avoiding all eye contact.

While the two men gave their names at the reception desk, Rebus and Clarke flashed their respective IDs and preceded them into the body of the building.

'Dempsey must be meeting them here,' Clarke said in an undertone.

'Nicer than the mortuary.'

'That's still where they'll end up, though . . .'

True, Rebus thought. He had been present

288

dozens of times as relations and friends—mums and dads; partners; lovers—watched the uncovering of the sheeted figure. They would blink away tears, maybe utter a gasp or a choking sound, and be asked to verify the identity of the person lying coldly inert in front of them. Never a task to be relished, and Rebus had always proved hopeless afterwards, not quite finding the right words, the comforting phrase. They usually all wanted the same reassurance: that he or she hadn't suffered.

It would have been quick. That was what you were supposed to say, no matter how untrue. Smashed-in skulls, cigarette burns, broken fingers and gouged eyes . . . *It would have been quick*.

'What do we do now?' Clarke was asking.

'Let's see what the boss thinks.'

She glanced at him. 'Told you you'd run out of song titles sooner or later.'

Page was on his phone in the teeming inquiry room. When he spotted Clarke and Rebus, he ended the call and made his way towards them.

'Where have you been?' he demanded.

'Buying boots,' Clarke answered. 'And finding rooms for tonight so we're well away from the media scrum. How did the press conference go?'

'She did well.' The praise sounded grudging. Page fixed Rebus with a look. 'She wants *you* to brief the team.'

'Why?'

'Because she's traced the timeline all the way back to you and your missing persons. That's what she needs from you: the details of all those cases.'

'Two of them we only just found out about.'

'The other three, then. I've already briefed on Annette McKie.'

'We're one body short,' Clarke added. 'Six A9 victims, five recovered.' It was her turn to look at Rebus. 'Are you going to tell them you think Sally Hazlitt's still alive?'

'I probably should,' Rebus determined. Then, to Page: 'When's this briefing scheduled for?'

'About five minutes from now.'

'I suppose if we hadn't turned up in time, you'd have been happy to fill my shoes?'

Page opened his mouth to say something, but thought better of it.

'I need to go for a slash,' Rebus said into the silence. Then, to Clarke: 'You going to tell him Hammell and Darryl have arrived?'

Clarke was doing just that as Rebus made his exit. As he headed down the corridor, however, he came face to face with Frank Hammell and Darryl Christie as a uniform led them towards Dempsey's office.

'For a retired crock,' Hammell said, placing him eventually, 'you don't half get about a bit.'

Rebus focused his attention on Darryl, who was only now looking up from his phone. 'Sorry about your sister,' he offered. 'How's your mum doing?'

'How do you think she's doing?' Hammell snarled. Rebus ignored him.

'What about you, Darryl? You all right?'

The young man nodded. 'What happens now?' he asked calmly.

'You'll be taken to the hospital for the identification.'

'And you're sure it's her?'

Rebus nodded slowly. Darryl's mouth twitched and he lowered his eyes to the screen of his phone again, fingers busy texting.

'Some bastard's going to pay big time,' Hammell spat.

'This probably isn't the place to be saying that,' Rebus warned him.

'It's true, though.' He stabbed a finger towards Rebus. 'And none of your lot better find themselves in my way.'

A door opened further along the corridor. Dempsey stood there, wondering what was taking her visitors so long.

'Is everything all right?' she called out.

Hammell had time for one last glare in Rebus's direction before shouldering past him and walking towards her. Rebus held a hand out towards Darryl Christie, but the young man ignored it, attention focused on his phone as he followed Hammell into Dempsey's office.

48

Rebus's presentation went as well as he could have wished. The team had plenty of questions for him, none of them stupid.

'Bright kids,' he commented afterwards to Clarke.

'It's how they make them these days.'

They had checked out of the hotel, driven to the guest house near the battlefield at Culloden, and inspected their rooms. There was no evening meal, so they'd headed into town and stopped at the nearest Indian restaurant. Page wasn't with them; he'd been invited to dine with Dempsey and a few other senior officers. When Clarke's phone rang, she wasn't at the table, having gone to visit the toilets. Rebus saw that the call was from Gayfield Square and decided to answer.

'It's Rebus,' he said.

'Is Siobhan there?'

'Who wants her?'

'Dave Ormiston—I'm the one whose desk you were given.'

'She'll be back in a minute. Is it anything I can help with?'

'Thomas Robertson has rejoined the land of the living.'

'Oh?'

'Aberdeen sent us the message. He's in hospital there.'

'What happened to him?'

'From what I can tell, he took a bit of a pasting from person or persons unknown.'

'Local police involved?'

'They found him next to some rubbish bins down by the docks. Unconscious, but with ID in his pocket. Credit cards and cash untouched, so not an obvious mugging.'

'He's going to be okay, though?'

'Sounds like.'

Rebus took out a pen and reached across the table for a paper napkin. 'What's the name of the hospital?' he asked. 'Plus, a name and contact number for someone in Aberdeen CID, if you have them.'

Ormiston gave him what he had, then asked how things were going in Inverness.

'Things are fine,' Rebus said.

'I saw you on the news—holding open the door for Frank Hammell.'

'Common courtesy.'

'Did you speak to him at all?'

'Why do you want to know?'

'No reason.' Ormiston made a sound as though he were clearing his throat.

'People usually have reasons for asking questions,' Rebus persisted.

'Not this time. You'll let Siobhan know about Thomas Robertson?'

'Of course,' Rebus said.

By the time Clarke returned, her phone was off and had been returned to its original position next to her glass of water. She was yawning, covering her mouth with the back of her hand.

'Minute my head hits that pillow,' she told him.

'I know what you mean,' Rebus pretended to agree. 'Reckon we should be getting back?'

She nodded, and signalled for their waiter to bring the bill. 'This is my shout, by the way,' she said. 'I can always claim it on expenses—and besides, I'm not the pensioner here . . .'

Having returned to the guest house, Rebus stayed in his room long enough to give his phone a bit of a charge and check the quickest route to Aberdeen. The A96 seemed to be the answer. It was a trip of a hundred miles, though, which caused him to hesitate. On the other hand, as soon as he was well enough, there was nothing to stop Robertson doing a runner. Tonight might be Rebus's only chance. As he crept down the stairs and out of the three-storey house, he wondered how he was going to break the news to the sleeping Saab.

*   *   *

It was well after eleven when he reached Aberdeen Royal Infirmary. He hadn't been to the city in years and didn't recognise any landmarks along the route. Oil was Aberdeen's core business, and the industrial units he passed all seemed to be oil-related. He got lost a couple of times before chancing on a sign that pointed him towards the hospital. He parked in the area reserved for ambulances and headed inside. The reception area was claustrophobic, and whoever manufactured beige paint had made a killing here. The bleary-eyed front desk sent him to the lifts, and he emerged a couple of floors up, pushing open the doors to the ward and explaining to the only duty nurse around that he was a police officer and needed to talk to a patient called Robertson. There were eight beds, seven of them filled. One man was awake, plugged into headphones and with a book held in front of him. The others all seemed to be asleep, one of them snoring loudly. There was a light over Thomas Robertson's bed, and Rebus switched it on, illuminating the pulpy face. Eyes blackened; chin gashed and sporting thick black stitches. The nose—presumably broken—had been strapped. There was a folder at the foot of the bed, and Rebus opened it. One broken toe, two broken fingers, one cracked rib, a tooth missing, damage to the kidneys . . .

'Someone did a job on you, Tommy,' Rebus said, pulling up a chair and sitting down. There was a jug of water on the cabinet next to the bed, and he poured himself a glass, gulping it down. His head was throbbing from the drive, palms tingling after so long at the steering wheel. He opened the cabinet and reached in for Robertson's wallet.

294

Credit cards and driving licence, plus forty pounds in cash.

No mugging, just as Ormiston had said. Rebus replaced the wallet. Handkerchief, small change, belt, watch—this last with its face smashed. He closed the cabinet again and leaned forward, so his mouth was inches from Robertson's ear.

'Tommy?' he said. 'Remember me?' He reached out a finger and pressed it against the sleeping man's temple. Robertson's eyes fluttered and he gave a low moan. 'Tommy,' Rebus repeated. 'Time to wake up.'

Robertson did so with a jolt, which quickly turned into a wince of pain, his whole body seeming to spasm.

'Evening,' Rebus said by way of greeting.

It took Robertson a few moments to get his bearings. He licked dry lips before fixing his puffy eyes on his visitor.

'Who are you?' he asked in a dry croak.

Rebus refilled the glass with water and held it to Robertson's lips so he could sip.

'The cop shop in Perth,' Rebus reminded him. 'I was the one standing by the wall.' He placed the glass back on the cabinet.

'What are you doing here?'

'I've just got a couple of questions about Frank Hammell.'

'Who?'

Rebus described Hammell and waited. Robertson blinked and tried to shake his head.

'No?' Rebus said. 'So maybe he's telling the truth for once when he says he doesn't know you either. Thing is, though, *somebody* did this.'

'I was jumped, that's all there is to it.' There was

a lot of sibilance when he spoke, the air whistling through the freshly made gap where a tooth used to be.

'Jumped?'

'Some wee bastards.'

'Wee bastards who didn't bother taking any of your stuff? And this happened down by the docks?'

'Docks?'

'Where do you think you are, Tommy?' Rebus gave a thin smile. 'You don't know, do you? They lifted you from behind the pub in Pitlochry and took you somewhere. Kept you there until they were sure you had nothing to do with Annette McKie—that's a bit of news for you, by the way: they've found her body in some woods up past Inverness. Four other bodies next to her. So you're off our list of contenders. Might explain why you're here rather than in a shallow grave somewhere.'

Rebus saw that he'd hit a chord. Robertson's eyes were suddenly fearful.

'What is it?'

'Nothing,' Robertson said, trying to shake his head. 'I keep telling you—I got jumped.'

'And which city did you get jumped in, Tommy? No, you were brought here and dumped here.' Rebus paused. 'Anyway, Hammell's probably finished with you now. But as a wee insurance policy, you need to tell me it was him.'

'How many times do I have to say it? I've never heard of the guy.'

The nurse was standing at the foot of the bed. 'Everything all right?' she asked in a stage whisper.

'I need to sleep,' Robertson told her.

'Of course you do.'

'Am I due another painkiller?'

296

'In two hours.'

'If I had it now, maybe I'd sleep through till morning.'

The nurse had placed a hand on Rebus's shoulder. 'You have to be leaving now, before you wake the other patients.'

'Five more minutes.'

But she was shaking her head.

'Off you go,' Robertson said.

'I can come back tomorrow.'

'Come back as often as you like. I'll tell you the exact same thing you heard tonight.' Robertson focused his attention on the nurse. 'It isn't right I'm being grilled like this. Not when I'm in so much pain . . .'

'I've driven a long way to see you, you little shite-bag.'

'You're leaving *right now*,' the nurse said, tightening her grip on Rebus's shoulder. 'Or I'll have you forcibly removed.'

Rebus debated whether it was worth standing his ground. Instead, he got to his feet.

'I'll see you around,' he told Robertson, pressing down on the back of the man's hand, the hand with the two strapped fingers. Robertson let out a wail loud enough to silence the snorer and wake the other patients.

'He might be needing that medication early after all,' Rebus informed the nurse, before making for the lifts.

* * *

That night, in a hotel room provided and paid for by Northern Constabulary, Darryl Christie sat at a desk with his laptop plugged in and his phone charging. He had already spoken to his mother and brothers, plus a neighbour who was keeping an eye on all three of them. Afterwards, he had called his father, telling him about the identification without bothering to add that Frank Hammell had also been present. Eventually it was the turn of Morris Gerald Cafferty.

'How are you holding up?' Cafferty asked.

'Never mind that. This blows a hole in your notion that it has anything to do with Frank.'

'Granted.'

'So why am I even talking to you?'

'Because whatever happens, you're still a kid with ambition.'

'I'm not a "kid". And all that stuff you told me about Frank's enemies—what made you think I wouldn't rank you among them?'

'Abduction's not my style, Darryl. Nobody innocent ever gets hurt.'

'Is that right?'

'Other people might disagree, but I like to think I have standards.'

'I'm not sure that squares with some of the stories about you.'

'Stories told by Hammell, no doubt.'

'Not just Frank, though. Lots of disappearances; lots of the wrong people ending up behind bars ...'

'These are changed days, Darryl.'

'Exactly my point. You belong in the history books, Cafferty.'

'Easy, son ...'

'I'm not your son—I'm not your son and I'm not a kid!'

'Whatever you say, Darryl. I know you're under a lot of strain and all.'

'You don't know the first thing about me.'

Christie ended the call and ignored the phone when Cafferty tried ringing back. He busied himself with his laptop, slotting home the memory stick, Cafferty's words echoing in his head.

Nobody innocent ever gets hurt . . .

Tell that to Thomas Robertson.

49

'You don't look like you slept much,' Clarke said next morning at breakfast.

Rebus was last down, having managed a rudimentary shave and a shower under a dribble of tepid water.

'Where's Page?' he asked.

'Already gone to HQ.' Clarke was trying not to bristle.

'I take it your services were not required.'

The owner of the guest house had started clearing the other two tables. She wore a blue check apron over her stylish clothes, and had made an effort with her make-up, not forgetting plenty of perfume. When she apologised that they were out of bacon, Rebus said he'd be happy with coffee and toast.

'Porridge? A poached egg, maybe?'

'Toast will be fine.'

When she had gone, Clarke held up a newspaper so Rebus could read the front page splash:

A9 KILLER—MASS GRAVE FOUND

'It's all over the radio too,' she added. 'Even managed to rustle up a few people who said they wouldn't be using that particular route for the foreseeable . . .'

'Do you get the feeling it's going to be another long day?'

'Reckon you'll manage without a nap at some point?'

'Me? I'm as chipper as they come.'

She had some flyers sitting on the table next to her, and Rebus started sifting through them.

'Dolphin-watching?'

'Mrs Scanlon says you don't need to pay— there's a place called Chanonry Point where they practically come to the shore.'

'Reckon we've got time to play tourists?'

'That depends on our dear leader.'

The landlady had returned with his coffee—just the one small cup. Rebus stared at it.

'Better bring the rest of the pot, Mrs Scanlon,' Siobhan Clarke advised.

*   *   *

Brigid Young's mother and sister lived in Inverness, and were filmed by the TV cameras as they left home to make the drive to Edderton, the mother carrying a small wreath and a framed photo of her missing daughter. Zoe Beddows's family had decided not to make the trip north, not until they had absolute confirmation that she had been found. A DNA swab had already been taken from her father. Nina Hazlitt had texted Rebus to say she was on the road and would Rebus meet her when she arrived? He hadn't replied as yet. A television had

300

been set up in the inquiry room so the team could keep up to date. The room itself was half empty— some were at Edderton, others at the mortuary or the forensic lab. Someone had pointed out Raigmore Hospital to Rebus—it was right around the corner from Northern Constabulary HQ. Phones drip-fed updates from all three locations. Looking out of the office window, Rebus could see a couple of camera crews and a posse of print journalists, plus curious locals with nothing better to occupy their time. Darryl Christie had formally identified his sister, and he too was on his way to Edderton, in the passenger seat of Hammell's Range Rover. One of the news channels had blown the budget on a helicopter, and it tracked the car's progress, cutting now and then to aerial shots of Edderton itself and the woods where the SOCOs and search teams were still at work. Ruby and her handler were on their way back to Aberdeen, services no longer deemed necessary. On the TV, Rebus saw the Portakabin, then the field he'd stumbled across in the dark. Between the treetops could just be made out the canopies covering the graves. There was no journalist on the helicopter itself, the running commentary coming from the studio anchor.

'And we're going now to our man at the scene, Richard Sorley. Richard, what's happening there?'

Rebus watched as the action shifted to the police cordon. The reporter held his microphone to his face, jostling for position as Hammell's car arrived and was let through the barrier, two stony-faced figures in the front. Its wheels spun as it moved off again, kicking up stones, the camera following its route up the single-track road. Back to the helicopter pictures as the Range Rover found its way blocked by a line of parked police vans. The two men got out. As usual, Darryl Christie seemed glued to his phone. Hammell appeared to give the helicopter the finger before plunging his hands into his pockets, striding in the direction of DCS Gillian Dempsey. She then led the way towards the track into the woods, the figures disappearing from view. Rebus realised Siobhan Clarke was standing next to him.

'Is Page out there?' he asked.

She nodded. 'Where else would he be?'

The studio anchor was back in business, announcing that he now had Nina Hazlitt on a video link. Her face appeared on a screen behind him. She was adjusting an earpiece. The caption had her location as Inverness.

'She's outside Raigmore,' Clarke said, identifying the backdrop, as Hazlitt began explaining to the anchor that she was readying to provide her own DNA to help investigators establish that her daughter Sally was among the victims. When the anchor reminded her that she had been the first to spot that the missing persons were linked by the A9, she nodded so briskly that her earpiece slipped out and she had to push it back in.

'I feel vindicated, Trevor,' she announced. 'Until recently I was dismissed as a crank by every police force I approached. I want once more to thank John Rebus, a retired detective inspector in Edinburgh, for pushing my case.'

'Isn't that nice?' Clarke said.

Rebus just grunted. One of the other officers in the room mimed a burst of applause.

'And you can bugger off too,' Rebus told him.

At the end of the interview, Nina Hazlitt removed the earpiece and handed it to a member of the news crew, before turning towards the doors of the hospital and walking through them, head held high.

'She's loving this,' Clarke commented. 'Maybe a bit too much.'

'She's waited a long time for the attention,' Rebus retorted. The camera seemed to want to follow her inside, but a member of the hospital's security team had other ideas. The studio anchor announced that they were returning to Edderton, where the helicopter was watching the white Range Rover reverse down the lane.

'Didn't take them long,' Clarke said.

'Not much to see.'

Another cut: this time to the cordon and Richard Sorley. The reporter craned his neck to watch as the Range Rover arrived at a spot where it could do a three-point turn. When it reached the crime-scene tape, it stopped and both Hammell and Christie got out. Hammell was dressed in his usual jeans and open-necked sports shirt with a gold chain around his neck. Darryl Christie was wearing a dark suit, white shirt, black tie, every inch the dignified bereaved. Blood had risen to Hammell's face and he was ready to talk to anyone who would listen.

'Whoever did this,' he told the reporters, 'they're going to hell. Whether they believe in it or not, that's where they're headed.' He stared straight into the lens of the camera. 'I'd like to see them swing from a fucking scaffold . . .'

At which point the sound feed was muted so that only the pictures remained. The anchor's

303

voice apologised to viewers before beginning a commentary based on what Hammell was saying.

'Mr Hammell,' he intoned, 'a close friend of the family and understandably upset by his visit to the crime scene . . .'

Rebus was watching closely. The incandescent Hammell was the focus of the camera's attention, but over his shoulder could be seen glimpses of Darryl Christie, his face showing no emotion whatsoever. When someone tried asking him a question, he simply shook his head. Hammell was now stabbing a finger towards the camera, as if he had the culprit himself in front of him.

'Wish I could lip-read,' Clarke was saying.

More microphones were being thrust in front of Hammell, but he was beginning to run out of steam. When Darryl Christie placed a hand on his arm, Hammell acknowledged him with a nod and the pair of them headed for the car. The studio had handed back to Richard Sorley, who was talking about 'the extraordinary tirade we've just witnessed here'. The Range Rover's horn sounded as it drove past the cordon and the scrum of journalists, slaloming before picking up speed along the main road.

'I'm going to have to interrupt you, Richard . . .'

And they were back outside Raigmore Hospital again as Nina Hazlitt emerged, teary-eyed and trembling with emotion, the gist being: her DNA was not required at this time and she would be contacted at some later date.

'How does that make you feel?' she was asked by the reporter with the microphone.

'Absolutely livid. I've placed my faith in the Scottish justice system and this feels like a slap in

304

the face, not just to me but to all the relatives out there . . .'

'Something tells me you'll be getting another text,' Clarke commented to Rebus. A small box had appeared at the top of the screen, showing Dempsey and James Page being driven away from Edderton in the back of a large black saloon car.

'Is there anything we should be doing?' one of the officers in the room asked.

'Look busy when they get here,' someone else suggested.

Five minutes later, Rebus's phone sounded. It was Nina Hazlitt, pretty much on cue. Clarke watched him as he shook his head slowly and let the call go to messaging. He stared from the window, but saw no sign of her. After three quarters of an hour, Dempsey and Page arrived. Dempsey gathered her team together and gave them an update. A stray pubic hair had been found on Annette McKie's body. A comparison was under way, but it didn't appear to be one of her own. DNA had been gathered from the families of Jemima Salton, Amy Mearns, Zoe Beddows and Brigid Young.

'Not Sally Hazlitt?' Clarke interrupted.

Dempsey shook her head. 'Pathologist doesn't think any of the bodies goes back that far. She's not even sure about 2002, when Brigid Young disappeared. If we end up with a body lacking a match, we'll bring Sally Hazlitt back into the running.'

Clarke nodded her understanding, and Dempsey went on with the briefing. Afterwards, Clarke and Rebus sought out James Page.

'We're feeling a bit marooned here,' Clarke

informed him.

'There's plenty you can be doing,' he snapped back, his eyes on Gillian Dempsey, making sure she didn't leave him behind.

'A bit of leadership might help.'

He directed a moment's furious attention towards Clarke. 'Would you prefer to be back in Edinburgh? That can always be arranged, you know.'

'You're acting like a groupie,' she said. 'Putting up with any old crap in exchange for proximity.' She turned and stormed out of the room. Rebus lingered, meeting Page's look.

'Something to add?' Page asked.

Rebus shook his head. 'Just enjoying the moment,' he explained with a smile.

Clarke wasn't difficult to find. She was seated in her car, hands gripping the steering wheel, staring hard at the windscreen. Rebus got into the passenger seat and closed the door.

'You all right?' he asked.

'Just fine.' But there was a tremor in her voice.

'It's not all his fault, you know.'

'It's me,' she said. 'In Edinburgh, I got used to being needed. Reached the point where I even started to believe I ran the show.'

'And now you're not even the drummer in the support band?'

Some of the tension melted from her face. 'Did I really just call him a groupie?'

'I believe you did.'

'I'll have to apologise for that.' She exhaled loudly. 'So what do we do now?'

'Maybe we should take a look at some dolphins.'

'You mean go for a drive?'

306

'Weather's starting to clear—there's even a bit of blue up there.' Rebus nodded towards the sky.

'Maybe we could take your car.'

Rebus looked at her, and in explanation she lifted her hands from the steering wheel. They were shaking.

'My car it is,' he said.

50

They drove over the Kessock Bridge and took a right on to the Black Isle. Another right at Fortrose took them to Chanonry Point. The Moray Firth was ahead of them, a golf course laid out either side of the single-track road, busy despite the gusts of wind.

'You ever played golf?' Clarke asked from the Saab's passenger seat.

'Christ, no.'

'You must have tried.'

'What? Because I'm Scottish?'

'I bet you have, though.'

Rebus thought back. 'When I was a kid,' he conceded. 'Couldn't get the hang of it.'

'It's an odd little country, this, isn't it?' Clarke was staring out of the window.

'Not so much of the "little".'

'Don't get all prickly. I just mean it's hard to fathom sometimes. I've lived here most of my life and I still don't understand the place.'

'What's to understand?'

'*Everything.*'

There was a car coming from the opposite direction. Rebus pulled into a passing place and

307

acknowledged the wave from the other driver. 'People are just people,' he said. 'Good, bad and indifferent. It's just that *we* tend to deal with the second group.' They had reached a turning circle with some parking spaces beyond. Rebus stopped the car. The water looked choppy, the beach made up of pebbles, seaweed and shells. There were gulls overhead, hovering as best they could. Vehicles had been parked, but there were no signs of anyone in them. Then, far over to the left, just past a lighthouse, Rebus saw figures standing by the edge of the shore.

'Looks like that's where the action is,' he said. 'You game?'

Siobhan Clarke was already opening her door and getting out, but he called her back.

'I've screwed things up between you and Page, haven't I?'

'Maybe.'

'It's because I don't want you selling yourself short, settling for second best.'

'You're not my dad, John.'

'I know that.' He paused. 'In fact, that's something else I wanted to tell you . . .'

'What?'

He looked out at the water. 'That trip I took— there *was* a reason I didn't want you along.'

'Oh?'

'I had a notion to visit Sammy.'

'And did you?'

He gave a slow nod. 'She wasn't at home, though.'

'Because you didn't tell her you were coming?'

'A slight oversight on my part. Thing is, Siobhan, I nearly lost her. Years back, before you joined

CID. Some nutcase got his hands on her . . .'

'So this is personal for you?' She nodded her understanding. 'Didn't they teach you at college—you don't get emotionally involved.' She stared at him as he shrugged. 'You're a complicated sod, aren't you?'

'Who isn't?'

'I thought you said people are just people?'

'And dolphins are just dolphins—so let's see if we can nab one.'

They walked side by side, Rebus with his coat zipped to his throat, wishing he had a hat of some kind as protection from the horizontal wind. As they got closer, he saw that half a dozen people were all facing the same direction, almost like statues, albeit statues with cameras. Someone had even brought a tripod and a zoom lens, plus binoculars, a folding chair and a flask. The resident expert, Rebus guessed, so he asked if there'd been any sightings. The man nodded in the direction everyone was facing. 'About thirty or forty feet into the firth,' he said. Rebus turned and watched too. Clarke had wrapped her arms around herself, cheeks reddened, squinting towards the water.

'Is that one?' she asked, pointing.

'Not yet,' the man said.

She kept looking as the man offered some advice: 'The harder you look, the more you start to see things—especially when you want to see them.'

'True enough,' Rebus agreed under his breath.

Siobhan's mouth opened in a gasp as a sleek pale-blue shape emerged almost exactly where the man had said it would. After a moment the creature disappeared again, but there seemed to be a second dolphin just behind it. And then a third. There were

309

laughs and whoops from the spectators.

'Feeding time,' the expert explained. 'When the current's right, they hang around here until their bellies are full.'

'Did you see?' Clarke was asking Rebus.

'I saw,' he said. But his attention had been caught by the opposite shore. There seemed to be battlements there.

'Fort George,' the man on the folding seat said, as if reading Rebus's mind. Then he got busy with his camera as the dolphins broke the surface again. Clarke had taken out her phone and snapped a photo, but was disappointed with the result. She angled the screen towards Rebus. Too far away, and the dolphins themselves too similar in colour to the water around them.

'Here,' the man said, handing her his binoculars. She thanked him and pressed them to her eyes, adjusting the focus. Rebus stood with his hands in his pockets. A couple of the onlookers were tourists—tanned faces, brand-new mountain jackets, bought to ward off anything the Scottish climate threw at them. They were grinning whenever anyone made eye contact. One woman had brought her dog, and she was soon off again, rounding the point and tossing a ball for the collie to fetch. After a couple of minutes Rebus retreated to the lighthouse's boundary wall, seeking enough shelter to get a cigarette lit. The show seemed to be over anyway. Clarke had handed back the binoculars and was being shown some of the photographer's collection of shots. She caught up with Rebus and they started walking towards the car.

'Fun?' he asked her.

She nodded. 'It's good to be reminded there's another world out there. Maybe we'd see seals, too, if we hung around long enough.'

'Or selkies, even.'

'Did you finish reading that book?'

He shook his head, dodging a puddle in the car park. There was a cairn in front of the Saab and he went to take a look at it. A plaque told him it was the work of a local school and was dedicated to the Brahan Seer.

'Now there's a coincidence,' Rebus said.

'What?'

Rebus nodded towards the cairn. 'He gets a mention in that book.'

'Who was he?'

'Supposedly prophesied stuff like oil rigs and the Caledonian Canal. But he might not even have existed.'

'Like Sawney Bean, you mean?'

'Exactly.' Rebus unlocked the Saab. As they closed the doors after them, he turned the ignition and got the heating going.

'Maybe we can just sit here for a minute,' Clarke said.

'Sure.'

She was wriggling the warmth back into her body. 'And you can tell me a story.'

'What kind of story?'

'From your book.'

'I didn't finish it.'

'Go on,' she encouraged him.

Rebus stared out towards the water while he made up his mind. 'There's one about a selkie, actually,' he said eventually. 'It's supposed to have happened in the south-west, on the coast outside

Kirkcudbright. Young lad there saw a creature emerge from the water and it scared him, so he killed it, which brought bad luck to the surrounding area. The local landowner didn't like that, but the villagers protected the boy.'

'They knew he was responsible?'

Rebus nodded. 'He'd owned up to his father. Anyway, the landowner decided the whole village had to be punished. He was going to starve them out. The boy saw only one answer to that—walked into the Solway Firth until the water closed over his head.'

'The curse was lifted?'

Rebus nodded again. 'But each night, his head rose above the water, staring towards land, eyes full of sadness. He'd become a selkie, and he knew that if he ever came ashore again, there might be another scared child waiting for him with a rock.' Rebus paused. 'The end.'

'And the moral of the story is . . .?'

He thought for a moment before shrugging. 'Does there need to be a moral?'

'Actions have consequences,' Clarke stated. 'That's what I take from it.'

'Plus there'll always be people who'll cover up for the guilty,' Rebus added, reaching into his pocket for his ringing phone.

'Hazlitt?' Clarke guessed.

'No,' Rebus said, checking the screen and then answering. 'What can I do for you, Peter?'

It was Peter Bliss, calling from SCRU. 'Just thought you'd want to know, that's us being put out to pasture.'

'The unit's for the chop?'

'Effective near-as-dammit immediately. You'll

want to start clearing your desk.'

'SCRU's being shut down,' Rebus explained to Clarke. Then, to Bliss: 'How's Elaine taking it?'

'She's philosophical.'

'And our Lord and Master?'

'Seems pretty confident that he's on the shortlist for the Crown Office job.'

'A shortlist of one, if he has his way.'

Bliss chuckled at the truth of this. 'So where are you anyway? Got somebody there?'

'I'm with Siobhan Clarke. We're up north.'

'Thought as much. TV cameras don't seem to be spotting you today, though.'

'One bullet I'm happy to dodge.' Rebus pointed through the windscreen, so that Clarke could share his sighting of another dolphin as it made its way towards the feeding grounds. 'But as of right now,' he told Bliss, 'we're actually sitting in my car watching a passing parade of dolphins.'

'At Chanonry Point? Then you're minutes away from where Gregor Magrath stays.'

'Oh aye?'

'Rosemarkie, it's called.'

'You've been there?'

'Just the once. Cottage facing the beach. Only red door on the street, I seem to recall.'

'Maybe we'll drop by.'

'Could you do that?' Bliss paused. 'I'm serious. Gregor's always wanting to know what we're up to at SCRU.'

'And you want *me* to be the one to tell him it's on its last legs?'

'Bit nicer than a phone call,' Bliss argued.

'And saves you the grief,' Rebus countered.

'You're a gentleman, John.'

313

'Otherwise known as an easy touch.'

'We'll have a night out when you get back. Toast the old place before it shows us the door.'

'Will Cowan be on the guest list?'

'What do you think?' Peter Bliss said, ending the call.

Clarke was on the lookout for more sea life.

'Might find some further up the coast,' Rebus suggested, starting the engine. 'Along with a retired detective and a cup of tea . . .'

Rosemarkie was only five minutes away. A narrow main street, a church and a pub. Rebus lost sight of the coastline, and signalled right, turning down a narrow lane until he hit the seafront. A row of houses faced the water, bookended by a children's park at one end and a restaurant at the other. The house with the red door was a cottage with dormer windows jutting out from its roof. There was an enclosed sun porch with enough space for a single armchair. The man seated there held a newspaper close to his eyes, peering hard at the print. There was a venerable olive-green Land Rover parked next to the house, and enough land for a foot-wide strip of weed-free garden. The man eventually realised that Rebus and Clarke weren't passers-by. He put his paper down and opened the door. He had heft, but the years had given him a stoop and slowed his movements. He would be in his mid sixties, his hair silver but neatly trimmed, his eyes small but piercing.

'Gregor Magrath?' Rebus said.

'That's me.'

'I'm John Rebus. This is Siobhan Clarke. Peter Bliss asked us to drop by.'

'Peter? I was speaking to him just a few days

back.'

'Well, he says hello.'

'Rebus?' Magrath studied him. 'I seem to know that name . . .' He thought for a moment. 'Lothian and Borders CID?'

Rebus bowed his head in acknowledgement. 'And Siobhan here is a serving DI.'

'So what brings you north?'

'Mind if we come in?'

'The place is a bit of a guddle . . .'

'I promise we won't look.'

Magrath led them inside. Past the front door, they were immediately in a small, overheated living room, with a kitchenette beyond. There was a patterned three-piece suite, a TV, and shelves filled with books and knick-knacks, including mementoes from Magrath's time on the force.

'You live here on your own?'

'Wife passed away many years back.'

'I think I remember Peter telling me,' Rebus said with a nod.

Clarke suggested that she make them a pot of tea. Magrath made to help her, but she told him she would manage. As she busied herself at the worktop, the two men sat down either side of the electric fire.

'Bills must be grim,' Rebus commented.

'Place isn't hard to heat. Good glazing helps.' Magrath slapped his hands against his knees. 'You were telling me why you're so far from home . . .'

'You must have seen it on the news,' Rebus said, glancing towards the blank screen of the TV. 'Or read about it, at least.'

'The missing women?' Magrath guessed.

'Five of whom might just have turned up.'

315

Magrath nodded solemnly. 'Bad business,' he commented, before calling out to Clarke that the sugar was in a bowl next to the bread bin.

'You've been living up here a while,' Rebus said.

'Ever since I retired.'

'It's a glorious location.' Rebus had risen to his feet and crossed to the window.

'It is that.'

'Are you from here originally?'

'No. Just always had a soft spot for the place. And how's Edinburgh these days? Any sign of those trams getting nearer?'

'They're still laying the tracks.'

'Waste of bloody money. Council never seems to have had its wits about it.'

'I work at SCRU,' Rebus announced, turning away from the window again.

'Maybe that's why I know the name. Peter probably mentioned you.'

'He probably did,' Rebus said. 'I've just got off the phone with him. He told me to let you know SCRU's days are numbered.'

'That Crown Office unit's taking over?' Magrath's mouth twitched. 'Doesn't really surprise me.'

'Shame to lose it, though.'

Magrath nodded slowly. 'I always saw it as my legacy. It meant I'd made a difference.'

Clarke had found a tray and was bringing everything through from the kitchen. 'Didn't see any biscuits,' she said.

'If I get them in, I just eat the lot,' Magrath explained.

When she glanced in Rebus's direction, Magrath knew why. 'Your colleague has broken the news,' he told her.

They drank the tea in silence for a moment, then Magrath asked how Bliss was keeping.

'Still breathing,' Rebus answered.

'And every one of them sounding like his last, eh?'

Rebus acknowledged the truth of this. 'Tell me something,' he said. 'During your time in charge, how many cases did you manage to close?'

Magrath thought for a moment. 'Just the two. Made progress on six more, but it never got as far as a prosecution.' He leaned forward a little. 'Actually, of those two, one fell into our lap—guy came forward to confess as soon as he heard we'd reopened the inquiry. I think it was a weight off his conscience.'

'We could do with a few more consciences in the world,' Clarke stated.

'That we could, lass.'

'Is that an old wooden truncheon?' Rebus asked, gesturing towards the bookshelves.

'From before your time, I'm sure.'

Rebus had walked over to the shelf in question. 'Mind if I . . .?' He picked it up and felt its heft. It was nicely weighted, with a leather wrist strap and grooves wide enough for his fingers. 'We're barely allowed handcuffs these days,' he commented.

'And pepper spray and extendable batons,' Clarke reminded him.

Rebus waved the truncheon in Magrath's direction. 'Ever use it?'

'Came in handy a few times, I have to admit.' Magrath leaned back in his chair. 'You came all this way just to tell me about SCRU?'

'Actually,' Clarke said, 'we were watching the

dolphins at Chanonry Point . . .'

'Bliss called me,' Rebus went on, 'and explained we were near your place.'

Magrath smiled and nodded to himself. 'He didn't want to be the one to break the news.'

Rebus replaced the truncheon on its shelf. There were family photos there, posed groupings in gilt-edged frames. 'You know Nina Hazlitt, don't you?'

Magrath seemed to take a second to place the name.

'Mother of Sally Hazlitt,' Rebus prompted him. 'She went missing from Aviemore at the Millennium.'

'Oh, yes.' Magrath nodded again. 'Memory's not what it was,' he apologised.

'She's been all over the media this past week or so,' Rebus added. 'She's full of praise for you.'

Magrath's eyes widened. 'Why would that be?'

'Because you gave her the benefit of the doubt when no one else would.'

'I listened to the woman's story.'

'And looked into it.'

'Yes, I suppose so. She heard about a woman vanishing from somewhere near Strathpeffer— convinced herself it might tie into her own daughter's disappearance.'

'Others weren't nearly as helpful, and she hasn't forgotten it.'

'I really don't think I did very much . . .?'

'All I'm saying is, don't be surprised if you're mentioned in dispatches.'

'I'd much rather she didn't say anything.'

'Mind if I ask why?'

'Because it's just one more case that went

318

nowhere.' Magrath had risen from his armchair, seeming to need the reassurance of the unchanging view from his window. 'Another in a long line of failures,' he said, more to himself than anyone else in the room.

'She may have been right, though,' Rebus said. 'About the abductions, I mean.'

'You have to wonder about the human race sometimes, don't you?' Magrath said with a sigh.

They stayed a few more minutes, Rebus listening as Magrath told Clarke about sightings of whales and explaining the difference between dolphins and porpoises. The man seemed at peace in his retirement, with its cottage, sea views and village life—it was just a pity none of it appealed to Rebus.

When they left, Magrath returned to his chair on the porch, giving them a wave before settling with his newspaper once again.

'Reckon the Land Rover's his?' Clarke asked.

'It's the right vintage.'

She looked at Rebus. 'Something wrong?'

'Not really.'

'You're lying.'

'I just think his memory's fine, that's all. And judging from the pile of papers by his chair, he keeps up with the news.'

'So?'

'So why pretend Nina Hazlitt's name meant nothing to him?'

51

On the way back to Inverness, Page sent Clarke a text suggesting dinner.

'You should take him up on it,' Rebus suggested. 'The two of you need to talk.'

'Can I take you along for moral support?'

Rebus shook his head. 'I need an early night.'

When they arrived at Northern Constabulary HQ, however, the first person he bumped into was Gavin Arnold.

'Can't keep you away, can we?' Arnold said, shaking Rebus's hand. Rebus introduced him to Clarke, giving her all the information she needed by explaining that 'Sergeant Arnold is one of the good guys.'

Arnold responded by asking if they fancied a drink later. Clarke told him she couldn't, while Rebus said he'd consider it.

'Well, you know where to find me, eh?'

'By the dartboard?' Rebus guessed.

Arnold nodded and explained that, like every other uniform in a fifty-mile radius, he had been drafted in to work on the inquiry, as a result of which the building was bursting at the seams.

'This should all be happening at Burnett Road,' he complained. 'That's where CID is.' He waved a hand around him. 'This is suits and bean-counters.'

'So why base the inquiry here?'

'*Because of* the suits and bean-counters—means they get to feel important as they walk past the cameras.'

The inquiry room was certainly filled with bodies.

Those who had been elsewhere were now gathered to listen to another of Dempsey's briefings. DNA matches were coming in, and she could now name two of the victims as Amy Mearns and Jemima Salton.

'The families are on their way here,' she said, 'to be told the findings.' Her voice was hoarse and she paused to take some water from a plastic bottle, clearing her throat afterwards. Her face was pale and exhausted; and somehow, Rebus knew, she had to find strength for these two meetings and the emotions they would bring. 'Any questions?' she asked.

'How long till we have positive IDs on the other victims?'

'Not long—hopefully tomorrow or the day after.'

'Cause of death?'

'That's still going to be hard to determine. I've requested a couple more pathologists from Aberdeen to speed things up.'

'What steps do we take next?'

'We continue door-to-door. Maybe some of the farms have CCTV we can look at; same with shops and garages. We need to talk to *everyone*.'

'All the evidence collected from the field and the woods . . .?'

'Is at the lab. Nothing to report so far.'

'The pubic hair . . .'

'Yes?'

'We know it doesn't belong to Annette McKie.'

Dempsey nodded. 'Once we get a DNA fingerprint from it, I'll be asking to take swabs from every male within shouting distance of Edderton.'

The officers in the room exchanged looks, knowing the amount of work this would entail.

'I know I'm asking a lot,' she said. 'But we need to be seen to be doing our utmost.'

Yes, Rebus thought to himself, because if nothing else, it might flush the killer into the open. He remembered the tactic he'd suggested at SCRU, and found himself proposing out loud that Dempsey tell the media there was DNA evidence, even if none existed. She stared him down.

'Have you considered approaching a criminal profiler, ma'am?' The question came from Siobhan Clarke, maybe to deflect attention away from Rebus. Dempsey met her gaze.

'I'm open to any *sensible* suggestions, DI Clarke.'

'It's just that there's been a lot of research done into what makes serial killers choose their particular disposal sites. The fact is, the victims came from a wide geographical area but ended up in that one spot.'

'Meaning it has some significance for the perpetrator?' Dempsey was nodding. 'I've already fielded a few e-mails on the subject. If anyone wants to suggest a friendly profiler who isn't going to break the bank . . .' She looked around the room. 'Or maybe DI Clarke could do an internet search and see what she comes up with?' Dempsey's eyes were fixed on Clarke again.

'Be happy to, ma'am.'

'Good.' Dempsey checked her watch. 'Well, if there are no more questions, I've got a couple of grieving families I need to prepare for . . .'

There were sympathetic sounds from around the room. Page was pushing past a few officers in order to get to Siobhan Clarke.

'Where have you been?' he asked.

'Here and there,' she answered.

'I was looking for you earlier.' He sounded disappointed in her.

'I was at the end of the phone.'

'Mine needs charging,' he muttered. 'Nobody seems to have the right adaptor. Did you get my text about dinner tonight?'

'She's delighted to accept,' Rebus interrupted, receiving a stern look from Clarke. 'And though I'd love to be there too, it so happens I have other plans.'

Having said which, he made his exit.

*   *   *

That evening, despite best intentions, Rebus took a cab from the guest house to the pub. He sat in the front and told the driver he never seemed to be able to find a parking space in Inverness.

'You should see it at weekends,' he was informed. 'Multi-storeys, supermarket car parks—full all day.'

'Place must be booming.'

The driver gave a snort. 'Wish I could say I was seeing some of the benefits.'

When Rebus walked into the Lochinver, Gavin Arnold was lining up an out-shot. His dart ended up just the wrong side of the wire and he continued to shake his head as he watched his opponent end the game with double seventeen. They exchanged handshakes and pats on the arm. Arnold saw Rebus and waved him towards the bar.

'What are you having?'

'An IPA would do the trick.'

'Two please, Sue,' Arnold said. Sue Holloway smiled a greeting at Rebus and got to work.

As they watched her pour, Rebus asked Arnold how things were going.

'I'm on doorstepping duties,' he replied. 'Reckon the shocks have gone on my car already, the number of farm tracks I've been up and down.'

'With no result to show for it?'

'Which DCS Dempsey insists is a result in itself. Narrowing things down, she calls it.'

'In a way, she's right.'

'It just makes for a bloody tedious day, that's all.'

'Stop moaning,' Holloway said. 'And these are on the house as a way of saying thanks.'

'For what?' Rebus asked.

'Trying to find the twisted bastard and stop him doing it again.'

'Cheers then,' Arnold said, clinking his glass against Rebus's before taking a sip. 'How about you, John? Any progress?'

'I seem to be surplus to requirements, Gavin. Spent half the day sightseeing.'

'Culloden?' Arnold guessed.

'Black Isle, actually.'

'If they widen the search any further, I'll end up there before long. What did you think of the place?'

'I saw some dolphins.'

'Did you go to Culbokie?' Arnold watched Rebus shake his head. 'Nice wee pub there with a beer garden looking over the Cromarty Firth.'

Rebus remembered how he knew the name—Culbokie was where Brigid Young had left her mobile phone the day she'd been abducted.

'Hey, Gav,' one of the other darts players called. 'You seeing this?'

The man meant the TV set above the door. It was tuned to a news channel. On the screen some

324

people were settling themselves around a table. Looked like another bar, this time with menus and napkins. Flashbulbs were going off, and at one point the news camera was jostled.

Rebus recognised Frank Hammell and Nina Hazlitt. They were shaking hands, as if they'd just been introduced to one another. Another couple were there too, not looking comfortable at the amount of attention and the proximity of the cameras.

'That's Brigid Young's sister and her man,' Arnold explained. Across the bottom of the screen ran the words A9 FAMILIES MEET.

'Isn't that the Claymore?' Sue Holloway said.

'Looks like,' Arnold admitted. Then, for Rebus's benefit: 'It's right across the road from here.'

Someone had gone to the door to check. Rebus, Arnold and half a dozen others decided to follow suit. Sure enough: an outside broadcast van with a satellite dish on its roof. And lots of lights moving around inside the Claymore Bar. Rebus crossed the street and peered through the window. He saw the table and the four figures seated at it. A man emerged from the back of the van and started setting up a tripod with a lamp at the top of it. He ran a cable back to the van and plugged it in, further illuminating the interior. Hammell glanced towards the window, his narrowed eyes meeting Rebus's. Then he turned back towards the microphones and continued with his speech. Rebus could see no sign of Darryl Christie. Nina Hazlitt was handed a drink from a tray. Brigid Young's sister had her hand clamped around that of the man next to her. As other gawpers closed in around him, Rebus retreated to the Lochinver. Arnold was

325

stationed in front of the TV, watching proceedings. Someone had turned the volume up.

'Impromptu press conference,' he stated. 'Dempsey won't be happy.'

'What have they been saying?' Rebus asked.

'Mr Hammell's complaining about a lack of effort; Ms Hazlitt wants to be swabbed for DNA.'

'And the other two?'

'Seem not to know what they've gotten into. You ready for a top-up?'

'My shout,' Rebus said, lifting Arnold's empty glass from him and making for the bar. When his phone buzzed, he reckoned he knew who it would be, but he turned towards the TV screen to check. Nina Hazlitt was talking. Frank Hammell could be seen next to her, studying the screen of his own phone. Rebus checked the message:

You still here?

He texted back, then paid for the drinks. It was a further half-hour before Hammell walked in. The only surprise was that he had brought Nina Hazlitt with him.

'This is Nina,' Hammell said.

'John knows me,' Hazlitt said. 'Though you might not know it from the way he's been behaving.'

This seemed to come as news to Hammell, who had a twenty-pound note in his hand, ready to attract Holloway's attention. Rebus looked around the bar. Everyone seemed to have recognised the visitors, while pretending to mind their own business. Arnold was halfway through another game of darts, his glance towards Rebus managing to pose both question and warning.

'Same again?' Hammell was asking Hazlitt.

'Why not?' she said.

'What about you, Rebus?'

'I'm fine as I am.' Rebus's eyes were on Hazlitt's. 'So how are you doing?'

'I'll be better when I get some news.'

'Tomorrow or the day after, that's what I'm hearing.'

'Then you know no more than we do,' she stated.

When Hammell handed her a glass, Rebus asked him where Darryl Christie was.

'Back in Edinburgh. Needs to be there for his mum.'

'Shouldn't that be your job too?'

Hammell glared at him. 'What about you? Boozing it up when there's a freak out there you should be catching.'

'I'm sure John's doing all he can,' Hazlitt broke in. 'Might explain why he's too busy to reply to messages . . .'

'I saw Thomas Robertson,' Rebus told Hammell. The man had ordered both a whisky and a pint, sinking an inch of the latter before adding the former to the mix.

'Remind me,' he said.

'The road worker from Pitlochry,' Rebus obliged.

'And why bother telling me?'

'He'd gone ten rounds with a battering ram.'

Hammell shrugged and took out his phone, checking its screen. Rebus turned his attention back to Nina Hazlitt. 'What was all that in aid of, across the road?'

'Media awareness,' she answered.

'Your idea or his?' Rebus nodded towards Hammell.

'Does it matter?'

It was Rebus's turn to shrug. Arnold was

327

gesturing from the dartboard, where he had just finished his game. Rebus walked over to him.

'Hell are you doing?' Arnold hissed.

'I can't help it if those two decide to wander in.'

'So it's just coincidence?' Arnold didn't sound convinced. 'You sure all the TV people have packed up? If this ever gets back to Dempsey . . .'

'I won't tell if you don't.' Rebus gave a wink and returned to the bar. Hammell asked him if he was finally ready for that drink. Rebus shook his head.

'Better be off. Another early start in the morning.'

'One more won't hurt,' Nina Hazlitt pressed, a certain amount of pleading in her eyes. Rebus couldn't tell if she wanted his company for its own sake, or was merely reluctant to be stuck alone with Hammell.

'Hey, guys!' The bar's door was wide open, someone standing there with their phone held up in front of them. Rebus, Hazlitt and Hammell couldn't help turning towards the voice. The young man smiled as he checked the quality of the photo he'd just taken, then offered a thumbs-up as he backed out on to the pavement, the door swinging shut after him.

Rebus had recognised Raymond, Dempsey's journalist nephew—and so had Gavin Arnold. The two men shared a look.

If this ever gets back . . .

'Maybe a whisky,' Rebus told Hammell.

'That's the stuff,' Hammell replied, waving towards Sue Holloway. The tension seemed to leave Hazlitt's body. She threw a smile in Rebus's direction, thanking him for staying . . .

He was in bed when he heard a knock at his door. Just shy of midnight, according to his watch. He got up and padded across the floor.

'Yes?' he prompted.

'It's me,' Siobhan Clarke said. 'Are you decent?'

Rebus looked around the small room. 'Give me a minute.' He pulled on his trousers and shirt, then opened the door.

'Not interrupting anything?'

'I should be so lucky. What's up?'

'Seen this?' She was holding up her phone so he could see the screen. It was a news feed from the local paper. The photo from the Lochinver was there, along with a subheading: *A9 Families Thirsty For Answers*.

'Not subtle, is he?' Rebus commented.

'Want to tell me about it?'

'I went out for a drink. Hammell and Hazlitt had been talking to reporters. They wandered into the pub and Tintin got busy with his phone.'

Clarke gave him much the same disbelieving look as Gavin Arnold.

'But to get to the important stuff,' he added, 'how did your meal go?'

'We were civil to one another.'

'Did you tell him you resent being dumped for the Chief Super?'

'Can we just drop it?' She sounded exhausted.

'Sorry,' Rebus said.

'I'll see you at breakfast.'

'If Dempsey's not sent me packing by then.' He gestured towards Clarke's phone.

'I might not be far behind. James says he's

struggling to find 'a viable role' for me.'

'He's a real charmer.'

Clarke checked the clock on her phone. 'Better get some sleep. Night, John.'

'Everything's going to work out,' he was telling her as he pushed the door shut. He listened as she crossed the landing and headed to her own eaves bedroom a further flight up. Another door opened and Rebus heard Page's voice asking her if she was all right.

'Fine,' was all she said, the stairs creaking as she climbed them.

52

Dempsey didn't wait for them to arrive at HQ. Her chauffeured car drew up as, post-breakfast, Rebus, Page and Clarke emerged from the guest house. Rebus, already in the process of lighting a cigarette, asked Dempsey if he needed a blindfold to go with it.

'What in God's name did you think you were doing?' she asked him.

'I was in a pub, having a quiet drink.' He'd had time to prepare this version of the story. 'Hammell and Hazlitt were across the road. After they'd posed for the cameras, they found themselves next to me at the bar. We know each other, so we said hello. That's when Raymond burst in and took his little paparazzi shot.'

'What's this about?' Page asked, frowning.

'Your officer,' Dempsey told him, 'is all over the internet.'

'Thanks to your nephew,' Rebus reminded her.

She ignored the jibe. 'So what did you tell them about the investigation?'

'What's to tell? I'm not exactly in the loop.'

Dempsey pointed at him, but her eyes were on Page. 'I want him gone, do you hear me?'

'Loud and clear,' Page responded. Dempsey was already getting back into the car. Her driver started pulling away.

'Thanks for backing me up there, boss,' Rebus commented.

'Go back inside,' Page said, 'get your stuff together and check out of your room—Gayfield Square will pick up the tab. We'll see you in Edinburgh.'

Rebus thought of things he could say, things like: 'I was solving murders when you were in your pram.' He didn't, though. He just gave a little bow of the head in Clarke's direction, as if to wish her the best of British, then flicked the cigarette to the ground and did as he was told.

When he re-emerged, Mrs Scanlon—make-up immaculate as usual—came with him and wished him well on the journey south. Page and Clarke were gone. Rebus watched as Mrs Scanlon closed the door, then decided on another cigarette before the off. When his phone rang, he considered not answering, but it was Gayfield Square.

'Who is it?' he asked.

'Christine Esson.'

'Hiya, Christine. If you've not already heard, I'll be joining you shortly.'

'Any news to report?'

'Way this thing's going, the internet'll know before I do.'

'I did see that photo of you with Hammell and Hazlitt . . .'

'And you thought you'd call me to gloat?'

'What is there to gloat about?'

'Nothing.' He crushed the butt of his cigarette underfoot and got into the Saab. Would *this* be the day it refused to start?

The engine growled into life; none of the dashboard's warning lights came on.

'So, anyway,' Esson was saying, 'I said I'd pass on her number.'

'Sorry, Christine, I missed the start of that. Whose number?'

'The woman who phoned wanting to speak to you about Sally Hazlitt.'

Rebus rolled his eyes. Another sighting. 'How much of a crank did she sound?'

'She seemed perfectly sane. Told me to give you her name and get you to call her.'

Rebus sighed, but reached into his pocket for his notebook and pen. When Esson read the woman's name out, he stiffened. Then he asked her to repeat it.

'Susie Mercer,' she obliged, keeping her intonation nice and clear.

'That's what I thought you said first time,' Rebus told her.

53

Glasgow.

Rebus had told the woman who called herself Susie Mercer: 'This has to be in person.'

She'd asked him why.

'I need to be sure.'

She was in Glasgow. A9 south, then M80 west. It was lunchtime before Rebus arrived, parking in a multi-storey near the bus station and walking the short distance to Buchanan Street. As arranged, he called her again.

'I'm here,' he said.

'Where?'

'Heading down Buchanan Street.'

'Turn left at Royal Exchange. You'll see a café there called Thompson's. Sit at the counter by the window.'

'I'm hardly James Bond material.'

'Just do it or I walk.'

So Rebus did it—ordered a coffee and an orange juice and sat with them, staring out at the passing parade of shoppers. Glasgow wasn't his patch. It was a sprawl compared to Edinburgh. As long as he stuck to a half-dozen streets, he could navigate his way around; outside that tight circumference, he'd be lost.

It was a good five minutes before she came in. She eased herself on to the stool next to him.

'Had to be sure you weren't bringing *her*,' she announced.

Rebus studied her. She'd cropped her hair and bleached it, then plucked her eyebrows till they almost ceased to exist. But the eyes and cheekbones were still those of her mother.

'You've gotten good at this down the years,' Rebus said, staring into the eyes of Sally Hazlitt.

'Not good enough,' she snapped back.

'That e-fit was a fair likeness, though—no wonder you panicked.' He paused. 'So do I call you

333

Sally, or Susie, or have you already fixed on a new name?'

She stared at him. 'Nina keeps mentioning you on the news. Then I saw that photo of the two of you . . .'

'And?'

'And she needs to be told to *stop*.'

'Stop looking for you or stop thinking you're a murder victim?'

Her eyes remained fixed on his. 'Both.'

'Why not tell her yourself?'

She shook her head. 'No way,' she said.

'Then tell me why you did it.' Rebus lifted the coffee to his mouth.

'First I need *you* to tell *me* something—why do you think she's doing it?'

'She's your mother. What other reason does she need?'

But Sally Hazlitt was shaking her head again. 'Has she told you anything about what our lives were like?'

Rebus thought for a moment. 'Your mum and dad were teachers. Lived in London . . .'

'That's as much as you know?'

'Crouch End, she told me—a nicer area than they should have been able to afford. A relative left some sort of legacy.' He paused. 'She's still in the same house, by the way, sharing with your Uncle Alfie at the moment. Your dad liked reading you stories when you were a kid.' He paused again, maintaining eye contact. 'You know he's dead?'

She nodded. 'Good riddance.' And at last Rebus thought he began to see. 'There's lots he liked teaching me,' she went on, meaningfully. 'Lots and lots.'

The silence lay between them until he broke it, his voice softening.

'Did you say anything to your mum at the time?'

'I didn't need to—she *knew*. That's the whole reason she wants to know if I'm still around. Because if I am, I might spill the beans.' She was looking down at the floor, eyes glistening.

'Why wait till Aviemore to make your move?'

It took her a moment to gather herself again. 'I knew I didn't want to study English at university—that had always been *his* idea. And the more we all sat around the chalet in Aviemore talking about the future, the more I knew I couldn't tell him to his face.'

Rebus nodded his understanding.

'He'd . . . stopped by that time. Stopped when I was fourteen.' She cleared her throat. 'Sounds crazy, but I thought back then it must be my fault, and that made it worse somehow. I'd spent the years since thinking how to punish him, and that night, December 31st, I had just enough Dutch courage in me—or gin at any rate. The whole thing felt so much easier, being in a strange place, hundreds of miles away from *them*.'

'But once you found out he was dead . . . ?'

'Too late by then. I knew I wasn't going back.'

'It can't be much fun, always living in fear of being recognised.'

'That's why you need to tell her to stop. I'm alive and I'm fine and I never want to see her or talk to her again.'

'It'd be a lot easier if you told her yourself.'

'Not for me it wouldn't.' She slid from the stool and stood in front of him. 'So will you do it?'

Rebus puffed out his cheeks. 'You're sure this is

the life you want?'

'It's what I've got.' She gave a shrug. 'Plenty of others out there worse off than me. You should know that.'

Rebus thought for a moment, then nodded his agreement.

'Thanks,' she said, managing a sliver of a smile. Rebus tried to think what else to say, but she was already at the door. Once outside, however, she hesitated, then came back in.

'Something else you've got wrong—I don't have an Uncle Alfie. Or an Uncle Anything, come to that.' She pulled open the door and left the café again, striding away with her bag slung over her shoulder, head held high, until the ranks of pedestrians swallowed her up and she was gone. Rebus took out his phone, adding her mobile number to his contacts list. She would probably change it, just as she would slip into a new identity, gifting herself a different past. He couldn't help but see it as a waste of a life—but then the life was hers to waste. With her number safely stowed, he slipped the phone back into his pocket and ran his hands down his cheeks as he replayed the meeting.

There's lots he liked teaching me . . .

I might still spill the beans . . .

I don't have an Uncle Alfie. Or an Uncle Anything, come to that . . .

'So who the hell is Alfie?' Rebus asked himself, staring at his reflection in the window.

Part Five

Smell of blood is everywhere—
Even in stone . . .

54

Rebus walked into the SCRU office at Fettes HQ and saw that the packing crates had arrived. Peter Bliss and Elaine Robison were busy with labels and inventories.

'Come to give us a hand?' Robison pleaded.

'This lot going to the Crown Office?' he asked, prodding one of the boxes with his toe.

'That's right,' Bliss said. 'And it'll all be in a damned sight better order than when it first arrived.'

'Don't worry,' Robison added, 'we've left one or two for you. Didn't want you to feel you were missing out.'

'Where's Danny Boy?'

'Another meeting with the bigwigs.'

'He's going to get the job, isn't he?'

'Looks like,' Bliss conceded.

'He'll be insufferable,' Rebus commented.

'Won't be our problem, though, will it? We'll be reduced to daytime TV and cold callers.'

'In place of cold cases,' Robison added with a smile. 'Though I might manage a wee holiday back to Australia first.' She picked up the photo of the Sydney Harbour Bridge from her desk and kissed it. Then, to Rebus: 'We were thinking next Friday for a meal and a drink.'

Rebus moved one of the empty crates from his chair and sat down at his desk. 'I'll have to check my diary,' he said.

'How was Inverness? TV made it look like a bit of a circus.'

'Nothing the media likes more than a new Sawney Bean to scare us with.'

'Who?'

'Cannibal—probably mythical.'

'Did you call in on Gregor Magrath?' Bliss asked.

Rebus nodded. 'And I passed along the news.'

'How did he take it?'

'Philosophically.'

'Picked a nice spot for himself up there, hasn't he?'

'Might be all right on a calm day . . .'

Bliss chuckled. 'Aye, before he retired, Gregor was always chasing the sun. Him and Margaret used to come back from Tenerife brown as berries.'

'Margaret was his wife?' Rebus guessed, remembering the photos on the bookcase. 'When did she die?'

'Couple of years before he took retirement. Bloody shame—he used to bring cruise brochures in, tell everyone where he and Margaret were going to go when he got the gold watch. How's he keeping?'

'Seems fine. You didn't work here when Nina Hazlitt met him, did you?'

'Don't think so. He'd have mentioned her.'

'It would have been 2004.'

'Just before my time, then.'

'He never discussed her with you?'

Bliss shook his head.

Someone rapped their knuckles against the open door. Rebus looked up and saw Malcolm Fox standing there.

'Can we have a word?' Fox asked.

'If you must,' Rebus responded.

'Maybe along the corridor . . .'

Rebus followed him to the Complaints' lair. Fox punched in the code for the lock, making sure to shield the combination from the visitor. The room was much the same size as SCRU, with an almost identical layout: desks and laptops and a window with a view on to Fettes Avenue. There was another suit waiting for them. He was Fox's age, but wirier, with ancient acne scars on one cheek. Rebus got the feeling this man would happily play bad cop to Fox's good—or vice versa. Fox introduced him as Tony Kaye, then asked Rebus to take a seat.

'I'm fine standing.'

Fox gave a shrug, then eased his backside on to the corner of Tony Kaye's desk.

'Thought you might still have been up north,' Fox said. 'That's why I phoned Inverness first, only to be told you'd been given the heave-ho.' His eyes drilled into Rebus's. 'Mind telling me why?'

'I was showing them up as amateurs. You know how prickly other forces get when that happens.'

'So it had nothing to do with Frank Hammell, then?'

'Why should it?'

'That photo of you and him enjoying a friendly drink,' Tony Kaye suggested.

'Just a coincidence.'

'Don't take us for mugs.'

Rebus switched his attention to Fox, waiting for the man to speak.

'Morris Gerald Cafferty,' Fox obliged, 'and now Francis Hammell. You don't half pick your friends, Rebus.'

'They're as much my friends as you are.'

'Funny, that,' said Kaye, 'because we've not been to any pubs with you, while you've been spotted

341

drinking with both of them.'

Rebus kept his eyes on Fox. 'We're wasting each other's time here.'

'SCRU's being wound up, I hear. That's you off the force again.' Fox paused. 'Unless you're serious about reapplying.'

'Being a civilian suddenly has its merits,' Rebus said, turning and heading for the door. 'Means I don't have to listen to you and your shit.'

'Enjoy the rest of your life, Rebus,' Kaye called out to him. 'What's left of it, that is . . .'

*   *   *

When he got home that evening, a note had been pushed under his door. He unfolded it. It was from MGC—Morris Gerald Cafferty—and it was just to let Rebus know how disappointed Cafferty was in him for 'consorting with scum like Frank Hammell', the word 'scum' underlined three times for emphasis. Rebus scooped up the rest of the mail and went into the living room. It felt stuffy, so he prised open one of the sash windows, then turned up the radiator to compensate. The hi-fi's turntable had been left switched on, rotating lazily. Rebus added a Bert Jansch album and lowered the stylus on to the vinyl. Then he started charging his phone before heading to the bedroom and emptying his overnight bag, filling a couple of polythene carriers with laundry. It would be another hour before the nearest launderette closed, so he decided to drop the stuff off—and collect some food on the way home. Leaving his phone behind and lifting the tone-arm from the record, he locked the flat and walked down the two flights of stairs.

'Yes, I know,' he apologised to the Saab as he approached it. He'd just tossed the laundry on to the back seat when he heard someone call his name. Tensing, he turned and saw Darryl Christie getting out of a black Mercedes M-Class. The driver stayed behind the steering wheel, but lowered his window the better to keep a close eye on proceedings. Rebus recognised him as the lippy doorman from Jo-Jo Binkie's—Marcus or something like that.

'Hello, Darryl,' Rebus said, resting his back against the Saab. 'Is it worth me asking how you come to know where I live?'

'This is the information age, if you hadn't noticed.'

'How's your mum doing? And the rest of the family?'

'There's a funeral needs planning.'

'There's also a friend of your mother's who needs calming down.'

'You think I'm bothered about him?'

'I think you've got a head on your shoulders. In a lot of ways, you're smarter than Frank Hammell. Someone needs to bring him back from Inverness.'

'Tomorrow,' Christie stated. He was dressed in the same dark suit, with a fresh white shirt but no tie. He slipped his hands into his trouser pockets and studied Rebus. 'Frank says you might be okay.'

'I'm flattered.'

'Despite being Cafferty's man.'

'I'm not.'

'Doesn't matter. Frank's wondering if you might keep your ears open, on behalf of the family.'

'Oh?'

'Any names that come into the frame—all we'd

343

need is a head start.'

'Frank wants his hands on them before they can be brought into custody?'

Christie nodded slowly. 'But I don't want that to happen.'

'No?'

'Things could get messy afterwards, and I don't want my mum being more upset than she already is.'

'Frank Hammell has a pretty good track record, Darryl. If he gets hold of someone, there's not going to be a trace of them afterwards—not for a long time.'

'This is different. I've not seen him lose it the way he's been doing.'

It was Rebus's turn to study the young man in front of him. 'You really *are* smarter, aren't you?'

'I'm just a bit more rational at this point in time. Plus it'll put my job on the line if he does something stupid.'

'It's more than that, though. I'd say you're canny by nature. My bet is, you kept your head down in school, did well in exams. But always watchful, learning how things are and what makes people tick.'

Darryl Christie offered a shrug of the shoulders. When he removed his hands from his pockets, he was holding a card in one. 'I've got lots of phones,' he said. 'If you ring this number, I'll know it's you.'

'You really think I'm going to hand over whoever did this?'

'A name and an address; that's all.' He looked through the windows of the Saab at the carrier bags on the rear seat. 'You never know—there might be the price of a washing machine in it . . .?'

Rebus watched him turn and head back to the Merc. No swagger to the walk, just an easy confidence. The driver's eyes were on Rebus, as if daring him to go against Christie's wishes, whatever those wishes might be. Rebus managed a wink as the window began to slide up, then got into the front seat of the Saab and started the engine. By the time he'd reversed out of his parking space and reached the junction at the foot of Arden Street, the Merc was nowhere to be seen.

The guy in the launderette told him it might be a couple of days. Rebus remonstrated that he didn't have a couple of days, to which the owner responded by waving his arms in the direction of the backlog of service washes.

'Way things are,' he said, 'I'd almost pay you to load the machine yourself.'

On the way back to the flat, it was a three-way contest between fish and chips, Indian and Chinese. Indian won, and Rebus stopped at Pataka's, ordering a rogan josh and saying he would wait. He was offered a lager but turned it down. The place was doing good business, the booths filled with couples sharing platters of food and bottles of chilled wine. There were three or four pubs within a two-minute walk, but Rebus flicked through that day's *Evening News* instead. By the time he'd finished, his food was ready. He drove back to Arden Street with Maggie Bell playing on the radio. He wondered if she was still going strong . . .

His kitchen filled with aromas as he opened the containers, scooping out the meat, sauce and rice on to a plate. There were beers in the cupboard, so he opened one and added it to the tray, which he carried through to the dining table. The living room felt a bit better, so he closed the window again and put the Bert Jansch album back on. His phone sounded, letting him know he had a message. He decided it could wait. A couple of minutes later, it issued another reminder and this time he got up to check the screen. One missed call; one voicemail.

It was Nina Hazlitt.

'Guess where I am,' she was saying.

55

They met at an old-fashioned bar behind the railway station. She was booked on to the sleeper service down to London, a couple of hours still to kill before boarding. She was seated at the bar when he arrived. The pint she'd bought him had been there some time and had gone flat. Rebus said it would be fine anyway.

'I thought you'd still be in Inverness,' she told him.

'Surplus to requirements.'

'They've identified all the bodies now?'

He nodded and took a sip of beer.

'No sign of Sally,' she went on, lowering her eyes.

'Meaning she's unconnected to the case,' he offered.

'But she *has* to be! Wasn't I the first person to see it?'

The barman cast a warning look towards them: this wasn't a place for raised voices. Rebus noticed that the couple at the table next to the window were readying to leave. He picked up his own glass and Nina Hazlitt's suitcase. After a moment she

346

followed him, carrying her vodka and tonic. When they were settled, she waited for him to meet her gaze. Her eyes were bloodshot, her face sallow and taut, lacking sleep and answers.

'What did you think of Frank Hammell?' Rebus asked.

'He seems very caring.'

'He's a gangster.'

'That's certainly what the papers imply.'

'He's not someone you want in your life.'

'He's not *in* my life.'

'The two of you looked pretty cosy in Inverness—which one of you arranged that bit of filming?'

'What does it matter?'

'Just trying to get things straight in my head.'

'I don't see that it's any of your concern, John.'

'Maybe not.' He paused. 'What about the other guy—I suppose he's none of my business either?'

She gave a sigh. 'Which 'guy' are we talking about now?'

'The one who lives with you—is his name really Alfie?'

'I told you, he's my brother.'

'You don't have any brothers, Nina.'

Her mouth opened a little. He watched as colour flooded her cheeks.

'What makes you say that?' she was eventually able to ask.

'I'm a cop; we're good at finding stuff out.' Rebus paused. 'So who is he?'

'He . . . lives with me.'

Rebus nodded slowly. 'Why did you lie?'

'I don't know.'

'Did you reckon your feminine charms wouldn't work on me if there was someone else in the

347

picture?'

She had lowered her eyes again. Her hands had dropped into her lap, resting there palms up. 'Perhaps,' she conceded quietly.

'Plus the grieving mother probably plays better with the media if there isn't somebody else waiting at home.'

'John . . .'

He gestured for her not to go on. He wasn't even halfway down the pint but knew he was going to leave it. His stomach felt queasy, filled with undigested meat and swelling rice. He rose to his feet. Nina Hazlitt didn't move. She seemed fascinated by her hands. Or maybe it was just that the pose had worked for her in the past. Rebus rested his knuckles against the edge of the small table and leaned down towards her, lowering his voice.

'She doesn't want to see you,' he told her. 'But for what it's worth, I don't think she's got any intention of telling the world about her father.'

Nina Hazlitt flinched, her head jerking up. 'Where is she?' she said.

Rebus shook his head as he straightened up.

'You've seen her?'

He was turning away towards the door. She was on her feet now. 'I'm begging you!' she called out. 'I just want to say sorry, that's all! Will you tell her I'm sorry? John! Will you tell her . . .?'

But Rebus had pulled open the door, leaving her world well and truly behind him.

During the drive back to his flat, he expected any number of calls or messages, but none came. Once he'd parked his car, he took out his phone and found the number for Sally Hazlitt's mobile. He

348

tapped in a text—*She says sorry*—and sent it, unsure if it would ever find a reader.

*   *   *

After Bert Jansch, it was the turn of the Stones, and after that some Gerry Rafferty. Rebus had emptied a fair amount of Highland Park into himself, and didn't know if it made him feel better or worse. He had taken the nylon plectrum from his pocket, the one made all those years ago by Jim Dunlop's company, and was rubbing it between his fingers while he did some thinking about Nina Hazlitt. Had he told her the truth out of simple spite? Would it have been better to leave it unsaid? He'd almost called his own daughter, just to hear her voice for five minutes, but it was too late in the day.

Five families, able finally to grieve properly, but with accompanying horror. Five victims plucked from the world, stripped and buried. Was their killer keeping his trophies—his store of clothing, purses, phones? Rebus really hoped so. He knew that Dempsey would make an appeal at her next press conference. It would be based on detailed descriptions of the women's belongings when they'd disappeared. He wondered if Dempsey was married—she didn't wear a ring, but that was hardly conclusive these days. Maybe she had children. Rebus's phone was on the arm of the chair and he kept checking it, wondering if he could maybe call Siobhan Clarke, just to tell her about his evening. Instead, he flipped the vinyl to side two, turned the volume down a shade, and trickled a final measure of malt into his glass.

The TV was playing silently: a news channel. The

349

A9 story had lost its top billing to a new political crisis in Europe. There was a fresh interview with Frank Hammell, but they only played half a minute of it. Already he was losing his novelty. When they cut back to the studio, a still frame of Hammell from the Edderton cordon was behind the newscaster's shoulder. Hammell's eyes bulged, flecks of saliva either side of his open mouth, finger stabbing at the viewer, as if ready to gouge out an eye. If a suspect ever did come to light, only to go missing, Hammell would get both blame and acclamation. Rebus was trying to work Hammell out. Was he so fiery because it was in his nature, or was he trying to impress Annette's mother? Did he maybe just like all the media attention? The other families had learned stoicism, or had come to embrace defeat. Not Frank Hammell, even though he *wasn't* family.

Not family.

Trailing Annette . . . arguing with her . . .

But not family.

Rebus considered this as he finished what was in his glass and decided against another. Instead, he made tea, and used it to wash down a couple of paracetamol. After which, despite the lateness of the hour, he called Frank Hammell. An automated female voice told him the number had not been recognised. He checked and tried again—same result. So he took Darryl Christie's card from his pocket and punched that number into his phone.

'Already?' Christie said, answering straight away.

'I need to speak to Hammell. I thought I had a number for him.'

'He changes it every few weeks—he's worried your lot might be tapping him. Is it anything I can

350

help with?'

'No.'

'Care to give me a clue?'

Rebus could hear soft music in the background. As far as he knew, Darryl still lived at home. Maybe he was in his bedroom. 'It's nothing important,' Rebus said.

'Do you always call people at midnight with stuff that isn't important?'

Christ, this kid was sharp. 'Sorry to bother you,' Rebus said, readying to end the call. But Christie told him to wait. He seemed to be weighing something up. Rebus heard sounds of glasses and coughing. Some sort of bar or club, but nowhere busy. The music sounded recorded.

'Is that jazz?' Rebus asked.

'You like jazz?'

'Not hugely. And I'd have thought you were about three decades too young for it.'

'Got a pen on you?'

'Yes.'

Christie recited Hammell's new number, which Rebus added to the back of the card before thanking him.

'I'll let you in on the secret of jazz,' the young man said, 'if you like.'

'Go on then.'

'It's all about control . . .'

When the music died, Rebus realised that Christie had ended the call.

He stared at the number jotted on the card, suddenly unwilling to talk to Hammell. He would sleep on it—after adding the number to the list of contacts on his phone.

There was an inch and a half of whisky left in the

351

bottle.

He decided to leave it there and call it a moral victory. 'It's all about control,' he said to himself, sliding the guitar pick back into his pocket and heading for bed.

56

Rebus was leaving the house next morning when a horn sounded. Hammell was beckoning to him from the white Range Rover Sport. Rebus crossed the road as Hammell wound the driver's-side window down.

'I need to change addresses,' Rebus complained. 'Seems every bugger in creation knows where I live. When did you get back?'

'Middle of the night. Didn't seem to be any point sticking around.' Hammell hadn't shaved for a couple of days, and hadn't had much sleep either. 'Darryl seemed to think you'd be calling me.'

'I was planning to.'

'Well, here I am.'

'Here you are,' Rebus couldn't help but agree. Hammell was waiting for more. Rebus looked up and down the empty street. 'Phone might be better, though . . .'

'Why?'

'Less chance of you being tried for assault.'

Hammell's eyes narrowed still further. 'Maybe you should just spit it out.'

Rebus considered his options. 'Okay then,' he said, leaning in towards the open window and lowering his voice. 'Is Annette McKie your

352

daughter?'

The car door swung out suddenly, catching Rebus a glancing blow as he backed away. By the time Hammell got out, Rebus had put some distance between them. They stood in the middle of the road, twelve feet apart.

'Hell are you saying?' Hammell snarled.

'Sure you want to do this here, Frank?' Rebus indicated the dozens of tenement windows either side of them.

'She's fifteen years old,' Hammell went on, taking a couple of steps towards Rebus, fists bunched. 'You saying I was doing her mum behind Derek's back?'

'I'm saying you're acting like a parent—tailing her, keeping tabs on her, giving her money, and then having fights about how she spends it and who she sees. And if that's not the case . . .'

'Which it's not,' Hammell spat.

'Then there's another scenario we need to discount.'

'And what's that?' Hammell's eyes were huge and he was breathing heavily, as if pumping himself up for combat.

'There's forensic evidence, Frank. A pubic hair that doesn't belong to Annette. Once the lab get a DNA profile, they're going to match it against her sexual history. They want to know if it belongs to whoever killed her, or just someone she'd been seeing.'

Rebus had backed away a couple of steps, but Hammell was no longer moving.

'So I have to ask, Frank—were you and Annette an item? Because if you were, then there's a good chance of that DNA coming straight back to you.

353

And meantime the team will have been tied up on a wild goose chase, giving the real killer more time to cover his tracks.'

'You're asking if I was sleeping with my girlfriend's daughter?'

Rebus didn't say anything.

'Is that what you're asking?' Hammell persisted. When Rebus stayed silent, he launched himself forward, his whole weight landing on Rebus, both men hitting the ground. Rebus felt all the air being punched out of his body. Hammell was trying to gain some purchase, Rebus rolling so he could dislodge his attacker. A delivery van had entered the street but stopped dead, its driver emerging to watch. Rebus gave Hammell a shove and started getting to his feet, but Hammell's foot caught him in the ribs and he went down again, grazing his knuckles against the tarmac.

'You piece of—'

Hammell didn't get the chance to finish the sentence. His groin was just the right height for a headbutt, and that was what Rebus delivered. Hammell gasped and pitched forward, Rebus grabbing him by the hair and pulling him down until his face met the road surface. The van driver had made tentative progress towards the two men.

'You need to break it up!' he cautioned. 'Somebody's going to be calling the police!'

Rebus was on his feet, heart racing, head pounding from where it had made contact with the ground. When he inhaled, his ribs complained. Hammell was on hands and knees, spitting dribbles of blood from his mouth. Rebus made sure there was distance between them and waited for the man to get up. Hammell's face was almost purple, bits of

354

grit stuck to it.

'Lost a fucking filling,' he said, wiping a string of blood and saliva from his chin. Rebus waved the van driver away without taking his eyes off his opponent. 'Probably one of my balls as well.' Hammell stared hard at Rebus. 'Dirty bastard of a fighter, aren't you?'

'Only way I was going to stop you, Frank,' Rebus said. 'Are we ready to talk now or what?'

Hammell had a finger hooked into his mouth, checking the damage. He gave a slow nod.

'Come up to mine, then. You can have a wash and a clean-up . . .'

Rebus led the way, out of breath by the time he reached his landing. His hand was shaking so much it took several attempts to retrieve his door key from his pocket and fit it into the lock. 'Bathroom's through there,' he said. The door closed and he heard the tap being turned. In the kitchen he switched the kettle on before checking the back of his head for a cut that wasn't there. He removed his jacket and unbuttoned his shirt. His ribs were sore when he touched them, and there'd be bruising later. He just hoped he hadn't cracked one. His shoes had been scraped by contact with the tarmac, but there was no obvious damage to his suit. He placed his hands under the cold tap and felt the immediate sting as he rinsed them clean. He had buttoned his shirt again and tucked it in by the time the kettle boiled. He made two mugs of black coffee and carried them through to the living room. When Hammell arrived, Rebus was seated at the dining table.

'Sugar?' he asked. Hammell shook his head and sat down, pretending to study the room so he wouldn't have to meet Rebus's eyes. There were nicks and abrasions on his face, but nothing too dramatic.

'I'm sorry,' Rebus said. 'But someone would have asked eventually.'

Hammell nodded slowly. He saw that Rebus had extended a hand across the table. With no great enthusiasm he took it, and the two men shook.

'My balls are nipping,' Hammell confessed.

Rebus repeated his apology and the two men started on their drinks. The bottle of Highland Park was over by the armchair, still containing a couple of good measures, but Rebus didn't offer and Hammell didn't ask.

'They can really get DNA from a pube?' Hammell enquired eventually. Rebus nodded. 'Well . . .' Hammell cleared his throat. 'I suppose it could belong to me.' He waited for Rebus to say something, but Rebus was blowing across the surface of his coffee, no judgement forthcoming. Hammell seemed to relax slightly. 'Things happen, you know? You're not always as in control as you think.'

'Did the two of you manage to keep it under wraps?'

'Would Gail still be seeing me otherwise?'

Rebus thought fleetingly of Nina and Sally Hazlitt, of families and the secrets they succeeded in keeping from the world. 'What about Darryl?'

Hammell shook his head. 'So what happens now?' he asked. 'Does this all have to come out?'

'Not the way you think.' Rebus considered for a moment. 'A DNA swab takes seconds. It can be done in private. If there's a match with the hair, it can be ruled out as evidence and the team can focus

356

their attention elsewhere.'

'Unless they decide to pin all five on me, of course.' Hammell's eyes were on Rebus now. 'Your pal Cafferty would love that.'

'Not going to happen,' Rebus stated.

'You really think this isn't going to get out? We both know what cop shops are like.'

'Was it a long-standing arrangement, you and Annette?'

Hammell glowered at him. 'Mind your own fucking business.'

'She wasn't pregnant, was she?'

'What?'

'She felt sick on the bus.'

Hammell shook his head. The landline started ringing, but Rebus ignored it.

'Could be important,' Hammell said.

'It's a pre-recorded message about a mis-sold payment protection plan that I never had in the first place.'

'That's detective work right there,' Hammell said.

'They're the only people who ever bother to call.'

As the ringing stopped, Hammell broke into a grim smile. 'This is all going to turn to shit,' he commented, 'yet somehow I can't bring myself to loathe your guts.' He started to get to his feet.

'I'll have a word with DI Clarke,' Rebus told him. 'Ask her to pass the message to DCS Dempsey direct. The swab can be done somewhere private— doesn't have to be a police station.'

Hammell studied him. 'Why would you want to help?' he asked.

'I'm a public servant, Mr Hammell, and you— whether I like it or not—are the public.' Rebus rose from his chair and the two men shook again.

'I'll have the beating of you next time, mind,' Hammell stated.

'I don't doubt that,' Rebus agreed, showing him to the door.

57

'You know what police stations are like,' Siobhan Clarke advised. She was still in Inverness; Rebus was standing next to his car, parked in the police bay outside Gayfield Square, phone pressed to his ear.

'That's what Hammell himself said. It's why you're the only one I'm telling, and why you should take it straight to Dempsey.'

'Even so . . .' She sounded sceptical. 'And it's not as though we owe Frank Hammell anything.'

'It's not just him, though, is it? Haven't Annette's family got enough on their plates?'

'I suppose.'

'Well then.' Rebus watched as a traffic warden approached. The man studied the sign on the Saab's dashboard and kept walking.

'Thing is, though,' Clarke was saying, 'if James finds out I went behind his back . . .'

'No reason why he should.'

'What's to stop Dempsey telling him?'

'You'll ask her not to. It's not like she won't owe you. Think how much of the budget she'd have wasted getting DNA from every bloke up there.' Rebus listened to her sigh. 'How's everything else?' he asked.

358

'Whole community around Edderton's been questioned. No light-bulb moments to report.'

'Hints of anyone protecting a nearest and dearest?'

'Nothing.'

'And the search?'

'Hasn't turned up a damned thing. I get the feeling Dempsey's going to give James and me our ticket home today.'

'Best talk to her quick, then—in person rather than on the phone.'

'I'm looking forward to seeing Edinburgh again.'

'It's been pining for you, believe me. It's crying on my shoulder as I speak.' Rebus arched his face towards the rain. It was only a shower, the sky to the west brightening already.

'So what are you up to today?' she asked him.

'Clearing my desk in *your* office, quickly followed by the desk in *my* office.'

'And that's it?'

'Game over, especially if the Complaints have their way.'

'You've done so much on this case, John. Someone needs to tell them that.'

'I'm sure my fan club's queuing up with testimonials.' He paused. 'So you'll talk to Dempsey?'

'She's bound to ask me how I know.'

'"Information received".'

'She won't like that.'

'Not much she can do about it—you're coming home soon. I've ordered balloons and everything.'

'Come to think of it, I've got to brief her anyway—serial killers and their disposal sites.'

'Did you dig up anything from the trusty

359

internet?'

'Only that there's usually a reason—the most basic being that it's in the vicinity of where they live. Or, to put it another way, their 'spatial behaviour' is 'empirically modelled'.'

'I preferred your first answer.'

'Thought you might.'

When they'd finished speaking, he headed upstairs. The office felt a bit like limbo. With Page and Clarke absent, and the case hijacked by Dempsey and her team, no one really had anything to do. Plenty of hard work; no real sense of achievement.

'Glad to see you so idle,' Rebus said, 'because I need a hand shifting all these boxes . . .'

In the end, Esson and Ogilvie helped take everything down to the Saab. Esson asked if the files were heading to Inverness. He told her he didn't know, and she suggested they be kept at Gayfield Square, just in case.

'If I'm not staying here, neither are they,' Rebus explained to her.

Afterwards, they celebrated with mugs of tea (and hot water) and the remnants of a packet of Bourbons.

'No new marvels to report from that computer of yours?' Rebus asked Esson.

She shook her head, taking tiny nibbles of her biscuit while Ogilvie dunked his in his tea before sucking the life from it.

'Best put your feet up while you can, then,' Rebus went on. 'Looks like Page might be back here by day's end.'

'And you're headed back to Fettes?' Ogilvie asked.

'Not for long—SCRU's been earmarked for closure.'

'So what'll you do?' The question had come from Esson. Rebus made show of shrugging his shoulders.

'Carpet bowls maybe; *Antiques Roadshow* reruns ...'

When she grinned, it made her look younger than ever.

'Been good working with the pair of you, though,' Rebus conceded, taking a last look around the office and gracing everyone with a wave as he made his exit. At the top of the stairs, he stopped and watched Dave Ormiston climb towards him, reading from a sheaf of papers. Ormiston spotted him and managed a thin smile.

'Is this me getting my desk back?' he asked.

Rebus nodded slowly.

'I'll say goodbye, then.' Ormiston's hand was out, but Rebus refused to take it and the man stiffened.

'Here's the thing,' Rebus said. 'All that nosiness of yours on the phone, it got me thinking about Big Ger Cafferty.'

'Oh aye?'

'See, Cafferty knew about that CCTV from the bus station when there was no way he should have.'

'It's an open secret he's a pal of yours.'

'But you and I know differently, don't we, Dave? We know he's got someone in his pocket—someone based right here.' Rebus leaned in towards Ormiston until their faces were only a couple of inches apart. 'Time you stopped being so chatty, or I might have to gather up a few brownie points from the Complaints. Ever seen them in action, Dave? They'll go through your phone and

361

computer. They'll look at your spending habits. They'll find stuff. And that'll be the big cheerie-bye to your pension.' Rebus paused. 'Fair warning—walk away from Cafferty, and keep walking.'

Back at the Saab, Rebus reached across the dashboard and lifted the POLICE OFFICIAL BUSINESS sign. He started up the steps, readying to hand it back at the front desk. Then he paused. After all, no one had requested it, had they?

He had only driven fifty or so yards in the direction of Broughton Street when his phone buzzed. It was Siobhan Clarke.

'Problem with Dempsey?' he guessed, lifting the phone to his ear.

'Are you near a television?'

'No.' He looked to left and right. Plenty of pubs he could dart into.

'I'll try for a screen-grab, then. Give me two minutes.'

The phone went dead. Rebus pulled over, slipped the sign back into place on the dashboard and walked into the nearest watering hole. When the barman asked what he could do for him, Rebus told him he could change channels for a start.

'Sky or BBC News,' he guessed.

There were no customers to complain, so the man did as he was told. When the BBC turned out to be focusing on a story about Afghanistan, he switched to Sky, where a reporter was interviewing Jim Mellon, the farmer from Edderton. But they were already cutting back to the studio, and Rebus hadn't even caught the headline. He got on his phone and told Clarke what he'd seen.

'I've sent you a photo,' she said. 'No 3G here, so it might take a while.'

362

'Has there been a break?'

'A break? No, they're just talking to the farmer for want of anybody more interesting. Half the news teams have already skedaddled back to wherever they came from. Call me when the picture gets there.'

'Can't you just tell me?'

'Might be nothing.' She paused. 'Probably is.'

The phone went dead again and Rebus stared at the screen, willing Clarke's message to arrive. The barman asked if he wanted a drink while he waited.

'Half of IPA, then,' Rebus obliged. It was poured, presented to him, paid for and demolished before his phone let him know he had one new message. When he opened it, he was looking at the scene from the TV interview—newscaster plus Mellon. They were in the farmyard, and close behind them stood a small white van with a name on the side in thick black capitals.

MAGRATH.

Rebus called Clarke back. 'Well?' he asked.

'Reckon it's coincidence?'

'Not such an unusual surname.'

'Actually it is—spelled that way. I just checked the local phone book.'

'You think Gregor Magrath runs some sort of business?'

'Google to the rescue—there's just one 'Magrath's' within about fifty miles. An electrician, based in Rosemarkie.'

Rebus was thoughtful. 'Did he act like an electrician to you?'

'Seemed more your typical pensioner. And the van wasn't there either, was it?'

'It's probably nothing,' Rebus told her. Then:

'Have you had a chance to speak to Dempsey yet?'

'Not quite, but she's in the building somewhere.'

'And you reckon you'll be back down here tonight? Want to meet for a drink?'

'Not a session, mind—just a drink?'

'Absolutely.'

'I'll call you.'

'I'm happy to bow out if Page makes a counter-offer.'

'Goodbye, John.'

He smiled at the phone and dropped it back into his pocket. The barman was standing behind the IPA pump, ready to offer a refill, but Rebus shook his head and left the pub.

At SCRU, Bliss and Robison helped him empty the car, Robison asking the same question Esson had: were the files going to Inverness?

'Quite possibly,' was all he said in reply.

At the very moment they deposited the last box on the floor, and stood up to wipe the sweat from their eyes and get their breathing back to normal, Daniel Cowan walked in from some meeting or other, looking both more dapper and more generally pleased with himself than ever.

'I'm not one to criticise,' he told them, 'but isn't our strategy to empty this office rather than fill it?'

'The A9 case,' Rebus informed him. Cowan looked suddenly interested, and even ran a finger along the edge of the topmost box. The A9 was a real investigation, current, live and in the news. There was a momentary longing in Cowan's eyes: he wanted it and could not have it. Moreover, if he took on a role at the Crown Office Cold Case Unit, he might never work a contemporary inquiry again.

'I was just going to treat the troops to a Kit Kat

in the canteen,' Rebus said.

'I'm not invited?' Cowan asked.

'I thought you'd want to stay put and make the phone call.'

Cowan looked at him. 'What phone call?'

'To Inverness—letting them know the files are here when they want them.'

Cowan's eyes brightened. 'Yes, I suppose it should be me that does that, shouldn't it?'

'We'll see you later, then,' Rebus said, leading Bliss and Robison from the room.

Once they were settled at a table, Rebus asked Bliss about Gregor Magrath's electrical skills.

'He could change a light bulb,' Bliss said. 'Not sure I'd trust him to wire a plug.'

Rebus explained about the van. 'Has he got any relatives up there?'

'None that I know of.'

'He'd have said, wouldn't he? I mean, the two of you have kept in touch—you've been to his house . . .'

'On the other hand, it might explain why he headed north rather than retiring somewhere with a bit of sun.'

'Suppose so.'

Robison bit into her apple, having turned down Rebus's offer of biscuits or crisps. 'Could just be someone with the same surname,' she offered between chews.

'Could be,' Rebus agreed.

'Meantime,' she went on, 'while the three of us are here, maybe we could decide where we want to go for our night out . . .'

58

That evening, Rebus met Siobhan Clarke at the Oxford Bar. They took a table in the back room and Rebus asked her if there was any more news from Inverness.

'The wheels are grinding,' she told him. 'More conscripts have been drafted in. Dempsey's widening the search area—locals are queuing up to help, along with a full complement of hunky firefighters.'

Rebus thought back to the original MisPer cases—lots of legwork, most of it so there could be no accusation of slacking.

'Thing is,' he cautioned, 'one of those locals could be hiding something.'

'She knows that. Every team of civvies has one of our lot attached, with orders to watch out for anyone acting nervous or odd.'

'And all this in the hope of finding clothes and belongings?'

'They have to be somewhere.'

Rebus nodded slowly and asked her if she'd spoken to Dempsey. Clarke nodded back, lifting her drink.

'I could see she wanted to ask me why I hadn't taken it to *my* boss.'

'But she didn't?'

'Just said she'd arrange for Hammell to be swabbed.'

'How did she react when you told her Annette and Hammell had been lovers?'

'A slight raising of the eyebrows.'

'And your source . . .?'

'Remains confidential.' Clarke paused. 'There's always a chance the hair *won't* belong to Hammell.'

'In which case, it becomes useful again,' Rebus agreed.

She took another sip of her drink. 'By the way, I phoned that electrician's—no answer. Still reckon it's a coincidence?'

'Peter Bliss has stayed in touch with Gregor Magrath. Doesn't see him as a sparky and isn't aware of any relatives in the area.' He thought for a moment, then reached for his phone.

'Who are you calling?'

'Jim Mellon—just remembered I've got his number here.'

It was Mellon's wife who answered. Her husband was in one of the barns and wouldn't be back for a while. Rebus gave her his number and asked if Mellon could phone him back.

'Nothing I can help you with, then?' she enquired.

'Actually, maybe you can. It's just that Mr Mellon was on TV earlier . . .'

'He's getting too much of a taste for it, if you ask me.'

'I was wondering about a van I saw parked in the farmyard behind him. It had the name Magrath on the side. I think it belongs to an electrician . . .?'

'Kenny Magrath,' she stated.

'Kenny Magrath,' Rebus repeated for Clarke's benefit. 'Lives in Rosemarkie, does he?'

'That's right.'

'It's just that I know another Magrath in Rosemarkie, name of Gregor.'

'Might be the brother.'

367

'The brother?' Rebus's eyes were on Clarke as he spoke.

'I'm sure Kenny's mentioned a brother.'

'That must be it,' Rebus said.

'Do you still want Jim to phone you?'

'I don't think that'll be necessary. You've been a great help, Mrs Mellon.'

Rebus ended the call, eyes still fixed on Siobhan Clarke.

'So?' she said.

'So Gregor Magrath retires and buys a place up north—despite the fact that he and his wife were always after holidays in the sun . . .'

'Making the Black Isle an odd choice.'

'Unless he has family there—which he does. But how come he never mentions as much to Peter Bliss? Even when Bliss visited, the brother never cropped up.'

'Maybe they'd had a falling-out somewhere down the line. It's not unknown in families.'

'But there were photos on the wall unit—a mum and dad with a couple of young kids, plus the same kids after they'd grown a bit. That has to have been the brother and his family.'

'Not necessarily.'

'I've always loved that positive attitude of yours.'

'That used to be my line.' She paused, then asked him what he reckoned it all meant.

'I'm not sure.'

'Worth another word in Dempsey's ear?'

He gave a shrug and concentrated on his beer. Clarke checked the time on her phone.

'A quick one?' Rebus suggested.

'Got a home life waiting for me,' she said with a shake of the head.

'Meaning . . .?'

'Post to open, bills to pay, washing to do.'

He nodded his understanding and glanced at his watch: he'd left it too late to collect his own laundry. 'We'll catch up again soon,' he said.

She had risen to her feet and extended her right hand towards him. Rebus took it and they shook, though it felt wrong, too formal. Was it her way of saying that their time together was done? Before he could ask, she was gone.

'Just you and me, eh?' he said to his pint glass. 'Same as it ever was.' Then he leaned back and focused his attention on the wall opposite, thinking some more about Gregor Magrath, and families, and secrets.

*   *   *

It was mid evening at Jo-Jo Binkie's. Frank Hammell had gone to see his dentist earlier for some repair work. Nobody had dared to ask him about the cuts on his face. He was watching from the balcony as the DJ twitched and danced behind his decks. Not that the man played records—it was all CDs, MP3s and laptops. The music wasn't to Hammell's taste, but Darryl was after a younger crowd, a crowd less careful with its money. The place was hipper these days, and people came from all over—sometimes in coaches from out west or Fife or the borders. A few dozen dancers gyrated below; Hammell checked out the talent. There was one skinny blonde, he could almost see down the front of her short, low-cut dress.

Almost.

A couple of staffers patrolled the periphery, on

the lookout for trouble. Hammell didn't know their names. They were new. Almost everybody was new. Darryl had explained—people not turning up on time; people bad-mouthing Hammell behind his back: they had to be replaced. People too old to handle the job; people who didn't pull their weight. Tonight, as Hammell had walked into his own club, he hadn't recognised a single person working the door. Even Rob the Reliable had gone AWOL. It was the same with the staff at his pubs: out with the old and in with the new. Darryl called it 'refreshing the brand'. Still, there was money coming in— no mean feat in a recession, as Darryl himself had suggested—and thanks to some creative accounting, not all of it went out again.

Hammell ran his tongue over the replacement filling. It didn't seem quite smooth, but he liked the coarseness. He felt movement next to him and turned to see Darryl himself standing there. Hammell patted the young man's upper arm in greeting.

'Not a bad crowd for a week night,' he said over the music.

'It'll get busier,' Darryl stated. He was in another new-looking suit, dark, with a pale-green shirt beneath.

'Where's Rob tonight?'

Darryl turned his attention from the dancers to his employer. 'I had to let him go,' he said.

Hammell lifted an eyebrow. 'What happened?'

'Nothing happened. But with you up north, it made it easier for me to tell him to take a walk. He got a bit of money, same as the others.'

'He was a good guy.'

'He was *your* guy, Frank, that was Rob's

370

problem.' Christie gestured towards the dance floor. 'Now it's all *my* guys.'

Hammell pulled back his shoulders and bunched his fists. 'What the fuck's going on?'

Darryl Christie answered with a cold smile. 'You're out, Frank, that's what's going on. I've got some paperwork arriving from your lawyer—now *my* lawyer, too. You're going to sell me your entire business for one pound sterling.'

'You little shit bag, get your arse out of here.' Hammell was standing toe to toe with him, flecks of saliva flying from his mouth. 'After all I've done for you? Ungrateful wee bastard.' He jerked a thumb towards the stairwell. 'Go on, before I rip your head from your fucking neck!'

'Look again,' Christie said calmly. Hammell looked, and saw three men appearing at the top of the stairs. Doormen. Men whose names and faces he didn't know. Darryl Christie's men.

'I've got everything,' Christie went on, his voice still icy calm. 'Passwords, account details, *everything*. The offshore banks, the numbers you don't think anyone knows about. It did for Al Capone and it'll do for you. Taxman'll have a field day.'

'What's your mum going to say?'

'Not one damned thing, because you're not going near her again. You're steering clear of my family from now on.' Christie paused. 'Unless you want me to tell her about you and my sister.'

Hammell's face froze.

'It was Annette who told me,' Christie went on. 'That's how she was—no way she could keep it to herself. I nearly whacked you over the back of the head for that—that and everything else.'

'There's not a chance in hell of me signing

371

anything.'

'Then a memory stick arrives at HMRC sometime tomorrow. Not even enough time for you to leave the country—not when I've got your passport in the same safe place as everything else.'

The three doormen were standing behind Hammell, awaiting orders. When Hammell made his move, they grabbed him by the shoulders, stopping him from getting to their employer.

'I made you who you are,' Hammell growled, trying to wrestle free. 'Gave you a job, took you to my house . . .'

'And pretty soon I'll have a house just like it,' Christie said. 'But there'll always be a difference between us.'

Hammell glared at him. 'What?' he couldn't help asking. Christie leaned closer.

'I won't trust *anyone*,' he confided, gesturing for the doormen to take Hammell to the office.

'I'm signing fuck all!' Hammell called out as he was led away. But he would sign, Darryl was sure of it. He rested his forearms on the balcony as he entered the text into his phone. It was to his father, and the message was succinct.

All done and dusted.

Even though he knew that wasn't quite the case.

59

Having managed a broken night's sleep, Rebus arrived at the Fettes HQ car park to find it half empty. The sky wasn't fully light yet, street lamps still burning. He locked his car and entered the building. The main reception was manned by the same officer who'd called up to SCRU that first day to tell him there was a visitor downstairs for DI Magrath. Another member of the team might have answered, or Rebus could have been on a cigarette break.

And everything would have been different.

He took the stairs rather than the lift—every little bit helped, as his doctor had told him at his last check-up. Even so, he needed the help of the banister and a breather at the halfway stage. The corridor was deserted, as were the offices he passed. He opened the door to SCRU and stood on the threshold. The place was frozen in time—half-filled crates; waste bin emptied by a cleaner and waiting to be used again; marker pens and paper clips; mugs needing to be rinsed. At his desk he found a clean sheet of paper, dated it, and jotted down the barest details of his meeting with Sally Hazlitt. Then he signed it and opened her case file, clipping it to the inside front cover. Cowan's desk, he noticed, was as tidy as ever—just in case any of the brass decided to drop by. There was a stapler with the name COWAN on it; Cowan had purchased it himself after each and every one of its predecessors had gone missing. Rebus lifted it from the desk and pocketed it, same as with the others, then headed out of the office and back down the stairs.

It wasn't a bad day for a drive and he wasn't in the mood for stopping. He'd filled the Saab on his way to Fettes and knew it was good for the trip north. He promised himself he would book the old warhorse in for a full service and valeting when this was all finished, a little reward for its efforts. Drumming his fingers against the steering wheel, Nazareth on the CD player, Rebus drove. He wasn't really thinking about anything other than the journey and its punctuations: the moment a particular section of dual carriageway ended; the passing of landmarks such as the Pitlochry roadworks and House of Bruar; familiar signposts pointing him to places he would most likely never visit, such as the Waltzing Waters and Killiecrankie. There was still a good covering of snow on most of the hills. Sheep continued to graze, inured to the passing parade of trucks, vans and cars. Rebus remembered Siobhan Clarke's words as they drove towards Chanonry Point: *it's an odd little country this . . . hard to fathom*. She'd accused him of coming over all defensive—well, it was a natural enough reaction, but in fact he agreed with her. A nation of five million huddled together as if cowed by the elements and the immensity of the landscape surrounding them, clinging to notions of community and shared history, some of them identified or hinted at in the book of legends Nina Hazlitt had given him. Even bogeymen were useful, because if there was a 'them', there was also an 'us', and if there was a 'them', there was someone to blame . . .

Aviemore.

Inverness.

Kessock Bridge.

Then Munlochy, Avoch, Fortrose.

Arriving finally at his destination: the row of houses fronting the coastline at Rosemarkie.

There was no sign of Gregor Magrath in the sun porch. The venerable olive-green Land Rover was parked in the same spot as before. Rebus knocked on the door of the cottage and waited. When there was no answer, he peered in through the living room window, noting no movement within. He could just about make out the framed photos on the bookcase. Straightening up, he fought the elements to get a cigarette lit, then stood beside his cooling Saab, gazing towards the distant shore. A dog was barking on the beach, way over to Rebus's right, its owner lagging many dozens of yards behind. There was a figure by the water's edge. Rebus shielded his eyes and watched as the man continued to trudge along the tide line. Not bothering to lock the car, he headed in the same direction, the wind flinging granules into his face.

'Mr Magrath!' he called. Magrath turned towards him, but then seemed to dismiss him. He had his back to Rebus when Rebus called his name a second time.

'You again.' Magrath sounded irritated. He was digging the toe of one shoe into the wet sand, watching each new indentation fill with seawater.

'What's the matter?' Rebus asked. 'Can't bear to look me in the eye?'

Magrath accepted the challenge, the two men standing in silence for a moment.

'How come nobody knows about your brother?' Rebus enquired, dropping his voice.

'Kenny? Everybody knows Kenny.'

Rebus nodded. 'Up here, maybe. But all the times you've spoken to Peter Bliss on the phone . . . and all the years you were at SCRU . . . and when Bliss visited you and I came to your house that last time . . .' Magrath had broken off eye contact, his interest shifting back to the beach beneath his feet. He opened his mouth but said nothing. The only

375

sounds were the breaking of the waves and the stropping of the wind.

'You've always been so interested in SCRU's caseload, pestering your pal Bliss for details.'

'Didn't I start the blessed thing?' Magrath complained.

'You did,' Rebus agreed. 'But I think there's more to it than that. A woman called Nina Hazlitt comes to your office one day, and soon afterwards you decide to retire—surprising everyone. SCRU is your baby, and suddenly you don't want it any more. You're moving north, moving near to your brother. Not that you're explaining it to anyone or mentioning his name . . .' When Magrath said nothing, Rebus went on. 'Nina Hazlitt came to see you because she thought she'd found a thread connecting her daughter's disappearance to that of Brigid Young. That thread was the A9 itself. She reckons you were kind to her, in that you listened to her story. But you yourself said it—you didn't make any actual progress, didn't manage to get anyone else interested in the case.' Rebus paused. 'I'm wondering if you even tried.'

Magrath flinched at this and began to trudge back up the beach, Rebus close behind.

'Your brother does some work at Jim Mellon's farm. He knows the area pretty well, I'd guess, the amount of driving he must do between jobs.'

'What are you getting at?' Magrath's pace had increased and he was breathing heavily.

'We both know,' Rebus said.

'I've not the faintest bloody idea!'

'Which house is Kenny's, Mr Magrath? I'd like to have a word with him.'

'Just leave us alone.'

376

'Mr Magrath . . .'

The man stopped and spun towards Rebus. 'Can I see your warrant card? I can't, can I? Because you're not a bloody cop! Maybe I should phone and register a complaint. Go back home, Rebus. Just leave us be!'

He stomped away again, Rebus at his heels.

'What is it you're afraid of?' Rebus enquired. He received no answer. 'Fine, if you want Dempsey and her team here, that can be arranged.'

Magrath had climbed the concrete steps connecting beach to roadway and was making for his cottage, taking a bunch of keys from his pocket.

'You brought Peter Bliss into SCRU,' Rebus persisted, 'so he could be your eyes and ears. That way you'd always know which cases were being reopened. Of course, you could have achieved the selfsame result by staying put, but you needed to be *here*, somewhere near your brother, rather than the hot countries you preferred. Blood's thicker than suntan oil, eh, Gregor?'

'I'm not listening to you.'

'Just think for a second,' Rebus argued. 'It's a lot easier this way.'

But the door was slammed shut in his face. He watched through the glass as Magrath opened a second door and disappeared into the body of the house. There was a newspaper on the chair inside the porch, folded open at the latest report on the Edderton case. The papers spilling across the floor seemed to be open at similar stories. Rebus thumped on the door with his fist, then rattled the letter box. After a few moments, he took a step back and approached the living room window, just in time to see Gregor Magrath drag the curtains

377

closed. He waited a full minute, then walked to the
next cottage along and rang the doorbell. A woman
who looked to be in her eighties answered, drying
her hands on a tea towel.

'Sorry,' Rebus told her with a smile, 'I was
looking for Mr Magrath.'

'He lives next door.'

'I mean Kenny—the electrician.'

She pointed along the street. 'The garden with
the swing,' she explained. 'But the front door's
round the far side.'

Rebus thanked her and began to stride along
the seafront. Beyond the row of cottages stood a
few modern detached houses with steeply sloping
gardens. The neighbour was right: these homes
backed on to the view. Someone had added an
octagonal conservatory to one, in front of which
stood a metal frame for a swing, but with its seat
missing, the frame itself rusting. Rebus headed
up the lane at the end of the promenade and then
took a left until he found the front door he was
looking for. He pressed the bell and heard it ringing
somewhere inside. A middle-aged woman opened
the door.

'Yes?' she said.

'I'm looking for Kenny Magrath.'

'He's at work. Is it to do with a job?'

'When will he be back?'

Her face remained friendly but puzzled. She had
a rounded, pleasing figure and curly auburn hair,
her eyes the same olive green as her brother-in-
law's Land Rover.

'Is it something I can help you with?' she asked.

Rebus took out his ID and held it towards her.
'I'm with the Edderton team,' he explained. 'Your

husband was out at Jim Mellon's farm yesterday.'

'That's right.'

'It just occurred to us, the job he does, he might have noticed any suspicious activity or a stranger in the area.'

'Well, he'd have said something, wouldn't he?' Her eyes had narrowed a little.

'Maybe he would,' Rebus countered. 'But sometimes you don't remember something until you're asked about it.'

'Really?' She took a moment to consider this. Rebus decided to fill the silence with another question.

'Have you lived here long, Mrs Magrath?'

'All my life.'

'Been married a while?'

'Don't remind me,' she said, making a joke of it.

Rebus managed a big, friendly smile. 'You've got a couple of kids?'

Her demeanour stiffened.

'I saw photos at Gregor Magrath's house,' he explained. 'Are they still at home?'

'They're in their twenties.' She had relaxed a little. 'One's in Inverness, the other Glasgow. So you've been talking to Gregor?'

'Not officially. I work with one of his old colleagues. The colleague told me to drop by and say hello.'

She seemed to have made up her mind about him. Taking a step back into the hall, she asked if he wanted to come in.

'I don't want to be any trouble.'

'No trouble,' she said. 'Kenny said he'd be home around one for a pit stop. The kettle's already on . . .'

379

The house was bright and well furnished. Plenty of framed photos on the living room walls, mostly of the offspring in every stage of development from cradle to graduation. Rebus tried not to look as though he was snooping.

'Does your husband work from a shop?' he asked.

'More a sort of shed—just somewhere he can store all his bits and pieces.'

'That's near here, is it?'

She nodded. 'Opposite the pub.' She paused. 'Sorry, I didn't seem to catch your name.'

'Rebus,' he said.

'Rebus?'

'It's Polish, if you care to go back far enough.'

'Lots of Poles in Scotland just now. Kenny's noticed it in the building trade.'

'He's got enough work, though?'

'Oh, yes. No complaints there.'

'Always local jobs?'

She looked at him, trying to fathom the reason for the question. Rebus tried out his smile again.

'Sorry, just me being nosy,' he said.

'Kenny has built a name for himself.' She poured tea from a pot and handed him the mug. There was a plate of shortbread, too, but he shook the offer away.

'He's in demand?'

'Always.' She took a sip of her own tea. Rebus's father would have called it a 'sergeant major's special'—the colour of mahogany and giving a tannic coating to the inside of the mouth. He studied some of the photographs.

'See much of your son and daughter?'

'When we can. It's easier with Joanne.'

380

'She's in Inverness?' Rebus guessed.

Mrs Magrath nodded. 'Though actually, Kenny saw Brendan a few weeks back.'

'And Brendan's in Glasgow?' Rebus checked.

'I couldn't go—had to visit a friend in Raigmore.'

'Quite a hike from here to the west, isn't it?' Rebus sympathised. He'd done that drive himself, after all. A9, then M80, Sally Hazlitt waiting for him at journey's end.

And if you needed petrol, you might leave the road at Pitlochry . . .

'A few weeks back, eh?' he added. 'Can you be more specific, Mrs Magrath?'

'Being nosy again?' Her tone had grown cool.

'Hard to switch off sometimes.'

'It was a Satur—'

She heard the van before he did. It was pulling up outside.

'A Saturday?' Rebus prompted. *Same day of the week Annette was abducted.* 'Just over three weeks ago, would that be, Mrs Magrath?'

'Kenny has a system—he'll tell you so himself. Leaves here early, lunch with Brendan, then he can start home and miss the football traffic.'

The motor revved once before juddering to a stop.

'That's good,' Rebus was saying. 'I must remember that.' *Leave Glasgow just after three . . . reach Pitlochry between half past four and five . . .*

An unoiled van door creaked open, then slammed shut. Mrs Magrath was on her feet when the front door rattled open.

'I've only got ten minutes,' a male voice boomed out. Kenny Magrath walked into the room, doing a double-take when he saw there was a stranger there.

'This is Detective Rebus,' his wife began to explain.

'I know who he is—just had Gregor nipping my ear about him.' A finger was pointed at Rebus. 'You're not welcome here.'

His wife looked from one man to the other. 'What's going on?'

Kenny Magrath's eyes were burning into Rebus's. He was taller and broader than his brother, and maybe ten years younger. A thick head of hair only now beginning to go silver at the temples. Chiselled face and deep-set eyes beneath bushy eyebrows. Rebus stood his ground, happy to continue the staring contest. He had risen to his feet and was sliding his hands into his trouser pockets, showing he was in no hurry to be anywhere else. The fingers of his right hand grazed the guitar pick.

'I'm asking you to leave.' Magrath gestured towards the door. Then, to his wife: 'Maggie, call the police.'

'But he *is* the police.'

'Not according to Gregor.'

Maggie Magrath looked at Rebus, feeling cheated and let down by the visitor.

'I'm attached to the Edderton inquiry,' Rebus stated, eyes never leaving Magrath's.

'He's from Edinburgh,' Magrath told his wife. 'Got no business being here, barging into people's homes ...'

Rebus was about to explain that he'd been invited in, but didn't want to get Maggie Magrath into any extra bother. 'We need to talk,' he told Magrath.

'No we don't.' Magrath took a step towards him.

'I still don't know what this is about,' his wife was complaining.

'It's about all those dead women, Mrs Magrath,' Rebus obliged.

Magrath bared his teeth and took another step forward. 'You want me to throw you out?'

Rebus knew that a struggle would make a mess of Maggie Magrath's impeccable room. His eyes were fixed on Magrath's.

'Maybe we should talk outside.'

'We're not talking anywhere!' Magrath clamped his fingers around Rebus's forearm.

'Let go of me,' Rebus said quietly.

'Answer me first.'

'I'm going,' Rebus assured him. 'Just as soon as you take your hand away and save me breaking it.'

'That sounds like a threat.' Magrath released his grip on Rebus's arm and stepped away from him. 'Best walk out of here while you still can.'

'Now who's making threats?'

'Not me,' Magrath told him. 'And I've got my wife as witness.'

Maggie Magrath couldn't look Rebus in the face, and he realised suddenly that she knew—knew or had had her suspicions. 'Just go,' she said, her voice cracking.

'One way or another, we'll talk,' Rebus told Kenny Magrath, making for the doorway.

'Like hell we will!' the man responded.

Outside sat the small white van with the name on the side: MAGRATH. There were windows in the back but they'd been painted over. Nothing in the front but a few loose tools and an out-of-date tabloid newspaper. Rebus tapped the details of

383

the licence plate into his phone's notebook before retracing his steps towards the seafront and his Saab.

60

'What are you doing here?' Gillian Dempsey asked.

'Trying to see you,' Rebus said. He'd been waiting for her outside Northern Constabulary HQ for over an hour. 'I got the front desk to buzz up to you.'

'I've been rather busy.' She was walking towards her car. Her driver already had the rear door open for her. Dempsey was trying to control the sheaf of papers tucked under her arm while still hanging on to her shoulder bag and briefcase. The few journalists waiting on the pavement seemed to know better than to expect any of their questions to be answered. They were kept at a distance anyway, courtesy of two uniformed officers who had somehow merited their thankless task.

'They wouldn't let me in,' Rebus went on, walking beside Dempsey. 'My ID wasn't good enough.'

'We've had our fair share of gawpers,' Dempsey explained. 'Even a few reporters trying their luck.'

'Including your nephew?' Rebus couldn't help asking. She stopped and gave him a hard stare.

'What is it you want, Rebus?'

'I think I'm on to something.'

'So write it up and Page can run it by me.'

'We need to cut a few corners here.'

'Why?'

384

'Because otherwise we're giving him time to dispose of any evidence.'

She thought for a moment. 'In other words, he knows you suspect him?'

'Sorry about that.'

Dempsey sighed and rolled her eyes. 'Get in the car,' she said. 'Let's hear what you've got to say.'

Rebus didn't know the destination or how long he might have, so he spoke quickly, making a few mistakes which he then had to go back and correct. Dempsey sat next to him, the armrest pulled down between them. Classical music was playing softly—her choice rather than the driver's, Rebus reckoned. She asked the occasional question, and only met his eyes when he'd finished talking.

'That's it?' she said. 'That's all you've got?'

'I've had worse hunches.'

'Oh, I can believe that.' She started checking messages on her phone. 'But we're up to our eyes. People are screaming for a result, and we've had every lunatic on the planet phoning us to assist—either shopping themselves or some neighbour they don't like. There are spiritualists who are in touch with the victims, and ghost-hunters who just need access to the site for a night. Every last shred has to be logged and added to the pile, and now you come riding back into town with a *hunch*?'

She shook her head slowly, then gave a laugh that only came, Rebus suspected, because the alternative would have been a bellow of frustration and rage.

'It's pretty straightforward,' Rebus reasoned. 'Search his home, garage and van. Check CCTV at the Pitlochry petrol station for the day Annette McKie disappeared. Then interview him concerning his whereabouts on the days the other women were abducted.'

'Well, I'm glad one of us has it all figured out.'

'Killers usually live in the vicinity of their disposal sites.'

'You got that from your friend Clarke.'

'Kenny Magrath *knows* Edderton.'

She studied him, as if for the very first time. 'You look exhausted,' she said. 'Exhausted *and* hung-over. When was the last time you can truthfully say you were thinking straight? Head lucid, no jumble or muddle?'

'Are we talking about me or you?'

'We're talking about you.'

'Because I can see how a case like this would grind you down until you just wanted it all to go away.'

'I've got work to do, Rebus. Actual work—not just jumping to conclusions. Don't forget, we may still be one body short—despite that previous 'hunch' of yours about Sally Hazlitt.'

'Sally Hazlitt's alive,' Rebus stated. 'I met up with her in Glasgow.'

'What?'

'She was running away from her father's attentions. As of now, she's still running.'

'Why am I only hearing this now?'

'Because it doesn't change the facts. There's a killer out there and I've just given you a name.'

'I need *more* than a name! I've got dozens of names! How dare you not tell me about meeting that girl!'

'You should have asked for the files,' he couldn't help snapping back at her.

Her face darkened further as she turned towards

her driver. 'Alex, stop the car! At once!' Then, to Rebus: 'This is where you get out.'

The car had screeched to a halt. Rebus made no effort to open the door.

'I'm telling you,' he ploughed on, 'the longer you leave this, the more stupid you're going to look.'

'Alex,' Dempsey said, her tone alerting her driver to what was needed. He got out and came round to Rebus's side of the car, hauling open the door.

'Bring him in,' Rebus was saying as Dempsey's man gripped him by his lapels. He shared a final few seconds of eye contact with her before finding himself on the pavement, the driver slamming the door closed. Rebus bent a little so he could peer in, but Dempsey was facing the other way.

'Cheers, Alex!' Rebus called out, giving the driver a little wave. 'Mind how you go!' The car signalled and moved off again, easing into the stream of traffic, leaving Rebus standing by the side of a busy arterial road.

Somewhere on the outskirts of Inverness, with no idea how to get back to his Saab.

'Nicely played yet again, John,' he muttered to himself, reaching into his pocket for his cigarettes.

In the end, it was a thirty-five-minute walk, with just the one fellow pedestrian issuing a set of erroneous directions . . .

*   *   *

The lock-up was easy to find—he just went to the pub and asked. The pub was on a sharp bend in the road at the northern end of Rosemarkie, at the top of the lane leading down to the beach and the homes of both Magrath brothers. The lock-up was

387

directly across from it, next to a modern bungalow, a low brick wall separating the two. There was a gravel parking area in front, and that was where Rebus's Saab ended up. The wooden doors to the garage were held fast by a padlock. There was just the one window, protected on the outside by chicken wire and with what looked like a polythene carrier bag pinned to the inside, blocking prying eyes. Rebus returned to his car and switched the CD player back on. Nothing to do but wait. He had purchased supplies at the pub—two packets of cheese and onion crisps and two small bags of salted peanuts. He still had a half-full bottle of water on the passenger seat. There was very little traffic. As far as he knew, the road led only to Cromarty. He checked the map and saw that it was the A832. With his finger he traced the route back to the A9, and from there all the way south to Perth. Then back up again, this time staying on the A9 until the Dornoch Firth, heading inland towards Tongue. His finger rested there as he remembered the view from Samantha's house, and the interior visible through the living room window, giving him hints and clues to her life. Durness and Laxford and Colaboll and Lairg, then Edderton. Rebus pressed the palm of his hand against the Saab's steering wheel.

'A lot of ground we've covered, old-timer,' he told the car.

When the CD ended, he tried the radio, but the signal came and went, leaving the choice of ceilidh music or nothing. So he swapped John Martyn for some early Wishbone Ash and leaned back in his seat, closing his eyes.

When he woke up, it was to absolute silence. His neck was stiff as he angled his head towards

388

his watch. He couldn't read the dial, so he switched
on his phone instead. Two in the morning. The
pub was in darkness. He took a slug of water and
got out, walking over to the lock-up and relieving
himself against its side wall. Back in the Saab, he
checked his phone for messages, but there weren't
any. He rubbed some feeling back into his arms and
legs. The temperature was not going to drop as far
as zero tonight: too much cloud cover. He stared at
the padlock on the door in front of him for a while,
then felt his vision blurring and closed his eyes
again.

61

A fist on the near-side window woke him. It was
growing light outside and he turned his head to see
Kenny Magrath's face inches from him. Magrath
was opening the door of the Saab.

'What the hell do you think you're up to?' the
man snarled.

'Stopping you moving anything.'

'Moving what?'

'Evidence.'

'You're off your damned head.'

'Seven in the morning—what else would you be
doing here?'

'Picking up what I need,' Magrath explained.
'Got a forty-minute drive ahead of me.' He stared
at Rebus for a moment longer, then shook his head
slowly and walked over to the padlock, digging
in his pocket for the key. 'Take a look,' he called
out. 'I won't even ask for a search warrant, with

389

you not being a cop and all.' The door was flung open; Magrath disappeared inside and switched on the light. Rebus got out of the car, stretching his spine while checking to left and right. Nobody else about. Not a single living soul. He walked to the doorway and stopped there. One wall consisted of home-made shelves filled with plastic tubs containing electrical parts: sockets, switches, fuses, junction boxes. A workbench stretched the length of the wall opposite, the one with the window above it. Either side of this window, tools hung from nails and hooks. There were broken appliances spread out on the bench, their components neatly arranged in what Rebus guessed was the order of dismantling. Magrath was stuffing packets of screws, washers and rawl plugs into his jacket.

'Getting a good butcher's?' he asked. 'Open the drawers if you like. And there are cardboard boxes and biscuit tins under the bench—you won't want to miss those.'

'Look at me,' Rebus said quietly. Magrath turned his head towards him. 'Have you heard the story of Dennis Nilsen?'

'Should I have?'

'They found human remains in the drains on his street. Moment he answered his door to CID, the detective knew.' Rebus paused. 'That was in London, but when I saw you yesterday, the same thing happened. I *know*, Kenny. I saw it in your eyes. Bear that in mind.' He paused again. 'So if you're going to use that screwdriver, this might be your only chance . . .'

Magrath looked down at his hand, and the tool clenched in it. He placed it back on the surface of the bench, taking his time.

'I can see you're methodical,' Rebus went on, eyes sweeping the garage. 'You're neat and you're careful. Explains why you've stayed off the radar all these years—that and having a brother who's tried his damnedest to keep an eye on you. But you're on the radar now, Kenny. Dead centre and with nothing else near you on the screen.'

'I haven't done anything.'

'You're thinking about them right now—especially Annette McKie. She's freshest in your mind. You're feeling your fingers around her throat.'

'You're mad.' Magrath looked around him, as if wondering if he'd forgotten anything. He pressed a hand to each of his bulging pockets, then moved towards Rebus. Rebus stepped back, so that Magrath could switch the light off and lock the door again.

'Did you tell Gregor, or did he somehow work it out? Maybe back when you were kids he saw the warning signs.'

'What signs?'

'Pulling the legs off frogs maybe; tying fireworks to the tails of cats and dogs . . .'

Magrath shook his head. 'That's not me—go ask him.'

'Maybe I will. It's about time he got this off his conscience. Same with your wife.'

'You leave Maggie out of this!'

'Bit late for that.'

'So help me I'll . . .' Magrath was just about keeping his rage in check. When he took a deep breath and exhaled, it sounded like a growl. Rebus stood his ground, awaiting the man's next move. Magrath seemed to consider his options, and ended

391

up turning away, striding towards his parked van.

'Where are you going, Kenny?'

No answer.

'You were in Pitlochry, weren't you?'

Magrath was getting into the van, avoiding eye contact. Rebus walked towards him slowly. The key was turned in the ignition; Magrath commenced a three-point turn. A minibus coming around the corner from the direction of Cromarty had to brake hard to avoid crashing into him. There were a handful of schoolkids in the back. The driver sounded his horn, but Magrath ignored him, the van roaring off in the direction of Fortrose. Rebus lit a breakfast cigarette and decided he'd done what he could. Two minutes later he was parking outside Gregor Magrath's cottage. The wind had dropped and there were the usual dog-walkers on the beach. Rebus caught a glimpse of something out to sea that could have been a dolphin or a seal. He thumped on Magrath's door and waited. Magrath came out to the porch and studied Rebus through the window.

'We need to talk about your brother,' Rebus called out to him.

The man shook his head slowly.

'Did you move here to stop him? If so, you did a piss-poor job.'

'Go away,' Magrath said.

'It was all right for the first year or so, but after that . . .'

'Go away!' Magrath was shouting now.

'It's all ending, Gregor,' Rebus persisted. 'Surely you can see that. Time to call a halt and save what's left of your reputation.'

'I'm not listening!'

'You've got to convince him—easier for all concerned if he turns himself in. Tell him he should think of Maggie, if nobody else . . .'

Gregor Magrath's look was full of loathing, but Rebus saw a trace of resignation too. The man turned away and went back indoors. Rebus bided his time and Magrath reappeared in the porch, this time brandishing the wooden truncheon.

'That won't do it,' Rebus told him with a shake of the head and the faintest of smiles. 'Not any longer. I know it's about protecting family—and maybe protecting your own name while you're at it. But moving up here hasn't stopped him. Time for the next step, Gregor.'

'Go to hell!'

Magrath disappeared inside again, and though Rebus stood there for a further few minutes, giving the door an occasional blow with his fist, he knew the man wasn't coming back this time. He returned to the Saab and called Siobhan Clarke in Edinburgh.

'Bit early for you,' she complained.

'Did I wake you?'

'Not quite.' He thought he could hear her sit up in bed. Her mouth seemed to be dry and she cleared her throat. 'So where's the fire?'

'I'm in Rosemarkie,' Rebus admitted.

'Doing what exactly?'

'It's Magrath's brother, Siobhan, I'd swear to it.'

'What?'

'Magrath moved north to try to keep a lid on it. The brother travels all over. He was in Glasgow the day Annette McKie was abducted, and he'd have driven up the A9 to get home.' Rebus rubbed his free hand across the stubble on his cheeks and chin.

393

'Wait a second.' He listened as she walked into another room. 'Can you prove any of this?'

'I told Dempsey, we need forensics on Magrath's van, plus searches of his home and garage.'

'You *told* Dempsey?'

'She's not going to bite unless I can give her something. That's why I thought of you.'

'Are you off your head?'

'Everybody seems to think so—but I *know* it's him.'

'That's not the way it works, John.' She paused, only now registering something he'd said a moment back. 'What do you need me for?'

'The phone number of that petrol station in Pitlochry. I want to take a look at their CCTV. If Annette hitched a lift in the town, Kenny Magrath must have *been* in the town.'

'He pulled off the A9 to fill up?'

'Maybe.'

She gave a lengthy sigh. He imagined her seated on the edge of her sofa, elbow on knee, hand pressed to forehead. Not quite ready to face the day yet, and already landed with this.

'The longer he has, the more chance we're giving him to dump anything that could be incriminating.'

'Hang on a minute, then,' she said, getting to her feet. She found the number and gave it to him twice while he jotted it down and checked it.

'Thanks, Siobhan.'

'I suppose Dempsey will have contacted James,' she commented.

'I dare say I'm in for yet another bollocking.'

'Except that you're not a cop any more.' She paused. 'Which means I shouldn't even be talking to you, and *you* shouldn't be doing this.'

394

'Aren't I naughty?' Rebus said with a tired smile. Then: 'I thought I saw a dolphin earlier.'

'Or maybe a selkie?'

'You implying I see things that aren't there, DI Clarke?'

'How many lies are you going to tell the petrol station?'

'As few as necessary. I'll talk to you later.'

'Always supposing they allow you more than one phone call,' she said.

Rebus managed another smile before punching in the number she had given him. But the petrol station's footage for the day of Annette McKie's disappearance was not available.

'You've already got it,' he was told.

'It's at Inverness?' Rebus nodded his comprehension, ended the call and tried another number.

'John?' Gavin Arnold answered. 'What can I do for you this fine, stress-free morning?'

'Raise those stress levels, maybe,' Rebus suggested.

'By doing what?'

'Bending a few rules,' Rebus answered, going on to explain his request.

62

Fox was usually first into the Complaints office, but not today. Tony Kaye was standing behind Fox's desk, holding a cardboard beaker of coffee in one hand and using the other to sift through one of the stacks of paperwork relating to John Rebus.

'Early bird,' Fox said, shrugging off his coat and hanging it up.

'Thought I'd maybe have a word before Joe Naysmith arrives.'

'Lost your phone?'

'I thought this was best done face to face.'

'Spit it out, then.'

Kaye rested a hand on one of the piles of paper. 'You know what I'm going to say.'

'You're going to tell me we're wasting our time.'

'The guy's old-school, Malcolm. It's amazing any of them still survive.'

'So he's some kind of endangered species and we should be feeding him bamboo?'

'A good hunter knows when not to pull the trigger.'

'You've seen the phone logs, Tony: is there any villain in the city he's *not* cosied up to?'

'DI Clarke said it—if Rebus is attached to the McKie case, he's got plenty of reasons for talking to Frank Hammell.'

'And Cafferty?'

'Used to be Hammell's employer.'

Fox shook his head slowly. 'The man's a liability—and dangerous with it.'

'That's for the board to decide.'

'With our input. Are you saying I put a halo over Rebus's head?'

'Just stick to the *facts*. Don't let it get personal.'

'Who says it's personal?'

'It is, though. You worked CID at St Leonard's, same time he did.'

'So?'

'I remember you once telling me, not every good detective fits in at Complaints.'

'Are you saying I couldn't hack it in CID?'

It was Kaye's turn to shake his head. 'I'm saying Rebus got results the old way, without seeming to earn them. He did that because he got close to some nasty people in a way you couldn't. *This* is what you're good at, Malcolm.' He tapped the desk. 'Rebus specialises in something a bit different—doesn't necessarily make him the enemy.'

'We've got to be accountable, Tony. Rebus and his ilk don't see that. In point of fact, I think he gets his jollies sticking two fingers up to the rest of us.'

'Doesn't make him the enemy,' Kaye repeated quietly.

Fox's phone vibrated, letting him know he had a message. He looked at the screen, then at his colleague.

'Have you mentioned any of this to the Chief?'

Kaye shook his head. 'Why?'

'Because he wants a word.' Fox's eyes scanned the mass of paperwork. There were boxes of it on the floor next to his desk. Thousands of pages detailing dozens of infractions. But dozens of arrests, too. And no smoking gun. Same with the notes at Fox's house—all of it circumstantial; easy to read into it anything you liked.

'You think it's about Rebus?' Tony Kaye was asking.

'What else?' Fox said, making for the door.

*   *   *

'They could bounce me down the stairs for this,' Arnold complained, meeting Rebus outside Northern Constabulary HQ.

Rebus held out a brown paper bag, which Arnold

397

took and opened, pulling out a croissant and biting into it. Then he gestured for Rebus to follow him into the building, where he was signed in as a visitor and handed a pass, 'to be worn at all times'.

Arnold was still chewing as they reached the inquiry room. He made another gesture—letting Rebus know he should wait there—before disappearing through the door. When he came out again, he was holding a clear plastic envelope containing several CD-sized silver disks.

'Laptop?' he asked.

Rebus shook his head.

Arnold gave a twitch of the mouth as if to indicate that he'd expected this. He led Rebus along the corridor until he found a room with an unused desk. He gave the mouse a nudge, activating the monitor, then entered his password.

'CaleyThis?' Rebus enquired.

'Short for Caledonian Thistle.' Arnold pulled out the chair and nodded for Rebus to sit down. The disk drive was on the floor beneath the desk, and he crouched in front of it, sliding home the first of the disks.

'Eight hours' worth,' he warned Rebus.

'Won't take me nearly that long.'

'Anybody asks, you tell them whatever story you like.'

'Keeping your name out of it?' Rebus guessed. Then he held out his hand. 'Thanks, Gavin.'

The two men shook, and Arnold left him to it.

Rebus reckoned he could focus on a specific hour of comings and goings on the petrol station's forecourt—thirty minutes either side of Annette McKie's arrival in Pitlochry. The first disk he tried was no help, being too early in the day. Ditto the second and third. When he got to the fourth, he fast-forwarded, keeping an eye on the clock in the corner of the screen. Eventually, when he was happy, he leaned forwards and watched intently.

* * *

Dempsey couldn't place him at first. When she did, her face tightened. 'How the hell did you get in here?'

Rebus had hidden the visitor's badge in his pocket. 'Not a crime, is it?' he asked.

'Actually, it probably is.'

He had found her in one of the meeting rooms. She had been seated but was now standing. The other officer was wondering what was going on. Dempsey dismissed the man with a wave and an announcement that they would finish their discussion later. Once she was alone with Rebus, she folded her arms and waited.

'I've got him,' was all Rebus said. She saw that he was holding a small silver object in one hand.

* * *

Both Magrath brothers, along with Kenny's wife Maggie, were brought in for questioning that same afternoon. Search warrants had been applied for, and Dempsey seemed to think they wouldn't be long arriving. Meantime, preliminary questions were being asked of neighbours in Rosemarkie.

The media had reacted quickly to the news. The ranks of reporters had swollen outside HQ, and a radio car was in position, a satellite dish on its roof. No TV as yet, or none that Rebus could see from the windows of the inquiry room. He had asked to be present at the interviews, but Dempsey had put the kibosh on it. He wasn't even a serving police officer—a lawyer could make 'potentially devastating' use of that.

'In fact,' she'd told him, 'best thing would be if you went back to Edinburgh. And remind me, how *did* you get in here in the first place?'

She'd said she would call him with news—she didn't want him to think she was ungrateful. But as yet it was all just supposition mixed with what might turn out to be coincidence.

And that was it: Rebus was dismissed.

He texted a brief thank you to Gavin Arnold, not being able to track him down in the flesh, and headed outdoors. Raymond, Dempsey's nephew, nodded a greeting and asked if he had any comment. The other journalists frowned and twitched, not knowing who Rebus was. They quickly gathered round Raymond, keen to be included. Rebus took his time getting a cigarette lit before he spoke.

'Persons of interest are currently being interviewed by DCS Dempsey and her team,' he obliged.

'Any names?'

Rebus kept his eyes on Raymond. The young man was pointing his phone, using it as a mic.

'The persons of interest are local,' Rebus went on. 'I don't doubt tongues are wagging . . .'

Then he got into his car and started the engine.

Was he heading home? He wasn't sure. First he drove to Rosemarkie and cruised past the lock-up. Kenny Magrath's van was parked in front, and Rebus stopped, getting out to peer through its windows again. It looked exactly the same as before, except for a Tupperware box and a Thermos—lunch prepared by Maggie, at a guess. A leftover sandwich was visible through the plastic. The lock-up itself still boasted its padlock. Rebus walked around the vehicle. It was small, with thin tyres, their tread reduced through use. Could a van like this have been driven into the woods at Edderton without getting stuck? Rebus checked for damage but didn't find any, just a bit of mud. The van was only a year or so old, judging by the number plate. He was walking around it again, checking more closely for non-existent scrapes and scuffs, when the forensics team arrived. There were four of them—two in a Ford Transit and two in a Vauxhall Astra. One of them recognised Rebus from the Portakabin at Edderton. He jutted out his chin and gave a twitch of the head, as much acknowledgement as Rebus was going to get.

Before anyone else could ask who he was or demand ID, Rebus garnered all the authority he could muster and explained that they would find the lock-up well organised and with few obvious hiding places.

'You might want to check the perimeter,' he added. 'If he's kept any trophies, I doubt they're going to be under your noses.'

'Why do you say that?' he was asked.

'I was here with him earlier. He seemed perfectly relaxed about a search of the place.'

The questioner nodded his understanding.

'Have all the warrants been signed?' Rebus enquired, receiving another nod for his efforts. 'Both brothers' homes?'

'That's right.'

'I think you might want to add the green Land Rover sitting outside Gregor Magrath's place. Not sure who it belongs to, but strikes me it should be checked. More of an all-terrain vehicle than this.' Rebus gestured towards the van.

'Why don't you arrange that, then?' the team leader asked.

'Not my job,' Rebus explained, retreating to the Saab.

63

He was back at Whicher's. Now that the initial fuss about the bodies had died down, they had rooms available, but Rebus wasn't sure he would be staying. Instead, he sat in the lounge, plugged in his phone for a recharge, and ordered a helping of steak pie and chips, along with a pot of tea.

During a trip to the toilets, he had a wash and studied himself in the mirror. He looked like a man who had slept in his car. At reception, they handed him a pack containing toothbrush, toothpaste, razor and shaving cream, and he returned to the toilets for a patch-up job.

With his belly full and another pot of tea on its way, he felt more human. There were plenty of papers to help him bide his time, plus the hotel's copy of *Cracking the Code*. He'd asked for the TV to be tuned to a news channel, but with the sound muted.

'No trouble at all, sir,' he'd been told by the waiter in the tartan waistcoat.

A couple of hours passed with no word from

Dempsey. Rebus checked that his phone was still getting a healthy signal. When it did eventually ring, caller ID told him it was Siobhan Clarke on the line. Rebus answered.

'Dempsey's just been having a word with James Page,' she told him. 'She's wondering if you're back in Edinburgh yet.'

'And?'

'And James spoke to DS Cowan at SCRU, but he hasn't seen you either.'

'Funny, that.'

'You're still in Inverness?'

'Of course I am.' He told her about the CCTV—Kenny Magrath stopping to refuel at the petrol station no more than five minutes after Annette McKie had left it on foot—then about Kenny and Gregor Magrath being taken in for questioning. 'Did Dempsey tell Page whether the interviews had finished?'

'No idea,' Clarke confessed.

'You and him not best buddies?'

'Leave it, John.'

'Pity—I really liked the guy.'

'You don't take a telling, do you?'

Rebus smiled to himself. 'Dempsey was supposed to be updating me,' he went on to explain. 'That's why I'm still here.'

'You really think this is it, don't you?'

'Hope springs eternal.'

'Well, I'm not sure Dempsey sounded like a woman on the verge of a breakthrough.'

Rebus had another caller. Number blocked. He told Clarke he'd phone her back.

'Rebus?' Gillian Dempsey said.

'Any news?'

403

'They've been questioned and released.'

'And?'

'And there's not much else to say. Kenny Magrath's work premises and van have been gone over—stuff's been sent to the lab but the team didn't sound hopeful. Same goes for both houses.'

'What about the Land Rover?'

Dempsey paused. 'That was *your* idea, was it? Well, our friendly sheriff signed an extra warrant, but again it looks clean.'

'Clean or cleaned?'

'Somebody may have cleaned it in recent memory,' she admitted. 'But not with the thoroughness you're implying. Besides, we know it was the van in Pitlochry rather than another vehicle, don't we?'

'What does he say about the stop for petrol?'

'He was on his way back from visiting his son in Glasgow and his tank was low.'

'You don't think that's quite a coincidence?'

'As it happens, I do, and so did he—he told his wife as much when Annette McKie became news, asked her if he should maybe come forward. She reasoned there wasn't much point if he hadn't seen anything.'

'Funny she didn't mention that to me.' Rebus closed his eyes and rubbed his hand across them.

'You think she's covering for him?'

'Sometimes that's what families do.'

'Well,' Dempsey went on, unless the lab finds something, we're at a bit of a dead end, aren't we?'

'Did you look at him in the interview room? I mean, *really* look him in the eye?'

'I did more than that. I had a psychologist watching the camera feed. They didn't see anything

404

that rang alarm bells. This is a family man, Rebus. Two grown-up kids and a doting wife. Neighbours full of praise and not so much as a speeding ticket to his name.'

'Will you at least do a bit more digging? Check where he was when the other victims were snatched ...'

'I've asked him. He's going to have to go back through his paperwork to find out.'

'Shouldn't that be *your* job?'

'We've sent an officer to the house to fetch it all,' she said coldly. 'But as of this moment, we're still at that same dead end.' She paused. 'Incidentally, can I ask where *you* are? Doesn't sound like you're driving.'

'I'm not. I stopped at House of Bruar for a break.'

'You're heading back to Edinburgh, then?'

'Just as you ordered.' Rebus rattled the cup in its saucer, so she could hear it. 'But you'll let me know if there's any news?'

'Of course. Oh, and by the way—giving that impromptu statement to my nephew? Not your brightest move, despite the manifest competition ...'

She hung up on him, and he set the phone down on the table next to the teapot. He was the only person in the lounge. The papers had been gone through from cover to cover, and the TV was still showing footage of some football manager's fall from grace. It seemed as if the story was on a fifteen-minute loop, same pictures each and every time, and nothing about Edderton, not even on the ticker tape of breaking news along the bottom of the screen.

'What the hell do I do now?' Rebus asked himself. The answer came to him. 'Cigarette,' he said, rising to his feet.

Forty minutes later, he was seated in the lounge again, staring into space, his mind swirling with thoughts, when he saw a face he knew: Gavin Arnold, in full uniform, cap tucked beneath one arm.

'What are you doing here?' Rebus asked him.

'Looking for you, at DCS Dempsey's behest. This was second on my list.'

'After?'

'The Lochinver.'

'Want to sit down?'

Arnold shook his head, looming over Rebus.

'I told her I was at House of Bruar,' Rebus went on.

'Seems she wasn't taken in. My orders are to escort you to the A9 and stick with you as far as Daviot.'

'I'm being run out of town by the sheriff?'

'That you are, Hopalong.'

'I didn't grass you up, Gavin.'

'I know that. But if she set her mind to it, it wouldn't take her five minutes to work out I'm the one who got you that visitor's pass.'

'Well, we'd better get you into her good books pronto, then.' Rebus rose to his feet and reached for his jacket. 'But if you should happen to hear anything on the grapevine . . .'

'You'd be grateful for a tip-off?' Arnold guessed with a smile. 'Tell me, is it possible for anyone to come to know you without them always feeling they're slipping their neck into a noose?'

'You'd have to ask my legion of friends.'

406

'Do you need to settle up?' Arnold nodded towards the teapot.

'Already done,' Rebus assured him.

'We're ready for the off, then.'

Rebus stopped in front of him, their faces mere inches apart. 'Kenny Magrath did it, Gavin. I've never been so sure of anything in my life.'

'Then we'll catch him,' Arnold said.

'Will we, though? We don't always, you know.'

As they passed the reception desk, Rebus thought of Sally Hazlitt and the alternative identity she'd created, far from friends and family, spending her life always in motion, never quite able to trust or settle or drop her guard.

*   *   *

Arnold's patrol car stayed on Rebus's tail until the Daviot signpost, then dropped back, flashing its headlights a couple of times as if to say a final, defining farewell.

Part Six

Woke up this morning, I had snow in my eyes
And I've been sleeping under terrible skies . . .

64

Nothing happened.

Rebus went into work each day and watched as more and more boxes were decanted. Men in overalls came with trolleys to take them away, and someone from the Crown Office Cold Case Unit arrived to thank them for their work and offer assurances that none of the cases on Lothian and Borders' books would be forgotten. This man seemed already to know Daniel Cowan, and the two of them disappeared for a long lunch. Afterwards, Cowan's cheeks were rosy and he had a wide smile for everyone in the room.

'You got the job, didn't you?' Elaine Robison asked, while Rebus and Peter Bliss feigned a lack of interest.

'Nothing's official yet.'

'You did, though,' she went on, and Cowan's smile grew broader.

SCRU was being wound up at the end of the week, but by Wednesday the shelves were empty. An IT technician went through their computers, saving files on to a single portable hard drive before deleting everything.

'Means we can recycle the units,' he explained.

Watching, Rebus was reminded of the scene in *2001*, the voice of HAL slowing down inexorably.

'To think of all the blood, sweat and tears,' Bliss commented.

Rebus had taken him out for a drink one evening, laying out his theories about Gregor and Kenny Magrath. Bliss had been reluctant to concede any of the possibilities proposed, and had eventually walked out of the bar, since when his attitude had been one of professional courtesy only. Rebus had left a note on his colleague's desk—*Just have a think back—does anything jar?*—which Bliss had crumpled into a ball and dropped into the waste-paper bin.

'You two,' Robison had chided them. 'Why can't you play nice?'

'He started it,' Rebus had answered, hoping to elicit a smile from Bliss.

A forlorn hope, as it turned out.

He spoke to Siobhan Clarke by phone, keeping up to date with the Inverness inquiry, Gavin Arnold having been warned—presumably by Dempsey—not to pass titbits to him. Clarke wasn't much help. Now that the Inverness team had all the information on Annette McKie from the Edinburgh end, James Page and his officers were being frozen out. Dempsey had even come south, reinterviewing Gail McKie, Frank Hammell and Thomas Redfern. A further request had seen the bus station's CCTV footage forwarded to Northern Constabulary HQ.

'None of which is going to help them,' Rebus had told Clarke. 'They're just scratching around for want of anything else to do.'

Nothing prejudicial had been found in either Magrath's van or the Land Rover. After exhaustive tests, nothing alien on or in Annette McKie's body could be linked to Kenny Magrath—the pubic hair had belonged to Frank Hammell. The funeral had eventually been allowed to go ahead, as had services for the other four victims. Watching the footage on TV—Darryl leading the mourners, his mother clinging to his arm, Hammell nowhere to be seen—Rebus realised he knew the cemetery: it was the same one where Jimmy Wallace was buried. He remembered that day, the pall-bearers called forward by number, the wailing widow, and Tommy Beamish sidling up to him.

Too many like Jimmy—gold watch, and soon after they're on a slab . . . Is that why you keep working . . .?

Well, of course it bloody was. What the hell was he going to do next week—take up fishing, or buy a dog? Or more likely sit staring at a gantry of drinks like some of the old-timers he knew, treating a stint at the pub almost as if it were a job in itself.

He'd met Malcolm Fox on the stairs one day, and Fox had stopped to tell him that the Complaints had ceased to have 'an active interest' in him.

'Oh?'

'For the moment, that is. So good luck with your application.'

'Aye, right.'

'I mean it,' Fox had said, eyes drilling into Rebus's. 'I *want* you back on the force. You'll screw up sooner rather than later and that's when we'll get to know one another better. I just pray you don't take the likes of Siobhan Clarke down with you . . .'

On the Thursday, Elaine Robison had tried to fix a time and place for farewell drinks the following night, but Peter Bliss had grown cool on the idea.

'I've got plans,' he'd said.

'The weekend, then?'

Bliss had shaken his head. 'Let's just call it a day, eh? It's not like we've anything to celebrate.'

'Peter . . .'

But Bliss had made up his mind. He couldn't

413

even find it in himself to meet Rebus's eyes. Not until the Friday afternoon, when they were emptying the contents of their desk drawers into carrier bags, readying to walk out of the office for the last time. Daniel Cowan had already said his goodbyes—he'd gone to a meeting of the new unit, a spring in his step. Robison was in the loo. Bliss had picked his moment and confronted Rebus.

'Gregor Magrath was one of the good guys,' he stated. 'In my books, he still is and always will be. What you're trying to do is take a dump all over his legacy. I won't have any part of that, and I'll never forgive you for it.'

'Have you talked to him?' Rebus asked.

'He's in agonies about this. Taken in for questioning on your say-so.' Colour was rising to Bliss's cheeks, his voice beginning to shake with emotion.

'He's been covering his brother's arse for years.'

'You're like a stuck record, Rebus.'

'Maybe so, but the song's still a smash. Magrath played you, Peter—is that what sticks in your craw?'

'The man deserves some dignity.'

'And what do the victims deserve, eh?'

Bliss made a guttural sound and snatched the carrier bag from his desk, shoving his way past Rebus and stalking down the corridor. Robison came back to find Rebus waiting for her.

'Guess this is it,' she said. Then she noted Bliss's absence.

'He was in a hurry,' Rebus apologised. She tried giving him a hard look, but her heart wasn't in it. They embraced and she pecked his cheek.

'Here's to fresh pastures,' she said, squeezing his arm. Rebus closed the door after them.

414

That evening, after one too many drinks, he made the usual call. The phone rang at the other end, and kept ringing until the automated voice told him to leave a message.

'We have to talk, Gregor. You know we do. This has to end.' Then he repeated his phone number before hanging up. The first half-dozen times, Magrath had actually answered, ending the call only when Rebus identified himself. Since then, however, he had let the machine pick up for him.

Rebus studied his reflection in the living room window. 'Friday night in the big city, eh?' he told it, as rain dribbled down the panes. The copies of the missing persons files were still sitting on his dining table, and he pulled out a chair and seated himself in front of them. One day soon he would feel able to bin them, but not just yet. So far nothing had been found that could place Kenny Magrath near the other women on the days they'd been abducted. His paperwork had proved incomplete, but then whose wasn't? He didn't keep a diary or hang on to calendars and notebooks, and neither did his wife. Rebus reached across to the bottle of beer and took a slug from it. His hand rested against a letter that had been sitting there a couple of days, the one inviting him to interview by Lothian and Borders Police Applications Board. There was a date for his medical, plus a sheet to be signed and returned, once its boxes had been ticked. Rebus read through it for the umpteenth time as he rubbed the guitar pick between his fingers.

'Maybe if I'd bought the actual bloody guitar,' he muttered to himself, before rising to his feet in search of a pen.

Cafferty's house was a detached Victorian mansion on a leafy street off Colinton Road. It sat in half an acre of grounds with its own coach house. There were plenty of public rooms, but Cafferty usually retreated to his study with its view of the back garden. There was a big old chair there that he'd owned since he was in his twenties. He sat in it to read books, and to think. Tonight he was thinking about Darryl Christie. Christie had invited him to Annette's funeral. Cafferty had duly turned up at the chapel, noting that the young man had brought some muscle with him—half a dozen faces Cafferty didn't know. Young but toughened—maybe army vets who'd bailed from Iraq or Afghanistan. They stood apart from the main phalanx of mourners and followed at a distance when the procession headed for the graveside, Darryl and his two younger brothers acting as pall-bearers with three other men.

No Frank Hammell. No Derek Christie.

The cop from up north was there. Cafferty didn't know her name, but he'd seen her on TV. He'd thought he might see Rebus, but that was another no-show. One of the thickset young men had made his way through the mourners towards Cafferty, leaning in to mutter in his ear that 'Mr Christie would like a word before you go.' Cafferty had hung back, watching people as they readied to go to the reception. Darryl had helped his mother into the limo, pecking her on the cheek and closing the door. Then he'd straightened his jacket and tie and headed for Cafferty. Cafferty held out a hand but Christie ignored it.

'You holding up?' Cafferty had felt it polite to ask.

'That's not the question you really want an answer to.'

'All right then—where's Frank Hammell?'

'He's out of the game. Signed all his businesses over to me.' Christie's eyes had come to rest on Cafferty's. 'Is that okay with you?'

'Why shouldn't it be?'

'Because you still want to feel like a player. But we both know that's not going to happen now. I've seen the way you operate, and that means I'm armed for any fight you want to start.'

'I'm past all that.'

'Those are the right words, but your brain needs to start believing them. I've studied hard, Cafferty, and I know which bits of this city Hammell controlled. As things stand, I'm not looking for a war—what's yours is still yours. Only thing that'll change that is if you decide this is a good time to try a bit of poaching or border-crossing. Do we understand one another?'

And only then had Christie reached out his hand towards Cafferty. The kid was eighteen! *Eighteen!* At eighteen, Cafferty had been no more than a foot soldier. And now he was being told what was what by a skinny waif with a Napoleon complex and a handful of paid minders to stop him coming to harm.

But he had shaken the hand nonetheless.

Now, as he sat in his study, he knew Darryl Christie had made the right move at the right time. The changeover had been smooth. Hammell was keeping his head down, but as yet no one was saying he wouldn't be seen alive.

417

What's yours is still yours . . . as things stand . . .

The cheek of the little bastard!

A clever sod, though; not to be underestimated or misjudged. Cafferty was embarrassed at the way he himself had played the whole thing—trying to be avuncular, an arm around a shoulder—when Darryl already had his plans in place, as cool and calculating as you liked.

It was to be admired, at least in the short term.

But when all was said and done, the lad was still in his teens. There were hard lessons he had not yet learned. Mistakes would be made, along with enemies. No one was untouchable.

No one.

Which was why Cafferty rose from his chair and checked that both front and back doors were bolted . . .

65

On Saturday morning, Rebus called Magrath again. This time, the phone did not ring. Instead, a different automated voice told him the number he had dialled had not been recognised and he should try again. He took more care the second time, but got the selfsame message.

'Changed your number, Gregor?' he asked quietly. Then he nodded to himself and went to take a shower.

By late lunchtime, he was parked on the seafront at Rosemarkie, directly opposite the cottage. He sounded his horn a few times, keeping watch on the windows for signs of life. All the curtains were closed. When he eventually went to check, brushing past the Land Rover, there was mail lying on the mat inside the porch. He went next door and the neighbour answered.

'Remember me?' Rebus asked. 'I was here before.'

The elderly woman agreed that yes, Rebus was not a stranger.

'Just wondering if you've seen hide or hair of Gregor.'

'He was at the shop yesterday, collecting his paper.'

'He's all right, then? It's just that he's not answering his door and the place looks deserted.'

'He's had reporters turning up at all hours,' the woman explained. 'And the phone, too—I can hear it ringing and ringing.' She paused, leaning in towards Rebus and lowering her voice. 'You heard what happened?'

Rebus nodded, as he felt was expected.

'Awful business, just awful. You never think these things will . . . Well, you know what I mean.'

'Plenty of talk in the village, I suppose.'

The woman tilted her head back. 'You wouldn't credit it.'

'Is everybody agreed it's beyond belief?' Rebus was doing his best to sound like a local himself. He had relaxed his stance and was resting his weight against the door frame, arms folded—just two old cronies having a chinwag.

'Beyond belief,' the woman echoed.

'No doubters?' Rebus raised an eyebrow. 'It's just that there usually are.'

'There's hardly a family around here Kenny Magrath hasn't helped out at one time or another.'

419

'I'm sure that's true, but all the same . . .'

But the woman was shaking her head in a resolute fashion.

'So you're all sticking together, looking after your own?' Rebus's tone had hardened. She frowned, took a step back and started to close the door on him.

'Has Gregor given you his new number, by any chance?'

The click of the door as it locked was his only reply. 'Nice speaking to you,' he muttered, returning to Magrath's cottage and hammering on the door.

The rain was falling again—huge sleety gobbets of the stuff, making slapping sounds as they hit his shoulders and back. He retreated to the Saab and sat there, waiting for the storm to pass. The sky was almost black, and he switched the wipers on. Hailstones now, bouncing off the surface of the road, coating it white. Rebus turned the engine on and put the car into reverse, backing seventy feet along the road until he was outside Kenny Magrath's garden. Again, the house looked deserted. The upstairs blinds were closed and the octagonal conservatory had no lights on. The windscreen was steaming up, so he turned the fan to high and opened his window an inch. After a few minutes, the hail stopped. The sky remained leaden, but there wasn't even rain, just a suffocating sense that a weight was being pressed down on the locality. Rebus sucked in lungfuls of air, and wiped sweat from his forehead and neck. He took a cigarette from the packet and realised his hands were trembling. He pressed them together, as if that might help. His heart was pounding, too.

'Not yet,' he said to his chest and the organs within. 'Not just yet, eh?'

He drove up the lane and took a left towards Kenny Magrath's front door. No van. The place definitely felt empty. Another short drive to the lock-up. Still no van. Maybe he worked Saturdays. Or he'd persuaded his wife they needed some time away—with brother Gregor in tow. A chance to check and recheck their stories. Hell, maybe they were just out shopping, a regular jaunt to Inverness or Dingwall. Photographs of both brothers had appeared in the media, but only for a day. They probably had little fear of being recognised outside their immediate community.

Rebus sat there drumming his fingers. He wondered what kind of weekend others were enjoying. Was Siobhan buying food, or off to watch Hibs? Was Daniel Cowan being measured for a suit for his new job? Did Gillian Dempsey have a family dinner planned, maybe with nephew Raymond on the guest list? Supermarkets would be thronged, cinemas preparing to entertain the masses. Lunchtime trade picking up in bars and restaurants, crosswords tackled, walking boots thrown into the backs of estate cars. Skiing and boating and golf. Swimming and indoor games. Kids with homework, adults with chores—queues at the car wash and petrol station. Everyone going about their business. Maybe the Edderton team had been granted enough of a budget to keep covering weekend shifts. But shifts comprising what, exactly? More interviews, paperwork and briefings? To no end other than a slightly swollen pay packet . . .

'What the hell are you doing, John?' he asked himself. Returning to Gregor Magrath's cottage, he wrote out a note and pinned it under one of the Land Rover's windscreen wipers.

All it said was: *This has to end.*

* * *

As he headed home, he noticed that the roadworks to the north of Pitlochry seemed to have finished. It wasn't just that no one was working—one of the Portakabins was being loaded on to a flatbed truck, and the Portaloos had already gone. He wondered what would happen to the men—did they have new projects waiting for them? A never-ending process of digging up and resurfacing?

'Join the club,' he said aloud.

And what of Thomas Robertson? Rebus had phoned Aberdeen Royal Infirmary a few days back, but of course Robertson was no longer a patient. Maybe he was back at the Tummel Arms, explaining to Gina Andrews why he'd lied to her about his conviction. Or maybe he was on the road to somewhere else, no real end point in mind.

Rebus saw that he was down to a quarter-tank of fuel, so he pulled into Pitlochry itself and crawled through the bustling centre until he reached the petrol station. As he started filling up, a voice called to him.

'What happened to the Audi?'

Rebus looked to the next pump along and recognised the rep he'd talked to when he'd been waiting for Clarke to ask her questions in the kiosk.

'Small world,' the man said with a smile

'Cigarette break after?' Rebus suggested. The man looked keen. They filled their tanks in silence, went into the kiosk to pay, and then met up on the pavement next to the main road. A coach party had arrived at the Bell's distillery and was being led into the visitors' centre. Rebus nodded towards the Saab. 'In answer to your question, I'm more the classic-car type.'

The man exhaled a long stream of smoke. 'Didn't catch your line of work last time we met.'

'I'm an ex-cop.'

'So what do you do now?'

'At the moment, I'm still getting used to it.' Rebus flicked ash on to the ground. 'You said you were in 'solutions'.'

'Posh term for sales,' the man admitted.

'You're working today?'

'Tomorrow as well, if anyone wants to see me. It's tough out there, if you hadn't noticed.'

'I'd noticed. What does your wife say?'

The man shrugged. 'We'll open a bottle of wine tonight, try to make the most of it.'

'Got kids?'

'One daughter.'

'Same as me, then.'

'Laurie's in her first year at high school.'

'Mine fled the nest long back.' Rebus paused, studying the tip of his cigarette. 'I don't see her much . . .' They watched the flow of traffic in and out of town. 'I think you told me you drive hundreds of miles a week.'

'Enough so I recognise faces and firms.' He nodded towards a lorry. 'Flowers from Holland. He'll drop off as far north as Aberdeen before heading back to the ferry.'

'I think I've seen him before, too,' Rebus said, remembering the lay-by and the van driver with the busted cigarette lighter.

'First year or two in the job,' the salesman was saying, 'I paid scant attention. In fact, probably no attention at all—far as I was concerned, it was all about me.' He sucked on his cigarette and exhaled. 'But then I'd find myself in the same cafés and petrol stops as people I'd seen before.'

'And you'd strike up conversations?'

The salesman nodded. 'Lonely old life otherwise, isn't it?'

'I suppose.'

'And you get to know spots, like the snack van parked next to the sign saying 'Welcome to the Highlands' . . .'

'The Slochd Summit,' Rebus chipped in.

'One thousand three hundred and twenty-eight feet above sea level,' the rep recited.

'Dewar's World of Whisky . . .'

'Ten miles off the A9.'

The two men shared a smile.

'I have to admit, though, I do like it. Not that I'd tell my wife that. Never feel quite at home when I'm stuck in an office, or even with my feet up in front of the telly.' He looked at Rebus. 'That probably sounds crazy.'

'Not really. When you're on the road, there's always a destination, and you know you're going to reach it one way or another.'

The salesman nodded. 'That's exactly right.'

They smoked in silence for a few moments, until the man coughed and cleared his throat.

'That girl who got murdered near here . . .'

'Annette McKie?'

He nodded again, more solemnly. 'Is that why you were here last time? I seem to remember your colleague asking questions in the kiosk.' He

424

watched as Rebus gave a twitch of agreement. 'I've picked up hitch-hikers in the past, always warned them about the dangers of travelling on their own. You used to see more of them, but they're still out there. I've made Laurie promise she won't ever do it.' He glanced up at Rebus. 'I know what you're thinking: we wrap them in cotton wool these days. I used to hitch lifts myself, back in the day—so did the missus—but it's all different now.'

'I suppose it is.'

'You reckon you'll ever catch the bastard?'

'Hard to say.'

'Even if you do, it's kid gloves in jails these days, isn't it?' He had finished his cigarette and began to stub it out under the toe of his shoe. Rebus had been considering possible answers to the question, but the salesman didn't seem to need one. 'Better hit the trail,' he was explaining. 'Job like mine, if you're not moving, you're not earning.' He gave a grin full of professionally whitened teeth. 'And those solutions won't sell themselves.'

The two men shook hands and returned to their vehicles. Rebus watched as the salesman drove off with a wave from his open window. He was heading north. Six- and seven-day weeks spent in a world that for him was permanent, for others fleeting, a place of lay-by sandwiches and pit stops for fuel, getting to know each road intimately, memorising short cuts, computing routes around snarl-ups, bumping into others whose routine was similar to his own, trading tips with them about the best fast food, the cheapest petrol, the cleanest facilities. Rebus had always thought of roads as simple, mute entities, but he knew differently now—they had individual identities and foibles. They pulsed with life. He stayed on the forecourt and pulled out his phone, punching in Samantha's number.

'It's me,' he said when she answered.

'Hey, Dad.'

'You okay to talk?'

'Nothing planned except a lazy weekend.'

'Lucky you. I just thought I'd call and see how you're doing.' He leaned back against the headrest, holding the phone close to his ear, content just to listen to her voice.

'Is everything all right?' she asked. 'It's just . . .'

'What?'

'Not like you to pick up the phone.'

'That doesn't mean I'm not thinking of you, Samantha. I think about you a lot.'

'I'm doing okay.'

'I know you are.'

'How about you? Any closer to catching that madman?'

'People keep asking me that.' He was remembering his words to the salesman: *there's always a destination, and you know you're going to reach it one way or another* . . .

'What do you tell them?'

'You really think he's a madman?'

'Has to be.'

'Sometimes it's hard to tell.'

'Gives me the creeps to think of him still out there. I've an appointment in Inverness in a few days with the IVF team. I've told Keith I'm not going without him.'

'You'll be fine.'

'Easy for you to say.'

'I suppose it is. Will you let me know how it goes at Raigmore?'

'Of course.'

'And maybe you and Keith should think about a weekend in Edinburgh. I could find you a hotel— my treat.'

'Are you sure you're feeling all right?'

'Enough of your cheek, young lady.'

He heard her laughter ringing in his ears.

66

That evening, he met Cafferty at the Tannery.

'Thanks for coming,' he said, buying the drinks before heading for a table.

'Is this where you offer an apology?' Cafferty asked.

'What sort of apology?'

'Last time we were in here, you were less than gracious.'

'I suppose that's one way of putting it.'

'So?'

'You're not going to tell me I hurt your feelings?'

Cafferty managed the thinnest of smiles. 'Maybe not,' he conceded. 'So why *did* you bring me here?'

Rebus reached into his pocket and unfolded a page torn from the *Scotsman*, flattening it out on the table. It was a report of Annette McKie's funeral, accompanied by a photograph of some of the mourners as they left the chapel, Cafferty among them.

'I was invited by the family,' Cafferty explained.

'I wasn't aware you knew them.'

'I know Darryl.'

'Since when? Not so long back, you didn't even

427

know he worked for Frank Hammell.'

'It was you who tipped me off.' Cafferty raised his glass as if in a toast.

'And between then and now, you've managed to worm your way into the family?'

'Darryl wanted me there.'

'Why, though?'

'Bit of business.' Cafferty took a sip of whisky, savouring it before swallowing.

'I didn't see Hammell among the guests.'

'Well you wouldn't.'

'Because he's been pushed out?' Rebus guessed. 'You turned Darryl against him?'

'You don't give the lad enough credit.'

'What does that mean?'

'Just that my help wasn't really needed. Young Darryl's had Frank Hammell in his sights from the word go.'

Rebus took a moment to digest this.

'I'd say he's going to give your lot a few headaches in the coming years, too,' Cafferty went on. 'Just as long as he stays smart and stays lucky.'

'So where's Hammell now?'

'Keeping his head down.'

'I don't buy it—Hammell's too big.'

'The kid's been chipping away at him from the ground up. Kicked out Hammell's men and brought in his own. And he did all of that without Hammell noticing, meaning he's been very clever. If Hammell *had* suspected, the kid would be lying in a forest somewhere.'

'Somewhere off the A9?'

'As good a place as any.'

Rebus shook his head slowly. 'Darryl had to have *your* backing.'

428

'Do you think I wouldn't be taking the credit if I could?'

'He's too young.'

'But sharp as a craft knife.'

'What was your plan—turn him against Hammell?'

'Maybe.'

'Stir things up a bit?'

'You're pretty good at that yourself—no wonder the Complaints are interested. Doesn't seem to have stopped our little get-togethers, though, does it? I reckon that's because you'd get bored otherwise.'

'Oh aye?'

Cafferty was nodding. 'Tell me something,' he said, leaning his elbows against the table. 'The argument Hammell had with the girl—any idea what it was about?'

'I know exactly what it was about.'

'But you're not going to tell me.'

'No, I'm not—and there's no point asking Ormiston, because I can tell you for a fact *he* doesn't know.'

The two men sized one another up. If there had been a chessboard between them, they might have been readying to call a draw—*another* draw in an ever-lengthening line of them. Cafferty finished his drink and got to his feet. 'One more?' he asked, heading for the bar without waiting for a reply. Having ordered for both of them, he listened as the door behind him rattled open and then closed again. When he turned, Rebus was gone, leaving behind a half-full glass and the photo from the funeral.

*   *   *

A forest somewhere . . .

As good a place as any . . .

A forest . . .

Back at his flat, Rebus tapped the number he had for Frank Hammell into his phone. It rang and rang without anyone answering. He tipped the dregs of the whisky bottle into his mouth and swallowed them down. He was standing by the living room window, its view unchanged. The two kids in the flat opposite were cross-legged on the carpet watching TV. He wondered what life held in store for them. An absent parent, perhaps. College or straight into work? Maybe unemployment. Meeting someone they really loved. And the last-chance saloon of IVF. Then they might become parents themselves, worrying about the future and wishing they could see what it held. His phone buzzed, Hammell's name appearing on the screen. Rebus hesitated, then decided to answer.

'I think we should meet,' he said.

'Why?' The voice sounded dry and hollow.

'Because I've heard about you and Darryl.'

'I never want to hear that little prick's name again!'

'You might have to,' Rebus stated calmly. 'What's more, I think it'll be worth it.'

'I'm not a grass, Rebus.'

'I'm not asking you to be one. I just need you to answer a question—it's not even a question about Darryl.'

'And?'

'And a spot of payback might well be

forthcoming.'

There was silence on the line as Hammell considered this. Rebus listened to him exhale. 'What's the question?'

'There may be a follow-up, depending on how you answer.'

'Just ask me the damned question.'

'Okay, then.' One of the kids opposite had come to the window. They waved at Rebus. He waved back. 'Where would you bury a body?' he asked Hammell, as the kid waved again, this time with a huge gap-toothed grin.

A forest . . .

*　　　*　　　*

Rebus was leaving his tenement building, pulling the door shut behind him, when he saw Siobhan Clarke standing on the pavement.

'Got Page with you?' he asked, looking to left and right.

'No.'

'So what can I do for you?'

'I was a bit worried, that's all.'

'Worried?'

'You've fallen off the radar.'

'Maybe it escaped your attention, but I'm not on the books any more.'

'All the same . . .'

'What?'

She studied him closely. 'I was right. You've got that look in your eyes. Something's brewing.'

'Nothing's brewing.'

'And suddenly he gets all defensive . . .'

He opened his arms in a show of innocence, but

431

he wasn't fooling her.

'Where are you off to?' she asked.

'Just out.'

'Mind if I tag along?'

'Yes.'

'Not heading to the pub, then.'

'Christ's sake, Siobhan . . .' Rebus made an exasperated sound. 'There's just something I have to do.'

'Does it happen to involve Kenny Magrath?'

'It might,' he conceded.

'And naturally you'll be sticking to the letter of the law?'

'I'm not the police; I'm not even a civvy *working* for the police.'

'And having a real-life detective along for the ride wouldn't help at all?'

He stared at her, then shook his head slowly. 'You should listen to Fox, Siobhan. To keep rising through the ranks, you need to steer well clear of the likes of me.' He prodded his chest with his thumb to drive the point home.

'A rise through the ranks that turns me into the likes of James Page or Malcolm Fox?' She made show of considering this. 'Somehow your way of doing things is just that bit more fun.'

'No,' he said, shaking his head again.

'Yes,' Clarke countered. 'Tell me what you've got in mind.'

Rebus rubbed at his jaw. 'If I do, will you bugger off home and leave me to it?'

It was her turn to shake her head.

'Thought not,' he said.

*   *   *

Frank Hammell was waiting for them in a fast-food restaurant next to a petrol station. The place was brightly lit, showing how much colour Hammell had lost from his face. His hair needed combing, and grey stubble showed on his cheeks. He was nursing a coffee, the burger in front of him not even half eaten, and his eyes darted everywhere, his whole body seeming to tense with each new customer through the door.

'You reckon he'll come after you?' Rebus asked, sliding into the cubicle. Clarke was fetching drinks from the counter—orange juice for her and tea for him.

'You didn't say you'd be bringing anyone,' Hammell snapped back.

'She's not here—not officially.' Rebus slid further over to make room for Clarke, who offered a nod of greeting to Hammell, a greeting he ignored, focusing on a couple of newcomers to the restaurant.

'I reckon the little turd's capable of anything,' he muttered eventually, in answer to Rebus's original question.

'Wouldn't he have made his move at the club?'

Hammell shook his head. 'Too many witnesses.'

'You've obviously given it some thought.'

'What else am I going to do? If I so much as pick up the phone to Gail, he says he'll tell her about Annette and me. He's even got keys to my house . . .' Hammell's eyes were filling with anger. 'If I can just get him on his own, I'll throttle the bastard.'

'Duly noted. But how about if *we* take him instead?'

Hammell looked at Rebus, as if seeing him for

433

the first time. 'Is this a set-up?'

'Definitely not.'

'What, then?'

'There's a result I'm after, and Darryl Christie's part of it.'

'I don't understand.'

'Best keep it that way.'

Hammell studied Rebus intently, then switched to Clarke and back to Rebus again. 'What do you need me to do?'

'Remember that question I asked?'

'Yes.'

Rebus reached into his pocket and took out the road map of Scotland.

'Just show me,' he said.

                   *   *   *

Afterwards, they walked Hammell back to the car park. He had yet to get rid of the Range Rover.

'Bit conspicuous,' Rebus warned him.

'Garage that sold me it offered fifteen to take it back,' Hammell complained. 'It's worth three times that.'

'All the same . . .'

Hammell gestured towards Rebus's Saab. 'Want to swap? Fifteen plus yours?'

'I can't do that, Frank.'

Hammell got into his own car, started the engine and headed at speed towards the main road. Rebus unlocked the Saab, Clarke sliding into the passenger seat.

'That would have been a good trade,' she said.

'The things me and this old beast have been through . . .' Rebus patted the steering wheel.

'Money doesn't come into it.'

'So what now?' she asked as she did up her seat belt.

'Now,' Rebus answered, 'we start planning.'

'Planning what, exactly?'

'How to give Kenny Magrath the fright of his life . . .'

67

He made the call Sunday lunchtime, using the number on the card Darryl Christie had given him. Whoever it was who answered, Rebus didn't recognise the voice.

'I need to speak to your boss,' he explained.

'What boss might that be?'

'Don't be daft, son. Give Darryl the name John Rebus and tell him to phone me back.'

Then he hung up and waited. Not quite three minutes had passed when his mobile trilled.

'I'm listening,' Darryl Christie said. No niceties; no small talk. Everything changed. Well, that was fine with Rebus.

'The guy you're looking for is Kenny Magrath. He lives with his wife in a house in Rosemarkie. I can give you the address.'

'I know about him,' Christie interrupted. 'It was all over the net—he's been checked out by Dempsey's lot and let go.'

'That's as may be,' Rebus said. 'But hear what I've got to say, then decide for yourself.'

'You've got two minutes.'

It took Rebus a bit longer than that to lay out

his reasoning: the van at the petrol station; the retirement of Gregor Magrath; the way Kenny Magrath had acted when confronted. There was silence on the line when he finished. Then Darryl Christie's voice:

'Why are you telling me?'

'Because I can't get to him—he's made too good a job of covering his tracks.'

'Are you taping this?'

'If I am, I'm about to sign my own arrest warrant. He has to disappear, Darryl. And it has to look like he's done a runner, otherwise the pair of us might come under the magnifying glass. Can't have his body being found.'

'Bodies have a habit of turning up, though, don't they?'

'Depends where they're left.'

'Are you inviting yourself to the party?'

'No,' Rebus assured him. 'The less you tell me, the better. Magrath has a workshop he uses—a garage, across from the pub at the far end of the village. Goes there first thing in the morning, and when he knocks off in the evening. I'd say evening would be best—it's nice and dark by five o'clock. His van can't be left behind, not if he's supposed to have scarpered in it.'

'You've given this some thought.'

'I've not had much else to do—you said it yourself, Dempsey proved less than useless when I went to her.'

'You know what I'll do to you if this is a stitch-up?'

'Yes.'

'This isn't some trick Cafferty's come up with?'

'No.'

'And what's stopping me from going straight to this bastard's house and kicking his door down?'

'For one thing, he has neighbours. For another, you'd have to do something about his wife. My way's better. You take him to woods somewhere— plenty of forests up north. I can suggest a few if you like . . .' Rebus's voice trailed off as he waited to see what Christie would say.

'Not necessary,' was the answer.

Which was good news: it meant he already had a spot in mind.

'I reckon he's a creature of habit,' Rebus went on, trying to keep the emotion out of his voice. 'Likes his dinner ready when he comes home. That means his wife will start to worry sooner rather than later. If he's half an hour behind schedule and not answering his phone, she's going to go out looking, and it won't be long after that before she calls it in.'

'Not a problem.'

'There's a place you can take the van?'

'Want me to tell you?'

'I just want to make sure this is done right—for both our sakes.'

'No qualms?'

'Not a one.'

'We're not going to speak again, you and me.'

'As long as I can close the file, I'm happy. Call it a little retirement present I'm giving myself.'

'If this works out, I might chip in a clock for your mantelpiece. On the other hand, if it doesn't . . .'

Darryl Christie ended the call without bothering to finish the threat. Rebus stared at his phone until the screen went blank.

'Well?' Siobhan Clarke said. She was standing in the living room, hands cupped around a mug

437

of coffee. Rebus rose from his chair and poured himself a drink, then thought better of it and pushed it aside. Instead he lit a cigarette, heading to the sash window and pulling it open so Clarke couldn't complain.

'Promising,' he decided, blowing smoke through the gap. 'No more than that.'

'Did he mention which forest?'

Rebus shook his head. 'But he knows about the one his old boss used from time to time. And it's perfect—not much more than forty-five minutes from the Black Isle. He won't want to be riding around roads he doesn't know with someone he's just abducted—not when there's a wife at home readying to call the police.'

'And the van?'

'I'm guessing dumped in a loch or sent for scrap.'

'Why not make it look like an accident? Van goes off the road with Magrath at the wheel?'

'Too much can go wrong—any half-decent scene-of-crime unit would smell something.'

Clarke lowered herself on to the sofa. Rebus's map was there, a circle drawn around a wooded area just outside Aviemore. 'He won't go rushing up there tonight?'

'Darryl's the careful sort—he's going to spend time mulling it over.'

'Meaning he might still get cold feet?'

'Always a possibility.'

'But you don't think so?'

'No.'

'And you don't think he'll touch Mrs Magrath?'

'He's not the type. He'll look for the flaws in the plan, maybe try to work out if there's any other way.'

'How many men will he take?'

'Two or three—one of them to drive away the van.'

'Do we need reinforcements? I could ask Christine or Ronnie . . .'

Rebus was shaking his head. 'I feel bad enough letting *you* get involved.'

'As if you had a choice.' She was smiling at him above the rim of the coffee mug.

'Remember: you're the only cop here. If Fox and his crew ever get wind of this . . .'

'I'd be scuppering my chances of joining the Complaints.'

'You want to work for Fox?'

'He told me I'd be good at it—I think he meant it in a kind way.'

'And?'

'And what?'

'Do you fancy it?'

'I'd have to take a vow of silence, wouldn't I?'

'About me, you mean?' Rebus blew another stream of smoke out of the window.

'The stuff I could tell them . . .'

'True enough,' he said, stubbing out the cigarette on the ledge before flicking it into the void.

68

On Monday, they were in position by three thirty, parked on Rosemarkie's narrow main street, Clarke's Audi tucked in between two other vehicles, pointing south. Rebus's reasoning: after grabbing Magrath, this was the way they would come—unless they wanted to end up in Cromarty.'

'Let's hope you're right,' Clarke had replied. The shop windows were illuminated, and locals walked past carrying bags of groceries. Rebus and Clarke had checked out Magrath's workshop, but there was nowhere to park that wasn't conspicuous. Rebus was passing the time explaining to Clarke that it was Darryl Christie who had abducted Thomas Robertson.

'Darryl's the one who's always surfing the web—that's how he'd have learned we'd lifted someone from the road crew at Pitlochry. Easy enough to find him, have him followed to the Tummel Arms and then snatch him.'

'And smack him about?'

'To get him to talk. But then comes news that it can't have been him after all, so they dump him in Aberdeen.'

'Why Aberdeen?'

Rebus watched as a car drove past—no one he knew inside. 'Maybe because Frank Hammell has friends there, meaning we'd go on thinking it was him behind it and not his spotty wee lieutenant.'

Clarke nodded her understanding.

'Something I wanted to ask you,' Rebus went on.

'What?'

'Fox told me he was easing off for the time being—you didn't have a word with him, did you?'

'No.'

'Says he wants me back in CID so he can nab me good and proper.'

'Do you believe him?'

'I'm not sure.'

'Have you signed the forms?'

'There's still a good chance I'll fail the physical.'

440

'Hard to disagree.'

'Thanks a bunch.'

Another car: driven by a young woman.

'Will Magrath pass by here?' Clarke asked.

'Depends where he's been working.'

'Assuming he's started back to work in the first place.'

'I didn't say the plan was perfect.' Rebus checked the time. Daylight was fading fast. When he looked up again, he saw the black Mercedes M-Class.

'Clickety-click,' he told Clarke, turning away so his face wouldn't be visible to anyone in the approaching vehicle. Clarke had her own head angled forward, as if fussing with the Audi's stereo.

'Four of them, I think,' she said as she straightened up again, peering into the rear-view mirror.

'Darryl in the passenger seat,' Rebus confirmed.

'Not a bad start.' She exhaled, releasing some of the tension. 'They're even a bit early.'

'They need time to scope the place out.'

'If Christie's the cautious sort, he'll be looking for traps.' She was starting the ignition.

'What's your thinking?'

'Move the car a bit further along, maybe tuck ourselves down a side road. We know what we're on the lookout for—a huge black Merc heading south.'

'You're worried they'll come back and spot us?'

'Yes.'

Rebus nodded his agreement. It didn't take long to find what they needed. They parked again, facing the main drag, and Clarke switched the engine off, before changing her mind and switching it on again.

'A bit of warmth,' she explained, turning the

heater up.

'Good idea.' The dashboard gave the outside temperature as five degrees. There would be a frost later—the skies were clear, a couple of stars already visible. Rebus held his hands in front of the air vent, rubbing them together.

Twenty minutes later, they both spotted Magrath's van, the name prominent on its side.

'Headed for the lock-up,' Rebus stated.

'There's still time for a change of strategy,' Clarke argued. 'Confront them then and there.'

Rebus was shaking his head. 'We need him scared, remember.'

'My way's less risky.'

'Just don't lose them.'

'Are you saying my driving's not up to it?'

Rebus gave her a look, then focused on the road. A couple of minutes for Kenny Magrath to reach the lock-up . . . bundled into the car . . . . They'd want to be quick. But what if someone from the pub had stepped out for a cigarette? Or a bus full of inquisitive locals was passing? Rebus had seldom known time to creep so slowly. And just as he was about to open his mouth and say something to that effect . . .

'Van!' Clarke called out. Heading back the way it had come, MAGRATH on its side. The shape behind the steering wheel was not Kenny Magrath—too short, too wiry. The black Merc was only a few seconds behind, its occupants hard to discern. Clarke began to follow, keeping her distance. When a delivery lorry came up behind her, she slowed to let it overtake. She'd studied the road map, knew there were few options for the Merc. There were manoeuvres the driver could make to check he wasn't being followed—slowing to a near stop; pulling over and biding his time; doubling back and finding a different route. But right now the Audi was hidden from view by the delivery lorry.

The first real decision came at Munlochy; the Merc stayed on the A832.

'Next it'll be the Tore roundabout,' Rebus said. 'Then the A9 south.'

'If your hunch is right,' Clarke cautioned.

'So little faith.' Rebus managed the beginnings of a smile, but Clarke knew he was nervous—it wasn't her driving that was making him grip the passenger-side door handle.

When they reached the dual carriageway, the convoy followed the signs to Inverness. Rebus craned his neck to see what was happening past the lorry.

'They're leaving it for dead,' he informed Clarke, so she signalled and moved out to overtake. The Mercedes had passed the van but seemed to want to stay close to it.

'They could be strangling Magrath right now, you know,' Clarke commented.

'They could,' Rebus agreed.

'Might have nothing but a corpse on our hands at the other end.'

'We might at that.'

'I don't suppose you'd lose much sleep.'

'I'm not a monster, Siobhan—but I suppose I'd cope somehow . . .'

Over the Kessock Bridge and into Inverness, staying on the A9 and heading south out of the city.

'So far so good,' Clarke said under her breath.

'You planning to stay on their tail all the way?'

'Give it another mile or two.'

After which she put her foot down, guiding the Audi into the outside lane and eventually overtaking the van, pulling in between it and the Merc before flooring the accelerator and passing that car, too. The clock said ninety-five as she watched the headlights behind her recede.

'They're keeping to a steady sixty-five.'

'Don't want to get pulled over, do they?' Rebus suggested.

A further few miles on, a sign indicated a lay-by. Clarke slowed the Audi to a stop behind an articulated lorry which was parked up for the night. She switched off the headlights and slouched down in her seat, Rebus doing the same as far as he was able. He could feel the sweat on his back, his shirt clinging to him.

'Here they come,' Clarke said, eyes on the wing mirror. Not just the Merc and the van, but a few other vehicles in their wake. It was completely dark now, no chance the Audi could have been clocked, not the speed the convoy was going. Clarke switched her lights on again and got back on the road.

'No shortage of disposal sites between here and there,' she offered.

'He's not got the experience, Siobhan. Something tells me he'll stick to what he knows, places he's been shown or told about.'

Twenty minutes later, they passed a sign telling them the Aviemore spur was just ahead.

'Where it all started,' Siobhan Clarke said.

'I suppose,' Rebus replied, watching as a few flakes of snow began to fall. A couple of cars were signalling to turn left.

'The Merc?' Clarke guessed.

'I'd put money on it—just not necessarily *my* money.'

But yes, the Merc was turning off, while the van stayed on the A9 and its appointment with a scrapyard or similar.

'We're sure Magrath's not trussed up in the back of his own van?' Clarke asked.

'As sure as we can be.'

The Audi followed the Merc, still a couple of other vehicles separating them.

'I think this is working,' Clarke offered. 'Insofar as they haven't spotted us.' All too soon, though, the covering vehicles were peeling off into new-build housing developments, leaving only the Merc and the Audi—fifty yards between them.

'Should I stop and let him get ahead?'

'I don't know,' Rebus admitted.

'We could overtake and block the route—don't tell me Magrath won't be scared rigid by now.'

'Not yet.'

She looked at him again. His eyes were fixed on the Merc, his left hand still gripping the door handle. They were in deepening countryside, heading away from Aviemore into a wilderness of mountain and forest.

'I could overtake again,' Clarke suggested, breaking off as she saw that, without signalling, the car in front was turning off the road on to a dirt track. There was a gate, but it had been left open. Clarke drove past and kept driving, while Rebus watched the 4x4's tail lights until they were swallowed up by trees.

'We're safe,' he said. Clarke stopped the car and did a three-point turn, switching off her lights and crawling towards the open gate.

'Just like Hammell said,' she muttered. The Merc had disappeared from view. Clarke slid down her window and listened for its engine. 'Still on the move.'

'Then we move, too.'

The Audi began to head cautiously up the track, both front windows lowered. Despite the flurries and the sharp night air, Rebus stuck his head out, watching and listening. The route wound uphill into a pine-scented forest, reminding him of Edderton. When they reached a fork, Clarke stopped the car, turning off the engine as a precaution.

'Hear anything?'

'No,' Rebus told her.

'No lights either.'

'You think they've stopped?' He had lowered his voice.

'Maybe.'

'Do we go left or right?'

'You tell me.'

'Ground's pretty well frozen—hard to tell if there are tracks there or not.'

'And you an ex-Boy Scout.'

Rebus considered for a moment. 'Right,' he said. Then: 'No, left.'

'Sure?'

'Fairly.'

'You mean you're guessing?'

'Fifty–fifty chance, Siobhan.'

'I don't think Magrath would be thrilled by those odds. How about we stick the lights on full beam and drive like hell?'

'Or go the rest of the way on foot.'

'On foot?' Her eyes had widened a little, her

brow furrowing.

'On foot.'

'Together or separately?'

'Bloody hell, Siobhan, do I have to make *all* the decisions?'

69

The bag was removed from Kenny Magrath's head. He'd been thumped a few times and his eyes stung. He blinked the world back into focus. There was a near-full moon in a hazy sky, and the smell of moss. Magrath was breathing through his nose, his mouth taped shut, hands bound behind him. Three men made a sort of triangle around him. They seemed very tall, until he worked out he was upright in a shallow grave. He tried to scream, a bubble of blood popping from one nostril. When he started scrabbling out of the pit, one of the men took a step forward and raised a shovel. Magrath knew what that meant, and stayed put. The car they'd brought him in stood a dozen or so yards away, lights dipped, illuminating the scene, picking out occasional slow-motion snowflakes.

'You killed my sister,' someone said. Magrath looked around, unable to pick out the speaker until Darryl Christie bent a little at the waist, establishing eye contact. He was dressed in a dark polo-neck, denims and trainers. Magrath shook his head, feeling a fresh wave of nausea as his brain throbbed with pain.

'This grave was dug for someone else,' Christie went on. 'Wrong guy that time. You're the one I've been looking for, so don't try to deny it.'

But Magrath couldn't help himself, his muffled voice rising in pitch. Christie turned away as if bored by the performance. He stretched a hand out towards the man next to him. The shovel was placed in it. Christie felt it for heft and balance, raised it over his shoulder and swung it a few times for practice. Magrath was reduced to weeping now, eyes screwed shut. His knees gave way and he landed heavily on the dirt, chin resting against the edge of the grave.

'Ssshhh,' Christie told him, like a parent to a child. Then he arched his body back, lifting the shovel high and bringing it down so that it connected with the ground directly in front of Magrath. Magrath's eyes flew open, focused on the implement's gleaming edge. Christie twisted it free and held the shovel in front of him as he crouched down, directly in front of the tearful, snot-nosed Magrath.

'You didn't think it was going to be quick, did you?' he asked. 'Plenty of damage to be done before then. All those lives you took. Just for kicks, eh? No real reason. Nothing that can be explained. It's not a prison they'll put you in, it's a nuthouse. Board games and daytime TV, walks in the garden and a friendly psychiatrist. Reckon that's fair, do you? All those lives you wrecked, the living as well as the dead. Time for some proper payback. Time for *you* to feel pain . . .' He rose again and lifted the shovel, but only to waist height this time, preparing to swing it at Kenny Magrath's head.

'That's enough!'

Christie swivelled towards the voice. Rebus had his hands bunched by his sides, as if spoiling for a

448

fight.

'What are you doing here?' Christie called out.

'Arresting you,' Siobhan Clarke said, stepping into the clearing and holding open her ID. Christie's men looked to their boss for instructions. Christie pointed at Rebus.

'You're the one who wanted this in the first place!' he complained.

Clarke ignored him, telling him he was under arrest. Christie had eyes only for Rebus, and those eyes were burning.

'Two of you against three of us?' he announced. 'Look around—plenty of room for a few more graves.'

'*He* might be stupid,' Clarke interrupted, gesturing towards Rebus, 'but I'm not. Back-up's about five minutes away.'

'What do we do?' one of Christie's men was asking his boss. Rebus recognised him: Marcus, doorman and driver. Christie took a moment to weigh up the options.

'We're going,' he said. Then, turning towards Magrath: 'This isn't over. You'll be seeing my face again.' He swung a kick, connecting with the side of Magrath's head, before starting to march towards the Mercedes. Clarke looked to Rebus, but Rebus wasn't moving. The two men began to follow their boss, Marcus forging ahead so he could hold open the car's passenger door. Christie gave Rebus a final baleful look, tossed the shovel on to the ground, and got in. After the doors had closed, Clarke took a step forward.

'We're letting them go?'

'Did you fancy our chances?' Rebus asked. He walked over to Magrath, peeling away the tape.

'They're getting away!' Magrath spluttered, flecks of pink saliva flying from his mouth. The engine of the Mercedes had roared into life, the car reversing back the way it had come.

'Yes,' Rebus said, starting to loosen the ties around Magrath's wrists.

'They were going to kill me.'

'We noticed.'

Magrath seemed confused. He looked from Rebus to Clarke and back again. 'You'll catch them, though? The back-up . . .'

'No back-up,' Rebus informed him. 'That was just DI Clarke saving our skins.'

'They were going to kill me,' Magrath repeated, more to himself than anyone else.

'A word of thanks wouldn't go amiss.'

'What?'

'Never mind.' Rebus grabbed Magrath by the arm, coaxing him out of the shallow grave.

'They took my van.'

'You won't be seeing it again.'

'They were going to—'

'So you keep saying.'

'Probably in shock,' Clarke explained.

Magrath realised he was being led from the clearing. 'Where are we going?'

'We're giving you a lift home—car's this way.'

'But they're this way too!'

'Best if we get a move on, then, before it dawns on them there's no cavalry in the vicinity.'

'Wait a minute,' Magrath said. 'Did you say a lift *home*?'

'Where else?'

Magrath stopped moving. 'I can't go home. They know where I live . . . where Maggie lives . . .?'

450

'They might leave her alone. It's *you* they're after.'

'Then why did you let them go?'

'Know what they'll say if questioned? They'll say they were just giving you a fright. That's *if* they say anything at all.'

'But you *saw* them!'

Rebus gave a shrug and fixed his eyes on Clarke. 'Seems that saving his hide isn't quite enough.'

'We've done what we can,' Clarke replied.

'You could always make a run for it,' Rebus suggested to the man in front of him. 'Get yourself a new identity. It would have to be a long way from here, though—Darryl Christie's got a lot of friends.'

'What about Maggie? And Gregor?'

'They've done what they can. Time for *you* to make a few decisions.'

Magrath looked around him, his mind reeling. He was trembling, and not just from the cold.

'I can't . . . I don't . . .'

'Your decision,' Rebus repeated, sliding his hands into his pockets. Magrath's eyes seemed to clear. He met Rebus's gaze.

'What do I do?' he asked. 'Tell me.'

'You're asking my advice?'

Magrath nodded and another tremor ran through him. Rebus gave a glance in Clarke's direction before seeming to think for a moment.

'I'll give it, then,' he said, 'but on one condition . . .'

Magrath blinked a couple of times. 'Yes?'

'You leave us out of it.'

Magrath's eyelids fluttered again. 'Out of what?'

'Your confession,' Rebus told him.

They dropped him outside the police station on
Burnett Road. Rebus had called ahead and Gavin
Arnold was waiting. Rebus and Clarke stayed in
the car and watched as Arnold led Kenny Magrath
inside. Rebus had his window down so he could
smoke a cigarette. His hand was shaking, but only a
little.

'He might change his mind, you know,' Clarke
said quietly.

'He might,' Rebus agreed. 'On the other hand, a
secure unit's about as safe from Darryl Christie as
he's likely to get.'

'You definitely got that across to him.' She
paused. 'Speaking of which . . .'

Rebus turned to face her. 'Christie?' He watched
as she nodded. 'Depends what Kenny Magrath says
in his statement. If he leaves out the forest . . .'

'Christie *was* going to kill him.'

'Entrapment, they'd call it in court.' Rebus
peered out through the windscreen towards the
darkness. 'I led him into it, after all.' Then: 'We
should get going before Dempsey arrives.'

'You're really planning to let Darryl Christie off
the hook?'

'I'm not the cop here, Siobhan.' He turned in her
direction again. 'Your call rather than mine.'

Clarke focused her attention on the door to the
police station and the illuminated POLICE sign
above it. 'They'll know someone got to him. Pretty
good chance your name will crop up.'

'Just so long as yours doesn't. Besides, I'm a
civilian, remember—I was watching his workshop
for want of anything better to do, saw him being

abducted and decided to follow, then ended up saving his skin. That's *if* he opts to throw my name into the pot.'

There was silence in the car for a moment, until Clarke broke it.

'We didn't ask him why he did it.'

'The killings or the photos?'

'Both, I suppose.'

'I doubt he knows the answer to that himself.'

More silence. Clarke was still facing away from Rebus when she spoke. 'For a moment there, when Christie raised that shovel, it flashed through my mind that you were going to let it happen.'

'Really?'

'Yes, really.'

'Magrath dead and Christie on a murder charge?'

'Yes.'

'Well, that would have been a result too, I suppose.'

'And it's results that matter rather than how you get them.'

'Used to be the way.'

'Not now, though?'

'Maybe not so much.' He leaned back in his seat. 'That grave wasn't meant for Magrath, you know.'

'No?'

Rebus shook his head. 'It was Thomas Robertson's. When I saw him in the hospital, I happened to mention a shallow grave. It spooked him, and now we know why—he'd been taken there and shown it. Scared him stupid . . .'

'But Christie let him go.'

Rebus nodded. 'Darryl's not a killer, Siobhan. Maybe one of his boys would have taken care of

453

Magrath, but whacking the ground with that shovel was as close as Darryl was going to get.' He seemed lost in thought for a moment. 'You know what this means, though?'

'I'm not sure.'

'It means I was right all along about that bloody song.'

He flicked the cigarette away as Clarke turned the key in the ignition.

'What song?' she was asking as Rebus began to wind the window up.